Winds of Shadow

The Wind Whispers Series: Book 1

To the Simon-May families,

Thank you for supporting my dream! What a blast to catch up! Best of luck with the grand kids and enjoy them!

Benjamin J. Stegenga

"I dedicate this to my family and friends who have shown me the support to grow as a writer. Each person in my life has impacted this story in one way or another; without them this vision would not be possible."

-Benjamin J. Stegenga

ISBN: 9798512090640

Prologue:

Ever since the oath had been sworn to protect the artifact, the tragic fate of the family Stormbringer was decided. Grandfather Orwick had told the youngest grandchild, Sean, the story of the Faithful Ancient 20, warriors of the light to defend the world against darkness and the Wanderers—the epitome of nightmares. In the story, Orwick told of his own feats among these Ancient warriors as a young lad, slaying Wanderers to keep the balance of good from tipping in the wrong direction. As the years wore on, and the battles were fewer, and the old soldier eventually settled down to the quiet life of a farmer. The 20 had sacrificed everything for the greater good and only a handful had survived. These brave warriors beseeched Orwick in offering a position destined to protect that which would save the world; or so Orwick told all who asked. The real truth much more complex.

Sitting on Orwick's knee, Sean would ask what it was they were protecting from the dark, but Orwick would only shake his head and tell his grandson to have faith. Orwick could not offer up the grim reality to someone so young; or the true nature of his involvement in the war. Sean lived in a world where even skilled swordsmen would fall short of those with true power of the elements. Orwick had been the strongest of the 20 in those powers of old. He knew each name and carried them deep in his heart; they would pass with him to the void. As the Proclaimer of Light, this was Orwick's duty, and the memory of the days gone by appeared within reach.

When the world was bright, the mountains seemed young, and the seas at peace. This is how the tale of Orwick Stormbringer begins. A young lord of an old family reaching back to the days when Grey Folk walked the surface, Orwick came to be the leader of a fellowship of other nobles. Eighteen members made up the group, women and men fighting alongside each other. All of similar heritage and nobility, they were fierce humans that possessed talents above others and rode the world in search of adventures. With every conquest, grew their glory of prowess in the field of battle as they fought bandits, wild beasts and even Giants in their Forest of Stone. One such quest proved almost too much for this group but it yielded a great and evil outcome.

Far to the South, across a blue sea, they ventured to a continent where the air boiled with sweltering heat. Orwick led the group on an expedition hunting monsters, dark beasts whose renown was well known to the Sea Folk. Upon crashing ashore, two warriors joined the party after saving Orwick from the waves' chilly depths. The two men were of Sea Folk descent and Orwick could sense strength in their fighting ability, so the Ancient 20 came together at long last. Setting off once more seeking adventures, they put the coast to their backs, sights set to felling a creature of darkness.

Preparations were for naught, as they nearly starved to death in the unknown continent. The 20 stumbled upon a dark tower of stone which seemed to absorb all light. In this tower lived an ancient wizard, who had lived alone for centuries. Wearing a hooded cloak, he beckoned the 20 travelers to accept his hospitality. In living on the Southern continent, the wizard studied mysteries of the world; energy ran rampant and the air worried Orwick. Here is how the Ancient 20 acquired what made them a legend, for the wizard tempted the warriors with an offer—a proposition of great reward but terrible consequence.

In an age long ago, the wizard discovered the elements once existed in a mortal state before their powers were bequeathed to the planet. The wizard's offer was to summon these once mortal beings, bringing them back into existence, granting powers unimagined to all who possessed the ability to handle them. In the tower of dark stone, the pact of the Ancient 20 was agreed upon without question, only Orwick being wary of the cost. For the wizard in all his years had become crafty without human interaction and cared not for the souls of these mortals at his door. Their blood is all the wizard cared for. Magic resonated from the depths like a bottomless pit.

What transpired still shook Orwick to the core—a blood oath had been taken between the 20 at the wizard's instructions. Their combined, latent power surged forth to the world, running wild around the chamber. Token objects placed in the chamber's center represented elements, and free energy flew into them to find a home. This is how the Elementals came to be once more, immortal beings bound to wander the world until the day the oath is broken; the crafty wizard had sealed their fate forever. The Ancient 20 became tied to the elements in a way that transcended ordinary magic, their essence filling the Elementals with life. To Orwick, however, the one who gained most of all seemed to be the wizard, and Orwick vowed to make things right.

When the blood oath was completed, power had been given to the Ancient 20, but it was the wizard's laughter which haunted Orwick. The wizard cackled madly, gleefully, for sealing the Elements awoke a terrible evil; total darkness being the wizard's ultimate goal. Being it was young, the darkness remained unknown to everyone but the wizard and Orwick alone. With a look Orwick watched the darkness seep into the wizards hood, laughter growing to a maniacal level. Though darkness would not manifest for many, many years, Orwick always lay waiting for such a day. Pushing the other Ancients to further their power birthed Orwick's title of Proclaimer of Light, locking in his role as leader to the Ancient 20.

War ravaged the continent years later, the Ancient 20 fighting to dispel the dark which grew with the wizard. Elementals aided the Ancient warriors and together they pushed back darkness to its eventual defeat. Orwick never believed the war truly was over, though, even with the Elementals' assistance. So much time had passed since that victory, and the crimes committed to achieve it weighed on Orwick more than any other Ancient.

Memory fading to the deep recess of Orwick's mind, he looked at Sean with wonder. This boy had potential to become the next in line to take on the role of Proclaimer of Light, a crafty solution to Orwick's predicament. Rebirth remained impossible, as Life had forsaken Orwick. To live another year in such a withered body depressed him. This crafty solution of inheritance had been Orwick's life work—years planning to yield a single heir worthy to right the wrongs committed by the dark wizard.

During Sean's youth, Orwick had left sword training to his son and focused on teaching the boy common practices like farming. No longer could Orwick wield a blade properly, its familiar weight useless in his hands. Another portion of the plan orchestrated by Orwick meant that their family heritage be left a mystery; even Orwick's son knew not all his father had accomplished. It was imperative to leave Sean in the dark on Ancient history, else Orwick feared the boy might repeat such mistakes as he. Only through small parables downplaying Orwick's role in the war could information be passed, and little Sean adored the tales spun. Taking to the adventure more so than the lesson taught, grim undertones were lost on the boy. Running off to play, Sean reenacted the fight scenes told, with sticks for swords, and Orwick would be left smiling, judging the next heir to be Proclaimer of Light. This boy had the greatest potential of them all—power even greater than Orwick himself.

Chapter 1: Ancient Faith

The fable became real as Sean grew into a young boy, no longer wielding wooden sticks for swords. Time on the family farm was spent farming fields in the summer months and learning to fight in the winter with his brothers. Being the youngest of five had given Sean a lot of firsthand experience to see that the story was definitely real as Wanderers attacked the farm. At the age of 14, Sean fought his first Wanderer and won at the expense of his eldest brother. The beast was of adult age, human-faced with black, lidless eyes accompanied by an abysmal stench that shook Sean's wits away. It tore through any of the defenses set up to repel intruders with ease. The beast reached Sean, the first on the foul creature; sword and staff in hand, blows were exchanged. The Wanderer knocked Sean to the ground with a swing of its claws and advanced on the defenseless boy. Sean's brother, Trey, dove over Sean as the second claw came down, crushing Trey's spine instead, and killing him instantly. Howling, Sean picked up his brother's sword and rammed the blade into the Wanderer's chest, piercing through its scaly armor. Shock wracked Sean's body after he realized what had happened and he finally got a personal look at what his family had been fighting.

Ten feet tall, the creature had scales the strength of steel covering its body whole. Combined with claws for hands and feet that could slice through bedrock, made it a formidable opponent. Wiping the blood from the blade, Sean gathered himself together and ran back to the house for help. From that moment on, he was no longer a child listening to grandfather's stories; Sean had become a part of the battle of good versus evil.

The wind blew loudly outside of the farmhouse, chilling Sean to the bone. Winter had forced people farther from the mountain than in most years past, making Stormbringer Farms one of the last in the area. No matter the weather, Sean had stayed to protect what his family had sworn to many years ago. Brother Trey was the first to die in the protection of the Artifact; several years later, Sean's brothers Zach and Eric followed him into the void. The deaths of Sean's older brothers left him alone to continue fighting the dark beasts, and the family mourned their loss.

A few years later, Sean's mother was attacked while traveling to town and left for dead on the side of the road, robbed by thieves. Shortly after, Sean's sister eloped with a merchant from town, hoping for a better life with fewer hardships. She left the mountain area without another look back and had not been heard from in over a year. Sean's father survived the following winter, but the strain from so many of his loved ones lost became too much to bear. One spring day he told Sean to keep the faith, for he was the strongest of them all and stepped outside, never to be seen again. The loneliness clung to a place where much happiness had been shared and memories made, leaving emptiness that tormented Sean.

    The darkness consumed him; each kill of a Wanderer furthered his hatred toward the beasts. It had seemed that the darker the year, the stronger the pull of the Artifact, and the hard winter seemed interminable. Sean had held hope that with the spring, the pull toward the Artifact would be diminished, providing the needed opportunity to finally leave the seclusion, even if only for a month. At the ripe age of 20, Sean planned on going into town and finding a woman to marry so that he could start a family of his own to bring back the happiness he once knew. Stoking the fire for warmth, his mind began to wander to what it was they protected. The possibilities of what it was and could do were endless. The one thing that Sean was sure of was that it had to be pure good or else it would not cause so much trouble. The opposite of destruction is creation, so he had always imagined it could help save the world from its ailments of bad crops, rockslides, floods and all the evil out there. This single idea kept Sean going; the faith that it could turn everything around and make up for those lives lost. A scraping noise outside brought him out of his brief reprieve; a sound known all too well as a telltale sign of trouble.

    "Not again! This makes four times this week!" Exclaimed Sean.

Chapter 2: Winters Wisps of Fate

A blood-curdling screech pierced the winter night air and sickened Sean. Gripping a short staff in one hand and the sword passed down from ancestors in the other, Sean faced the front door, ready. The sword hummed as he swung it through the air, making a slight breeze as it passed. It felt alive in his hands, as if it could sense the blood to come. Slowly, Sean turned his head to the side to pick up the soft scrape of the eternal foe that slayed his family trudging through fallen snow. Anticipation building, the Wanderer fell silent, puzzling Sean. The sound of an owl hooting in the thicket to the West of the house, a mouse scurrying to find protection in his home and the heavy breathing from his own chest were all that could be heard. Had Sean imagined it all? Was his mind playing tricks again?

Suddenly the door burst open as the Wanderer howled again, clawed feet protruding. Splinters flew past as the Wanderer kicked in the door, large chunks heading straight toward Sean. Dodging the wood pieces with ease, Sean assumed his fighting stance and braced for a first strike…..that never came. With a strangled grunt, the creature fell through the open doorway and lay still on the wooden floor. Sean lifted his eyes to see the Wanderer, a pitchfork sticking out of its back. Another shape moved a bit into the light of his house and pulled the pitchfork free with a sickening sound, black blood dripping from the tines. Light from the lit lamps cast dark shadows, hiding the stranger who claimed the kill, but Sean had other worries on his mind.

Sean walked up to the body, and, to ensure that the beast was truly dead, severed the head with a flash of the sword. Looking up, he finally noticed who the kill belonged to and shock spread across his face. In front of Sean stood a woman with a triumphant look in her sky-blue eyes and a smile that showed calm even in the face of danger. She had a sense of nobility about her, and her face had the beauty of an angel. Her shoulder length blonde hair looked travel-worn along with her dark green dress that had once been a fine silk. She stood shoulder height to Sean and if he had to guess she was a year younger than him. His eyes returned to those big sky blue eyes and when they locked a feeling of something long forgotten came to him. The smile slowly faded from that angelic face and she collapsed from pure exhaustion.

Catching her, Sean gently laid her near the hearth, melted snow falling from her to the rug below. Her skin was ice cold, and would not last long if he did not act quickly. Throwing another log onto the fire, he covered her in a thick blanket and noticed things he hadn't seen on the dark porch. Several scratches along her dress showed signs of fighting and some quick escapes into the mountain brush. From where, Sean may never know, but they would have to get treated before infection set in. With calm urgency, Sean set himself to dressing the wounds.

Opening a chest, Sean pulled free a timber box of bandages and alcohol, and poured water from the pitcher, gingerly applying water and alcohol to the cloth bandage but Sean's hand froze inches from pressing it to the first cut. 'Chivalry be damned! This woman will have to understand,' Sean thought before applying the cloth. A small shudder escaped the lips of the woman and Sean carefully let it sit on the largest cut, making more bandages ready. After the major wounds had been treated, Sean stood in the kitchen, examining the chaos.

The main room of the farmhouse held a kitchen, a small wooden dining table, and the rest taken up by the family living room with a few rocking chairs. Now a corpse sat inches from the table and its stench sickened Sean more with each passing moment. Sean had long since stopped keeping rugs in the rest of the house, for getting out black blood from a wounded Wanderer was nigh impossible, but he looked disapprovingly at the pools on the bare birch floor. Walking to the Wanderer, Sean grabbed the talon legs and dragged the beast from his front porch to the side of the house. Coming back for the head, Sean noticed that the strange girl was standing in the doorway, a blanket covering her slender body and a flushed face looking directly at him. Sean could see that the bandages were tied tightly to the larger wounds as the girl adjusted the blanket, not out of nervousness, but from the cold.

Striding to where the head lay, Sean was silent, only grunting, when she turned away and headed back for the warm hearth. The silent game Sean could play, after being alone all winter and now having another body in the house felt alien. Quickly he picked up the head and disposed of it in the snow next to where its bottom half lay. No time for a fire now; there was too much moisture about and oil was a precious commodity this late in the winter. The Wanderer's body would have to lie in the shallow snow until it could be burned. Heading to the barn, Sean grabbed his tools and a new door to replace the one that had splintered all over his floor. Nothing fancy with this one, it seemed like all of the good doors he put up got trashed and he was tired of creating something beautiful just to see it destroyed by evil.

Once on the porch with all necessary tools, Sean could hear the girl humming a light tune his grandfather Orwick had sung during the dark times. The melody had always brought images of the first days of spring where the town would hold a festival, and all the winter worries were no more. Sean's mind drifted to those days of the festival and the people who resided at the base of the mountain.

Their mountain neighbors would all gather at night to share stories of hunting in the winter and of times long past, retold as legends. Everyone would gather at the Stormbringer farm on the last night to hear the magical tales Orwick could tell about fierce battles with heroes and the Dark Force. A few folks with talent might play musical instruments to accompany the stories. Sean had learned to play the flute some years back, much to Orwick's delight.

Every story told was different right up to the year Orwick passed away peacefully. The last one foretold of the next heroes and heroines to rise in the great battle that was to come. There was seriousness in Orwick's raspy voice under the humor as he pointed to children, even Sean, and wove them into picturesque scenes of great triumph over foes so unrealistic it became comical. If Sean recalled correctly, it centered on an immortal wandering bard who sold songs for drinks and fought monsters while he was drunk, tripping over his lute more so than hitting a scaly Wanderer. As the bard journeyed, the children joined forces to help aid the man in his quest for the perfect adventure. At each stumble of the bard over his lute while trying to hit a foe, Sean would play a mix of notes, bringing laughter from the children and adults alike. They had called it Orwick's greatest story ever told and spoke of it as they laid his body to rest some days later.

The festival's tradition continued several years afterward, but fewer showed up as times became harder and every story told of hardships or bad luck. Now the harshness of this winter meant there would be no tales, laughter or music this year. This realization brought Sean back to the reality at hand, sending cold shivers down his spine. No longer was Sean a kid with big eyes who would one day become a hero; he had responsibilities that would not be taken care of by standing around.

Slamming the door into the frame, Sean began sizing it up for the correct spot to place the hinges. Glancing to the fire, Sean could see the strange girl sitting upright with her back to him. Her humming continued breathing life into the room until it was barely audible and then came quiet, leaving an emptiness that exemplified how Sean had felt all winter. Lowering the hammer, Sean debated broaching the void, unsure how his voice would hold after being silent so long.

"You're welcome for saving you," she began in a raspy voice. "That one was still a few years from full grown but just as dangerous."

"Hmph" Sean snorted.

Rather than answer, Sean returned to hammering the door in place, cold air causing goose bumps on his arms. Morning was far off, and Sean had no intention of sleeping in a cold house. 'Light, I will have to offer her a place to stay too, won't I?' Sean pondered while pretending to line up the hammer with a nail.

Stealing a gaze from the flames, Taylor focused on the silent, ungrateful man that had rescued her from utter exhaustion and a cold death. 'This can't be the one I am looking for; he is just a farm boy with a sword.' She began to take him in fully, and noticed things that had been initially overlooked. Broad shoulders spoke of many days in a field tending crops, but they had a grace to them that showed hours spent practicing with a weapon and developed muscles underneath that could handle the most complex sword strokes with ease. Room for growth, of course—that showed clear as day—but at least there was a beginning to this boy's knowledge. He was about a head taller than her, with auburn hair, a winter stubble, and greenish brown eyes that took in every detail of the room. The facial expression was grim, hard like stone, as if acquired from years of fighting and loss.

Taylor looked away to inspect the little house. Its main room consisted of a kitchen holding a metal stove with a pipe sticking out of the roof, a small dining table, and the living room which seemed to be the most decorative. A staircase led to a second floor. The living room interested Taylor. Six rocking chairs had been placed around the rug facing the fire, interspersed with little chests. Hanging lamps reflected off the soft wood panels of the walls. The Eastern wall was broken up by a large glass window overlooking the mountain, although now in the darkness, nothing was to be seen. . There were no painting or tapestries to provide color; only the colored rug Taylor sat on broke up the gray monotony, its well-worn threads had been weaved together in hues of blue, green, red and even some yellow; Taylor wondered if it had depicted some great event from long ago.

Taylor's eyes returned to the man who had spoken less to her than the Wanderer itself. What should have given him away as a warrior was the way his body moved; fluid motions that had purpose and shouted danger even without a sword. The sword hanging from his hip was......impossible!

"That is quite the interesting blade. It carries a mark on the hilt long forgotten by men and Ancients alike but with a history that runs deeper than this mountain. My name is Taylor, of the House of Luding. Protector to the Ancients and the secrets that they keep until death."

Sean's hammer didn't miss a beat as it struck the nail into the door in one swoop. Blood drained from his face and his heart beat as if were about to pound out of his chest, thoughts running wildly through his mind: 'Another Protector on a night such as this? Could it be true, or had he finally gone mad?' Taking a breath to steady his nerves, Sean knew this 'Taylor' could be an enemy to the Light. But he had little choice except to respond, for never before was the term 'Protector' used by anyone outside the family.

"I am Sean, Protector of the Bear Mountains and of the secrets that are contained within its depths. This blade has been passed from Protector to Protector in my bloodline and knows only the blood of Wanderers. The mark has little meaning to me, for its truth has never been revealed—not even to my grandfather." Sean responded begrudgingly, in barely a whisper.

Turning back to the door, Sean continued to hinge the blasted thing to the frame. He had never been prepared for this. No other Protector had ever wandered into his part of the world, nor had he sought them out before. It was said that Protectors could not leave their post unless it was destroyed, and even then it was their duty to die in honor there. A life outside of death was unfathomable, if not impossible.

Sean looked to the fire and saw Taylor sitting there, eyebrows knit in deep concentration staring deep into the red glow of the coals. Why of all nights had she come and stumbled upon his doorstep when spring was around the corner? It took Sean all winter to get the courage to plan on leaving the house for a short period of time and now this! It was unthinkable to leave the Artifact unguarded, especially when someone who held knowledge of the honored title sat so close by. He had never been told of Protectors attacking others for their charge, but it was a mad world nowadays and anything could be possible. Should Sean trust this Taylor or did he have to get rid of her?

Taylor began whispering into the coals, her mind racing at what Sean had revealed and the possibility of what it could mean. Her trance was interrupted. When she turned to the door, Taylor saw Sean looking at her, his jaw open and eyes glazed over. There was no way he could be what Taylor spent years seeking; the one she wanted would never freeze like this fool. The whole reason that she left her charge was to find an Ancient in this land, but it could not be him. Sure, traces of ancient power surrounded him and seemed to be ingrained in the marrow of his bones, but there was no apparent source. Maybe in a few generations, Sean's line could become partly Ancient with the right breeding but only one test remained, and it was an easy one: to make a human appear like an Ancient.

"The wind strips the valley barren; the earth swallows the oceans and fire blazes in the forests. Do you have the key to the salvation of light?" Recited Taylor.

Sean's hand started trembling and the hammer clattered to the floor as the last line was sung. The clatter echoed through his bones and seemed to be the only thing that made any noise in the chilly night. His trembling hand came to rest upon the smooth oak door, keeping reality from spinning out of control as he looked upon the grain patterns in the wood.

Taylor stood up, turning her back on the fire. She walked a short distance, coming to stand by Sean's side. Gently she reached out to embrace him, fearing that the strain of it all was too much to handle. The blade of his ancestors began to pulsate, glowing slightly in its sheath. When her fingers touched the rough wool shirt on his back, it was all she could do not to pull away. His body trembled from pent up emotion that was known all too well. Taylor had felt it long ago and the memory of it was enough to make her almost experience it all over again.

It was so overwhelming—the release of worry, excitement, relief, joy, anger and happiness from knowing that all you had sacrificed over the years protecting something that might or might not save the world. It showed an end to suffering and a start to life that was meant for death. 'So, Sean would think,' Taylor thought, 'little does he know our service does not end here and we are just pawns in my master's plan; in this there will be much pain ahead.'

"The key to the salvation of light resides in human beings, but only the greatest, chosen by the Ancients, may use it," responded Sean in a haggardly voice. "Greatness is earned when the world has beaten them to the end of hope, through such trials few can survive or know."

The response had flowed out of him like water from a spring in the earth, naturally and fluidly with a sweet taste to it. Never before had these words formed in Sean's head, but it felt right to say them aloud and a sensation came to life inside; one long forgotten until today. Then there was a stranger feeling; one that didn't seem to belong to him but of another person. Knowledge about places and things that Sean had never seen rooted in his mind as if it were always there just out of reach. The gentle touch on his shoulder retreated; the feeling that was flowing into him subsided, leaving a feeling of sadness.

'Had she always been there at his back reaching out to comfort him? How much time passed while staring at the world in this new perspective as if being alive for the first time?' Sean's mind spun through these thoughts in a dizzying fashion. Turning, Sean saw that Taylor had pulled away as if he were diseased. How could he have been so blind to his feelings for her? It seemed like they were buried deep in his bones. Reaching out to capture that contact again, the world turned upside down. Falling..........

Sean awoke on the floor, his head in Taylor's lap as she comforted him with a damp cloth on his forehead and hummed 'Winterman's Glee.' The tune was a strong one; capable of revitalizing anyone suffering fatigue if properly sung. Her skin was warm despite the cold still creeping through the unfinished door. Sean's body flushed with raw heat; pure emotion that could not be contained. Taylor's eyes were shut; the humming made her appear even more beautiful than before. Golden blonde hair fell away at the shoulders, framing that perfect face so close to his. The closeness was almost too much; body warmth pressing against him and the silk dress caressing his cheek.

Reaching with his left hand, Sean found the cool floor and pressed down, moving so that his face was even with hers. 'Taylor, what is this between us, and do you feel it as well?' Sean wondered deeply. At that moment, Taylor's eyes fluttered open and locked with Sean's; eyes so sky blue that he could have flown to the heavens in them. The scared look had retreated, replaced with a look of musing; at what, Sean did not care. All that Sean knew was that if he died right then, he would be happier than any man in the world, for an angel was looking after him. Inch by inch, Sean closed the gap between their faces and Taylor did not pull back from him; lust filled her eyes as they kissed.

Sean had kissed girls in town in his younger years and was even chased off of a farm for getting too close with one of the daughters; but none of it had a feeling like this. Sean felt whole when their lips touched, and all of the passion in him drained out into this one kiss. He wanted this moment to last forever; together with Taylor till the world broke apart and darkness claimed the land.

What felt like decades were actually seconds, and Taylor pulled away from Sean. His muscles burned as if from a fever and his head was aching from all that had happened. Again, Taylor put his head in her lap, a wet cloth to alleviate the pain. Slowly the lights grew dim as his heavy eyelids closed, and all Sean could hear was a soft hum that reminded him of her lips, and of the perfect kiss.

After an hour, Taylor woke from the trance-like state that she always achieved while humming. What had just happened? There was still a mystery, and not even the dreams seemed to make any sense. Sean was full of emotion one moment and the next reciting the ancient verse unlocking his mind to the world. But after that was……a mystery she wasn't sure could be solved until an Ancient could be consulted. The faint trickle of Ancient power from Sean could be felt right off the skin; barely perceptible, but there nonetheless. That sensation of tugging was still making Taylor's skin crawl. It seemed like Sean was drinking in the world from everything she had seen. It was as if he was a malnourished human consuming whatever was in reach to quell that hunger which had awoken inside. If contact hadn't been broken when it had, she might not have seen the next sunrise. Sean stirred slightly, head still in Taylor's lap.

"'Please don't wake up," Taylor whispered. "It took all of my energy last time to put you to sleep. Never thought Ancients could get so grabby, either."

That joke made Taylor smile. There had been something unspoken between them since she showed up killing that Wanderer. His shocked face when the pitchfork pierced the Warrior Wanderer's body was priceless. It wasn't as if Sean were bad looking; he was actually quite cute. It was just that Taylor had been around courts with Lords and Ladies. Once you have seen one you have seen them all and the top pick on any Lord could go to Taylor if it was what she wanted.

Serving an Ancient had some advantages to the job, certainly, but being stuck in all of those palaces with people who would think the world would bend to them was enough to drive anyone crazy. Taylor's mistress slept for years on end, waking long enough to make sure that the humans remembered who was really in charge and to give the next orders for their vessels. Taylor had been chasing down the man, now resting beside her, for several years with little success until this chilling night.

There had been talk in the village that Sean was too stubborn to remain on the mountain alone with no family. They had told Taylor before the winter that Sean should have followed his sister's lead venturing into the world. Up until Sean had recited the key to Light's salvation, Taylor feared tracking Sean's lost sister might be Taylor's next assignment. Another one of Ancient blood to improve the genetic line, if the girl had it in her, though it would have been up to Taylor's mistress to decide such matters. News of the death of one member from the original Ancient 20 had been disheartening to Taylor, but the idea that Sean possessed the abilities require ... Taylor shivered.

'And I kissed him!' Taylor wanted to scream aloud, but it would disturb Sean, so she held the thought inside. The kiss might land Taylor in trouble; she may have to complete penance until after the war; a warrior sidelined as a maiden—what a fitting thing! 'It was a good kiss, even you can't deny that or else he would not have lasted that long with me...' Taylor let the thought trail off.

Staring into Sean's sleeping face, Taylor began to piece Sean together, youngest of his family and the last surviving member to keep faith in the Light. Brushing the bangs from his forehead, Taylor bent down and gave him a kiss on the exposed warm skin, for what reason she was not sure but it seemed the right thing to do. Gently, she put Sean's head beneath a blanket and got up to stoke the dying fire. There was a chill in the air that needed to be taken care of, and it wasn't from the crooked hanging door.

Sean began to wake up and felt the soft pelt of a blanket under his cheek. 'Soft pelt?' With a start he woke to see the sunlight peeking through the window next to the fire and thick black smoke outside. With a groggy twist of his body, Sean moved to a kneeling position and almost fell back down to the floor. Every part of him felt like he had just plowed all of their fields, and his head seemed as if it were about to split open, as if he had drunk himself to near death the night before. Staggering to his feet, the world tipped again, but this time it remained right side up and the familiar smell of burned flesh came to Sean.

Walking to the window, Sean saw the source of the smell; Taylor was burning the corpse five feet from the house. Mustering his effort, he made it to the door just as she opened it and stepped inside. He tried to speak, but all that came out was a gurgling sound. Laughing, Taylor went to the table and grabbed a glass of water for Sean. Taylor held out the glass, Sean made a grab for it and she pulled it back.

"What, use up all of your saliva last night, lover boy?" chided Taylor, giggling "Don't have enough to at least say good morning?"

Taylor took the glass and downed it in front of Sean before returning the empty glass next to the pitcher. Satisfied at accomplishing so much in the morning light while Sean had slept, Taylor could not help but feel giddy. Walking to the fire, she threw a log on to the coals and flames leapt up.

"Please don't drown yourself trying to quench that thirst; I can only save you so many times." With a wink, Taylor sat next to the hearth and poked at the fire.

Pouring a glass of water, Sean drank slowly at first and did almost choke. After some sputtering, he got the water down. Looking to the hearth, he saw that Taylor still had that mischievous smile on her face. Turning away, Sean poured another glass and went to examine the door that had somehow gotten finished during the night. Sloppy work, but at least it was up and working properly….for now. Taking his time, Sean made it to his favorite chair, all the while looking at this angel (possibly devil in the daytime), and poked at the fire as if he didn't have a care in the world.

"I guess I should thank you for helping me last night with the Wanderer and for taking care of me ..." Sean began, words trailing off.

"Didn't think that the kiss was *that* good. You seemed pretty out of it and just kind of slobbered in the general area of my mouth." Taylor gibed.

"Well…I wasn't really myself last night. I don't know what I was at all," remarked Sean, becoming flustered. "What did you do to me, by the way? One moment I was fine and the next I could barely stand."

Trying not to laugh, Taylor responded, "You had what we like to call an awakening. Each Protector can transcend the human condition into something ... more desirable; all it takes is to get woken up. Not a difficult thing to do but it does require your entire body to turn on itself and create anew. This allows you to tap that Ancient blood in your veins and control the power to a degree. However, the ability to heal faster than normal humans, and a few other tricks, are still beyond you for the moment."

"Ancient blood? My family are simple farmers; our heritage is the fields," said Sean. "And we were tasked with being Protectors ..."

"Well, I will let my mistress sort this out then; just know the only downside to what happened is that if you are not faithful to the core, then the transformation can kill you," Taylor replied, evading Sean's inquiry. "Few have done that, but that's mostly because unfaithful Protectors choose not to go through with becoming awoken. In two days, you will be feeling better than normal."

Getting up from his chair, Sean went back to the window to look at the day, and to ponder what happened the previous night. So much happened—memories that weren't his, invading his mind—and….and that kiss. 'What got into him? Never has he been that impulsive…but Taylor did not fight it, either, and she is joking about it, so it must not have been that bad,' Sean thought as the sun crested the horizon. Then another thought came to mind, but it made no sense at all: claim the Artifact. Sean's family had never talked about it really, how the days of protecting would end for them, but it had to be that someone would eventually take it, or they would die trying to stop it from being taken to darkness till the world crumbled?

"You want me to proclaim ownership of the Artifact, don't you?" Sean asked, slowly turning toward Taylor.

"That is up to you. Is that what your mind and heart are telling you to do, Sean?" responded Taylor, "If so, why not do it? Maybe you are meant for more than just protecting this thing that your family has sacrificed so much for."

"Hmph. I have never seen it before nor have any of my ancestors. To protect faithfully is the oath I swore, and to break it would destroy everything my family has sacrificed."

Taylor moved to Sean's side, gently embracing his shoulder while feeling his head to see if the fever had yet broken. The skin was warm to the touch, but the fever had rescinded to its last vestiges and cold air found its way through the poorly fitted door. There it was deep beneath the surface, a faint sense of untapped energy waiting, and the meaning eluded her. This boy warranted further observation, for were the power to be inappropriately used, it would spell disaster to the balance of Light and Dark.

Shaking Taylor off, Sean moved to hang the door properly. Glancing to the table at his sword he noticed it no longer glowed as it had the night before. There were too many uncertainties floating around in his pounding head and it took every ounce of strength to focus on the task at hand.

Several minutes passed before Sean succeeded in fitting the door snugly into the frame, which warmed the room significantly. It almost resembled the home Sean had grown up in; of course, the stench of that wretched beast lingered, ruining the illusion. Sean returned the tools to the barn, and as he came back, he pulled a dress from a chest. It belonged to Eric's wife; not as fine as the dress Taylor was wearing, but one made of good, sturdy wool. This would prove warmer than the current ripped garment draped around her body. The memory of it being worn at the Mountain Festival resurfaced, making the room appear dark. With a shake, Sean pushed the memory away.

"Here, I hope this fits well enough. You are similar in height to its previous owner and you would catch a cold death in that ripped thing," Sean said, offering the dress to Taylor.

Graciously, Taylor accepted the garment, gingerly relinquishing it from his hands, and for a moment she noticed something familiar. It was dyed a forest green, like pine needles, and there was a slight embroidery of yellow thread at the hem of the sleeves. The wool would be rough against her skin, but the warmth would be a welcome comfort. The split that went up the middle allowed for free movement and could be worn while on horse or foot.

Slowly, Taylor began to undo the knot in her silk dress at the back, the fabric becoming loose and dropping on the floor, as Sean quickly turned his back, face beat red from her audacity and lack of privacy. Sean had not the stomach for such indecency—the bandages were bad enough!

An amused smile touched Taylor's lips; Sean looked ready to faint from embarrassment. This farm boy would learn a lot of the world indeed and be faced with much more brazen actions once they reached the city. Gently the old dress was folded, and Taylor donned the new one. Such a shame that the run up the mountain had left the silk in tatters; maybe a seamstress could salvage something from the material. Anything was possible with the proper court seamstress, and silk was quite valuable in these parts.

"I am finished dressing; you can turn around now," Taylor said seductively.

With deliberate caution, Sean turned back to see Taylor standing there, clothed in the new gown. His mother would be turning in her grave had she known what had transpired! Taylor spun around on the rug, testing how freely the dress moved. She lifted the skirts up slightly; to avoid any further embarrassment, Sean went to stand by the hearth, his hands outstretched for warmth. Throwing another log onto the fire, sparks sprung up and the wood popped. Not another noise came from either of them, and all that could be heard was the sound of the wind. A tugging sensation in Sean was growing, and no matter how much he tried to ignore the feeling, it only came back stronger.

Slowly, Sean walked to the far wall as if from instinct and not of choice. A single unlit lamp hung on this wall, but there was more to this wall than those outside of the family knew. Grabbing the lamp by the base, Sean gave the lamp seven turns; twice right, once left, and four times right. A sound of grinding gears filled the room and a panel of the wall slid down. Sean could find this panel in his sleep, for it had been shown to him numerous times by his grandfather. Gears grinding to a halt brought back the silence again. The panel was gone now. All that remained was a narrow gap, wide enough for one hand. Inhaling deeply, Sean reached forward precariously to grasp what lay within, hidden from the world.

Exhaling in a rush, Sean pulled his hand free, palm facing up. Holding it tightly to his chest, Sean stepped back from the hole, from which one could see only darkness. As was taught to the family, the secret inside could not be revealed to any unworthy souls.

"If you are as you say you are, then pass the trial that lies ahead. Only the just and worthy are allowed to know this secret," whispered Sean. "I offer caution however, for it will see through deception and claim a price that must be paid."

Taylor nodded and strode forward to the hole, straining her eyes with all the might she possessed to view what lay in the blackness. Reaching in with her right hand, palm up, as Sean had done, the fingers disappeared, then her palm, and finally her wrist. The hole felt......alive. A spark of light cut through the darkness, filling the room. The sensation increased with the intensity of fire. Gasping, Taylor remained still as a statue while pain throttled over her palm to a point she feared passing out.

As quick as the light had started, it was gone, leaving the room looking gloomy and the sudden brightness causing Taylor to blink several times. With the fading light, the pain subsided, causing tears to form at the corner of her eyes as relief flooded over her body. Gently removing her hand, palm up, from the hole and blackness, she expected it to be scorched beyond recognition, preparing for the worst......

Chapter 3: Trust in Mysteries

    Disbelief. Utter disbelief sprang across Taylor's face when her hand was free of the dark hole and saw that it remained untouched except for a small symbol etched into the center of her palm. The symbol for the Ancients, what Sean had on the sword he carried. It faintly glowed as if it was a firefly in summer, humming and illuminating with the beat of her heart. Sean lowered his palm to her, revealing the same symbol, but for one difference—his hand contained something … else and did not glow as hers did. A sensation that it was missing light was the only explanation Taylor had for the state of Sean's symbol. The extra addition to Sean's was something Taylor had seen somewhere…. her blood ran cold. 'That symbol is for the Proclaimer of Light!!' Taylor's mind burst with questions, none of which Sean was able to answer.

    Relief sprang over Sean's face upon seeing the symbol etched on Taylor's palm, light pulsing like a heartbeat and the worry of the world disappeared with it, warming his face even more. Truly this was a person who Sean could trust, but the symbol on Taylor's palm was different for some reason. Before Sean could ask why, Taylor spoke up, taking charge.

    "You see, I am telling you the truth," quipped Taylor. "Why the doubt if I spoke the ritual chant?"

    "One cannot be too careful in this day and age; I had to be sure. There are too many unknowns for my liking and few answers coming from you. However, this is proof enough of who you are and that you do believe," responded Sean. "In truth, this is as far as I have ever seen for the trial; it is something that my family has done for centuries by the will of the Ancients."

    The panel slid back into position as Sean lit the lantern, and the wall appeared whole once again. A sense of unease settled upon his shoulders, making the scalp tingle slightly; excitement was present as well, but what could this mean? The familiar tugging sensation came to Sean and rather than fight it he followed its direction. First though Sean had to think on all this and take a moment to let his mind catch up.

    Stepping into the kitchen, Sean grabbed bread and cheese, for neither of them had eaten in some time. Filling a pitcher with tea, Sean brought the food to the table and he set places for them both, the first meal with another soul in over a year. A poor excuse for a meal, but there was little energy to complain and he had too many questions on his mind to cook. Sean beckoned to the empty chair for Taylor to sit; out of manners he waited till she settled before taking the chair across from her, and he handed her a plate.

Taylor eagerly wolfed it down, then took a second and third portion. Sean ate with the same intensity, as quiet settled over both of them again, the fire crackling to break the silence. Where to start was the real question, but Taylor seemed entranced by the symbol and in deep thought. Chastising himself for staring at Taylor, Sean closed his eyes to mull over what had happened. It had always been said that once the trial had been passed by a member of the Ancients, he had a duty to reveal the Artifact. There was no precedent, however, if the Ancient sent on an emissary to retrieve it; even one that had passed the trials. He rolled the last morsel of bread between his fingers, as Taylor finally spoke.

"After much thought, you must come with me back to my mistress. There is great potential in you and to waste it would be a true shame, for the war rages and the Light is in dire distress," Taylor spoke softly. "My mistress will give a hero's welcome and the Artifact can be delivered safely to her. This job would be wasted for only me; it is a dangerous task requiring allies to accomplish. I can see you are wondering what to do next and am afraid the conundrum will cause you to faint again."

"A tempting offer, but this is where I know, and it is my home. It is all I have known my whole life and what I saw in your mind when we … linked, the world seemed strange, dangerous," Sean said slowly.

"Is it truly more dangerous than sitting here year after year on your own? Do you think this place will remain untouched for long? Even now the shadow reaches the mountain to a degree not known since before the 20 rode out to face it. The powers of Light must gather to face the foe and you have the ability to be a part of it, for even now, my mistress is beginning the preparations. Along the way, I will teach you what I can so that you do not appear foolish; this is my promise."

An answer came slowly from Sean, for such an inconceivable notion to leave what he knew, what his family had always known, could not be coerced. It was then a memory came from long ago of Orwick speaking of the future. He had warned Sean that fate is a mysterious thing and it never guarantees a choice can be made. Sometimes it lets you dip your toes in the water and other times it thrusts you into the icy depths.

"My grandfather taught me that fate can be mysterious, and if this is not proof, then I must be blind. Before my decision is made, and we depart, there is more that I must show you, but only if you are willing."

"I am willing; does this mean you are going with me?" Taylor asked hopefully.

Arising from the table, Sean strode to the far wall of the kitchen and carefully took down two sacks hanging from the wall. Opening cupboards, he began to fill them with supplies as if to answer Taylor's question, staying silent all the while. Keeping it light for the precarious journey down the mountain, Sean grabbed a small pouch with the family gold and what little trinkets he could take with them. Taylor watched as Sean carefully selected what to bring, the sacks packed with food and small items that meant the world to him. Tying the first sack close, Sean returned to the table with the second open for Taylor.

"Here, take this sack of supplies with you; there is much unease in the air and I fear we may not have the means to come back up here," Sean said while depositing the sack on the table. "I plan to take a secret path to the village below; my grandfather has spoken of it before. Follow me, we go to the Inner."

Strapping the sword to his belt and putting the sack on the other side, Sean headed to the fireplace and the slowly burning embers of a dying fire. With care, Sean extinguished the coals with water while Taylor gathered her sword from outside on the porch and gently placed the dress in the sack. Coming back to meet up with Sean, he took a look at the blade on her hip. Its design was similar to Sean's own sword, but the blade seemed to be newer than the family blade Sean wielded. Set for the journey inward, Sean led the way, adrenaline pulsing through his veins at what lay in the families cellar and the Artifact protected.

Following Sean to the back of the house, Taylor watched as he took a last look around at the family home. Picking up a torch from the nearby wall, Taylor lit it with a lamp, holding the end steadily until it burst into flame. Taylor knew not what lay in the 'Inner' as he called it, but his leaving meant the end to a long journey of shame for Taylor. The excitement at having the impossible within her reach, and high praise from her mistress looming overhead.

Sean found the wall on which a crack ran along inconspicuously, instructions on its location given so long ago it felt unreal. Balling up his right hand, Sean tapped three times on the crack in the wall, revealing another secret panel and the sound of stiff gears grating throughout the house. Holding his breath as the panel slid away, Sean was unsure what to expect as the glint of a lever became caught in the torchlight.

Reaching out, Sean pulled the lever down, looking to Taylor as it reached the final moments of motion. Eyes locking, a glint of excitement danced in the eyes of what Sean had thought to be an angel. 'Maybe she is a devil after all ...' ran through his head when the lever clicked in place.

Chapter 4: The Inner

A rush of air blew past the two of them as a stone slab below the wall began to shudder and shake. Ever so slowly it receded to open a staircase into darkness, and Sean took the lead, grabbing the torch from Taylor. Sticking close behind Sean, Taylor descended into the Earth, unsure what was next but unafraid. The mark on her hand began to illuminate, increasing in brightness the deeper they went, and the only light available was Sean.

The cellar smelled of spring air and life, exactly the opposite of what Taylor had expected from a home in the deep mountains. After such a long winter it was a welcome reprieve, and made her itch for actual spring to finally rear its head. When the bottom landing was reached after what felt an eternity in the dark, the air felt warmer than normal.

It was here that Sean took the torch to the wall on their right and Taylor waited in anticipation of what was to come next. Slowly lowering the flame, Sean brushed a trough of oil which ignited a flame that raced along the room. Carefully placing the torch in a bracket, Sean removed his boots from his feet to leave them bare. Cautiously following his lead again, Taylor removed her boots as well and when her foot touched the ground to feel……

Grass! It was as if spring was inexplicably the permanent season in this dark cellar in the earth. Moving forward slowly, Sean took careful steps to keep the precious vegetation undamaged as if stalking prey in the woods. It was such an amazing thing that Taylor felt joy bursting from inside her. The Inner spread far before Taylor's eyes and the sight was nearly too much to handle. Green grass ran along the cellar for 200 feet in all directions. In the center stood a pond of water next to a tree; one of the most beautiful things she had ever laid eyes on. To think something so magical had thrived under such unusual conditions; how this Artifact could change the world.

Sean was dumbfounded by the scene sprawling before him, a sanctuary of spring so pure it made perfect sense why the Wanderers always attacked. Eyes adjusting to the dim light from the trough of lit oil, Sean could make out a small pond with a tree sitting next to it. Being that they protected an Artifact, Sean had expected some sort of altar or a chest like in the stories, but nature's beauty was even better. A fog bubbled out of the water at the far end of the pond, billowing its tendrils across the glassy reflection of the cellars ceiling painted on the water. In a moment, it had engulfed Taylor along with Sean, thickening like wool obscuring each other's faces. An eerie quiet crept between them to the point where the slow exhale of breath was all that seemed to pierce the veil, causing the hair on the back of Sean's neck to stand on end.

After what seemed an eternity, another noise began to fold into the fog; it almost was a whisper of air tickling his ear. Swatting behind his head, the palm grasped at air and only succeeded in stirring the fog. Then it struck. A deep bellow emanated from the trunk of the tree; rising, falling, all the while vibrating the fog. Sean squinted to make out an odd shape sitting next to the tree on an upturned log.

It was there a path began to clear in the fog leaving a trail and revealing the source of the noise. The most bizarre-looking creature stood before Sean covered in vines, moss, and flowers. If he had ever heard of a creature such as this in stories told by his grandfather, it definitely would have rung a bell. But nothing came to mind, causing Sean to approach cautiously, keeping a watchful eye on the vines as they twirled toward the sky in rhythm with the bellow. A bare branch from the tree perched to the face of the creature revealed to Sean how the tree created such a noise as it reminded him of a giant horn.

Step – Sean's pulse quickened as his legs seemed locked in place. Step – time seemed to slow down around him. Step – only the pond to his right and tree in front were visible; Taylor was nowhere to be seen. Step – what was going to happen? Can this creature be trusted? Step – the sword strapped to his side began to hum, matching the sway of the bellow. Step – the world stopped and the tree bellowed one final note, fading into silence, leaving a feeling of sadness.

Sean was only five feet from the creature now, able to see it was completely made of vines and other vegetation. Where hair grew on a man, moss grew wild and unkempt instead. Buds covered what appeared to be arms, some of the flowers blooming and a sweet aroma wafted from the petals. But the feature which interested Sean the most had to be the face.

A dark oak wood mask, polished by the years, protruded beneath a mat of moss on its crown. Two holes gave way for the creatures shallow green eyes, with a sunken look and blackness around. The mask gave a humanoid appearance to the face but that did not comfort Sean; it only intensified the intimidation he was feeling at the moment. When he finally got past the eyes that seemed to see into his soul, the mouth was where Sean's gaze settled. Vines crawled in and out of the hole near the bottom. Attaching to the bare branch, it would wrap around an opening which let air push through the tree, creating the sound.

Reaching out its right branch, like a hand with upturned palm, its vine fingers beckoned Sean to come closer still. On the creature's command a second log came from the ground, seemingly out of nowhere, offering a second seat for Sean, forcing his decision to continue onward. On a day for oddities, this could only be added to the list of unexplainable events. Hopefully, it was all real; otherwise Sean's imagination had a sick sense of humor. Bracing to feel the rough texture of wood on his rear, Sean was pleased to discover the log could almost pass as a padded chair. It seemed to grow, contour and perfectly stabilize for maximum comfort to the point he wanted to keep the log always; maybe a nice parting gift.

Relinquishing its summons, the creature shuddered, croaked and groaned, loosening knots that seemed older than the earth. A calm once again ensued, and Sean finally realized that the feeling came from what sat in front of him. It was then that the whisper of air tugged at his ear once more, but this time it came across crystal clear. A rustle of leaves, bowing of wood and a creak that could have resembled language but instead reminded Sean of the forest during the spring winds. Closing his eyes to hear better, the darkness was illuminated with the green glow of its two eyes under the mask. The brightness showed greater with each creak and groan until bursting at the seam, making it nearly unbearable.

"Creeeeeeaaaaaaakk…….creeaaakkk….crreee-derstand…me…..now….?"

His mouth dropping open, Sean was left speechless.
"Will….take…..as ……understanding……."
Communicating with a slow nod, Sean clamped his jaw shut.
"Hold…out…..right…hand…..something….to…..give…"

Chapter 5: Artifact of Old

As if in a trance, Sean complied begrudgingly, placing his right hand forward with the palm up. The Ancient glowing symbol was now softly pulsing to match Sean's heart and the creature reached out with its right vine tendril till mere inches of air separated it from Sean's hand. The vines unfurled to wrap around Sean's hand, encompassing it entirely, rough bark scratching the surface of his skin. What passed through this bond transcended rational thought and was bigger than any one being to Sean. It was almost as if the entire meaning of life was contained in this transaction. However hard Sean tried to grasp it, it was just beyond his reach; and just like that the connection broke between them.

The vines uncoiled, releasing Sean's hand, allowing them to resume their original forms, disconnecting the bond. The creature nodded in approval of the exchange; a pleased light glowed silently in its eyes. Flexing his digits, Sean investigated to ensure all aspects remained unchanged, finding a new Ancient symbol etched and glowing on top of his hand now. Greeting complete, the creature decided it time to remove the mask exposing what lay underneath. Sean watched with anticipation as a vine wrapped upward to cover the mask and pull it free.

Vines wriggled beneath the mask, woven like muscles to give birth for eye holes and a mouth, but the cheeks were hollow. The same green energy which filled the creature's eyes with light surrounded the rest of its face giving it a ghastly, ghost-like appearance. Sean imagined that a strong wind could dispel its form entirely, scattering pieces to the air with ease. Sean seared the details in his mind but failed to comprehend if such a thing were even feasible. The air tugged at Sean's ear once more but this time a deep strength emboldened its speech.

"My appearance startles you; I apologize for this. It is all that I am, all that I shall be, all that I wish and all that is needed. My formal name takes three days to creak out, but we neither have the time or composition to instruct you on all the nuances of communication. Simply refer to me as the Element of Life, for everything about me is the preservation of all life. By the power of Light, I serve the Ancient 20 in wait for this day, to pass along traditions for your preparations.

Many years ago, it was foretold by your grandfather, Orwick, that a descendant should require the rites be taught. Never had I thought the time would be upon us in such a frightful manner that I lack both time and ability to do this properly. At this moment, a deep magic works to give us some of both, in a hope to steel thyself. If you have not puzzled this yet then there is much ground to cover; what do you know of the Artifact?"

"All I have known of the Artifact is that its power can change the world; my family has sacrificed much to protect this power," Sean spoke softly. "Wanderers and strange company have forced my entry to such sacred beauty, I feel I have failed my line entirely."

"Worry not young Sean, grandson of Orwick. Fate has a peculiar way of working out," the Life Elemental spoke, creaks accompanying each word.

"May I ask, what brings you to reside in my family's root cellar?" Sean asked, bracing for retribution at such a bold question.

The Life Elemental chuckled, images of leaves blowing in the wind traversed through Sean's mind. Afraid to disrupt the hopeful answer, Sean waited on the edge of his stump seat. Eyes on the Ancient symbol on the top of his hand, the view of vines unnerved Sean greatly.

"I am the Artifact your family has spent years protecting, one of the few of my kind to roam the world. You may call us Elementals. There are six in total alive; this is the rite I am meant to teach you, Sean." Life Elemental's answer came to Sean in a whisper. "We are Life, Earth, Water, Air, Fire and Death—the essential components of our world. It is fated for you to conquer all six, a task which would kill any mortal man. Even Ancients faced great difficulties in controlling two of these abilities, let alone six."

Sean listened intently at what the Life Elemental spoke of. Having control of greater power than ever imagined was humbling to Sean. Until two days ago, he had been just a Protector to this 'Artifact' and a decent swordsman at best. Now he was confronted by the possibility that the adventures told by his grandfather lay right within reach.

"We are the teachers of power, but most of all, I only may teach the strongest of them, for Life is not something to trifle with. The cost that comes from using Life energy is one that equalizes in the user, bringing them closer to eternal slumber," Life said as his tone turned dark. "Great power always comes at great cost. Forever remember that."

Sean nodded and with a gulp he realized all the while Life spoke Sean had not even breathed. Inhaling deeply, Sean listened as the Elemental spoke of the world long ago, how the Ancients came into power and the role Orwick played leading up to the first war of Light versus Dark. Hate filled its tone at mention of the wizard who tricked the 20 into their blood oath, birthing the elements to mortal forms. Sean's mouth hung open at all Life spoke of. These were not fairy tales to be told around a fire, but the history of how the world came to be in its current position.

For 100 years, the Ancient 20 remained in the South learning to control their power and gaining knowledge from the Elementals. In their efforts, the landscape began to take on a different shape in a way that became hospitable for comfort; no more blighting heat to take away their senses and dry them like leather. The 20 lived, laughed, and enjoyed their world but never returned to the wizard; they feared him and the wrath he felt for changing his world. Of course, as the story goes, this peace would not hold, and soon word of darkness spreading in the deep South reached the ears of the Ancient 20.

It is here that the legendary tale of the Ancient 20 came to be, as they rode out to face what was released in their folly to gain power. All were ready to destroy the darkness with their newfound abilities and were giddy with excitement to test the limit of what they had been studying. Save Orwick whose face looked grim, knowing full well the challenge might cost more than the 20 were willing to pay. Life assured Sean that this information was of the greatest importance for it was the key to understanding the world Sean was about to be thrust into. With every story, it must come to an end for the next one to begin; or continue…..

"Sean, this is where you come into play; I warned Orwick much as I have given you a warning not to abuse the power granted. It seems the crafty man found a way around rebirth in offering you, sole heir to the title of Proclaimer, an Inheritance of the grandest scale." Life coiled vines to give its face a stern look. "Let you not waste this opportunity to right the balance of Light and Dark."

"By the Light of the 20, I will heed your words to the best of my ability," Sean intoned, bowing deeply to the Elemental. Tears threatened to grace Sean's cheeks at how much his grandfather had sacrificed, sadness at being unable to speak of Orwick's deeds resonated throughout Sean.

Chapter 6: Folly of the Ancient

"Alas, it seems our foe, Time, is against us, but then there are tricks which can aid your training that time cannot touch. Enemies are at the doorstep of this sacred grove; you must not flee by the way above, for your strength has only sprouted. Remember the cost of power, my young Proclaimer, and use wisely what is given to you. Learn from the Ancients of their victories and their folly." Life's tone became as bright as sunlight in the spring. "In meditation you may find me with enough practice, when my brethren are awoken, our spirit shall be strong enough to teach you in this manner. The shrines tether us to this world and can be used to communicate as well; it is where our essence gathers the strongest. May the Light bless you and your escape….."

On those last words, the Life Elemental dissipated with the fog in the grove, the tree returning to its original form. Sean mulled over everything told to him as Taylor began to stir from her frozen slumber. 'Learn from the Ancients…' Life's voice floated into Sean; an inkling of understanding crept into his brain.

'It seems the right choice has been made to follow this…girl.' Sean thought watching as the world took on its usual color and the other side became clear, fog no longer dampening the grove. Sounds of scraping above in the kitchen were now heard by Sean, accompanied by a howl or two added into the mix. Wood snapping came next as the beasts started to tear at the house he had lived in his whole life. Taylor stood at Sean's side, a look of uncertainty on her face, while eyes began searching for a way out. Nerves prickled Sean. Trapping them down below the earth with no clear exit was less than ideal. Taking a deep breath, Sean concentrated to find how they both could escape and a tugging sensation at the pit of his stomach took over his nervousness.

Sean was infused with new power, so strong that he felt alive almost to the point of bursting out of his skin. Looking up, Sean could see six of the creatures above, the energy of their bodies pulsing darkly. The tallest one came upon the floor where the stairs laid hidden and stomped the stone slab to smithereens. Glancing back to the grove, Sean started his search for the secret way out, momentarily stopping to check on Taylor; her body radiated pure energy as bright as the sun. It seemed to be frozen in place, yet a trickle moved about here and there like a dancing flame. Tearing his eyes away, Sean looked to the tree, finding a small hole at the base of the trunk. Tenderly he reached out with his hand and energy flowed into the hole, causing it to grow larger, finally stopping when it was as large as a grown man.

Gulping, Sean grabbed Taylor by the arm, leading her to the newly grown exit. Without protest, she ducked into the hole finding vines underneath to assist in the descent. Sean glanced toward the stairs again, seeing the dark forms of energy at the final door about to break it down. As the crack of splintered stone rang throughout the grove, Sean checked to make sure Taylor had made it down safely, only to find her tangled among the vines. Drawing his sword, Sean took up a stance preparing to meet the uninvited guests in his home. The blade hummed in anticipation for blood of the Wanderers. Sean noticed the Ancient symbol glowed slightly in the dark.

"Weird," Sean muttered.

The first Wanderer burst through the door bellowing a stone-cracking scream at Sean, mouth frothing at the sight of him. Taylor finally was untangled and was almost down the escape tunnel; her eyes shot up to Sean at the noise. It seemed bloodshed could not be avoided; she dropped the last few feet, finding solid ground and fresh air at the end of the tunnel.

"Hurry up!!" Yelled Taylor from below, barely audible to Sean.

The beast inched forward. Sean could not hope to escape without some type of distraction, especially because three more were following it, and were now close behind. Roaring, Sean swung the blade at the Wanderer's head. It had not expected a strike so fast, and cold steel found its neck. Before the head could hit the floor, Sean took another pose, ready to take on the next.

"Observe this next move, young one; I shall show you the path..." whispered in Sean's ear.

The next three Wanderers started to morph, power channeling through Sean he watched as they turned into trees. Feet first as roots to a trunk, they roared in terror until the bark of a trunk spread over the mouth freezing the jaws in a permanent howl, leaves sprouting for hair. It amazed Sean, turning something so dark into...Life. As Sean turned to enter the hole and escape the cellar his body nearly collapsed to the ground. That sweet power barely trickling in him, its potency staggering; Sean gasped to catch breath trudging slowly forward.

"Great power comes at a great cost..." Sean again heard whispered again.

Turning the Wanderers into trees drained Sean greatly but he could not fail, the world depended on his escaping this situation.

Firming his resolve, Sean placed his left leg in the hole, followed by his right leg and found a little ledge to stand on inside the tree. Grasping a vine, Sean descended to the pitch-black depths, eyes focused on the makeshift rope before him; oblivious to the other two Wanderers who stood at the grove's entrance. They were too afraid to advance on the prey who escaped.

Clumsily, Sean quickly climbed down, wasting no more time wondering if they would try to follow. Releasing the power, he saw the tree close up leaving greater darkness. Gripping the vine, Sean slid down to the bottom, hands burning from the friction as he abandoned a slow descent. Landing to find soft earth below, Sean could see Taylor waiting, a look of worry on her face and her sword drawn.

"Put that away, now. We must run until this place is a distant memory," Sean said with remorse at losing his inheritance, the farmhouse above.

'No, my home will be the price I have to pay, for I have found my true inheritance,' Sean thought while blowing air on his hands to cool them. He knew that the Wanderers might destroy the timber, but the Stormbringer farm would forever be carried in his heart. Winning the war, Sean could return and rebuild it better than before—a consolation for his sacrifice.

Following Sean's instructions, Taylor sheathed the sword and let him take charge into the tunnel ahead. 'This farm boy is more special than I ever could imagine; I wonder what happened above?' Ran through her head, her mind drifting to that kiss. Taylor worried about what lay ahead on the road; this many Wanderers so far north had to be noticed by someone; human or Ancient. 'Is the village safe still?' Taylor shook her head, dispelling the terrible thought.

"There is hope yet in this world, and he lies before me, no matter the foolishness of Ancients," Taylor whispered to herself, but Sean heard every word and remained silent.

Into the darkness the two went, unsure what would be found on the other side or what else fate had in store in this journey. Taylor wished they were in the Land of Stars already, back under her mistress' protection and good grace after years searching for the Proclaimer of Light. All Sean knew was that the world once known would never be the same again; nor did he want it to be.

"Good, the world is vast and full of wonder. Do not squander it as I have, my Sean…" Orwick's voice came forth in Sean's head, shaking him to the core.

Chapter 7: Flight

The tunnel opened to the night sky; fresh air filled Sean and Taylor's lungs as they breathed in deeply. No noises of pursuit followed, which made the journey in darkness unsettling to them both. More than once Taylor nearly reached out to ensure Sean still was there. The woods told Sean they still were in the Bear Mountains, stars twinkling in the dark canvas above put them west of the farm.

Sighing with relief when no sounds of enemies came, Sean caught Taylor's eye, nodding to head west and to the closest village. Taking off in a slow run, the pair skirted through trees, doing their best to remain stealthy in the dark and snow-covered ground. Cool wind nipped at their necks, making Sean wish for a thicker cloak to travel in rather than the leather jacket. Taylor shivered slightly and taking out the silk dress, she wrapped it around her like a scarf. Clouds covered the moon which made it harder to see trunks and slowing their pace slightly. Taylor yanked at Sean's shoulder forcing him to look up in time to see a stone tower ahead. It was falling apart, abandoned for years, but Sean had not remembered seeing it before this day on any hunting excursions in these woods. 'We must be way off the path to the village; better cut north slightly,' Sean thought. Adjusting their trajectory, they made a wide berth of the haunting tower, heading northwest. The moon peeking from behind the clouds, offered just enough light to make their journey possible. Morning would be coming in a few more hours and Sean wanted to be running adjacent to the path in case they were being pursued by the Wanderers who remained.

When the sun reached its midmorning height, Sean stopped. They had covered half the distance but weariness forced a break. Finding a clearing surrounded by underbrush, Sean built a small fire to warm his aching body. Along the way they stumbled on an abandoned farm and scavenged supplies left behind, scoring an extra flint, a small hatchet, two short dull knives and oil to make a few torches. The clothing found was worn out, but a few blankets still held value to them, and Sean could fashion traveling cloaks from the material. The farther down the mountain they traveled, the warmer it would get, though nighttime was still quite chilly, and Sean dared not die of hypothermia.

Meager food meant small rations to Taylor and Sean who ate it ravenously, stomachs growling for another helping. Exhaustion on both of their faces, Sean volunteered to take the first watch, Taylor making him promise to wake her in a few hours. While she slipped off into sleep with a log for pillow, Sean got up and stretched. Deciding to make use of the time, he gathered more wood to burn and then started meditating. Birds chirped, squirrels chattered among themselves and leaves rustled gently in breeze. Concentrating harder, Sean heard other sounds. 50 feet from where Taylor was sleeping, a twig snapped which caused Sean to look intently in that direction to find a doe and two fawns. Settling back into the trance, he thought of all which transpired the last day.

Sean still found it hard to believe, him being the Proclaimer of Light! Had his grandfather planned everything so perfectly or was this fate? Letting the question hang in his mind, it drifted to the journey after sighting the tower. The two straggling Wanderers had eventually caught up to them, screeching in the night their bloodless scream. None answered the call, but it still made both Sean and Taylor nervous to the bone. Stopping where the trees allowed enough room to swing swords side by side they set up an ambush point. After waiting for what seemed an hour, the beasts' scent wafted toward the pair, alerting them to be ready for a battle.

Sean gripped the hilt tightly, cutting off circulation, and as he heard a footstep close enough, he attacked. The first swing, aimed at the head, missed by inches. Sean blocked a strike and parried with one of his own. Dodging another swing from the foes' blade, Sean stabbed at its chest, finding his target. The blade penetrated deep as the beast spit up black blood, fighting for one last swing until it collapsed, dead. Drawing the sword blade from its body, Sean watched as Taylor finished hers off in a flourish, taking its head clean off. Panting, they both ran off, leaving the fallen Wanderers behind to rot among the trees. Keeping vigilant, they heard no other signs of Wanderers, but so far, luck had not been on their side.

Over the reflection, Sean saw how tired Taylor was, staying up for such a long period of time after already being weary from the journey up the mountain. The unfamiliar terrain meant taking a trail which added a few days to the journey. Sean was aware that the game trails could get a person there in three days. Taylor's trip must have been about five by the state of her dress when she first met Sean. Add on fighting Wanderers while caring for Sean after awakening his latent power...exhaustion barely described how Taylor must have felt.

Letting Taylor sleep for an extra two hours, Sean eventually woke her up to take watch. Eyelids drooping, the last hour forced his chivalry to end which brought an angry look from Taylor when she saw how far the sun had moved. Sitting up crossly, Taylor did not say a word and Sean lay on the ground falling asleep instantly. Dreams filled with the Wanderers made the rest pure torture; occasionally, fights broke out with Wanderers, focusing his mind enough to give it a real feeling, almost like a memory long forgotten. Those vivid fights left Sean in a cold sweat, for no matter how hard he tried to kill them, more filled the void.

A shaking shoulder brought Sean out of the dream world to see Taylor standing there, bread in hand. Accepting it, he rolled over to a sitting position tracking the sun overhead. Night was falling. Taylor let Sean sleep extra as payback but he did not mind it. If anything, he appreciated the extra rest and his body told him it needed even more.

Neither said a word, enjoying the silence which gave the camp a normal feeling, almost peaceful. The woods around settled for night, but Sean knew the enemy to be nocturnal and they would need to follow suit. In the last light of the day, Sean tied together one of the blankets corners, and with a small stick, bundled them to make a cloak. Grabbing the second blanket, Sean repeated the steps, offering it to Taylor who accepted it graciously.

Banking the fire with dirt to put it out, a new thought occurred to Sean. Taking some green twigs, he added them to the dying coals to create a smoke distraction in case Wanderers were tracking their path. Getting up, he gathered the small bag of supplies. Taylor followed suit and Sean set the course once more toward civilization; 'Maybe a hot meal,' he thought glumly as his stomach rumbled loudly. Cloaks swished as they parted brush and headed off in the same northwest direction. Sean imagined they had to be close to the main trail by now.

The moon covered by clouds forced a slow pace, Taylor consistently checking their back even though the darkness only returned the stare. Only once did she try to talk, but Sean put his finger to his lips—too dangerous. On the night went without any interruptions or sounds of Wanderers, but Sean could not relent. Any twig snapping brought his sword half out in preparation for a fight, eyes frantically searching shadows. At around midnight—hard to tell without any moon—the main path was reached with no signs of life there. The stone hurt Sean's feet after walking on soft grass for so long, but the absence of trees to dodge was a benefit. Setting a comfortable pace, they hurried along, taking care to walk gently, so as to reduce the thud of their boots.

A few more hours of walking and Sean decided it was safe enough to make camp to get a bit more rest. Going off the path, Sean came upon a spot where the ground seemed flat enough to sleep on, and with ample brush cover surrounding them for protection. Without a word, Taylor lay down first, and was asleep in minutes. Sean took up the usual post of guard. This stop would be short—no time to waste arguing who rested when. As the moon broke free, he woke Taylor to make the switch, and as his head hit the ground, Sean's dreams began once more....

Sean stood in the cellar again, fog surrounding the pond and a familiar shape sat below the tree. Walking forward, Sean found the Life Elemental waiting patiently, deep in thought, no horn of welcome this time. As Sean opened his mouth to speak, it spoke to him:

"I wondered when you would come to me again."

"Where am I?" Sean asked. "Is this a dream?"

"Insightful Sean, this is a dream that we are using to communicate, and the space is my sanctuary or link to this world. I have come to teach you techniques that will aid your training in the days to come, for few Ancients can show the path of Life." The Elemental's words creaked like a tree just as it had when they first met. It continued. "To understand Life you must know the life of each creature viewed, beginning to end. The Wanderers you fight, for example, are born to be the bane of Light, bred in the darkest pits, far south. They must fight for the right to venture in daylight above. Only the strongest survive to make the world a dark place. To die in the name of darkness is their greatest honor."

"Do Wanderers wish to exterminate all other forms of life, then?" Sean asked.

"They do, in fact, wish to see all forms of life destroyed. Wanderers are not human, despite some common characteristics, but the true origin is a secret even to me," Life answered. "I tell you this so that you can discover and learn more through your experiences. Study Wanderers in the years to come so you can know your enemy. Apply this drive to other subjects of similar intrigue; simply seek them out to expand your mind."

"Expand my mind? Already I feel it is overflowing from the past few days," Sean responded glumly.

Life reached out a vine to touch Sean's shoulder, offering support at understanding the young Ancient's predicament. How little Orwick had done to prepare the boy for taking on the challenges of the world. If not for the pressing nature of the looming shadows, Life would have broken the dream connection right then and there.

"Sean, it is understandable that you feel this way, but keep striving onward and know you are not alone. Your destination is a strong ally to the Light, and their aid may help you find the solutions to the questions raging in your mind." Life's tone was gentle and warm, like a breeze. "Now that we have gone over training the mind, it is high time the power is discussed. It is a manifestation of your mental energy and physical energy; one supplies the power while the other its use."

"So that is why I must expand my mind?" Sean asked, still confused.

"Yes, spot on, Meditation is a tool that will assist you in finding this power, but manifesting it is a different story because you must bend the power to your will. Turning enemies into trees originates from a simple thought, but shaping it is so complex." Life spoke slowly, to be understood. "One must first turn the skin to bark, plant the roots and shape the cells to be a plant, not an animal. Although it is a type of magic, a caster has to know where to shape the energy first; in this case, taking their own Life energy and converting it to another."

"Shaping the energy to another?" Sean's head was spinning.

"Correct, now sensing Life energy is the practice I want you to continue, focus the power and use your eyes to see the energy. Worry not about shaping it to another form—that comes with growth in my element," Life's tone became firm to drive the point home. "Feeling Life energy will make you stretch muscles long dormant and enhance your strength, stamina, eyesight and hearing. I warn you to avoid changing energy into complex organisms; it takes a toll as you must have felt when you turned Wanderers to trees. It was my example showcasing the downside of this power; something even your grandfather, Orwick, struggled to understand."

"Are all the element powers this confusing?" Sean asked.

"Ha! They are not, but each is just as deadly if used inappropriately. Worry not, Sean. You will get the hang of it. My students will guide you in the use as well, for now think on the components of Life, as we must part ways…" Life's sentence trailed off.

"But wait, I have questions!!" Sean shouted. The dream began to fade as he was shaken awake.

Alert, Sean jumped up with his sword in hand, surprising Taylor nearly to death. She pulled out a small knife by habit. Taking in that he no longer sat by the pond, Sean slumped back to the cold ground. 'Just when I thought it could not get any more confusing, the Life Elemental drops knowledge about shaping energy.' Sean's mind was spinning wildly as he thought, 'When will my brain stop hurting?' Morning had come, sunlight glistening off snow on tree branches like jewels made Sean glad they had chosen this spot to stop and rest. The long nights traveling and waking sleep made Sean lose track of the day. but it felt a lifetime.

"Are you all right, Sean?" Taylor asked worriedly.

"Yes, only an odd dream. You would think after all this excitement nothing could set me off, but here I am looking like a fool again...."

Worry disappeared from her face. Taylor jokingly responded "Be glad that I did not have to use water to get you up, lazy bones. I have been trying to wake you up for some time. Nothing would work! It was like you were in some kind of…trance."

"How were things? Any sign of Wanderers or bandits?" Sean asked, dodging the topic of a trance.

"Nothing to report; all seemed quiet but I did stumble upon a few trap lines around us. Figured with it being morning we best not lollygag here while you get beauty sleep," Taylor jabbed.

Rolling his eyes, Sean got up, took stock of what supplies they had left and started to walk back over to the path. Along the way, Taylor pointed to the empty traps, proof of her valid concern to leave since they had not just been abandoned—each seemed freshly set to Sean. His head pounded like he had had too much wine the night before, and it gave him pause.

"My head feels like it is stuffed full of wool," Sean complained aloud.

Snorting, Taylor handed him a skin of water. "Here, this should help some. I found a stream a little ways out and filled it up in the early light."

Graciously accepting, Sean drank the water with vigor, the pain subsiding slightly with each gulp. He caught Taylor studying him with interest. Removing the skin, Sean wiped away the last drops on his mouth.

"What?" Sean asked her innocently.

"It seems we need to discuss what happened when you shoved me down the hole in the sanctuary. First somehow a hole opens in the tree creating an escape tunnel and then you take down four Wanderers alone?"

"Well, I had help if I must be honest. The first I slew with sword and the other three….. got turned into trees."

"WHAT?!? Trees?? How is that possible??"

"It seems that I was chosen for the task and am the Proclaimer of Light," Sean began slowly, telling the story of what happened in detail as they continued down the road. A lot he kept back, but the story held her interest enough that Taylor did not suspect there was more to be told.

"Trees, well if we ever need a boat or canoe, guess you are the guy to call upon," Taylor joked, stealing back the waterskin from Sean.

With that, silence fell between them once more and Sean heard voices talking up ahead. Not loud voices, but strange accents drifted in their direction, forcing Sean to leave the road. Friend or foe, he was soon to find out and Taylor prepared for the worst, cautiously drawing her knife. Sean fingered the sword at his hip but kept it sheathed; its steel could give them away if an enemy did lurk ahead. Cold wind biting at their cheeks, both ready for war, they climbed into some bushes, waiting for the source of voices to expose themselves.

Chapter 8: A Changed World

    Sean's legs started to burn from crouching for so long. They had sat still for over an hour, waiting on the voices, but they disappeared. Slowly edging through the brush back onto the path after stretching, Sean started to look for any signs of Wanderers or for the source of the voices they'd heard. Coast clear, they quietly resumed the march toward the direction of where the voices had come. Pushing away a limb, Sean discovered nothing but a new trap off the trail. Closing his eyes, Sean concentrated feeling a trickle of Life power come to him, sending it to his eyes. He then opened them to see a new world sparkling in front of him. Lights like candles danced around, the tree's energy was large and steady, flowing from the ground up to the leaves on the branches. The animal's energy, Sean observed, was small and quick, flickering in a circular motion, starting at the chest. Whenever Sean lingered too long on one thing it felt like the energy was responding; the light would begin to pulsate at his mental touch.

    A scent in the air caught Sean's attention, taking away full focus from the lights of the Life around. Smoke coming off the path to their south drifted on the wind, gray wisps cleared the tree coverage and Sean tensed up, deciding the next move. Signaling Taylor, they moved back to the trees and much as a predator stalks its prey, they advanced. Closer to the village, the smell and sign of smoke would not be out of place, but it was still miles off yet.

    100 feet from the smoke they stopped. Sean, using the fast growing Life power, searched until he found a clearing where a group of men were sitting around a fire. Seven signs of humans came into focus. There was no obvious sign that they were enemies. Still, something peculiar about the way they all grouped together bothered Sean and he could not put his finger on why.

    Taylor held her breath, waiting to hear what Sean saw. She tugged at his sleeve to attract his attention. Turning toward Taylor, Sean's eyes were glowing green, sending a shiver down Taylor's spine. Not daring to speak aloud, Taylor nodded at the clearing ahead where the smoke came from.

    "Could be a hunting party," Sean whispered.

    Then a twig snapped behind them. Taylor tensed up, ready to strike, but no screech or yell rose in the air that might signal a Wanderer. Being upwind from the smoke, it was impossible to tell for the final check. Slowly in unison they both turned heads around to find a large man in furs standing a few short feet away; bow drawn with an arrow aimed at Sean. Raising hands, showing no weapons, Sean stood, turning his whole body till it faced the man. Taylor took a yank on the arm to drop the knife and follow his lead, but they both stood waiting on the stranger to speak.

The man had considerable girth and size; a large white wolf pelt draped on his body gave the image of a true mountain man. The wolf head sat on the man's head as a hat and Taylor wondered if it was decorative or if it truly protected the man from the cold. To Taylor it seemed too small for the head it was perched upon and she stifled a laugh.

Sean took in the large man, eyeing the two hand sword on his hip and how the 6-foot frame seemed capable enough of handling the blade. Quickly, Sean let the Life energy drop, and his vision returned to normal.

Releasing the bowstrings tension to half drawn, the man approached carefully, keeping a watch on Taylor and Sean for sudden moves. The wolf head bobbed from side to side as the man began inspecting them thoroughly. Now Sean could see the man's skin was a darker hue than his own, a short black beard covered the stranger's face. Despite the growth, Sean could see wrinkles around the mouth which gave Sean the impression the man took to laughing more than anger or violence. The strangers eyes stopped on Sean's sword, widening at the Ancient symbol etched to the hilt.

"How goes it, fellow traveler?" Came a musical voice of the man as he lowered the bow completely, smile spreading over his face. "You look hungry and cold, a hard road traveled in these mountains with such light provisions. Please come join my camp, for the 20 bless us, it seems."

The man brushed past Sean and Taylor heading in the direction of the seven others around the fire. Tension no longer clung in the air and the man gave not a second thought to inviting two strangers to supper. Even after holding an arrow to Sean, it seemed the man had moved past the whole event at the sight of Sean's sword. Taylor wondered how much of a friend to the Light this man truly was; the accent seemed familiar for some reason.

Taylor nodded to Sean, signaling they should follow, and the offer of a hot meal had both of their stomachs growling loudly. Catching up to the man, Taylor saw he held the bow on one arm, and a line of rabbits fresh from the trap in the other. On the back of the wolf pelt an image was dyed into the white; a green tree with roots reaching all the way to the tail. It was truly beautiful and only strengthened the feeling Taylor had that she should know its origin.

Sean tried his best to lessen the building tension inside, but after the last few days of strange events, meeting this man in the woods only made things worse. Sean could read that the man had spent years trapping, hunting and living in the woods just by the way he walked. But an edge of worry that the man led them to a well-placed trap prickled Sean's mind; the friendly tone surely was a shock given the man's size and yet it did not ease the feeling. Taylor seemed undisturbed by the man's presence and so Sean would follow her lead more so than the man in the white wolf pelt.

Walking together the last few feet into camp, the man was greeted by the others with jubilant hellos from each of the seven companions. Offering Sean an empty log at the fire, he took it with a nod of thanks and Taylor sat next to him. Their camp was truly spectacular; six large trunks from trees freshly cut were placed around the fire for seating, white tents dotted the perimeter with domed tops and a bundle of cages filled the space between. One area was set up to dry and tan furs, the smell of salty brine wafted over top of the smoke from the fire. A wagon with skids like canoes on the bottom sat near the tanning area piled with the furs Sean guessed they had trapped since setting up shop.

While Sean looked over the camp the man deposited his catch to another man for cleaning. Taking the bowstring off the man in white wolf fur put both bow and string away in a case, ensuring that the string was properly sealed. He returned to the fire and took the next empty log, holding his hands out to the flames, ignoring the looks from the other men. They sat barely breathing, let alone talking, each gripping knives, which unnerved Sean. After a while a few looked at the newcomers, their eyes eventually seeing the Ancient symbol on Sean's sword. It took all of Sean's will not to wriggle under their scrutinizing gazes, and instead of staring back he looked to the fire.

The man who cleaned the rabbits returned and dropped one at each man's feet, except Sean, Taylor and the strange man in white wolf fur. Every single one took their knives and with a silent nod they began skinning the animals with quick precision. As they went about the task, a few shouted jokes to another on how slow they skinned or the fur wasted; they spoke so fast with odd words that it was hard to follow. Glad to no longer be the focus of their attention, Sean began to watch them at work with awe. Inspecting the men, Sean found they each wore a wolf pelt of different colors. Sean would bet the same symbol was embroidered on the back, like the white wolf pelt. Every man had a similar face and beard to the first man, so it was starting to make sense why they all wore different colors. Sean would be hard pressed to tell them apart otherwise, even though a few stood at different heights. One truly identical pair wore the same black wolf pelt, yet different color wolf heads. Sean figured out they had to be twins; there used to be a pair of identical boys on the mountain and Sean could remember the trouble they would cause.

After warming hands a while, the man wearing the white wolf pelt brought them down for proper introductions. Taylor took the offered hand and cusped it as they shook. Sean, unsure what to do, followed suit. The usual greeting used by the villagers was to clasp arms, but Sean feared this custom might be rude to the strangers on the mountain.

"Welcome to my fire and home away from home. I am Jorseph and these are my brothers," Jorseph said, pointing to the rest of the men. "We have come from a long ways north to trap furs of the Bear Mountains. Sadly, not a bear yet but hope one stumbles upon our path and regrets it!"

This brought cheers from Jorseph's brothers with further joking insults Sean did not catch. Taylor looked just as perplexed by this but kept her face composed. They were still at work with their knives, fervently skinning the rabbits, mounds of pelts piling up next to them all. A few began to whittle sticks into spear tips, which Sean hoped would be for cooking the freshly cleaned meat, and not for them. Deciding it proper to return the introduction he worked on what to say without sounding a complete fool; Sean had prayed Taylor would go first but it seemed she held her mouth clamped tightly shut. Unsure if Taylor would speak, Sean took the charge and it seemed fitting since these woods were his home.

"My name is Sean, further up the mountain is my farm and home, born in these mountains I have spent my days learning the woods. Two days journey northeast you will find a small mountain where the bears like to hibernate in caves. Being that this winter has stretched so long it is a wonder if they ever will wake to roam again."

"It is an honor to meet a native of this realm. We have been trapping for weeks but haven't seen a soul until today. My youngest had stories of this mountain being cursed, but I told him if it was cursed, why would we catch more rabbits than a ziggy fish lays eggs." This brought on more laughter and jostling of the brothers.

"Most of the mountain dwellers left some time ago because of the harsh winter, I fear that not another person wanders these woods. But tell me, did the villagers not inform you of this when you passed through the main road?" Sean asked.

Joking came to an abrupt halt as each brother looked to the others, unsure how to respond. Joseph even seemed taken aback by the question, Taylor sat taken aback, just as confused as Sean. An uneasy feeling grew in the pit of her stomach. The increased Wanderer activity had worried her about the state of the village inhabitants.

"Is something amiss at the vill-" Sean began.

"The village be blazed boy, its inhabitants slaughtered and only charred timbers with whispers of ghosts remain. May the 20 protect their souls." A chant repeating the phrase followed around before Joseph continued, "We did not stay long, it is best avoided if possible, for the sight is not taken in lightly."

Seans heart dropped. The village he had traded with and visited his whole life, gone without a word reaching him. He truly had been the last survivor on the mountain and would have never known until the thaw of spring. Memory of the first girl Sean danced with at the festival floated in his mind, along with several families who knew Stormbringer's well. 'Gone.' The word repeated in Sean's mind over and over. It felt as if his world had been ripped wide open; again, in how many days, Sean lost count. Sitting there in silence, Jorseph told as best he could what may have happened, his brothers starting to cook the rabbits as he talked.

The trapping party had come from the north a few weeks back by the way of a small river instead of the main road that led to the village. Upon collecting enough furs to sell, they had ventured to the local village less than a week ago in hopes of finding a market to unload wares on the friendly folk. Coming to the village by the main road they found tracks that indicated a horde of Wanderers came to the village and ran amok. From the bodies strewn about, it looked as if the beasts began killing all that crossed their path.

Fires seemed to be set around the perimeter, the village's attempt to drive the monsters away. No sign of a formal army to defeat the Wanderers could be found, so Jorseph surmised that sacrifice was the only option to let some villagers flee. This was in vain, for torn apart wagons had been found 200 feet from the village. Jorseph spared

Sean the particular details on the bodies found abandoned, with buildings in ruin.

Sean really had been the first person Jorseph had met from the mountains, for no survivors were found living in the expanse between the largest mountain and the village. Taylor's face turned to icy calm as Jorseph spoke and Sean could only wonder why she had not told him. Numb, Sean got up from the log and walked to a tree 15 feet away where he emptied his stomach until nothing was left.

"How can one find hope in such a bleak and dreary world of darkness?" Sean whispered.

Chapter 9: Strange Friends and Stranger Customs

Sean felt hollow; all his family, friends and community wiped out by Wanderers. So many lost because of the power that ran through his veins. How cruel that death followed Life. 'Why had Taylor not told me?' Sean thought darkly, balling up a fist and punching the bark of the tree in anger. Walking back to the fire, Sean said not a word as he sat on one of the logs across from Taylor. In his absence, the men had finished skinning their meal and it sat on skewers roasting over the fire. More wood was thrown on, but it did little to help Sean and the cold penetrating through to his bones.

Rabbit was divided up among the group; more joking between the men. Taylor conversed with them as well, joining in their talks of home—a country called Bischke. The rabbit had taken on the taste ash in Sean's mouth and the jokes fell dead upon his ears. 'Gone.' The word repeated in Sean's mind over and over again till he felt the bile in the back of his throat once more. Standing, Sean walked away between the pines, finding a smaller clearing to be alone and to process.

Too many faces and voices ran through Sean's head; friendly greetings with offers to sup when finally Sean was all alone on the mountain; butchers who purchased grain to feed their livestock at harvest time; Derek, the grain warehouse manager, who always gave Sean a better price than the other farmers; David, the blacksmith, whom everyone went to for repairs. The girls who had a twinkle in their eye just for him; and their mothers who kept an eye on him for reasons of their own. All were gone now, and Sean could never atone for their deaths. Even the snap of a broken twig behind him did not interrupt Sean's state of grief. 'Good, let them come with a blade in the back,' Sean thought darkly.

"If you can't stomach this, then how will you last when greater atrocities occur acquiring the other elements?" Asked Taylor, "let alone when we enter battle with an army of soldiers?"

"How could you not tell me?" Rasped Sean in a whisper.

"I had no idea; things were fine in the village when I left and they all spoke so highly of you..." Taylor's voice trailed off. "It did cross my mind the day those extra Wanderers attacked and you claimed the ... 'Artifact' but I held out hope they were safe."

"Who are you? No more half-truths or lies." Sean spat the words out like venom.

"I am Taylor, servant to those of the original Ancient 20, Protector of the stone shrine, and keeper of my mistress's secrets. That is all I can say for now." Taylor said gently. "Sean, I have not deceived you; in truth I am unable to tell you more, for my mistress forbids it and her words are law."

"Why come for me? Since meeting you I have only felt more pain."

With those words, Sean punched the tree trunk, his knuckle bleeding from the force and cold air. Anger like a swarm of bees raged inside. Turning to face Taylor, Sean's heart skipped a beat. A tear streaked down the right side of Taylor's face. Even when crying she looked beautiful, and Sean saw a new side of Taylor—the battle angel. Taylor's concern for the villagers' safety was apparent on her angelic face. Sean had never seen her this vulnerable before. Sean held another emotion besides anger; there was joy, too, but he could not say that aloud.

"Darkness like this grows in the world and my mistress sent me to find you. Her reasons are her own, but you are needed."

"Needed for what?"

Taylor stared at Sean with a dumbfounded look. Sean blushed, forgetting already what he had obtained. Taking his hand in hers, Taylor peered into Sean's eyes and he felt that connection again, much like the first-time meeting.

"The 20 are gathering and they need their Proclaimer. That is the message to relay, and once we reach my mistress you may ask these questions that plague you. I can lead you there."

More plans and games played by those immortal beings. Since claiming the Ancients' power, Sean realized he was being controlled by the actions of others. It did not anger him at first since it all meant that they were able to meet, but the continued shrouded mystery of Taylor's mistress fueled the anger inside. How badly Sean wanted Taylor to spill everything right then and there; answer the questions looming overhead. However, it was the dedication to her mistress that made Sean love the girl all the more.

"I will think about this, but now I need quiet for meditation," Sean huffed.

Letting his hand slip free, Taylor stalked back to Jorseph's fire, pulling the cloak tight to drive the point home. Alone again, Sean opened his mind to the connection of Life energy, seeing the trees' Life but sharper. He pulled at it and a new branch formed, sprouting fresh pine needles, and along with it, Sean's own energy drained away. Looking at the fire he saw nine signs of energy, each holding a unique energy flow. Taylor's glowed brighter than the rest and its pattern shifted at a faster pace than the others. Jorseph's swirled in a constant state of unrest, almost wanting to match Taylor's energy; Sean wondered … A voice boomed in Sean's head:

"Do not disturb human flow; it comes with a steep price."

With that, Sean quickly lost the connection, and all returned to normal. There was nothing further to think about; any plans of going to the village for support were gone. All Sean could do was go with Taylor to her mistress's place and get answers. Seeing the world would not be a bad change of pace either, as nothing kept Sean tied to the mountain anymore. One thing was certain; Jorseph could offer more information on the outside world and he would not be bound to some nameless mistress. Slowly, Sean walked over to the fire and sat down next to Jorseph on the log. Ignoring the quizzical look from Taylor, Sean struck up conversation with the traveler.

"I thank you for your fire and hospitality. My family farm is northeast, a one- or two-day walk, and if you are ever there, make yourself at home," Sean said. "Jorseph, you mentioned coming by river, and I noticed your wagon had some strange pieces of wood attached to the bottom. What are they?"

"Ah those are so it can float! The wagon wheels change out for paddles and it bops us around on top of the water. It's faster than walking with all our wares," Jorseph said, pointing to the wagon and making a motion of rowing with the wheels. This brought laughs from his brothers around who all joined in the motion.

"That is quite the amazing wagon! I will have to look it up next time I find myself in Bischke," joked Sean.

"Ha! When you do, be sure to also look up the seven brothers, Jorseph, as we are all known. Bischke is a wonderful country, by the way," Jorseph added, as his eyes wandered to the sky above. "Some call it the birthplace of wolves and so we wear their pelts in their honor."

"I wondered why; they do little for the cold in these mountains," Sean replied. "What of the tree symbol on its back?"

"Hmm, that is our family crest—stretches back to the days of the Ancient 20—our own symbol like that on your sword," Jorseph added, nodding to Sean's blade.

"You noticed that. Well, not too long ago, I thought of it as a family crest; how things have changed …" Sean's voice trailed off.

"You pressing South still then, eh? My fire is always welcome to you and this fine lady. Sorry if my news disturbed you." Jorseph bowed with his head slightly, the wolf head appearing to look directly at Sean.

"Southwest out of the mountains. There is a nothing left for me here. The news would have been found out eventually, but thank you for easing into it like you did."

"My pleasure, Sean. One piece of advice; at the base of the mountain running for miles is a bramble wall. Its edges can scrape steel and tear off limbs. Be wary of it, for the thing extends deep and there are only two ways to cross it by land. The first is a toll bridge on the top; soldiers of Hammerfell control it and it is not cheap. The second is a path. Plants overgrow the path at night, yet retreat when daylight comes. Both are treacherous to cross, for either way there is danger."

With a hard stare, Jorseph drove the point—a secret meaning. Sean had never encountered soldiers before; the mountains had no king—only nature as the ruler. A tax collector had not been seen in many years, either. Sean had assumed the area at the base of the mountain held the same freedom. Taylor came over at the mention of the brambles and sat next to Sean. Looking at her, Sean could see they had to be on the way. Despite the hospitality of the fire, their journey was still long from over. Turning back to Jorseph, Sean grasped the man by the forearm in the custom of the villagers and the man returned the gesture.

"I will be wary; again, thank you for your wisdom. Excellent bear a day north; big creatures with an amazing coat. I recommend checking it out if interested," Sean suggested.

"I shall consider the advice. Peace favor you and may the 20 Protect you," intoned Jorseph.

"You and your brothers as well."

"May you find home someday and honor the return of the Life Giving Tree, Jorseph," said Taylor.

With a startled look sprawled across Jorseph's face, he kissed Taylor's hand and murmured in her ear. For how long had Sean left them alone? They parted the camp of brothers, but not before Jorseph shoved cooked meat and small pelts into Taylor's supply bag and they began the trek southeast. Both walked in silence until dusk, covering more distance by following the road, but they were still a day from the village. Stopping at an old farmhouse, Sean decided it would provide shelter for the night. Escaping the cold was welcome, and as Sean built a small fire, Taylor set about scavenging the place for anything of value.

Coming up empty, she sat next to the fire with a sour expression and Sean handed her a piece of meat. Broaching the topic of Jorseph's warnings, Sean wondered if Taylor could speak on the matter of the toll to cross.

"What did he mean about the soldiers?" Sean asked between bites.

With deep thought, Taylor answered, after swallowing a hunk of roasted rabbit. Sean had to understand the world and would eventually run into Hammerfell kingdom whether she liked it or not. Taylor's mistress might be forgiving, especially since Jorseph already had eluded to the toll charged.

"Southwest of the mountain in the kingdom of Hammerfell, boys are made to serve as guards at the age of sixteen. Girls are made apprentices to a craft until it is mastered and then they marry a retired soldier. The boys must serve until the age of 25; then, they may re-enlist by choice to be an officer," Taylor spoke matter-of-factly. "Otherwise, they return home and find a suitable occupation."

"What does that have to do with me?" Sean pressed.

"Well, it applies to both of us. Foreigners from the mountain realm become indentured to their prospective areas for 10 years, unless they are able to trade or buy their way out. I am not a citizen, so we both would need a trade to bribe the guards. Only this border has such a massive toll," Taylor answered, "and leaving the country is not their worry, but coming back *is*."

"Then the bramble path is our only option. I wonder if my power can control them for our safety," Sean mused.

"That would help us tremendously, but we can talk about it more when we get some rest," Taylor yawned.

With that, the fire was reduced to coals and they settled in for the night. Barring the door with a wood plank, Sean felt comfortable enough to forego standing watch. Exhaustion raked both Sean and Taylor, so neither objected to the lack of a guard while sleeping. Tomorrow worried Sean. They should reach the village by mid-morning and news of its demise still stung like a fresh wound. His dreams were filled with the faces of the perished, turning sleep into a running nightmare.

Morning light broke through the farmhouse window, waking Taylor who had tossed and turned all night long. The strain of being so secretive was taking its toll more than even the rapid flight up and down the mountain. Nudging Sean awake with a foot, they prepared to head out on the road and make it to the village. Birds chirped in the air, giving them a sense of the coming spring; melting snow falling off tree limbs gave Sean quite a fright. Taylor had not the energy to even laugh at the boy. Her mind was wrought with sadness as she mourned those poor villagers. All had been eerily quiet since their fateful meeting with Jorseph; almost as if Sean did not trust her. Putting on a brave face, Taylor stowed away those feelings and focused instead on the task at hand; before Sean, she had done just fine in the wild by herself.

  Sean stopped in the middle of the path; crossing over the next hill would take them to the village. Normally at this point in the day, sounds of life could be heard. Sean strained his ears hoping to find those welcoming noises. Only the chirping of the birds answered Sean's wish. Taylor tugged at his arm to keep him moving forward. Cresting the hill, Sean took in the pure destruction; its sight was even worse than Jorseph had described.

  Sean gasped as he looked upon the ashes where once a small mountain village had stood only a season before. The blacksmith's forge on the edge of town standing open to the air, stone walls, fragile to the touch, outlined the beautiful shop Sean remembered visiting since childhood. A splintered anvil sat charred with soot from the flames. Upon seeing it, Sean could hear the hammer fall on horseshoes while Dave worked the metal to bend to his will. The rest of the buildings on the outskirts of town were unrecognizable, half burned timber stood in shambles on the verge of collapse. The small grain mill positioned on the river, running through the village, was only distinguished by the skeleton of metal from the giant wheel that ground flour. Sean's heart sank; truly the flames had claimed all.

  Further in was much the same, only scorched metal could be found in piles of ash like ghosts of the people who lived there. Sean anxiously looked for the Mayor's house which had been the only true stone home in the area, and much to his sadness, the rubble was spread far. When the house stood, it held a beautiful array of stones that changed color in the sunlight. The pride and joy for this small village as each piece of stonework had come from the river after years of polishing. Now only the color of black reflected back in the sunlight, and Sean wanted to weep. The whole time Sean was vigilant for any bodies or bones in the piles of ash surrounding them, he wanted to offer the dead a final burial. Not a bone or body would be found, giving Sean hope that there might be survivors, proving Jorseph wrong.

Taylor took in the devastation of a place that had been so welcoming and friendly. A small village, it held a unique charm never seen before on her previous travels. The inn was a quaint building with only a room or two and a common room that felt more like a family dining room than a banquet hall. Stopping at the ruins, Taylor dug out a metal star that had been attached to the pillar that held up its porch. This had signified that those inside the inn were friends to the Ancients and she had felt such joy in finding aid. Now it was a memento to carry onward. Someday she would find a proper home for the thing in memory of the laughs shared with the innkeeper. Catching up to Sean they pushed inward to the center square, the heart of the burned village.

Entering the village square Sean was visibly distraught. As he looked in each direction at every burned house, barn and wagon in sight. Still no sign of any dead bodies in the wreckage and Sean scanned with Life, unsure what he could do, but it was better than nothing. Sean smiled as he watched Taylor deposit a metal star in her bag of supplies. Even those passing by had felt such a connection to this place. It truly warmed Sean, despite the cold.

"I must do more than avenge my family, Taylor; for the honor of house, Stormbringer Light must vanquish Shadow…" Sean vowed.

Taylor only placed a hand on Sean's shoulder; no words could be said to offer relief or lessen the sadness. She knew the sacrifice involved with protecting the Light from the Dark all too well. Subconsciously, Taylor's hand went to the sword at her hip. The blade was more than just a weapon; it was a reminder of the cost that came with protecting the ones you love.

Sean's whisper fell away into the silence of the once boisterous village. Pain, loss, tragedy; all these people's lives lost because of Sean's family. Heavy the penance to redeem countless families and friends who died by the hand of Wanderers—a daunting task which Sean did not plan on shirking from; even if it killed him, these deaths would be avenged. Taking a deep breath, Sean continued on toward the fields beyond the charred village.

Standing on the edge of the field, Sean could see mounds of dirt lined up in neat rows— unmarked graves of the ones who had fallen. Where winter wheat should be planted, the dead lay as if ready to harvest instead. The ground spewed dust when Sean's knees fell heavily, as his shock turned to rage and he beat fists on the dirt. He felt utterly useless. Had Orwick just told Sean about the Life Elemental and his role in the war so much bloodshed could have been avoided. If Sean had only come to the Village rather than waiting for the winter to end then countless lives would be here to welcome them instead. The list of 'what ifs' mounted in Sean's head and each one received a punch in the dirt.

Knuckles bleeding, Sean finally stopped raining blows at his invisible foe; Taylor did not interfere, afraid he might lash at her, as well. Sean stood shakily as the rage subsided, but the anger had not gone away. Sean seared the anger in his mind in a single thought—'master your gifts and avenge the dead'. Wrapping his bloody hands in a torn piece of cloth, Sean turned away from the field, heading to the grove nearby and worked out what he wanted to do.

Taylor watched as Sean wrapped his hands in a cloth. She wanted to tell him to clean the wounds first but the look in his eyes prevented her from doing so. Instead, she watched as Sean walked to a grove of trees nearby. Interested in knowing his plan, Taylor prayed it not a reckless one; she could not lose the charge in her care again.

Sean returned to the field of graves with his hands cupped. Dirt spilled out of them and a small sapling sprouted in the soil. Placing the dirt on the ground, Sean summoned the power of Life to his fingers and the little tree's roots dug into the cold ground. Feeding it energy with tender care, the sapling grew to knee height, Sean struggled to maintain composure as the thing soaked up energy like dry clay drinking water. Satisfied the tree would grow when spring came, Sean cut off the energy and marveled at the work accomplished. A little apple tree stood sprouting leaves among the dead—Sean's offering to their sacrifice for associating with the family Stormbringer. Smiling, Sean collapsed to the ground and the sound of Taylor's boots running in the snow was all he heard as sleep came to his weary body.

Taylor watched in awe while Sean nursed a sapling to maturity, his eyes green with power and face contorted in a struggle to maintain control. As the new tree reached knee level, Taylor wanted to yell for Sean to stop, but this was his duty and she dared not interrupt. New branches quivered one last time before they stopped growing and Sean collapsed to the ground. Taylor ran forward, too late to catch him, but she would be there to keep him safe so Sean could rest properly. Stopping in a clearing near the river, Taylor waited patiently for Sean to stir. The peacefulness was too much; how could such a tragedy have occurred, when all was so calm? Taking out a knife, Taylor whittled a stick, keeping hands busy to distract her mind from the haunting memory of her own brush with death in service of the Light.

Sean awoke to the sound of water bubbling over rocks. The sun sat in the sky past noon. What day Sean was unsure, but his body ached to sleep more. Sitting up, Sean could see the village a distance off and Taylor had selected his favorite grove. This was the best fishing spot in the village. Sean had spent hours soaking up the sun in the summer catching next to nothing. The memory brought a single tear to his cheek and Sean wiped it away. 'No more crying, do you want Taylor making fun of you?' Sean thought with a laugh. They ate a little and afterward Sean felt much better, stamina returning. It was decided to leave the village behind. Taylor never mentioned how foolish Sean had been for the delay, but something told him she appreciated what Sean did for the people who had died. The setting sun spread far in front of the two travelers who were ready to distance themselves from the haunting memories in their minds. Sean left the village behind, resolved to protect people like this and Sean was intent to follow through without hesitation.

Taylor pulled him aside on the third day of travel after the village. The road had become increasingly travel worn. The forest seemed to press in on itself, giving an ambience of doom.

"A little farther ahead is the ladder to the toll path. Past it lies our route over ground and if anything like what we were warned of, it is a dangerous path. We should camp here for the night," said Taylor.

Sean responded with a silent nod and began the trek to find a campsite and game, away from the path. In a little alcove surrounded by trees, they lit a campfire and Sean went to hunt. Not many rabbits, but squirrels and birds a plenty. Returning to their camp with his haul, Sean dropped down on the outskirts, taking a knife from belt. He skinned the squirrels with ease. Taylor had collected firewood for the night while he hunted and for the first time in a long time, the camp felt ... homey. The trouble that lay ahead dissipated, leaving only Sean and Taylor with a fire in between. The sun was setting behind Taylor and the fire cast a warm glow, brightening her face. 'Such beauty,' thought Sean.

Taylor's eyes locked with his. Blushing slightly, she quickly turned her head and Sean did the same. So much had happened in a short time. Everything had turned upside down. All Sean could do was focus on the task ahead, their kiss from what felt long ago flitting at the edge of his memory. Sean realized after looking up that Taylor had, in essence, moved on, as she carefully sharpened the knife usually kept concealed beneath her dress. Sean had come to know of it and of Taylor's skill when had she killed a snake days earlier.

"Ack!" Sean exclaimed. The knife had slipped, nicking his thumb. A small droplet of red blood oozed from the wound. Wiping the hand and sticking his thumb in his mouth to stop the pain, the humming stopped. Staring with amusement at Sean, Taylor sat with her blade suspended above her thumb, mocking the cut he just sustained. Hastily he took his thumb away from his mouth. 'Just like a child! Mocks instead of offering compassion!'

Sulking, Sean skewered his clean game and carefully set their dinner over the fire. Scraping followed by humming came from Taylor once more as she resumed sharpening the knife. Dusk faded to night as stars twinkled in the black sky. Sean turned the meat over, waiting for the inevitable critique from Taylor. The scraping of the knife faded, but the humming continued. Taylor was perched on a log gently threading a needle with thread, torn silk dress on her lap. Most could not be salvaged, yet still she worked to sew holes shut and fix what she was able. Where Taylor might have gotten a sewing kit Sean would never know, but seeing the care taken to repair the damaged gown was enlightening. Taylor was always surprising Sean, and he could not put a finger on what role she played for her mistress.

"I know that inquisitive look. Ask away."

"What was your position at your mistress's side?"

"I was educated in the manners of court. My mistress relied heavily on any insight I could glean as a servant, and through this, I became an apprentice."

"An apprentice? As a seamstress? Court ears? A master of shadows?" Chided Sean.

"No. As a matter of fact, I was apprenticed to become a Protector; a position every servant aspires to. This task is of the highest order. A protector must leave the Realm, mission in hand, to become a beacon of light," replied Taylor, lying to Sean.

"Then how is it that an apprentice sits at the same fire as I? Surely your skills have not yet been fully realized?" Sean asked.

"Sadly, it is above my station to divulge such information. But know that your guess is right and dire circumstances forced my position along. It is sheer luck that I share a fire with one such as yourself."

"What is this realm you speak of? It is only nations that I know by name, taught long ago by my grandfather. Never was there a mention of realms."

"That as well shall be answered, but our journey takes us to what is called the Realm of Stars. It is my home…" Taylor trailed off, staring into the fire.

Sean remained quiet in hopes that more would be revealed but Taylor resumed humming again. Some light was shed on the mystery of his companion, but still the questions regarding this strange beauty swirled around him. Dinner followed in the same manner with slight berating on meal preparation. Sean decided to find more firewood, for tension had built between them and the solitude would be welcome.

Taking in the stars and the forest at night, Sean cleared his head. Settling beneath the boughs of an oak tree, he started meditating in hopes of talking with the Elemental. After a time failing to communicate, it seemed no matter what Sean tried, the Element was not answering. He returned exasperated and with an arm load of wood. Taylor had settled down to sleep so he stood watch, alone with his thoughts again, and an opportunity to train.

Taking slow breaths, Sean tapped deep into the power of Life and a new world swam in his vision. Energy of animals lurking in the night; a wolf checking the glow from their fire, an owl hunting a hare. He started to distinguish insects from plant energy and even encouraged growth where needed on a tree to stop a branch from forming disjointed and weak. Then, at the moment a hill of ants had killed a spider, there came a large life force, blinding him. Shaking, Sean released the power of Life to see Taylor's face in front of his own.

"My watch. Sleep, you need it," Taylor said as she rested on a tree trunk, her cloak pulled tight.

Sean believed dreams were a fool's premonitions, but nightmares gave him foreboding. This night was no different and it forced a restless sleep as the vivid terrors tore him apart. A puppet on strings dancing to unseen masters going against Sean's will no matter how he tried to pull free. Their shadowy faces laughed at each tug and Sean's struggling attempt to go against their wishes, ignoring his screams to be released. Taylor was there holding him at one point; dream or reality, Sean did not know. On that angelic face was pain and joy in such great contrast that he wept.

Waking to a gentle nudge, Sean casually checked for those tears to find mere traces of moisture. Taylor banked the fire, avoiding eye contact, but stayed always in his view. Camp packed, fire out, they set out to find a path that could mean death or salvation. Sean was not afraid, knowing enough about his power and what it could cost them.

Tapping the blade at his hip gave enough reassurance to keep moving forward.

The path was well hidden, for King Hammer ordered it so. Taylor had explained on the way from their campsite that King Hammer kept a tight rein on this border to keep folks away from the bramble path. Trapping travelers into servitude meant less money to pay an army and his subjects benefited from not fighting wars. According to Taylor the purpose of the bramble path was smuggling, and to provide stealth for people who entered the nation of Hammer in secret; both conditions they met.

Slicing through a group of brambles, their path appeared ahead as stone columns supporting an archway. Dark vines seeming to writhe like serpents wound around them as Sean and Taylor entered. Enough light filtered through to create a murky dusk; wind whipped out of the corridor carrying with it the stench of death. No creatures were around, resulting in an eerie silence that only heightened their feeling of impending doom. Deeper in, the path veered sharply to the right, then left, right until all sense of direction was gone. Onward they trekked while morning changed to afternoon and the air became stifling. Around what must have been 3:00 in the afternoon, Taylor found a marker stone saying this point was halfway. 'Halfway!' Sean found the news disturbing ... and frightening.

During this adventure, Sean had nearly been pricked three times and Taylor once. Greater care was taken to clear the path and Sean's blade sheared the vile thorns with ease. Time was against the pair as darkness enveloped their path and it felt almost as if the vines were following them.

"Sean, listen closely. There isn't much time left before this place is sealed along with us in it. Quicken the pace and sheathe your blade else your chopping gets slower," Taylor said while drawing her own sword.

Urgency filled Taylor's swings of the blade, clearing their way of the poisonous vines. Reaching a brisk pace, Sean dipped into Life power, pointing to growing foliage while Taylor hacked away. Rounding the last corner was the exit; sun setting behind the small opening.

"Run!" exclaimed Sean.

Taking the lead in a single file they fled as Sean drew his sword. Vines and thorns crept closer, and succeeded in covering the exit, trapping the two in twilight. Channeling his power, Sean summoned energy to his fingers, coating hands so as to touch the thorns. The vile energy from the vines made Sean sick, but there was no time for that now. Out of instinct, sparking the energy in his fingers toward the vine caused it to shudder, and as hope faded, the thick vines fell. The recoil of dark energy to Life power angered the vines and around Sean they vibrated. Taking it as a cue to leave, Taylor pulled Sean forward to the opening before being trapped in darkness.

Fresh air engulfed Sean and Taylor, and with a final slash, they were free. Exhaustion forced them to camp off the path in a small clearing, a meager meal split between them of leftover squirrel, since fire would be dangerous. Taylor took first watch. Using his power and cutting the undergrowth had left Sean exhausted. She needed to allow him time to recover from the day. 'Dirt makes an excellent bed for a dead man,' thought Sean with a chuckle, passing out immediately.

Blissfully asleep, Sean didn't have the merest hint of a nightmare, and on waking, his joints appeared to be rejuvenated. Morning had come without a disturbance which concerned Sean who looked in dismay to find Taylor at watch. Although she looked tired, Sean thought he detected the faintest smile on her face at what had been accomplished. They had made it through, narrowly escaping with their lives; a feat accomplished by the hardiest travelers and vagrants running from the law. This thought of them being outlaws dawned on Sean and the smile slowly spread to his lips, washing away the last dregs of weariness. Standing up, he walked toward Taylor, extending a hand to help her up. Accepting graciously, Taylor stood, slightly unsteadily; understandable after a night of no sleep after such a harrowing day.

"We have to find a better camp for you to rest. I do not want soldiers stumbling on us," Sean steadied Taylor, too tired to argue. "Plus, animals seem scarce and we need a good meal."

Taylor responded by rolling her eyes and setting off further away from the vines until that place was just a memory. The chatter of wildlife resumed when a clearing surrounded by young oaks came into view about half a league away. She collapsed on Sean's chest when they stopped to investigate, legs barely keeping her upright. This journey so far had sapped the strength from her body; her feet were rocks, and every root found them. Maybe staying guard all night was too much… 'But he needed it more after using Life,' Taylor wearily thought. Pushing off Sean with exaggerated strength, Taylor picked what seemed the comfiest spot and lay down, pulling close her cloak. What Taylor would give for a bed roll, something to pick up when they stopped at the City of Engshl. Sean came into view carrying wood for a fire. Taylor figured he had set traps to check later. Tinder box in hand, she closed her eyes as flames licked the small twigs. Taylor settled into a deep sleep, knowing that her protector would watch over her. 'I found him...'

Sean set the smallest log on his growing fire, careful to keep the air flow going so that smoke would not accumulate. Traps set waiting for prey; he took blade in hand swinging through various forms. His foe was one small oak whose trunk became rapidly stripped from the sword's connection. Whirring steel through the air, Sean felt the slightest drop in speed on his slash; lack of practice with sore shoulders meant more reps till it felt perfect. When the last whack faded, Sean returned to the fire to throw on another log. Settling down in a shady spot he began to clean the sword. After wiping the hilt, Sean noticed small lettering right below the guard in elegant script; something he had never seen before. The inscription read: "for the light, by the light. This light is thy birthright." Furthermore, it appeared that the Ancient symbol had a faint glow, getting brighter as the fire grew. Strange, as Sean could not remember the blade looking this way before, the script, a new feature. 'I wonder if this is tied to my meeting the Life elemental,' Sean wondered.

By mid afternoon, Taylor still had not moved. Sean started training with Life energy in hopes of learning more. The Elemental still did not answer, no matter how much he asked. The sound of soldiers came from their old camp; good thing Sean had retraced and covered their tracks. Using Life vision, Sean confirmed the soldiers presence, muscles tensed for a quick escape if necessary. Lucky that they sat downwind, and that little smoke came from the fire. Eventually the soldiers moved on patrol, but Sean did not relax, staying attentive. Every twig snap or animal chirp alarmed him. New territory was supposed to be exciting; not nerve-wracking.

Evening had fallen when Taylor awoke abruptly, taking in her new surroundings. Sean looked up to see her sit up and stretch. She relaxed after locking eyes with Sean, cheeks turning red slightly. Catch from the traps Sean had set laid near the fire, cleaned and ready to go. 'Why was he so rigid,' wondered Taylor.

"Progress report? Anything particularly interesting happen while I slept?" Asked Taylor. She had now stood and was walking toward the fire.

Sean relayed what transpired with the scouts and why he was on high alert. Nodding in understanding, Taylor started peering around the camp, checking for scouts. It felt as if spectral eyes were peering out from every shadow; she pulled her cloak closer around her. Every noise caused the hair on the back of her neck to stand on end. It was clear now why Sean looked like a coiled spring.

"Well, that explains the lack of cooking at least," Taylor grabbed a poled rabbit, carefully placing it on the fire.

"I would not recommend it; something is… off still, and it scares me."

"Better to die full than live with regrets. Here, put this on your side to cook."

She handed Sean the laden skewers until the fire was surrounded by poles of squirrel, rabbit, small birds and a kind of … rodent? Fire crackled as grease dripped off their meal, wind wafting the smell of cooking meat. Stars peeked through, in the night sky, constellations forming; some Taylor recognized but others… this land had odd formations. It took a moment, but she found her quarry in the sky telling them which way to go. Far to the southwest a sparkling pink star could be seen as well as which direction to head.

"Sean, look to the southwest. Do you see that pink star? Larger than the others around, sparkling? It is a part of a larger constellation named Hinabi's Star—ten stars forming a drawn star and at the top sits that pink beauty. It lies in the direction of our destination. It seems we are close to where I camped passing through to you." Taylor turned a skewer. "Given our travel distance and time, we might need to travel at night by the road tomorrow."

"Would that be safe? What of Hammer and his men; are they not still a threat?"

"Keep discreet, and they should not be a problem; however, we might want to travel without weapons; especially once we cross the Great River which runs through his domain. It acts as a boundary between the capital territory and the Bear Mountains."

"The Great River? How large is this river and can we swim it?" Inquired Sean.

"Water stretches to the horizon, so swimming is out; no bridge either. So, a ferry is our best option; or, rather *would* be…" Taylor's voice trailed off.

"*Would* be? What's wrong with the ferry? More indentured servitude," scoffed Sean.

"I kind of… bailed on a debt offered for crossing. They wouldn't take my money because it lacked Hammer's image. So, I ran… for three days madly until reaching that hill yonder."

Pointing in the distance for Sean to see, Taylor then continued "I have a plan already forming but we can talk about it on the road. Dinner seems done."

Silence filled the camp, a familiar passenger on the journey Sean thought, biting a hunk of rabbit. Between mouthfuls, Sean educated Taylor on the stars above. The Three-eyed Scorpion, Two Maidens Rowing, and his personal favorite, the Bright Knight; a system that had been made in his grandfather's honor, or so the story goes. New constellations like Hinabi's star popped up here and there. Sean would love to learn them all. Being the furthest point from home, it would be more than just new stars in the sky to learn. Politics in Hammer's kingdom made Sean wonder if those realms had their own set of rules. Sean wanted to ask, but Taylor always put up a stone wall, guarding her from his inquiries.

The meal was finished, and wood stacked for a small fire that night. A chilling wind blew through, raising the hackles of Sean's neck. Uneasiness to top their meal like a rancid dessert, he began to drift asleep. Taylor's low humming continued to run through his mind and into his dreams: a field of dead Wanderers, 20 riding horses laughing as the creatures fell before them. Every face distorted save one: a man at the front who portrayed Orwick at a young age. Raising a fist split the ground open, swallowing everything, Sean included. Before Sean smacked the surface, his body jolted upright; sword in hand, pointing it at Taylor.

"Good, you are awake," She whispered, lowering the tip of the blade. "Company has come. Wanderers, by the look and smell. We must flee; hurry!"

Scooping the small number of belongings, both rushed into the night as silently as possible, leaving the campfire burning to lure the creatures in. Sword hilt strapped to his side now made moving easier and the blade gleamed in the moonless night. 30 feet away came the screech of a hunter missing its prey followed by scuffling of underbrush in their direction. Activating his Life vision, Sean encountered a party of ten Wanderers.

They both readied to ambush the pursuers, for running did not seem to be a viable option. Taylor positioned herself to stab the first with a knife, sword at the ready, while Sean cleared his mind to prepare for the fight of their lives. Sean's sword hummed with anticipation, eager for blood. Like a lightning strike, Taylor stabbed the first creature through its skull; a sickening gush sputtered from the mouth and it fell.

Sean sliced the head off the next one in one sweep, black oily blood spattering everything as the blade completed its arc.

Taking turns killing the next creatures, Sean used the slight reprieve to survey the larger creatures. They were wary at what would happen when they found their trackers had been slaughtered. Four remained, all eight feet tall, and that unforgettable, unmistakable stench wafting in. Anticipation in the air for the next move made time seem to slow. Bellowing like a frozen pine snapping in deep winter, a middle creature urged forward, finding Sean's blade pierce its midsection. With a flourish, Sean ripped through the wanderer's chest. It was all the motivation the other three needed to bull rush Sean and Taylor all at once. She felled another one that came through the middle, like its brethren spawn before, and as the body came down, it nearly fell on top of her. The other two came on either side of the ambush and Sean found himself locked in combat with the foul beast.

Jabbing, blocking, parrying, he went to work pushing the monster backward until "schling" his blade parted the head from the body. Turning toward the last, Sean saw the creature slip on bodies now littering the ground, and Taylor's sword pierced through the skull, adding a new hole to a face that only its twisted mother could love. Sean scanned the area again to be sure no other enemies lurked. Taylor approached, panting for breath, sword still half raised.

"All clear, but we need to leave as soon as possible; no telling who else may be lurking around here." Sean directed.

"Ten wanderers at night? Who knows, we might get our own star system," Taylor joked.

After cleaning themselves and their equipment of any blood, the pair set off toward the pink star. Neither wished to stop more than a moment; not until the sound of water reached their ears. It was a brisk pace for the two, already battle-weary, but adrenaline coursed through their bodies, keeping them moving. Close to the bank now, Taylor pointed to the ferry house sitting desolate. Creeping around to the dock they found one boat but no oars. Sean searched carefully around the house trying to not make a sound when finally, luck: missing oars. Remorse settled over him as they paddled into the river. Stars made navigating the great water easy. Both sighed with relief after having escaped the first stage of this journey.

Taylor grinned at Sean, "A savior, companion, knight and now a thief. Oh, the tales that shall be sung of us!"

Water lapping at the sides and oars swishing were all that could be heard after her joke.

'What have I become?' pondered Sean, eyebrows furrowing as he threw himself into the task of rowing.

Early dawn broke as the other shore neared and there were no pursuers to hasten the landing. Shallow enough, Sean jumped out of the boat to wade in the rest of the way, arms aching. Splash! Taylor was next to him, all supplies in hand.

"Start filling rocks in the boat, have to sink it or a patrol will find it. This is the part I knew you wouldn't like…"

Groaning, Sean complied until it filled with water and sunk to the bottom. 'I will make this right by my honor,' he swore silently, as a man's livelihood sank to the riverbed and then joined Taylor on shore. Stepping on sand, Sean realized that this had to be the farthest from home he had ever been. An excitement grew as Taylor led the way to their next destination; a "small city" she called it. No time to dry clothes; both trudged on, to Sean's discomfort, squishing in boots and wringing his shirt. Several hill tops came then went as the pair skirted in the trees to avoid being seen. According to Taylor, there was no danger but better to be safe until out of Hammer's domain.

A main road was finally reached and away went the weapons as commerce traffic joined them. They passed a number of farms, with crops already planted. An occasional farmer waved, and making Sean feel nostalgic.

Eventually he could only look forward to forgetting what had been left behind; 'She forgot farmer,' he thought, Taylor's naming joke rolling over and over again in his head. The people now travelling towards Engshl (Engi-shl) as part of their party seemed road worn. They talked of soldiers demanding taxes and taking whatever they wanted. Others said wanderers had destroyed their ancestors' farm, leaving them to venture south for protection as refugees. Closer to the city came traders, carts laden with goods to sell and big guards carrying wooden clubs wearing leather studded armor. Sean drank it all in, awed at seeing so many people headed in the same direction.

White gleaming walls became visible as the sun tipped passed high noon and Sean would have stopped, if it were not for Taylor elbowing his stomach. The "small city" stood larger than anything he had ever seen. River trade could be seen near the east wall as the road curved south. They saw many narrow, long vessels on the water, some empty and others filled for market. A packed road made for the promise of what existed inside: endless possibility. Before the road could turn east again, Taylor took Sean aside down to the river's edge. Here she hailed a barge half filled with goods, a star on the side and with a sign of her hand the operator bowed slightly, offering passage.

Sean had a list of questions and this topped them all, but he knew better than to ask. When underway he turned to find Taylor studying him closely, picking him apart until it felt she knew everything.

"This is my cousin Buford of the Star Mountains and he is visiting for culture," she told the boatman. "Be sure a pole finds those hands, Buford. We can hardly expect a free ride."

"It is a pleasure, my lady Elaine, no need for him to work. A strong current carries us forward and managed by me, no trouble," replied the boatman.

"If you insist, then please do drop the 'lady' business. I am Elaine, a girl from the Star Mountains by arranged marriage," she replied in kind. "No fancy dress this time to force me in a pricey inn. What fortune you happened by, Robert, in my time of need."

"Was told to take a trip early hence the light load, otherwise would be stuffed in a barrel," and Robert laughed loudly.

The barge slowed near the wharf gate, as Robert taught Sean, to allow three guards near, all reeking of cheese, wine and unkempt men. A spindly guard with a 3-day-old stubble and hook nose inspected Sean, questioning him until Taylor (Elaine) handed him papers for Buford of Star Mountains and Elaine of Star Mountains.

With a sniff and scoff, the guards allowed the barge onward to their business of off-loading cargo. Easing to a dock spot, Sean tossed a line to be pulled in for mooring. Dock hands rushed about, lashing the lines tight. Robert pulled a bag from his tunic, handing it to a man wearing a yellow vest over a bare chest. Smiling, the man weighed the purse, bowed and ran off inside a shop. Disembarking onto the weathered dock, Sean helped Taylor join him on land.

"Buford, stay close, mind you. We have to see our companion off before a hot meal," she chided because it was her always complaining of meals.

Men around the dock in earshot snickered at this comment adding insults of their own until Sean was red in the face. When the boat wanted to shove off, they bade farewell to Robert and then set off to find a room in the bustling, noisy city.

The smell of fish dominated the wharf, spices a close second in competition and until leaving it behind did Sean get a true taste of city life. Sweating bodies, blight splattered in alleys, a mass of refugees huddled together; these were the lucky ones. Taylor explained this was referred to as "the gutter" in hushed tones, for most ended up here when no work in the trade could be found. Soldiers recruited men into service here occasionally, but only in times that the streets seemed to bulge to near capacity. After some winding travel and a few pickpockets, they entered the city proper.

Here the streets seemed cleaned daily, no stragglers in alleyways lurking for a mark to steal from. Merchants with actual shops lined between houses, and performers working for supper on corners. The air was cleaner but turned Sean's nose the same, for it felt stale, above musty barely. Directions to a fair inn had been given and soon found, named the Drunken Pole; a clever sailor joke it seemed. Inside they found a medium-sized common holding six long tables able to sit ten to a side, partially occupied by patrons done for the day and into the ale. Tending bar stood a short brown-haired woman, who spent her nights running an inn of sailors, evident in her features. The bright clean apron shone like the walls of the city, marking her as patron of the inn. Renting the last room with their story of culture and city business received them half an eyebrow raise from Madge, the patron. Several young serving girls scurried about bringing ale or food to customers taking every chance to check Sean out. One look from Madge sent them running to tasks at hand yet there stood a moon-eyed girl that always found her eyes back on him and a tongue sticking out behind Madge's back. Stifling a laugh, Sean grabbed their gear as Madge lead the pair up to their room. Fresh, hot water followed to take the road from them as she put it; for Madge could sense their long journey; really it let her dig more information out of the strangers.

Three times it took bidding farewell with thanks until Madge left the travel-worn pair alone in their small single-bed quarters. On the third time, Sean nearly picked the small woman up to force her out, but something told Sean that the diminutive woman would wind up bending him over her knee, so he decided to shut the door on her instead. Taylor clasped her hand over Sean's mouth and put a finger to her lips to subdue his outburst, pointing with her free hand to the shut door then pointing to her ears. Harnessing Life, he looked in the hall to find Madge slinking down the hall on her way to the common room once more. With her out of earshot, Sean told Taylor they were alone for the time being, and she slowly relinquished her grip.

"Well, what a fine start to my first visit here!!" Sean hissed in a whisper, "Taylor what kind of name is Buford? I fear no need for such deception."

"Quiet or I will muzzle you again," interrupted Taylor coldly, voice barely audible. "There was no time to prepare you. Buford was the best fit—trust me. As for the barge, all will be answered once we are safe out of this city; keep names under tongue or lose it, mind you, for our agents lives depend on secrecy. Names lead to questions we have little desire to answer under Hammers kingdom and can lead us to irons."

Fuming, Sean thought it over carefully before continuing the tirade, "Still, why a mute!? Are you that afraid of me talking?"

"Gaahh, you are worse than a child! Listen to accents and change yours, otherwise, grunts will have to suffice. Which if I recall, is something you do quite well; your mountain accent can only stir up trouble. Now cover up your hands with gloves to hide the sword marks from the hilt and let us get food. It smelled as divine as the 20 down there." Taylor turned to pour hot water in the basin with that last comment, signaling their discussion over to Sean who ran fingers through his hair trying to understand it all.

"Fine. Holding you to answers when we leave and for the record no cursing the 20 as it seems—mmm, you forget who is in your present company!" Sean pulled a glove on with force to match the last comment.

"Ha! Believe that I am with a thief and you had better get used to it; most curse the 20 here for hiding away and leaving the world to its whims. Though they know not what lies outside of their little Hamlet."

Washing up in the small basin and dressing for the common room, Taylor said nothing more to Sean, regarding Ancients or their journey that day. Opening the door to their room, Taylor led the way toward the smell of delicious food and music began to reach Sean's ears the closer they got to the stairs. Reaching the bottom of the stairs, Sean took in the vast difference this room had compared to when they first arrived. Taylor, unperturbed, found an empty table near the opposite wall in view of the front door. Evening fast approaching had brought more travelers into the common room to drown their day and sing the night away with loud songs. In the back, sailors slapped barmaids backsides as they sang shanties of the open sea, and spilled more ale *on* them than *in* them. Finding his senses, Sean stopped staring at the boisterous crowd and rushed to sit opposite Taylor who had already received a glass of honey-colored wine. As Sean sat at the table, a serving girl rushed to ask what he would like to drink in which Taylor promptly replied "he'll have an ale," giving Sean no time to open his mouth and reveal the lie. She returned in a hurry, dropping the flagon in front of Sean and with a smile she darted away just as fast; the smile, though, made his face red. Watching her scamper over to a group of serving girls near the bar Sean saw as she pointed to their table and all three girls turned to smile at once. Catching their eyes caused Sean to turn a deeper shade of red and the trio giggled in unison before scurrying away to other tables. 'Giggled!' he thought taking a big drink of ale to calm down. They did not stop there, though. It became a game as the three took turns getting as close to the table without touching Sean and then make the lad bump into them instead. After a fourth time playing this game, Sean let out a low grunt that sent a girl fleeing to the kitchen. Grateful about being left alone in peace, Sean looked up to see Taylor menacingly holding a knife in hand, glaring at him with deadly beauty. Emphasis on deadly. Embarrassed at thinking his grunt had anything to do with the girls departure, Sean downed the remaining ale and motioned to Madge for another flagon.

  The food arrived, and to Sean it tasted as divine as the 20, if not better, for the roasted chicken had been spiced with an exotic tasting dry heat. Hearty vegetables that seemed unfamiliar to Sean stacked next to it coated in a similar spice complemented the chicken well. He could only imagine a meal such as this would take months to prepare in the mountains, and would certainly not have such exotic spices. Yet here it sat in front of him at a moment's notice with more to come if he called for another helping, which nearly happened if not for the bread. Fresh, warm bread smothered in a butter cheese spread topped it off to fill Sean's stomach so that his pants became too tight. Draining another flagon of ale, a crisp fall taste with a hint of apples this time around left Sean satisfied and warm cheeked with a hand slapping the table to the rhythm of the music that filled the common room. The sailors shanty caught his ear as they sang a tale of a mermaid as pretty as the sunset over the ocean but voice scratchy as wool that scared sailors away. During a second verse, warm arms wrapped around, squeezing the gorged meal sitting snugly in his stomach. Catching him by surprise, he half hoped the arms belonged to Taylor in an attempt to get a rise from Sean; but in turning around, his smile froze. There sat Taylor, open mouthed, holding a piece of bread in mid-bite, staring in shock at what was behind him. That normally would be a priceless look, yet the moon eyed girl hanging off Sean made the situation murderous. Quickly standing up and untangling himself from those warm arms, Sean checked the damage done by the girl; however, Elaine resumed eating as if nothing had happened. Taking his leave, Sean headed upstairs, but not before noticing Taylor holding that knife subtly under the table. He had enough trouble for one night. Shortly, Taylor followed, wordlessly, as she entered the room, making sure to step on Sean at least a few times where he lay on the floor pretending to sleep. Using Life, he checked to make sure no one had followed her upstairs and a small frame could be seen slipping silently down the hallway; not much sleep would come that night for fear of an ambush by the serving girls. In Sean's mind, this was worse than his usual nightmares.

 Morning came with a note under the door with a slight star in the corner of the parchment so faint it disappeared when held in direct sunlight. Taylor swiped it fast from Sean, stuffing it in her dress with the other important documents. A light breakfast of porridge, cheese and bread had Sean wanting more chicken, but they bade farewell to Madge, and promising to visit again.

 A commotion outside drew Sean's attention down toward the gutter. A line of soldiers parading volunteers to their barracks almost made Sean lose his breakfast. Old, young, weak or strong, these men were being marched onward, regardless of the protestations of both the volunteers and their families.

 "Easy, they will not hesitate to take you with them," warned Taylor.

 Sean settled back to let them pass but never relaxed. Nods of encouragement to those who held heads up high all the while praying for them. And though the people seemed to agree that the refugees do not deserve a break, it was also agreed that it was a waste of time to make them soldiers. Before uttering a retort, Taylor took his hand to lead them away which was fine by Sean for this city sickened him. Passing the shops meant to host the Lords and Ladies Taylor took him to the front gate. A set of armor caught Sean's eye but there was not a minute to spare. 'Perhaps another time,' he thought.

Chapter 10: Light of the Stars

Fresh clean air broke through as the city gates came closer with each step forward. A breeze touched Taylor's cheek teasing her muscles, tensed up from being inside the city of Engshl. It took effort to remain at a leisurely pace as to avoid attention but everything ached to leave the "city" faster. Journeys here always displeased her because so many people lay packed in the walls with nowhere to go. The city had a stench you could never escape- no matter the time of day. Designers had sadly forgotten that thing called air flow when building that rat nest Taylor thought letting out a loud sigh. At least Sean had done surprisingly well in a new city- for a farm boy that is.

A horse merchant, dressed for desert travel, whom Taylor had sought the previous night, returned to her, ignoring Sean (who looked as relieved as she for the breeze). Offering sale slips, Taylor took them without a second glance at the man. How foolish to leave a message at her room? 'This man will be dealt with accordingly by my Master; that is certain.' Bowing, the man departed, leaving Taylor and Sean to saddle horses with their equipment and provisions. This leg of their journey would be easy, but horses need replenishment, and the clay outside the plains offers little for grass. Without a word, Taylor spurred the horse to a fast trot, forcing Sean to awkwardly catch up to her. This being Hammer domain caution was everything. If not careful, her companion's head would be to the gallows and his body spread across the land.

"It appears my horse was named Bucksnot, not fitting for a woman's steed. How about Majesty instead?" Noted Taylor to Sean who remained stoic.

The man barely spoke except in grunts and exclamations. So frustrating! 'A royal court will eat him alive!'

"What is your horse's name? The Mighty Backwind? Heard the same merchant say yours eats beef for the extra speed," continued Taylor, laughing harder; "or the Great Left Footer. That would be the talk of the town."

A smile from Sean broke that stone wall!

"Was thinking Ground Shaker more appropriate; droppings so large it causes earth tremors," replied Sean.

Taylor laughed until she was nearly in tears until she heard mumbling from Sean.

"Some new name to share? Please go on, my dear rider of Ground Shaker."

"I said his name shall be Star Shaker, a name fitting to our journey."

"Alas, a winner it seems! Majesty and Star Shaker, two formidable steeds rode by less formidable folk!"

They followed the trail in silence from then on, Taylor keeping a close eye on Sean, studying everything. 'No matter my feelings, Mistress comes first above this man.' A single patrol could be seen north heading west to the training grounds. As if a weight had been lifted, the grass was greener, the birds sang and the world felt right to Taylor.

"Welcome Sean, this begins the Land of Stars where the 20 are worshipped as truth, not legend. We are free of the shackles held by humanity! Can you feel it?!" Taylor excitedly kicked her horse which sped to a gallop, leaving Sean spitting dust. Exhilaration of home enveloped each sense as she sped to the first stop. Stopping a league away, the farm boy caught up, covered head to toe in dust and open mouthed to hurl an insult when Taylor shot him a playful glance, turning his face red. 'Too easily flustered, she thought smugly.

"You see the outpost ahead? Here we are properly equipped to start the pilgrimage to my Mistress. Questions bubble in your mind, but do not ask them here; even the Land of Stars should not have topics discussed. Onward, hiya!"

Leaving him without allowing him to get in a word, it always seemed to thrill Taylor. She had dismounted at the outpost, a simple stone castle with a short tower. When Sean caught up again, he had no retort—only a dull, grim expression. By the time he had dismounted and quit gawking at the post sentries, they greeted Taylor.

"Elijah! Breonna! Ho there! My visit may be short but let us make the best of it by the 20," began Taylor in the informal greeting.

"Taylor! Ho there! A stranger as well to these parts, eh? May the 20 have blessed your travel!" Responded the twins in unison.

"Ah, as well as one can hope beyond our borders! May we enter to shake the dust; especially this stranger, ha!"

With great poise, the twins jumped off the tower, landing in unison. Elijah, the male, stood 5'10", with sandy blonde hair and freckled face. Breonna, the female, stood an inch shorter. Jet black hair framed her face. Fraternal, not identical twins—both had a look of natural athleticism in their ease movement, a latent speed beneath for enemies. Two respected warriors and guards, their post never taken.

Taylor figured them to be nearly a century old, however no one could tell because they looked 20.

Clasping hands, the two lead Taylor inside, nearly dragging her, chatting about the rough road and state of her dress. She then introduced Sean, still named Buford by Taylor's command.

"No one may know of you yet; best kept between us no doubt," she told him.

Overjoyed, the twins were meeting Buford and from the furthest reaches of Star Mountains no less! Every minute was bliss, rejuvenating aches unknown since Taylor started out. Immediately a small feast was prepared fresh with veggies and fruits to boot, fitting of their return.

"You see Buford, we try to not eat animals here in the Land of Stars. Yet fish are a necessity because their nutrients keep us young. You will see!" Explained Elijah.

Taylor overheard as Breonna rummaged about for a new silk dress and armor for Taylor. Changed, they joined the men for the meal and ate until not one more bite could be eaten. The twins gave advice on court etiquette to Sean all the while, since formal introductions meant everything in the Land of Stars.

"When first greeting a new face, begin by saying 'may the ancestral 20 bless you and your travels, stranger!' Social hierarchy dictates who speaks first, honor to those above who begin the greeting to one below; yet that rarely happens."

"Except when it involves valiant deeds!"

"Yes, yes, that was my next sentence, sister."

"And the proper return greeting, 'may the 20 bless our meeting, stranger, and future encounters as friends.'"

"Breonna, you forgot."

"Oh yes, and to add to it, 'May the 20 bless your travels!'"

"Mind you, that is for formal greetings outside court," interjected Taylor. "With royalty, it is 'by the blessing of Ancestral 20, may your reign last forever in rebirth, in defense of the Light.'"

"To which they shall respond 'in Life or Death your blessing shall be accepted and may thine Light protect as thou serves against the Shadow in the name of the 20.'"

"It is rumored that a blessing from all 20 grants immortal life and a power unlike any other. Sadly, that is a young man's quest to falter on folly. May the 20 protect us," Elijah said.

"May the 20 protect us all," shouted Breonna and Taylor, Taylor shooting Sean a dirty for not repeating it.

"...May the 20 protect us all," Sean finally mumbled.

"But wait! A young man's quest? Surely you must be the same age as I!"

Elijah and Breonna exchanged glances and then began cackling aloud until both wept tears of joy.

"It is not wise asking one his age here; that is sacred knowledge. It reveals one's bloodline, and things age differently here in the Land of Stars. That is why most animals are not eaten, for they are ancient, most unable to create life now. Keep that in mind as you meet strangers." Elijah looked to Breonna, then said, "We celebrated a century last month."

Taylor could not believe the audacity of Sean and how close she was. Blushing, Taylor cleared her throat, finishing her wine.

"In honor of your birthday, by the Light of the Ancestral 20, I can trust you to keep a secret?" Inquired Sean.

"By the honor of the Ancestral 20, we hold this oath," the twins spoke in unison. "But what secret among friends?"

'Oh no! Do not do it, Sean screamed Taylor in her head. 'They are clever on oaths!'

"Between us three friends you swear?"

"Yes, yes, yes!" they replied eagerly.

"In Life and Death your blessings shall be accepted and may thy dormant Light protect thee as thou serve against the Shadow. In the name of Ancient 20 upon steeds of Star and Earth in the final shadow of Darkness. By my honor as Proclaimer of Light, take thy blessing forth to thy life and death as I am reborn."

"My name strike fear to the Shadow and enemies, Sean, chosen of the Ancient 20." With this, Sean channeled Life, adding years to each life where possible.

Taylor's jaw dropped—such an oath, and Ancient to the first rites! Her ears had to be playing tricks. Elijah and Breonna stared in disbelief at what had just transpired. When their mouths retracted after several attempts to speak, they uttered "By your Divine Right, may you live forever to defeat the Shadow and in an hour of need call on the oath for your blessing to be realized. Life or Death, may the Ancient 20 protect us."

Taylor was in disbelief. Elijah scrambled for the best wine cask and fitting armor of a King. Breonna averted her gaze, jumping at each noise, and eventually leaving to check the perimeter. When alone, Taylor turned to Sean sheepishly seeing the farm boy no longer but a future leader by Divine right. 'The smug bastard! Thinks himself clever!'

"This will not please my Mistress," Taylor said. "Discretion is a must. Even those oaths shall not stop the news, for they are crafty beyond years, you child! What, stop snickering!"

"It was worth seeing you speechless for once! What started as a variation on your blessing for Royalty, the next thing you know, it became an oath," Sean responded coolly.

"Elijah and Breonna are bound to you now with that oath of yours! My Mistress has not held servants like this in hundreds of years and here you are."

"I told you, Star Shaker is my horse's name for a reason. From what I have seen, things may have to be changed and I will usher in the new age; or at the least, help guide it."

"Why is it fools have the largest mouths? You will deal with the consequences, mark my words on the 20!"

With a huff, Taylor turned and stormed outside. Breonna sat there, weeping tears of exhilaration and joy for receiving the greatest gift of all time. The highest honor that will spin tales for generations to come. Placing an arm around her, Taylor relished in that joy remembering how she found that one-time farm boy and feeling his presence 'like a true Ancient.' Dusk fell with them embracing what happened, enjoying the night sky as stars twinkled to life. 'Star Shaker; fitting name indeed.'

Inside, Sean sat, proud of the oath and blessing he had given to these amazing people.

"Whatever Taylor said, it felt righteous."

Elijah came back with a goblet and cask of wine and both toasted the joyous news. Armor came next as a gift for Sean. Intricate scrollwork covered the shoulders, gold on silver, with a bright star symbol in gold in the middle of the chest. From the star came gold tendrils like roots of a tree and smaller stamped stars down the back. A helm contained one gold star above the eyebrows on silver again in a way that when light when the light hit it, the star seemed to glow. Greaves had a star on each, silver plated to leather for use and movement in battle. Armor fit for a King belonging to an Ancient long ago stored in case of a need such as this. They toasted the armor, drinking more until the room was spinning for Sean. After another glass, he asked: "Why is it that you never refer to people as humans here?

Pardon my lack in knowledge but we do not have this custom where I am from."

Elijah, swirling his wine, spoke slowly, "you see, oh great Ancient one, the Land of Stars is home to people of different bloodlines. Not all are pure humans, yet we are all the same blood. We choose to be known as people instead; it is our birthright to do so. I feel that is the best answer I can give for a far more educated mind is needed on the subject."

"Thank you, that does help greatly in dealing with the people of the Land of Stars. A toast to you, Elijah!"

Taylor and Breonna rejoined the celebration a bit longer; then beds were brought out for sleeping. Sean could not believe all he had learned and the fun after such a harrowing journey. It felt like home here. As eyes shut, dreams began...

The world stretched below Sean. He could see the outpost they were at all the way to Hammer's Kingdom and to the south, a great castle of star light. Along the way stood a mountain which drew him to an old stone building. Power pulsed beneath his feet, ancient as the ground. In a blink he was floating, further south at a peculiar temple that seemed to be floating as well. Here the energy had an old feeling as well, but floating all around him. Blink. Water surrounded him, the ocean raging to control him as he saw a temple below the depths. Blink. Near the edge of the wild, to the South, he found himself in a volcano of fire, destructive, powerful and an altar in the middle. Blink. Rising from the Earth stood a dark tower as black as night, seemingly a world away. Blink...

Everything hurt. Head pounded, body ached, and mouth felt like cotton. When he came to, Elijah and Breonna were nowhere to be found; only Taylor tapping her foot impatiently at Sean to rise. Easing up to a sitting position, the foot tapping increased and each strike seemed to get worse.

"It is about time you woke. Drank a bit too much, huh? Great start, Master of Star Shaker!" Taylor's voice grew louder with each word "Now we have to push faster than I want and thanks to you, the horses will be miserable."

"Please, lower-"

"No! Now, up!"

At snail speed, he rose and dressed, all the while suffering. "All my power for this to go away," mumbled Sean. Saying farewell to the twins, thanking them for all their hospitality, Taylor and Sean headed out again on the road, replenished for the remaining journey ahead of them. Sean broke the silence by talking of his dream and what it meant—the locations, and how the power felt. Taylor furrowed her brow, refusing to discuss any detail, except for in time it will be revealed. The aches wore off as repeated intervals of galloping to a trot covered several leagues. He thought that, in a mountain stood the stone building, but Taylor ignored him, moving forward to meet her Mistress. The Land of Stars had impressive rock formations which cropped up the farther south they traveled. By the end of the first day, they had traversed a mostly rocky clay terrain. A novice guide would find it rather difficult. Luckily though, Taylor seemed to know every trail that wound through the country. Taylor and Sean had stopped once again just for the night near a lake to catch fish for dinner and to give the horses some much needed rest. While setting up camp, a great antlered beast wandered up to get a drink. While the beast allowed Taylor to pet it, it had impressed Sean a great deal as she explained he was the eldest of a long line of Zilda beasts, the size of an elk, and antlers as large as Sean. Departing as quickly as it had come, things settled down and an uneventful evening passed. Though the night was calm, it seemed as if Taylor had remained on edge, keeping a vigilant eye out for Wanderers. The next morning, after pestering Taylor to explain more of their surroundings, she finally decided to teach Sean what was around them. Traversing terrain such as this was alien to him, having grown up knowing mountains and the plant life quite different, as they had to survive on less moisture in cracked clay. It at least offered a release to Sean from the silence and horse hooves as they set out from the first night camping in the wilderness.

  Their journey continued this way, Taylor pointing out plant life that was edible, campsites for a safe night of sleep and food or water. They hadn't come across any other inhabitable outposts or buildings; only wild places along the trail. As the sun drew closer to the horizon, she allowed Sean to make a decision on where to set up camp as a test of sorts, and laughing at the suggestion, insisting on a better location for water. In protest, Sean decided to stay quiet, making sure to turn his back to the fire and meditate on the lessons, not wishing to look foolish in front of her again. Taylor took the opportunity to toss little pebbles at him now and again until the moon rose to its peak, but receiving no reaction, it proved boring and the night went along without any Wanderers in sight. Taking off the next morning, Sean did his best to prove what he had learned, and received only a slight amount of razzing on the pronunciations. When a stone tower came into view, Taylor quit talking, no matter how much Sean persisted, and to make matters worse, she insisted on even taking the long route away from the tower to prevent Sean from exploring. He made a mental note of its location so as to visit when given the chance, for a feeling tugged at the back of his mind as if pulling Sean there.

"Fine! I give up here trying to learn the history of what we called legend. You withhold the information. We'll wait and have quite a word with this Mistress of yours."

It was the fourth day when Taylor abruptly reined in Majesty; Sean followed her lead listening for anything. Using the Power of Life, he conducted a scan of the area yet nothing showed and here she sat. Turning to Taylor, Sean began to ask what the issue was when she whispered softly, "From this moment on, I no longer have the same freedom or time alone with only you. Be wary binding Oaths to yourself or others—it causes more trouble than it helps. Remember, you are in control. Listen to advice but make the best judgment call; I know you can. When we reach the top of this rise, every part of our relationship changes and your life as well. Ready?"

"Surprised you let me make the choice on this. Half expected an ambush," Sean joked. "My Oath binds me by the 20; let us forge ahead."

His head nodding in understanding, Taylor continued forward knowing a contingent escort would be upon them shortly. 'Good luck, farm boy!' Atop the rise, Sean took in Star Valley, capital city to the Land of Stars. To the east lay a small stone outpost, but further south sat a gleaming tower of white peaked with gold. To the west sat the Queen of Stars palace, beautiful in every aspect and shimmering with a faint light as stars at dusk. Winding their way up the mountain to greet Sean and Taylor rode a contingent of 20 soldiers adorned in armor Sean had never known existed; steel greaves branded with stars wrapped upwards on their arms and no chest plate. Each had strapped short swords to their legs, battle axes, maces, or bows on backs, covered by a steel plate. Reminding Sean of beetles, his lips twitched up towards the sky when the helms came into view. Two stars portrayed on each side curving up to mimic flying; however, it augmented the beetle look that Sean had snickered about.

"Cut it out," hissed Taylor, jabbing Sean in the gut.

More motion at the bottom of the mountain piqued his interest—one large dust cloud rushed toward them up the side, no path to aid the traveler. Nearing the top of the rise, Sean met a woman in her middle years standing at the center of what appeared to be a rock platform, and a man in armor such as what had been given to Sean, peering straight up at him intensely. Back to the woman, Sean saw calmness in the face, composure at the impending meeting, a fairly cute nose with a mouth to match but the eyes were shining as bright as a star which made Sean tremble. 'Is that an Ancient? Do I look like that as well?' Now Sean was certain the duo rode on a platform made of rock that began slowing as the distance grew short. The man stood at 6'7", with broad shoulders, ready to pounce on any fool who dared attack his ward. His right hand remained on the sword attached to his hip. Stopping the platform next to Sean, the woman advanced on foot, alone with eyes brimming in that same glowing light. At around Taylor's height, the woman appeared regal and wise despite her young face. Physical strength unnecessary for most opponents would run at her presence and self-composure alone. Gulping subtly, Sean gathered his wits while dusting off his trousers, attempting to look casual.

'Taylor seems no worse for wear; however, something is different,' mused the woman as she closed the gap in a final step. 'This boy she found, I can sense his talent...'

Taylor bowed deeply and Sean followed only after she yanked on his pants a few times. A sound of amusement escaped the lips of the strange woman in front of them which only brought Sean more apprehension. After a few moments, Sean raised his head to find her inspecting his face with great scrutiny.

"Rise, Taylor, my servant. May the 20 have blessed your journey and those to come from here on out. It appears your quest has been fruitful." Glancing to Sean, she said, "come join my halls, oh guest of honor."

Gingerly, Sean followed on foot toward the platform, Taylor in toe and avoiding his gaze, keeping eerily quiet. Soldiers had taken the reins of Majesty and Star Shaker, peering at the strange man; but more eyes followed Taylor than Sean had expected. Eventually, with a lurch, the platform descended the mountain slowly to start, but then picked up speed. Disjointed at first, Sean grew to relax as the feeling of falling dissipated with each passing second. Nobody spoke a word, but he did observe this woman's power, for it commanded their travel as if the ground were water. Seamlessly, the rock rolled near the platform edge, not slowing or cracking; almost like water on a pond. Concentration was second nature to this woman. She looked out over the valley and before he knew it, they were traveling over the plain toward a palace the size of a city; well, the size of Engshl, at least. Mounds popped up around them closer to the Palace where in people came out of their sides to wave. Slowing the platform into a slot of open Earth, the woman stopped it, and like a puzzle piece, it locked into place. She dropped the power and walked briskly forward, leaving Sean scrambling to catch up. Guards on either side saluted the party arms over chest wearing the beetle armor.

'Well, better not put this off any longer, time for answers lie ahead' Sean thought and entered the Palace of Stars toward destiny.

Chapter 11: Palace of Stars

    To say the beginning of Sean's stay was relaxing would be a lie. Rushed into a bath he was scrubbed head to toe by giggling servant girls which left his face as red as the clay outside. After being cleaned until he felt like a newborn, the girls trimmed his hair, beard and nails till the simple farm boy disappeared and a young lord emerged. Next came dressing Sean. They tried silks but they were too tight with his broad shoulders. Only upon threats of nudity did the girls bring cotton trousers, black as night, covered in gold scrollwork, a tunic white as snow with a gold star on each shoulder. New leather boots completed the look with only a slight grimace at needing to break them in. One placed a red scarf around his neck and another placed a sword on his waist, polished and cleaned as well. The symbol glowed slightly on the sword as it had since coming here to the Star Valley. Before Sean could sit down to ponder its glow, they whisked him off down corridors, causing him to lose track of what turns had been taken until he stood in front of a large set of doors. The giant doors looked like the sky at dawn, twinkling stars included. Looking around, Sean saw he had been left alone in the hall admiring the intricate artwork of each star when the doors began to swing open.

    A grand hall became visible before Sean's eyes in the crack of opening doors, bright white walls, fluted columns lining the walkway with lit torches; and at the far end sat the Queen of Stars; Sean's jaw dropped as she was the same Ancient woman from earlier that wielded power with ease. Appearing regal in a white and gold gown with what seemed to be a crown made of real stars glowing on top of her head. Taylor stood to her right, 20 guards lined the carpet and the man in armor sat to the left. Stepping in, Sean felt all eyes locked on each movement that pulled him forward, nervously. Harps played a dreamy song that sounded like the one Taylor always hummed next to their fire on the road underneath actual stars which soothed his nerves. Doors swung shut as Sean was halfway down the carpet, but he pressed on with no further doubt.

    Stopping at the dais in front, Sean could feel everyone holding their breath in anticipation; who would speak first? As Sean began a low bow, the Queen rose from her chair, stepping down to circle Sean. He froze mid-bow before deciding to straighten up, holding his head high like the Ancient he was meant to become. Reaching his hand toward the blade at his hip, Sean saw the Queen's face soften slightly. Her hand began to reach forward as if to trace the symbol on its hilt before it fell back to her side. Composing herself with dignity, the Queen retreated back to memorize his face as if searching to find a secret Sean knew not. Taylor watched anxiously, washing hands to free her nerves, feeling helpless during their silent exchange. Smiling, the Queen retreated up a step of the dais and spoke loudly for all to hear:

"Welcome, weary traveler, stranger to these halls; may the 20 bless your journey and protect you from the shadow in the name of light. I am the Queen of the Stars, Eyonka, Queen by right and of the Original 20 Ancients. May I ask your name?" Her voice echoed around the chamber, drowning the music of the harps.

The gathered all hushed, for their Queen had uttered first denoting Sean's importance. Each waited in anticipation how the boy would respond, knowing that a greeting of thorns had been set with Eyonka's Queen by right nonsense. Any Ancient could see that, let alone a hall filled with lords and ladies of the court. It made Sean boil with frustration until a single thought popped in his head clear as day 'A test it seems? Then I shall do as my horse is named and shake the stars to their core.'

Gathering Life, he channeled it through his body until it felt as if he would burst at the seams. Opening his eyes wide, the Queen nearly fell backwards, for Sean was illuminated as bright as any star, and those gathered shielded their eyes from his light. Unsheathing his sword with practiced ease, the Ancient symbol glowed a radiant light. The guards rushed in, hands to swords, but the man (Sean assumed to be a general) prevented them from taking action. Taylor looked concerned. 'Ha!' thought Sean.

"My name is Sean of Bear Mountains, chosen by the Ancients to save the Light of humanity and all people. Destroyer of Shadow Beasts, Protector of the Artifact, and by my birthright Proclaimer of the Light as heir to the Ancient post held by Orwick Stormbringer!" Boomed Sean.

With force, he thrust his sword into the air, as his power surged toward the ceiling in a manner that frightened all but one: the Queen of Stars. Nodding defeat, she strode toward Sean, reaching out her hand to press her thumb on his forehead. Drawing the symbol of the Ancients, Eyonka started muttering quietly so only Sean could hear the words; then Eyonka backed away a short distance. Taylor's jaw dropped open and every guard kneeled down in awe at their Queen's actions. Sean lowered his sword slowly, making sure to carefully sheathe it in the hilt.

He then relinquished control over Life energy, letting the last vestiges of power drain from his body.

"Well then, my vessel has done well in finding you. Such power, like Orwick...Now! Come with me for you are ready to fully awake your true potential. All Ancients must die to be born anew; otherwise, what separates us from the mortals?" With a wink, the Queen clapped her hands together.

A small door to his left opened, revealing that night had fallen and a single staircase down the valley could be seen. In the distance, Sean could see a tower of white, gleaming as a beacon in the darkness. Cool, fresh air came through the opening and the smell of clay along with it brought a change of pace to the stifling hall.

"Follow the stairs and enter the tower. All shall be explained by a friend; failure to do so means death in the Star Lands by my decree."

Growling, Sean trudged out into the night and down the stairs without hesitation. Every eye watching this boy leave on a personal quest. Taylor wanted to rush forward but was unable to budge. "He did it..." she whispered.

The Queen settled back in the throne, sipping from a chalice. 'This boy is Orwick all right, but doubtful he remembers so.'

"Taylor!" Eyonka's voice rose enough for the guards to hear.

"Yes, my Queen?!" Taylor shouted, caught off guard.

"Prepare to venture below. I want to take a stroll."

"As you command, my Queen."

The two followed Sean quietly in the night. The soldiers felt displeasure at being left behind. Taylor had to hold back running ahead; it was torture as they descended each step slowly. 'Please be careful,' thought Taylor, her heart beating fast. Her Mistress placed a comforting hand on Taylor, and arm-in-arm, they traveled together.

"It is in the hands of Light; have faith, young one," the Queen whispered. "It seems we have much to discuss after all this is done."

With that said, silence enveloped the two and the night got darker. Taylor was left speechless. 'Could she know?'

Chapter 12: Ancient Determination

Clouds drifted in front of the moon. Luckily for Sean, the glow of the tower in front of him provided enough light to see the stairs in front. Nerves ate away at his stomach and his heart pounded loudly, disrupting the quiet of footsteps on stone. This place gave him the creeps for some reason and a sense of someone watching from a distance could not be shaken. Stairs ended 100 feet below the palace hall, where crunchy clay sat firm under his leather boots. Walking forward, Sean finally took in the size of the tower in front of him. Sitting on a lake, its shadow reflected on the surface of the water. Sean began circling to find an entrance, but none could be found. Frustrated, Sean sat on a rock to look above at the top of the tower. 'Maybe an entrance high above?' Near the top he could barely make out an opening of a balcony, but there was no way to it.

"Maybe if I were a bird," Sean muttered.

Thinking over the Queen's statement again was no help either. Sean went to the lake, taking a drink from the cold water. Staring absently at the lake's surface, he saw lights dancing below the ripples, not from the towers reflection. 'Could it be an entrance now buried?' Thought Sean. Tracing the edge of the tower on the water side, he noticed where those lights were coming from. As the moon became clear again, so did a small tunnel underwater, near the edge, the source of the small lights. Gathering a deep breath, Sean plunged into the frigid depths. He was certainly no stranger to swimming, but this tunnel was set deep into the lake. Touching bottom, he opened his eyes to see the tunnel leveling out, leading toward the tower. Kicking frantically off the lake floor, Sean returned to the surface, gasping for breath. 'Too deep for me to make it!!' Sean screamed inside his mind as a creeping sense of dread set in. Once his breathing returned to normal, he mulled the Queen's words once more, searching for a deeper meaning.

'Failure to enter meant certain death.' Sean regained his breath once more, determined to make it this time now, for failing was not an option. The plunge felt much longer, but this time he knew what direction to go in and there wasn't spare a second to waste. Touching the sandy bottom, he kicked down the tunnel in the murky water, the trapped air beginning to burn his lungs but ahead sat a chamber of light. 'Almost...there' he thought releasing a few bubbles of air, stretching hand out for salvation and promise of relief from the watery depths. Darkness began to envelope his vision, air running thin and the room was just within reach....and that is when Sean heard a mad cackling before everything went black. Water suspended a motionless body in desperate need of air and muffled "thunk" as he floated to the ceiling of the submerged tunnel.

"All Ancients must die to be born anew, otherwise what separates us from mortals?" The Queen's words echoed hauntingly in his mind before unconsciousness set in.

Sean opened his eyes finding a world empty of all save a faint light which glowed around him. 'Did I die?' Sean wondered. Taking in the surrounding white world, he could not see another soul or an indicator he was, in fact, dead; yet he was not truly alive, either. His body buzzed, vibrating with power like the day he awoke with Taylor. It felt real enough, but that same light seemed to come from his bare torso. Turning once more, Sean was startled to find the Life Elemental who sat quietly eyes closed before Sean almost in a trance Then he spoke in that same voice of tree branches rustling in a wind mixed with pops like new saplings:

"Welcome my young Ancient, to the plane between Life and Death, where rebirth is requested and judgment passed on those we deem worthy to rise to mortal form again. It appears since our last meeting you have come far; memories jumbled together slowly, forming whole, and yet you continue as Sean without aid of their knowledge. Orwick chose his heir wisely, someone that stands on two feet without a crutch to aid them." Life chuckled dryly at his anecdote and Sean dared not move a muscle. "Now my young Ancient, your worth has been judged and I shall awaken you, but before departing, let us talk some. This tower that houses your physical body, or vessel, is called the Tower of Resurrection—a direct conduit between worlds—a place first used to rebirth Ancient vessels when mortal wounds occurred in battle against the shadow long ago. It is also used to transfer a consciousness to a new body as years wear down upon Ancients. That is Ancient birthright locked by the oath and contract. Other chambers now exist as portals to this world, yet this was created by Orwick in the age after their confrontation with the Shadow. The blade you carry is a key to rebirth. Others forged blades of similar origin, but yours is unique as it lets you use any chamber you may stumble across. Guard it well, for if used wrong, it could be disastrous.

The Shadow grows stronger as each day passes. Gather those of the 20 which remain and march south with haste. You must visit the shrines shown to you along the way to unlock your true power and become Proclaimer of Light."

"Wait, those were real? A mountain, air, water and volcano? I thought those were just a dream," Sean blurted out loud, his voice rippling like a dream.

"They are real and calling to you at this exact moment in hopes this Shadow may be defeated as the last war. The Land of Stars announced your arrival to them as soon as you crossed its borders. Trust the Queen, she is a formidable ally to have and was a great advisor to Orwick during the war. Learn what you can from her, but remember that she has an agenda as well."

"Why would she offer me aid? From the start, she laid a trap with a greeting of thorns from which I barely escaped unscathed."

"For the love of Orwick she would move the mountains; she will see him in you. It is your path that shall save the world and those around must learn to accept help when given or strike out alone."

"If only I knew what path to take ... How do I channel my grandfather's memories?"

"That will have to be found by you; no other Ancient has done what he has done—passing power like an inheritance. These days are filled with much mystery not seen in some time and often answers to questions produce only more questions. As a parting gift to you, I grant power to your body. Stab wounds will not drain you of Life, nor will fire or water. We must part I am afraid; use these gifts wisely and call upon me in meditation."

"But there is so much more to learn and ask! I cannot leave now!"

"Answers to questions make more questions to answer; finding them provides full understanding. Go forth, tell your Queen a storm gathers, and so should the 20. You, Sean, must find my brethren. The Light rides upon you, my young Ancient. Learn all you can…"

The Elementals eyes opened wide revealing the green of grass. Reaching forward with a vine to Sean's forehead, he marked the Ancient symbol, and the world of light spun away. A floating sensation enveloped Sean's ethereal body with the power of Life pulsing greatly as each moment passed like an eternity.

Chapter 13: Jubilation of Rebirth

Sean breathed in deeply and found himself lying on a soft feather bed in a room surrounded by glowing stones. He felt strong as Life energy surged through his veins. Never before had Sean channeled this much. Moving out of bed he found white marble stairs leading up to the Tower's main chamber. Here Sean took the room in with wonder: A wall of water fell from the ceiling to the pool he had been swimming toward; those same glow stones lined the walls to the corners and ran from the floor up to the ceiling. Seeing no other doors leading outside, it left a single possible exit. 'Only one way out, then,' Sean thought as he dove into the pool of water that had defeated him what seemed a lifetime ago. This time he didn't gasp for air as he left the tunnel, leaving the tower interior behind. Popping up to the surface of the lake, Sean found Taylor sitting there with the Queen of Stars. Taylor looked worried, and the Queen was triumphant at seeing Sean emerge unscathed.

"It seems I was right—talent you have. Welcome back to life and among our ranks, my young Ancient. Hope that you received the answers that you were looking for," chimed the Queen. "It seems your body agrees with being Ancient; exhilarating, yes?"

"I have more strength than I ever thought possible, yet it seems like there is more to come. The storm gathers, so should the 20, for Light must ride again," responded Sean.

Taken aback, the Queen nodded in agreement, responding "Riders shall be sent immediately but let us get some breakfast. Morning is upon us and I heard Taylor's stomach growling loudly."

"Mistress!"

"Was I mistaken an hour ago, or was it nerves for this boy only?"

Turning bright red, Taylor stood upright and offered an arm assisting her Mistress up. Squeezing as water from his tunic Sean locked arms with both the Queen and Taylor and the three began climbing the stairs. 'Serves Taylor right after how she tortured me the whole journey here,' he thought laughing to himself. Eventually, the grand hall came into view as their party topped the final step. The Tower of Resurrection was behind them as a memory of what was. Entering the hall with the sun creeping above the horizon to welcome cheers which rang through the hall at their return. Lords and Ladies bowed, making Taylor squirm in Sean's arm. Servants poured into the hall, carrying trays laden with food, large jugs of wine and musicians of various instruments in tow. Soft music serenaded those around with tones that set a mood of jubilation. They feasted on wine, bread, cheese, fruits, and fish well into the afternoon as the Queen introduced Sean to nobles and merchants. At first opportunity, Taylor had broken free from Sean, leaving him alone to a world never known, among strangers wanting to gain as much knowledge of him as possible. After the sun was at its zenith, his head spun from all the names and wine, both of which seemed infinite. With a loud clap, the Queen dismissed the festivities to get some rest, which Sean thought a profound idea. All this commotion had been overwhelming and each glass of wine went down faster than the last. Composing himself as a servant led Sean out of the hall down corridors, he lost track of their path until they reached a rather large room at the palace. To one side was a 4-poster bed; on the other side, a set of double doors. Sean knew nothing about what was behind the doors, but it was the bed which drew him in. The mattress had to be the softest bed of goose feathers ever, and sleep came to him instantly; a deep dreamless rest.

Chapter 14: Knowledge of Ancients

The sound of a crisp bell woke Sean from his rest; night had descended outside his window and a server girl appeared to wake him with an urgent message. Finding he had fallen asleep fully clothed (boots included), Sean grew red with embarrassment at being so disrespectful towards his hosts' hospitality. 'I cannot become entitled like some kind of Lord,' Sean thought in a berating tone. Dispensing a scroll to Sean, the serving girl went outside to wait patiently for Sean to change clothes in privacy. Taking care breaking the seal on the scroll he read "Sean, at your earliest convenience I summon you to my study for there is much to discuss in private - Ey.". Selecting a simple light blue cotton tunic along with a pair of brown cotton trousers from his wardrobe, Sean dressed clumsily, still a little drunk from the feast earlier and strapping sword to waist he looked in a standing mirror. The image reflected back took Sean off guard for he looked ... regal, almost like a noble. Remembering why he had been woken up, Sean strode to the door, and opening it he found the same serving girl near the door patiently waiting.

"My presence has been requested by the Queen of Stars, please take me to her private study," Sean said, and the girl nodded and started off, but then stopped suddenly.

The girl had said weapons were not permitted, yet Sean took the sword at waist regardless. It took a stare from Sean before she finally began moving them down corridors, and this time he did his best to remember the path taken. After the 20th turn Sean gave up, deciding instead to take in the art tapestries that hung from walls in some hope that these markers could guide him in the future. Some were of scenery and others of grand cities, yet none of actual people, which he thought odd. Reaching the chambers corridor, a giant painting at its end stuck out to Sean more than the rest: 20 humans riding horses into battle against shadow figures, each person wielding swords much like that on his hip, and an aura of energy encircling heads. A deep sense of remembrance of what truly happened and disgust at the depiction surged to the surface but he shook it away, deciding to focus on what lies ahead. Entering the chamber after the serving girl knocked, bowed and disappeared, Sean saw the Queen bent over a desk with book open and parchment to her right. The study was as large as his own room and well-lit by the same glowing stones as the tower had—not a torch or lamp to be found. Bookshelves covered three walls and to the Eastern open wall lay a window of stained glass, with an image of a star engulfing the Ancient symbol. Sean prepared to speak when …

"Welcome Sean, drink?" Offered the Queen.

"Many thanks but I had enough wine earlier at my welcome party." Sean replied.

"Punch then, chilled please," asked the Queen of a serving girl near the door.

In no time, goblets filled with chilled punch sat poured on the Queen's desk, her focus still on what lay on the table and not Sean. Then with a flick of a hand, the girl departed the study, hastily bowing to Sean in the process. Silence ensued, only interrupted by a flick of quill on parchment and turning of dry pages, Sean's patience wearing thin at each passing second. Unable to bear the torture, he decided it best to begin. "My Queen, has word been sent to gather?"

"To business then, just as Orwick would be, for not a moment of repose can be found," she mocked dryly. "Yes, my fastest dispatchers departed this afternoon; however some of the 20 are… prickly to visitors. I summoned you to this study to officially offer my home as your own; it has a vast library of books that await to be read and the best swordsman to spar with as well."

"A fine offer that I graciously accept; there are many mysteries to find answers to and allies to acquire," Sean responded, already prepared to accept this hospitality after meeting with the Life elemental.

With a satisfied nod, the Queen sat, taking the chalice of punch. "It seems you are not dense, that is good. I had feared the worst upon hearing of your upbringing in the mountains, but to hear you had been alone for so long…solitude can have an adverse effect on the mind. Tell me, what request can I aid in first?"

"If I may be so bold, what of Taylor?" Sean blurted before thinking it through, heart beating wildly.

This piqued the Queen's interest. She took a long sip before responding: "Taylor, what about her?"

"Would it be so much to ask she be my tutor here, guide to the Land of Stars? So far she has taught me so much that I wish her to continue our studies."

"A wise thought, one that crossed my mind once or twice. Taylor is my best vessel, trusted servant and offers much knowledge to teach being of the court for many years. I will allow this but there are some topics that she knows nothing of. For example, the Power we wield as Ancients I shall teach you directly; yes?"

"I accept humbly, thank you. All I can learn aids the Light and anything to eliminate this feeling of being a newborn is welcome."

"To start your education, take this book written by Orwick on explaining the Elements. It was a personal journal left in my possession which I have treasured all these years, but it is yours by right. Taylor headed out from the palace some time ago and is out visiting the Shrine of Stone. The first step on your path is to visit the Shrine of Stone, start by heading to her with a guard as a guide. Your horse is ready for the trip and we have no time to waste!"

Bowing slightly, Sean took the journal with care and left Eyonka's study behind. The serving girl outside brought Sean once more to his chambers to gather up the armor he had originally come with and wrapped them in a bed roll. Departing the room, she next led him to the stable where a guard sat on a horse, holding the reins of Star Shaker. In silence, Sean mounted and off they went to the Shrine as the moon rose high in the sky. The night air sobered Sean up and only by moonlight did the two travel north, taking a trail around the hill that only a day ago had brought Sean here. Horse hooves rang out in the night as Sean leaned forward in anticipation of what lay ahead: a new power.

Chapter 15: Mind the Heave

Riding all night into the dawn, they only stopped once to rest and to water the horses. Slowing to an easy trot after mounting the horses, Sean pulled the journal out. Finding a section about the temples he began reading the section of their current destination:

Temple of Stone
The Elemental of Stone grants the power to move Earth upon an Ancient and shape it to their design. Hidden in a mountain system on the North Edge of the Land of Stars it acts as a barrier between the Ancients and mortal humans. Erected by the strongest on Earth, Eyonka, after the fall of Shadow and Wanderer War. The Guardian accepted its new home and slumbers deep beneath the ground. It is important for one to take caution and "Beware the Heave."

Putting the journal away to ponder what he had just read, its last sentence swirling around Sean's head. 'Beware the Heave? Figures these must be rigged with traps, but should it not recognize Sean?' He thought deeply. It mentioned no specifics as to what the temple looked like or who the Elemental really was. This lack of information disturbed Sean but a spark of excitement at the unknown slowly burned. Kicking the horse into a faster trot, Sean surprised the guard who took a moment to react and catch up to take the lead over.

The guard signaled to pick up speed, and Sean kicked Star Shaker, bringing him to a mild gallop, keeping pace. He saw signs of Taylor and his journey prior, the mountains like he saw in his dream coming into view. Topping the rise, he saw the stone building Taylor had made sure to avoid with Majesty tied next to it. Saluting his arm over his chest, the guard turned around to leave him and began the trek back, saying not a word. Pulling up next to Majesty, Sean stopped then dismounted Star Shaker and tied off on the same post. Brushing the horses snout affectionately, he headed into the stone building where he heard Taylor humming that same song. The building was empty which caused Sean to use Life trying to find where the source of humming came from. On a ledge behind the stone building, Taylor sat sharpening a knife as was her routine when killing time. Jumping quietly up to the ledge she sat, Sean crept up to scare her and as he prepared to shake her... Without missing a beat, the point of Taylor's knife was at his neck.

"Fine, I surrender." Sean said jokingly.

"You will need stronger will than that to face the next task," responded Taylor, blade still at his throat.

Backing up a step, Sean maneuvered around the knife, countering with one of his own. Smiling wide, she hid the blade in a fold of her dress, Sean returned his to the right boot and he jumped down. Before he could offer assistance, Taylor dropped down, and walked off without a word toward a tree. Sean stumbled to catch up to her under the shade of the tree, questioning where she was headed.

"Wait, do we not need to go in?" Sean asked confused.

"That is a decoy shrine; we must head into the Mountain for the true Shrine. This way and do not dawdle; mind the heave." Taylor said in a hushed tone barely above a whisper.

Sean paused only a moment; 'was it a coincidence she said heave?' before he stepped forward to follow below in the mountain. A breeze from inside the cave entrance made it seem as if it were exhaling. It appeared to run long and deep into the mountainside. Pebbles trickled to the ground, forcing Sean to look up, ensuring no larger rocks were falling. When all was clear, he entered the darkness, eyes adjusting to the dim light, he nearly bumped into Taylor. Saying not a word about Sean's clumsiness, she continued forward undisturbed by constant air flowing past their faces. The tunnel descended slowly at first, but becoming steeper, the further they traveled. As Sean questioned how much longer they would be walking, his feet hit ground level and the walls opened up wide. Taylor lit low torches using flint and steel to offer light in the darkness, revealing to Sean the true Shrine.

Behind boulders sat the entrance outlined by marble columns, dark rock pillars filling the space in between from floor to the ceiling above. A low ceiling forced Sean to duck slightly. Taylor remained outside the entrance masking her concern for Sean by playing with her dagger. Briefly making eye contact with Taylor, Sean nodded and pressed a step onward as another gust of air burst forth. The warm air stung his cheeks, forcing him to squint. 'Is it just me or is the cave getting smaller?' He wondered, darkness around seeming to close in. As the wind subsided, he opened his eyes wide to find the cave had actually opened up more. Reaching an arm out to the side, Sean found the wall had moved back a foot or two, confirming suspicions that it had changed, but adding more questions as to why. Hurrying along before it could close in again, Sean did his best to move forward in the dim light. He wanted to get as far in as possible before the next wave of air could hit again; no reason to think it would, only instinct.

"That must be the heave," he mumbled sullenly to nobody in particular.

Deeper he went, disturbing pebbles along the way, a feeling of potent energy around him. His pulse quickened. This time Sean felt the next push build beneath his feet at first, bracing an arm to the wall as a gust of air and warm dirt blew past his face. The air forced him to the ground in a kneeling position as the walls closed in on Sean. This time in the light he saw how the ground retracted around him to its original place, allowing him to stand hunched over once more. 'It is as if the mountain were breathing! Alive, like…' Rushing forward so as not to be trapped in a kneeling position again, Sean pushed further into a cavern like an arrow, nearly falling victim to a pool of bubbling magma.

"Best not test my impervious face to fire," he joked morbidly. 'Taylor would not like that,' a quiet voice thought.

Standing upright, Sean brushed the dirt from his pants to take in the whole cavern. From the light provided by magma pools, its magnificent beauty took his breath away. Ceiling stretched to a peak 500 meters away, stalactites with razor-sharp points hung menacingly; they made Sean shiver. In the middle of the cavern rose a smaller mountaintop. Sean could see its steep slope rise like a needle. Stalagmites decorated it like ghostly trees with magma surrounding its base as a moat. He walked forward a step and the ground vibrated making a humming sound and the magma bubbled more intensely. Pebbles fell from the ceiling in response to the tremor, Sean did not dare look up for fear he'd flee the danger. He had to move onward for missing the creature who could shake a mountain meant giving up on the world. He kept eyes locked dead ahead, taking each step till the moat of magma was reached.

With a howl loud as air rushed forward, nearly blowing Sean out of the cave. Finding the source of such powerful wind, Sean could see it came from a widening crack 15 feet away on the mountain side. Planting feet firmly in the ground, Sean drew his sword; The symbol glowed in the dimly lit cave. Roaring, he tapped into Life energy and thrust his sword forward as its blade began splitting the debris-filled air. What seemed an eternity passed. Sean was unyielding but sword arm beginning to tremble at the strain. A last gust erupted with force then ended as the crack slowly closed, leaving unbroken mountainside once more. Sean's arm fell to the side, adrenaline dissipating fast, and only then could he tell how fatiguing the task actually was. Gathering a deep breath, he stepped forward once again, sword still in hand. Sean raised its tip level and pointed to the mountain in front of him where the gap was located. His spine prickling and tingling, Sean bellowed out:.

"I am Sean of Bear Mountains, Protector of Life, Ancient of the 20 and savior of Mankind. I proclaim this to you in the name of the Light; awaken by my command Earth Elemental!"

The cry rang out, echoing around the cavern; his words of Power shook free a few pebbles from the ceiling. The Ancient symbol on his sword blazed to life. A mirrored symbol carved in the stone began to glow from the edges where the sword tip had pointed. Then two large ledges of stone began to move up on either side of the symbol etched in light. Golden orbs larger than Sean appeared under ledges like eyes, the air from the crevice had started up again. Diamond stalactites and stalagmites made like teeth poking through, 'Is that the Elemental?!' Sean wondered in shock. A sound of grating rock came as the mouth opened wide, and the vibrating earth became louder until Sean found it unbearable. It seemed the entire cavern would collapse on top of him in a moment's notice unless he could stop it. That is, if the formed face of stones and gems did not gobble Sean whole first!

"Mind the Heave!" Sean shouted before the rock could deafen or crush him.

Quiet. All noise then left the cavern, the rock stopped moving and Sean heard only his haggard breathing. Out of the mouth billowed fog as a figure stepped from the white smoke; sharp edges outlined its figure as it trudged towards Sean. Legs that never lifted moved this creature closer to Sean; then a memory of Taylor seeing it the first time overpowered his brain. A mud-colored creature covered in gems, the awe she felt was immense. How it spoke with rock noises rather than the common tongue and her Mistress responding in kind, eventually translating to Taylor. Sean could almost understand the dialogue of rocks, using descriptions and images to communicate the speaker's message. Slow like a changing landscape when explaining and fast as a rockslide when receiving a displeasing answer. The exchange fascinated Sean who drank in every rocky syllable trying to decipher what was being said, but only some flashes of imagery came through.

Sean gasped loudly, and his mind returned to the cave, the creature from his memory standing before him. Standing 7 feet tall, it appeared to be an extension of the earth itself and a humanoid face stared at Sean. Fewer gems coated the Elemental's brown body now, but still they shined as brilliant as when Taylor saw it long ago. Sheathing his sword to scabbard, Sean kneeled to this molder of land, the Earth Elemental.

"My journey has been far, but it ends further on to the south. By the 20 I have come to learn and speak with you, wise Earth Elemental. May the Light favor our meeting." For some reason, Sean's throat itched as if in need of water.

Rumbling rock turned to a chuckle in Sean's ear, with imagery of a mountain range during a mild earthquake behind it.

"Rise and stand tall, my young Ancient. Do thou understand Rock tongue? Orwick was wasted on the language, preferring that fast Terran tongue; yet you listen with more patience." More rumbling and an image of a slow moving stone permeated from the Elemental. "The Bear Mountains you say? I have not seen those ranges in over two generations! I left when the trees were babes and the Mountain tops bald. Ha!"

An image of them bald made Sean gasp, then laugh for they did not seem frightening as he remembered his home, almost vulnerable more than anything with how the Elemental remembered. 'I can understand!' He thought excitedly, 'I wonder if I am sending imagery too?! This language may be harder than I expected!'

"Relax, young Sean. Understanding Rock tongue is one thing, yet speaking another. For now I shall read your mind and communicate there; please continue the practice of Rock tongue however, for this language tires me; I find it unpleasant."

'I thank you for the kindness; my throat thanks you as well.'

Nodding in acceptance, the Elemental went on, "It is true, I taught your grandfather Orwick, yet he was deemed worthy of such knowledge. Appreciation of the language is not enough; users of ground power must have wills of iron, nerves stronger than steel and a gut made of rock. These attributes grant command of the ground and the ability to lift a mountain. You have much grit but are still too young; not battle tested enough to stand the trials this power commands. Come back another time and I will teach you…"

"I will not! The shadows gather, growing stronger each day and their reach extends to areas of light! Mine mountains remain desolate of life from this threat of darkness, Wanderers killed most of my kin folk. Time is one luxury I cannot afford, let alone the world. You must teach me!" Rumbled Sean.

"Boy…" grumbled the Elemental.

"I shall not leave this spot; no matter the hot air you push at me. Upon first entering this chamber I thought I had the wrong temple for a moment until a pebble hit me!"

The sound of crashing rocks filled the cavern from the ceiling to ground. "Orwick's blood, all right! Such audacity to insult me in thine own temple of stone! One stalactite from above could end your life and the hope of this world!"

At this threat, a death spike fell toward Sean who remained steadfast in place and did not flinch a muscle as it crashed next to him. Calmly brushing fallen dirt from his shoulder, Sean stepped forward to close the gap.

"I said, train me. I am the Proclaimer of Light!"

Another stalactite fell from the ceiling, this time cutting into the stone floor by the Elemental. Grinning widely, the creature raised its fist and struck out to break it into a pile of rubble.

"You have passed the test, young Sean of Bear Mountains. Take my power and learn to move boulders and then shake Earth until the Shadow dies, leaving Light to rule the land. I shall train you further in the power as promised, but there is much that must happen before this may occur. When you can break the pillar as I, then seek me out once again." the Elemental rumbled, "leave this cavern now, I have awoken and the gnomes must remember my presence. They will fight for the Light this time to answer an unpaid oath."

Power surged inside of Sean in each cell; that sensational feeling much like when first awakened to his Ancient ability. It was different this time around in that his body felt weighed down, grounded and yet it hindered not his speed. Various types of Earth he never knew were in the cave could be sensed around them. Focusing on a single mineral, he could point where they laid buried. Gravel, shoal, sand, clay… the list went on and Sean shook his head as if sifting through while absorbing all the information. When the power dissipated, leaving Sean empty, he still could point it all out without looking. As normal sensation returned, a lingering beat remained almost like the ground's pulsing heartbeat. Looking up from the floor, Sean discovered the Elemental gone, but its laugh still echoed around the cavern like a specter. Turning around, Sean left the shrine behind, exiting without any air blowing on him and tunnel walls holding steady. Rocks he had missed before stuck into his mind and Sean avoided tripping himself. 'I will never lose my footing again!' He thought eagerly as the path illuminated itself in a new way.

****

'What is taking him so long? Did he get my hidden message?' Wondered Taylor who grown bored at each passing minute; worry changing into anxiety every breath. Sean had been gone nearly a half hour and the trip to the shrine cavern was only a few minutes' walk from what she remembered.

"The cave quit breathing some time ago. Maybe Sean was yelling and needs help," mumbled Taylor. "Better not to interfere …"

Taylor had been the Protector of the Stone Temple since she could wield a sword. Being brought to wander the stone shrine from a young age, Taylor made it her mission to look out for any intruders on the sacred ground and her Mistress even trained Taylor personally with a sword, followed by hand-to-hand combat here below ground. Each fight ended the same, no matter how much they battled in mini-spar sessions: Taylor always losing to her royal Queen of Stars. Then the day came when Taylor was introduced to a creature older than dirt itself… it shook her to the very core. No matter how many times Taylor saw the Earth Elemental, its sight unnerved her greatly. The creature was kind, despite being made of stone, as it would give her trinkets of gems and other gifts from time to time. Once it even sparred with Taylor, beating her of course, but after their spar the Earth Elemental spoke, saying someday she might make a great Ancient. This comment is what unnerved Taylor the most, and after that her Mistress allowed none past the fake shrine. "Until today," came out in a whisper from Taylor absentmindedly.

"Where is it that farm boy?" She muttered in annoyance, kicking a rock away.

A final crash echoed down the hallway as the rock skidded to a halt some distance away. In the fading noise, Taylor's mind began wandering back several years earlier, to a time before leaving on a mission to find Sean …

Taylor stood on the dais of the Great Hall in the Palace of Stars tending to her Queen during court; she scoffed as another Lord winked at her while kissing her Mistress's hand. The Snot Lord (as she always had names for Lords) had come here on a good will mission. He wanted to venture the pure Star Lands and kill a Wanderer like the stories of old. Stifling a laugh at his request, she thought 'this Lord's courage appears to be that of snow; strong when danger is cold and gone when hot.' A Wanderer had not come into their territory for some time, but reports of other Ancients said different. Allies were important to her Mistress for some reason even though with a sweep of one hand she could level mountains. 'Waste of time in my opinion, I miss the-' Taylor began until her thought was interrupted.

"Yes, Mistress!" yelled Taylor running forward with a slight curtsy.

Snot Lord sat smug faced waiting patiently to see what would transpire; if he requested that she take in the sites, Taylor would have no choice but to obey. 'Please no, here is another offer at a Kingdom to be rescinded an hour later while on trail. Then he becomes another victim to my torture for proposing it, not worth the time...' thought trailed off as Taylor snapped attention back to her Queen.

"It appears our dear Lord has asked for the best scout to take tour of the lands in our humble realm. Wanderers to fight, and such; dreams of grand stories it seems," her Queen said with a twinkle. "As you are not scheduled to guard until a fortnight from now, I must oblige his request. When can you ride south?"

Keeping her composure, Taylor thought, 'I hate when she acts this way to foster support.' However, she responded with all the decorum of any lady of the court: "In the morning, my Queen, however not to dissuade a trip with such a fine (gag) Lord, reports mention nothing to our south. Why not show the land north on his way home?"

"Well as you know, the south always has Wanderers, my Lady," chimed Snot Lord. "This blade begs to bathe in blood and earn a name for itself."

He bolstered the comment displaying the sword ostentatiously; almost provocatively. Despite the fine blade, Lord Snot seemed weak with a weapon from years of lounging rather than training. Clean armor, like new, as if it were freshly forged specifically for his journey south, added to Taylor's suspicion about his lack of skill.

"A fine sword, my Lord, yet stands short of anything above a warrior class Wanderer blade from what reports I have read. May the 20 protect us from Hunters on our journey south to match those stories of old," Taylor commented with a hint of sarcasm directed toward the Lord's foolish ambition. "The morning is when we shall depart if we may, be ready at the stables by sunrise. My Queen?"

Nodding in agreement at Taylor's recommendation, the Queen dismissed Taylor from her presence and eyes came back to rest on the Lord, but Eyonka's mind on the verbal battle. 'Not him...' the Queen mused weighing the man that sat in front of her. What she looked for in each of these noblemen who came to beseech an audience with the Queen of Stars offered a unique opportunity to search for Orwick or even a slight presence of the Ancient. A few showed great promise, given their bloodlines, but none resonated with her power, nor did they show interest in becoming more than mortal. Returning attention to the Lord Hammer in her presence at the moment, Eyonka continued to exchange pleasantries until finally bid the man farewell to chambers for rest before his journey in the morning.

Taylor and Lord Snot departed that morning at first light with their horses' saddlebags filled to bursting which annoyed Taylor slightly. The journey being only 5 days in length meant this extra weight to keep the Lord in comfort would surely slow them down and exhaust the horses. Stifling a bitter remark, Taylor kicked her horse into a fast gallop heading southeast, hoping his horse would be left behind in the dust. It took a few minutes, but soon he caught up, riding awkwardly in the saddle taking care to brush specks of dirt from his hair. Seeing his disgust with being dirty made Taylor smile; 'This is going to be a long five days' she thought amusedly.

After three days riding with the Snot Lord, two advances and offers of an Earldom from the noble, Taylor finally began the slow process of torture. It mainly consisted of her verbally jabbing him at every opportunity when his guard was lowered and taking his guard down with flirty looks. It was tiresome but gave Taylor something to occupy her during their boring journey south; a trip taken a thousand times with other lords and always the same outcome. By the time they made camp, the Lord glumly dismounted his horse while Taylor set up a picket line, unloaded gear, laid out bed rolls and lit a fire. So far, there'd been no sign of a Wanderer which pleased Taylor to no end, but each day of the clay landscape and dry trails dampened the Lord's mood. For dinner, they ate berries, bread topped with cheese; Snot ate jerky that he had packed away for emergencies. It took only one knife pull to teach Snot that animals were not to be hunted and he was a fast learner. After eating, she settled the horses from the day's ride, making sure each received food and plenty of water while she gently brushed their coats. Snot sat watching idly, eyelids drooping lazily and darkness had not fully set, only twilight. Returning to the fire, she found the hero snoring with a whistle, forcing Taylor to scoff 'Another night guarding my Prince ensuring he remains safe and sound,' she thought sarcastically. Taking a blanket in hand to fight the coming cold night, Taylor sat down on a log herself and soon began to doze off …

With a jump, Taylor shook off the cold memory back to reality, arm positioned to draw her sword as the other brought her trusty hidden knife out. Adrenaline pumped through her veins as Taylor intently listened for any sign that Sean was coming from the dark depths. A light shuffle could be heard and Taylor's instincts took off as she jumped forward into the dark, all senses firing at their maximum when: whack!

Falling to the cave floor she saw Sean doing the same, his eyes rolled back inside his head, their collision had knocked him out cold. "Ouch!" she yelled, her voice echoing around the tunnel. Taylor felt her head for a lump. Only a small goose egg, it seemed luck on Taylor's side coming out of the encounter marginally hurt. Picking herself up off the cave floor, Taylor tried to wake Sean up but it seemed he was unconscious, but alive. Hauling the big oaf outside was no easy chore, yet after walking the tunnel for what felt an hour it opened up and they were in the bright sunlight once more. Breathing a sigh of relief, Taylor deposited Sean to the ground, taking care to rest him against the mountain wall. During the trip, Sean's breathing had lessened more and more till only shallow gasps were heard, which caused Taylor to worry he was dying, until she felt his hand pressed firmly to her chest. 'Always grabby!' Taylor thought, taken aback, but somehow the motion seemed to calm her nerves. Removing his hand, she started to hum, knowing its sound would awaken Sean as it had the night of their first meeting. All the dragging and exertion to leave the cave left Taylor only enough strength to hum a few bars, her mind not fully into performing the sweet melody.

The melody reached Sean's ears, and he began slowly opening his eyes. Disorientation could clearly be seen on the young Ancient's face and Sean found the sun blinding him. Squinting, he searched for Taylor who sat close by, humming the tune that awoke him. Eyes locked, Sean took in the picture of beauty before him: even the hiding concern in those blue eyes, blonde hair lit up by the sun to almost radiate fire, he pondered if time could stop so he might stare at Taylor forever. But something else seemed to trouble Taylor more than just Sean's condition. Struggling to gather courage, Sean took the leap to change their relationship forever; a daring bold that had been coming since their fateful meeting.

"What's wrong?" Sean asked worriedly. "Are you okay?"

Chapter 16: Taylor's Atonement

The cold memory came flooding back to Taylor at once in a rush; of the tragedy which nearly broke her whole mind and body. Grasping at any chance to maintain her composure, she shook her head no, her voice losing all strength and it scared her how it might betray true feelings, but then unable to contain it any longer, she burst out "Never would I have imagined my duty to come to an end. Its … It's so freeing, yet…. the cost of getting here has been great."

Sean could sense her pain pouring forward without restraint, suffering alone as he had for so many years. The loss experienced at protecting something with their life, and costing other lives even to reach this point. A tingle in Sean's mind grew each moment and before he could help stop the torrent, it came into his mind: Taylor's memory that haunted her every moment since its inception.

Cold air crept past Taylor, fire long gone, its dying embers offering little heat and only a pop as sparks of the fading hearth fell. She pulled the blanket closer to ward off this unwelcome visitor to camp and debated throwing more wood on the fire. Next came a gust of wind and with it brought a stench of death in the cold causing her to crinkle her nose. As she began to rouse from a dreamless sleep, a blood curdling screech broke the silence, close to the horses. This forced Taylor wide awake to find a Hunter Wanderer over the horses' bodies, claws dripping blood, and the beast howled to the moon in ecstasy at the kill. The Hunter stood 10 feet tall; being alone meant that this monster was trying to become a Skulker by returning to its clan with the head of a human. 'Such an attack in the Land of Stars has been unheard of for over two hundred years!' Taylor thought, mind racing desperately. Rolling upright, Taylor drew her sword. The beast, upon hearing the noise of steel, turned and bellowed again in Taylor's direction, issuing the challenge of battle. As Taylor predicted, Lord Snot cowered in his bedroll, frightened by being face-to-face with his quarry. His sword was out of reach, for the fool took safety and comfort for granted like the pampered royalty he was. 'What, no boasting? Sword showing? Where is that arrogance?' Taylor thought while laughing maniacally at her wit in the face of danger, jumping forward into the fray, wanting to strike at the Hunter first and draw its attention away, Taylor prayed to the Ancients that they may survive the night.

Taylor ferociously fought, dodging those dripping claws, striking her blade to its chest, narrowly missing flesh, blocking the second claw and dispelling the beast's confidence in getting an easy kill. Snarling, he had drawn a dark, two-handed sword free of a ragged sheath and his stench was gut wrenching, filling Taylor's nostrils with each breath. The dark blade swung with such deadly grace it almost caught Taylor twice— a near miss on her head and left arm. A few more strikes forced Taylor back, handicapped by the presence of the sniveling coward, Lord Snot. No matter the injury to herself, it was on Taylor to protect him, for she could not leave him defenseless; could she?

That single moment of hesitation allowed the Hunter to kick Taylor aside with ease, breaking ribs. She spit out blood, pain enveloping her mind. It advanced on the now kneeling Lord who had scrambled toward his sword. With trembling hands, he had half-managed to pull it out of its sheath, snot dripping from his nose.

Swish! The Hunter's blade found the lords neck in a fluid motion, separating body from head, and seemingly slow motion, Taylor saw blood spurt from the corpse. Catching the head midair, the Wanderer let Snot's headless body fall and kicked it at Taylor who was slowly rising with strained movements. Dropping once more to the cold ground because of the dead body, Taylor cried out loud, blood pooling in front of her eyes. That sole cry turned to an enraged snarl. Fighting the pain, she waivered on the edge of consciousness ... Without thinking, by instinct alone, she stood and charged the beast, using every ounce of strength left and embracing the pain.

Unwilling to relinquish his trophy, the Hunter clumsily blocked Taylor at the last moment as the sword lunged forward. Taylor came back, fighting with a flurry of sword strikes, no longer worried for her own safety, and no need to protect her dead charge. Slashing downwards across its body, following up with a slash up to the arm, Taylor used momentum to begin pushing the Hunter one step back and then another. Luck finally as Taylor struck with a blow that knocked the sword from the Hunters hand and the blade skittered across rocks. Angry, the Hunter swung its free fist at Taylor's already broken ribs in hopes of dealing a fatal blow with its glistening claws. Blocking the melee strike with the sharp edge of her blade, Taylor cut through its hand, releasing black sludge like blood, and the creature howled in pain. As the Hunter dropped the Lord's head, Taylor found an opening and stabbed it in the heart, killing the beast. Panting heavily, Taylor shoved its disgusting body to the ground, pulling free her sword, pain threatening to overwhelm her. Calming breath was far from easy as each intake of air caused more pain, but still Taylor remained in control of her conscious thought. No other Wanderers came to the aid of this Hunter's final bellow, but she stood vigilant, nonetheless. Morning approached slowly, the early light of dawn visiting first before the sun rose a quarter of the way up, yet Taylor sat waiting, staring at the head of Lord Snot.

"I told you to fight, damn you!" She muttered over and over again to its lifeless gaze, eyes judging her failure at the duty bestowed. "Maybe my sword's name should be 'hindsight'" she joked darkly. "Better yet, 'Revenger'…" as Taylor's chin fell to her chest, the name she knew the sword would be called escaped into the wind like an ill-fated whisper.

"Fate Avenger …that shall be your name" and the shadowy name made Taylor's spine tingle. "And that shall be my legacy."

"Fate Avenger…." Sean whispered to the wind without thinking.

Upon hearing its name uttered, Taylor's eyes opened wide and she curled up around Sean, crying well into the afternoon till not a drop of moisture was left. Dusk was nearing when Taylor pulled out of the trauma from long ago, locked eyes with Sean and kissed him deeply, catching the farm boy off guard. Magical as the first time their lips met, neither wanted to break free of their found connection. Traveling back to the castle was out of the question. Sean was still recovering from the trial with the Earth Elemental and Taylor emotionally spent, it would be disaster if they were attacked. Taking Sean's hand in hers, Taylor pulled him from the ground and the pair brushed dirt from their clothes before intertwining hands, not out of necessity, but comfort. Taylor led the way up a cliff to where they would camp, forgoing a night under the stars as the sky threatened rain. Going into the stone Shrine decoy, Sean saw a single bed for the protector to stay when duty required. Taylor lit a fire in the small hearth, taking small twigs and adding them until a flame roared to life. Meanwhile, Sean arranged dinner from the stores he had packed away in saddlebags before heading out to the shrine. It seemed he was the only one to think of a meal though he had no doubt Taylor would find sustenance in the wilds. All the while, Sean's mind whirled at how he could have been privy to such an intimate thought. Were these his powers? It could be quite troublesome; best to find out more later on when they were safe at the Castle of Stars. After the fire was lit and dinner arranged, Taylor and Sean sat down to eat, only to push around their food, not looking up. 'Ha! This time it was Taylor who could not control herself!' Thought Sean. 'But …wow.'

Clearing his throat, Sean reached out his right hand to Taylor who did not recoil. Looking up, Sean dared to see how Taylor reacted to his boldness, her face turning red as each second ticked by, but Taylor locked eyes with Sean, welcoming his presence and support. All the years spent searching alone had placed a jagged edge around Taylor who feared to let anyone see weakness, yet Sean could see it plain as day and rather than pulling back it bolstered their connection. Her redemption found by stumbling into the farmhouse on a boy (man, really) naive to the world around; but it was in this moment she felt a bond that could transcend time itself which melted this jagged edge away. All throughout their journey to this point, Taylor never imagined being so vulnerable to someone who controlled the fate of the world.

"Look, we do not have to talk about it… but I have to say, everything will be okay. No matter what lies ahead I am with you and by my honor there will be no need for that blade to avenge my fate." Sean emphasized this by squeezing her hand to solidify his support as Taylor fought back another round of tears.

"You are full of surprises, farm boy, thank you," Taylor whispered.

Emotion swelling, Taylor moved to Sean's side of the table and without fear of consequences, she kissed him again. Taking his hand, Taylor pulled gently leading the way to where the sole bed lay and Sean got up from the table, following Taylor, his heart racing as if it would beat right out of his chest. Rain could be heard softly falling on the mountain outside, chorus driving the pair forward into an unknown journey which they alone would share. Neither spoke for fear it may break the spell binding their union, and Sean dismissed the worry of what was to come in the morning.

That night, a storm rolled through, gentle rain became a downpour with thunder that echoed off the mountains. When morning broke, the sun shone, and the raindrops glistened on the rocks and foliage to give the wild terrain a sparkling dazzle. Taylor woke with the morning light and taking a long look at Sean who lay snoring loudly she left him to sleep in peace and stepped outside to meet the day. Taylor knew that Sean had seen her encounter with the Hunter but not of the aftermath to follow. Lord Hammerfell (no longer would she call him Snot Lord) was son to King Hammer—his only heir to the throne—and her punishment on Lord Hammerfell's death was banishment to find Orwick, a task Taylor had never thought to complete, a cruel joke on the part of her mistress who thought the old Ancient long dead.

"Thank you, Sean. Though you may not be Orwick, it is because of you I am able to return home in triumph." Taylor mused "I gave you the best nickname of them all."

Wiping away a tear, Taylor mounted Majesty for 'a quick detour, then home.' Galloping away on her mare, she left behind Sean and the decoy shrine in a cloud of dust heading southeast to retrieve a discarded piece of her: Fate Avenger. Grasping the sword at her hip for strength, Taylor fingered its hilt as a reminder of what sword she wore and the cost of wearing it: the twin sword Doomed Fate, a gift from her mistress upon banishment. Southeast Majesty rode on toward the site of the bloodshed where she left Fate Avenger. This trip must be done alone as Wanderer sightings had been reported by scouts who roamed the Land of Stars since the dark incident. Taylor would not allow another to die for that blade which held a title of ominous shadow.

Chapter 17 : Recovered Pride

Sean stirred awake as sunlight streamed in through a small window, the smell of rain the night before wafting into the shrine decoy on the wind. His arm moved to where Taylor lay the night before to find nothing but air and a bedroll barely warm. Opening his eyes wide in alarm, Sean could see the shrine was empty save him and what little gear he'd brought for the journey. Fire, long from a memory of embers, had remained untouched, giving the stone structure a cold feeling despite the warm morning light. 'Where could Taylor have gone?' He thought, mind racing and eyes searching for any sign of a struggle. Frantically, Sean scrambled to dress, foregoing any armor for the sake of expediency. Sean hastily put his sword on his hip. Exiting the structure like a deer running from a wolf, Sean saw only Star Shaker tied to the post outside and his pulse quickened. Grabbing the reins, Sean mounted the steed, setting off following the tracks left in the ground, softened from the rain, heading southeast. Subconsciously, like breathing, he dipped into the power feeling the ground to guide their course and Star Shaker shot off at a full gallop tracking Taylor. The tracks were only a few hours old. Taylor may know this land better than he did, but Sean hoped his new power would help him close the gap. An uneasy stomach foretold danger, like the nights Sean spent alone in the mountains when a Wanderer would strike. It hastened his resolve to save the one thing that meant anything to him since leaving that cold, distant mountain.

The sun moved across the clear sky; moisture long gone as the rays began baking the clay beneath Majesty's hooves. Taylor could not spare a moment, for this feeling of unease was building in her stomach, spreading out and upward throughout the body. 'I should not have left Sean alone, this place is unfamiliar to him if the fool chooses to follow me,' she mulled over in her mind. 'Should have laid a false trail instead of rushing off like a child.' A bump made her snap back to reality and looking back on the trail behind her she could barely make out a small cloud of dust racing in the distance.

"Damn!" Taylor cursed through gritted teeth. "The fool followed me!"

Kicking Majesty faster, Taylor started to think how to lose Sean in hopes that he would abandon his pursuit. A cave would not work given his awakening to the Earth Element and no other paths were close. Time was against Taylor for she lacked preparation to spend days in the wild and a scouting party sighting her meant trouble for those soldiers who were loyal to the Ancient mistresses orders. 'Outrunning him will be the only way,' Taylor grimly thought, driving heels and whipping reigns to spur every ounce of strength Majesty could offer.

Determination is all that kept Sean in the saddle despite the mad dash threatening to bounce him off at each change in the terrain. Sean would ride all night to catch Taylor and make her explain why she felt the need to abandon him without so much as a note. 'Why leave?' He thought while avoiding a boulder in the path. Star Shaker sprinted wildly, obeying his commands without hesitation. Gingerly Sean fed the steed energy of Life to continue onward faster. The dust trail only a few miles ahead showed signs of slowing each step forward 'What I would give to fly,' Sean pondered for only a moment before focusing on the chase at hand.

Wind whipped Taylor's face. Her horse had been losing speed at the hard pace, and she looked up to see a dust cloud in front. Dirt flew through the air in a cyclone, roving dust storms were prevalent this far south and an experienced scout could feel them coming. The scouts with nerves of steel used them to their advantage in tracking prey or in some cases losing a trail.

"This might work!" Taylor yelled out, she was one of steel and needed the edge to lose Sean.

Sean squinted toward the horizon, making out a much larger dust cloud than he remembered seeing before. Continuing forward, the distance closing and cloud getting larger until Sean brought Star Shaker to a halt. Up ahead, the cloud he tracked was a dust devil and he dared to not push his luck at how immortal Ancients were. He frantically looked for tracks or any sign of Taylor, but the ground yielded nearly nothing … only a single track heading toward the tornado. Circling carefully, keeping a safe distance away, Sean continued his scan, but it was unfruitful. Scowling, he turned his horse to a stream nearby for a quick rest.

"No way a dust tornado could take her," Sean murmured to Star Shaker. "Taylor is clever though, for using it to hide her destination."

Staring at the stream, Sean reached down, cupping the cool water in his hand. Bringing it up, Sean began to splash some on a face that felt as if it were on fire from the sun high above. Star Shaker drank gulps of this cool water, lulling Sean into a trance state, the noise of trickling stream drowning his ears. 'Where are you? Where would you go rather than the Castle?' Sean pondered and then another memory not of his own surfaced.

Taylor sat on the ground in front of the Queen looking worse for wear, stress of the attack days before and no sleep evident on her face all while holding a severed head Sean recognized too well: Snot Lord. The Queen looked on Taylor menacingly. They were on an edge of a mountain range, further south than Taylor's camp where the Hunters corpse lay. Sean could almost make out a small stone tower that seemed to draw Life energy toward it 'A resurrection chamber perhaps?' He thought, drinking in every detail with feverish eyes. Taylor looked on the edge of crying. Breathing was shallow but the pain was mostly gone now; the broken ribs no longer a concern ... or was it Sean's imagination? Raising a sword to her, the Queen spoke softly, no louder than a whisper, but as heavy as stone in the words' meaning.

"For failing to protect your charge the penalty should be death. Our tenuous relations to the Hammer kingdom are no more and the world lurches toward darkness because of your failure. Given the circumstances of a Hunter nearing the age of Skulker being responsible for this deed is the only reason a small amount of mercy shall be shown."

Taylor sobbed again; composure long gone, for the words stung worse than a blade to the heart. The thought of death for the dishonor was all that kept Taylor's poor wits together, no matter that it would be the permanent end of her life; to do such a disservice to her mistress was incalculable. Taylor clung to the severed head as a child does a blanket, waiting to hear punishment worse than death to be imposed.

"I charge you to venture into the world alone, your task is to find and retrieve Orwick Stormbringer to the Land of Stars. Darkness approaches our land in ways not seen since the war of Shadow; great danger will befall us without him at our side. Take this sword from my hand and be gone. Do not return until he is found," the Queen of Stars boomed this loudly for all to hear. Mercy it was called, to the onlookers it a fate of unfathomable pain and suffering as the Ancient had disappeared long ago, and many believed to be dead.

Taylor wept silent tears at this order and took the offered blade by its sharp edge, hands bleeding as it cut her palms with deep gashes. When she held the sword by the hilt, Taylor's body writhed uncontrollably, and the Lord's head fell to the ground; its lifeless face staring to the sky. Sean gasped at the horror and felt her pain as if it were his own, the terrible agony at being cast out of the one home Taylor had ever known. Darkly the Queen looked on as her favorite servant collapsed like a dying star. Hands clasped tightly to the Queen's side, balled into fists that shook not with rage but... 'sadness?' Sean could not be sure, and before he had a chance to think further, Eyonka spoke.

"This sword has been named Doomed Fate; with it rides hope by the Light you may complete this quest given. May the 20 guide and protect you, Taylor, for this task is of great importance," the Queen's tone dropped to a mere whisper, and for Taylor alone, she uttered a single phrase: "good luck."

The Lord's body then was raised by soldiers, one collecting the now freed head and quickly a procession led by the Queen left Taylor behind, kneeling on the mountain's edge. Now that judgment was passed and coming to her senses, Taylor rose, turned, and drew Fate Avenger out. No more tears would be shed in front of the army and her Mistress, the blade a dark reminder as to what transpired, and its sight filled Taylor with rage. With a heave, Taylor threw the blade over the mountain and it sailed through the air, steel shining off the sun. Clanging of metal on stone as it fell to the bottom of the mountain played the procession away and the memory slowly faded from Sean's mind.

Sean blinked away the memory, the noise of the creek babbling and Star Shaker breathing welcomed after that painful vision. To the South, his eyes gazed, making what he could of the horizon to find the mountain range seen through Taylor's eyes. Sighing, Sean mounted Star Shaker again and with a spur to the horse he set off, seeking any indication of the memories precise location. 'Why must you go there, a place so full of pain?' Sean wondered as the horse hooves on clay carried them onward.

Taylor was hard pressed to believe her luck at finding the dust tornado and escaping it unscathed. Skirting around was tough but rewarding because the dust should cover her tracks from Sean, power or no power. Despite the urgency, Taylor had to rest Majesty for the poor thing was exhausted, so there they sat by a hidden well and Taylor measured her time left in the day. Facing southeast the mountains' silhouette could be seen; it would be dark by the time she reached their base. Praying to the 20, Taylor hoped luck would hold out, a watch tower just a league away from her destination meant sleeping inside rather than in a damp cave. Mounting Majesty, break over, Taylor continued onward looking back, checking what trail was left behind them every so often. Confident they weren't being followed, Taylor turned around to face destiny and reclaim the pride she had tossed aside so long ago. With grim determination, Taylor spurred Majesty into a slower gallop than the mad dash at the start of the day. By her calculations, night should fall soon, and a small chill crept down her spine.

Sean's intuition from the memory led him southeast, and finding a small well, confirmed he was on the right path as he found a hoof print from Majesty. Renewed vigor filled him to the brim and Sean drew Life to bolster his weariness and he released some more to Star Shaker. 'Let us catch them before dark,' Sean thought. The horse jutted forward in faster strides heading southeast toward Taylor. 'I will not let you run away!'

Dark had fallen as Taylor fumbled on the mountains, searching crevices and rocks using only the dim light of the moon, obscured by an overcast sky. Fire would signal her presence to everything within a hundred yards; at night she could be stealthy and that suited her fine, especially since no patrols knew she was out there, and Taylor could not be bothered by their meddling. Majesty sat 20 yards away at the base of the mountain taking a long-needed rest, breathing ragged and when tethered to a tree, the creature nipped at Taylor for driving so hard. Clouds moved, revealing a full moon which aided Taylor's search for Fate Avenger immensely. A slight shimmer of metal 10 feet up the cliff caught her eye and carefully she moved toward it. Covered in spots by a layer of moss, Taylor found the sword, more tears streaked down as she tenderly grasped its handle. Pulling slowly, she freed it from the prison of stone revealing more of the steel which reflected moonlight, giving an eerie glow to the blade. Fingering the Ancient symbol on the hilt it felt right in her hand somehow; almost at home. Breathing a sigh of relief, Taylor stood, careful not to scrape the sword on any rocks as the night lay quiet around her. Suddenly she heard a rock fall to the left, 15 feet down, noise echoing to break the silence. Glancing around for what had dislodged the rock, Taylor braced herself for a potential ambush, heart pounding loudly.

Clouds covered the moon, leaving only dim light when Sean crept to the mountain's edge, eyes glowing as he channeled the power of Earth to see the rocky terrain ahead. Seam left Star Shaker back a ways for increased stealth, he snuck past Majesty, careful not to stir the mare and giving away his presence. Sean wanted to make sure Taylor could not escape again, and while Channeling Earth he felt the vibrations of her footsteps moving up the slope and then stopping without reason. The moon came out as clouds cleared the sky, Taylor started to move up to the left and paused again, Sean held his breath in 'watching' her. With each pause, Sean would tense up, ready to spring forward into action, throwing caution to the wind and disregarding his vantage point below. Then from the base, Sean made out a glint of steel in moonlight and his fear took over all rational thought as he rushed up the slope. Halfway up the slope came the sound of a rock falling, followed by more vibrations, much smaller than Taylor's footsteps. Looking to find its source, Sean's heart dropped, throat tightening as four pairs of eyes gleamed above Taylor out of the rocks; she seemed unaware of their presence. Sean then reacted without thinking and the ground beneath began to propel his body forward at a faster pace, earth shaking with each step.

 Straining her eyes to see what disturbed the rock, Taylor frantically searched the slope above and below her, to no avail. Pulse quickening as if a battle were imminent, Taylor grasped at any noise which could give a clue to where she was being ambushed or even if there was truly an ambush! Since departing to retrieve Fate Avenger, Taylor had been a bit jumpy; her imagination ran wild. As Taylor began to disregard the threat, a "chi-chi-chi" noise finally reached her and throwing caution to the wind she started down the mountain slope at a decent pace. Glancing back to where the sword was found, Taylor could see four pairs of eyes appear gleaming red in the dark—'Wraiths!' They scuttled toward their prey. Taylor screamed from surprise as she tripped to the ground, catching herself on a rock to cushion the fall. A blur accompanied by shifting earth rushed past Taylor toward the creatures Sean roared as he swung his sword at the first Wraith. It reared back but Sean's sword was too quick and sliced the head clean off leaving a wriggling body. The other three Wraith's retreated slightly, chittering deviously; in unison they squealed loudly into the night air. A roar up the mountain answered their call, followed by three more below, warning Sean that Wanderers were nearby. Sean helped Taylor up, and they both nodded, knowing a fight was to come. They would have to attack the remaining Wraiths. The little buggers were fast but lacked foresight in combat, pincers chomping at the bit to find flesh, and they squirmed between rocks as they approached Sean and Taylor.

 After killing the Wraiths with ease, Sean and Taylor climbed down the mountain at a quick pace, hearing roars get closer every step. When on solid ground, they took up a stance standing back-to-back toward the oncoming Wanderers roar with grim expressions. An avalanche of rocks came down the slope as the first Wanderer skittered to a halt, now at the base of the mountain it bellowed, issuing a challenge to Sean. Taylor kept eyes focused to their left, right and center letting Sean handle their flank. On level ground it stood eight feet tall, the stench making Sean gag. A toothy grin spread over its face as it lunged, attacking Sean with a half-moon axe. Sean blocked, parried, and began a counterattack, using his sword strokes. Wind over water, Fire on the plains and the opening came allowing Sean opportunity so he stabbed the beast where its heart should be. The grin faded from the dead Wanderer's face as its body dropped to the ground with a thump. This time it was Taylor's turn to fight as three Wanderers came into view, utter shock and rage on their faces at seeing the death of their comrade. Smiling wide, Taylor drew Doomed Fate in her other hand. 'Three on one; I like those odds' she thoughts as she rushed up to the next Wanderer, dispatching it with ease. Sean looked on to the battle in awe of her dual wielding skill. Sean's blade hummed for battle as always, begging to cut another Wanderer down. Soon Taylor had dispatched the second Wanderer in a similar fashion, using both blades as Sean prepared to help face off against the largest Wanderer; a Skulker, if he heard Taylor correctly.

Taylor led the charge into combat, the beast blocking the strikes with its giant two-hand sword, knocking her backwards. Sean then stepped in, sending it back with a few crafty feints, clouds then moved over the moon to darken the sky which brought a smile to Sean's lips and the Skulker chuckled, welcoming the black of night. Though darkness could not stop Sean, he felt the steps of this beast with his new power, and it gave him a greater advantage than sight. Sean pressed on, barraging the creature as Taylor flanked Skulker, preparing a final blow to take it down without getting close to its deadly sword. Opportunity came, and Taylor struck, slashing with both swords at its back. Skulker howled in pain, dropping its sword to reach claws behind to strike at Taylor. Bringing swords around, Taylor ducked the claws and stabbed through the Skulkers chest, making the beast sputter black blood. To finish the kill, Sean slashed his sword separating head from body in a clean motion that pushed the Skulker to the ground on its back. Yanking Doomed Fate and Fate Avenger free, Taylor came to Sean's side, both stood there panting for air, revolted by the stench.

"We make a pretty good team, Farm Boy," Taylor managed between breaths.

"I guess it's fortunate my being here. I'm not sure dual wielding would have been enough to take him down," Sean joked, pointing the tip of his blade at the headless Wanderer. "A Skulker, you say?"

"Yes, a dimwitted one it seems. For had the group rushed us at once, the battle would have had a different outcome," Taylor explained, choosing to ignore his jab at running off.

"He was controlling the others?" Asked Sean.

"Correct. Wow, you do have a lot to learn, more than the Queen let on," Taylor said, taking on the tone she used when explaining the simplest things on their journey to the Land of Stars. "They are merciless, General class beasts, most larger than this one."

Sean pictured an 11-foot monster staring down at him and it sent a shiver down his spine. Once they caught their breath, they gathered up both Star Shaker and Majesty heading northwest on foot, leaving the Wanderers' bodies to rot. Neither spoke a word. All of Sean's anger from before had dissipated with the battle, and he just enjoyed the walk. The shining pink star was guiding them in between cloud cover and Sean was sensing the ground for rocks in the path. It seemed easier every time Sean used the power and his ground sight spread further out the more he channeled. 'Soon I will be able to move the ground as the Queen did. I'd prefer that to walking right about now,' Sean glumly thought. Another hour or so walking then Taylor mounted Majesty and Sean followed suit. The horses were tired, but Sean trickled Life into them and they began a slow trot onward.

Morning broke with the sun peeking above the horizon, casting shadows in front of them. Sean could maneuver a bit to change the shadow, and make it look as if he was a Wanderer, which brought a laugh from Taylor. Stopping at the hidden well to water the horses, both ate bread and cheese; Sean splashed his face with cool water and began to freshen up, for the fight left a lingering stench. Taylor took to brushing and massaging Majesty and the mares aching muscles, all while avoiding Sean's eye. The sword Taylor and Sean nearly died retrieving was strapped on the back of the saddle, no longer covered in moss. It intrigued Sean; this sword looked identical to Doomed Fate Taylor currently wielded, yet… the metal seemed older.

"What is the story behind the two swords?" Sean asked, breaking the silence.

"Well…" she started slowly, "One blade was forged for wielding by an Ancient and the other for their faithful servant. The pair is meant to be used in such order; however, my mistress has a twisted sense of humor."

Waiting for her to go on, Sean drank a bit more water letting the subject hang in the air between. He knew if he pressed her on the subject, she would only clam up and it must be her choice to continue on. Finally, Taylor relented and began telling the origin story of Doomed Fate and Fate Avenger; Sean kept quiet on knowing how Doomed Fate came to be in Taylor's possession.

"My Queen gave the Ancient blade to me and kept the other for herself. Fate Avenger had no name before that night with Lord Hammerfell dying, my Queen did not find it fitting to name a blade as most Ancients never named their sword. So you are aware all Ancient-forged blades are blessed with power, thirst for battle and have a sharper edge than most weapons. Knowing full well I never could use its true power is the cruel joke of my mistress; it forced me to fight with master level sword skills. After banishment I decided on its name along with the choice to discard Fate Avenger and wield the proper blade as atonement. Doomed Fate came to my possession with its name as every predecessor to wield it has died save my mistress and now me. The sword was a sign of shame, but an offer of hope to my eventual return. Now Doomed Fate signifies my redemption back into the Court of Stars for finding you, Sean."

Taylor's words spoke more than just the meaning of her blades—it showed the arrogance of most Ancients but also that a shred of humanity existed in these immortal legends. Sean never thought about why his sword had remained nameless; it always was the family's sacred treasure and their best weapon against Wanderers. Right there Sean made a vow to never forgo his humanity, no matter the power achieved to fight Shadow, and this promise reverberated to his soul.

"I had no idea," Sean responded in awe.

"I retrieved Fate Avenger out of pride, to symbolize how I have grown from that lowest point in my life so long ago," Taylor admitted to Sean, opening up and letting the jagged edge melt before she continued with a smile. "Now as for the dual wield... I have always enjoyed using two swords. The rush in pushing enemies backward, music as both hum in the air makes a fight rather enjoyable."

"Better dual wield next time we spar then, I do not want you holding back," Sean responded with a grin.

Mounting horses, they continued toward the Palace of Stars, the silence a welcome comfort for they were still alive together. Eventually Taylor gave more tips on traversing the clay plains and all the hidden wells Sean could make use of. More so Taylor did this to keep them both awake, sleep now past due even without the activity of a fight and she only needed to repeat herself a few times to wake Sean whose eyes drooped heavily. Eventually by mid-morning a sentry squad out on patrol stopped Sean and Taylor to inquire what the pair were doing half asleep in the saddle. Relaying the battle story to these soldiers took some time, but by the end of it, half of them rode onward to check it out with haste. The other half escorted Taylor and Sean at a slow pace, allowing the pair to rest in their saddle; the look of awe in the soldiers' eyes beamed brightly. Tale of two warriors who lived after killing a Skulker would spread that night at each tavern to be sure; it was the responsibility of the soldiers to do so. Before that could happen though, they had a duty to return these valiant heroes alive to the Palace of Stars.

Chapter 18: Knowledge and Power

The conquest of Taylor and Sean spread wide across the land, first by small whispers that crescendoed into large ballads by every bard. Defenders of the realm earned feasts, ceremonies and private audiences by any noble of notoriety followed in honor of the triumph; all of which interrupting Sean and his studies. It took a royal order from the Queen to disband the pestering nobles of foreign lands who wanted to meet the Proclaimer of Light and hero to the People. Excitement from soldiers did not dissipate; only the higher ranks seemed less than thrilled about Sean's rise to popularity with the enlisted. A ripple in their long careers of extinguished servitude disrupted their advancement by raising the bar of valor. Parties sent out to patrol hoped to kill Wanderers to get a song written about them, and Sean prayed for their safety. Without their advantage of power to aid in the fight, the outcome could have been quite different in fighting the Skulker. When Sean at last had time to devote to studying, he spent every moment honing his skills. Whether it was in the library or training with swords, his progress was evident; it was learning the elemental powers which worried him, for these improvements came slowly. Now Sean could throw rocks and quake the ground which the Queen called a vast improvement but still he yearned for control of the ground that she had held from years of experience. Sean's control of Life became refined per the journal notes left by his grandfather alone. Meditating never brought back the Elemental to guide him. Taylor quizzed Sean on Ancient trivia each day to be sure he could hold the title with head held high. Much like the trips when she taught wildlife while riding, Taylor put Sean through the wringer on Ancient houses and her knowledge left him in awe. Names, places and events stirred Sean's memory like remembering something long forgotten, unused for some time, and the experience felt unnerving.

"How many Ancient houses are left that we know of?"

"13 houses—well, 14 counting me."

"How many remain active to serve the light?"

"Now at 11, hopefully more given time as Shadow approaches."

Nodding in satisfaction at the answers given, Taylor started in on other trivia about the world at large.

"What parts of the mainland are held by Terran Kings?"

"Hammerfell and Arise. The latter is an ally to the Light."

"What of the Sea Terrans?"

"They have no king to speak of; they are a society guided by Ancients. This is mostly due to their lives being on open water as tribal codes dictate."

The last bit left Taylor's mouth open slightly. 'That was not in our studies…' Snapping her mouth shut before Sean could poke fun, she continued on.

"Number of realms and their names."

"Six in total: The Light Realm, Sea Realm, Desert Realm, Mountain Realm, Forest Hills Realm and Plains Realm."

"What lies south, deep across the Sea Realm?"

Sean hesitated; this topic had not come up before as the Queen deemed it an advanced topic. "There in the Southern hemisphere lies our enemy; the Untamed South is home to the Ancients' training grounds…birthplace to the Wanderers"

'Is he remembering bits and pieces, or has he done advanced reading? Interesting.' Thought Taylor. "What are the element Powers? Their shrines?"

"Life, Earth, Water, Air, Fire and Death; six elements in total. Each Shrine is south of us, minus Earth."

"Exceptional job today, let's go practice sword fighting." Taylor emphasized this by closing the book loudly and stretching her arms to the ceiling.

Being the private library to the Queen, the two of them had free range to leave any resource materials without fear of being scolded. However, after each session Sean made sure to return books to their place which drove Taylor insane; maybe she was just hardened to proper manners since this is where she spent a lot of her formative years. A lady serving court was expected to know more than just proper etiquette, and Taylor's mistress always harped "A pretty thing with no brain is a shame"; the words made her skin crawl. Taking leave of the dusty shelves, Taylor let Sean keep tidying up and decided to stretch before their exercise. As the door shut, Taylor thought she made sight of a shadowy figure in the stacks.

"Always watching and listening, aren't you Nesar?" Taylor mumbled to herself in the empty corridor.

The training yard cleared as Taylor and Sean strode to the center facing each other while holding wooden swords. Taylor took it upon herself to begin teaching Sean dual-wielding; starting off with only fighting using the non-dominant hand. Sean had worked until the sword moved naturally; not perfect, but good enough to hide which hand he favored. Next came learning combos with strokes of the blade and what breathing to pace out energy as to maintain stamina. Blocking, the most challenging for Sean, became easier when they started using wooden practice swords rather than sticks. The edges and flat of the blade gave a better foothold to stop strikes, something Taylor had perfected from years of practice. Taylor gave no quarter to Sean. From the start, she used practice swords while he was stuck using sticks. One afternoon, a frustrated Sean snapped and pointed out the difference in their weapons. Taylor responded by taking up a set of sticks herself. Leaving massive welts all over Sean, he never complained about the weapon choice again and instead invested energy into mastering the techniques. After a few weeks of sparring, a crowd would come to watch their daily contest. The Queen detested this at first, but Sean feared the bruises he would receive with no audience, and backed Taylor's decision to fight publicly. Though not once had Sean beat Taylor, he had quickly gained skill and had learned to fight with two blades. Sean's measure of success was less bruising at each cross of swords and how Taylor actually needed to concentrate, the furrowed brow a dead giveaway.

    Bow practice was too easy for Sean but Taylor insisted that this be a daily exercise; not all enemies could be killed by sword alone. Soon Sean worked in Life energy to the practice session by creating apples to shoot down from trees when they would need escape into nature, away from the soldiers' archery pit. To help round out Sean's already impressive single sword fighting, Taylor made sure to enlist the best, and that admittedly was not her. Sparring was done by other soldiers, mainly a captain by the name Cogarth who kept Sean in check. Cogarth's speed and quick wits in a fight left a few welts on Sean, not to mention that no matter the terrain, Cogarth stood unshaken. On occasion, the man joined Taylor and Sean for a walk outside to hunt or even just enjoy the beautiful mountains all around them. Cogarth always kept his life private before coming to the Land of Stars; though his tan did make Sean wonder where he had been born. One night on a walk by themselves, Taylor told Sean the truth: Cogarth had come from the Sea Terrans, pledged to the Queen in servitude as a soldier and he made a name of himself in combat. Rumor said that Wanderers had killed his family, but Cogarth would not say, and Sean cared to avoid asking, knowing the pain all too well. Pleasant company to be had no matter the mysterious origins, Sean did not pester Cogarth about his past and in it a kinship formed between the two fighters. Taylor had pushed the relationship a bit more. She said Sean was getting on her last nerve and needed a break so she would leave them alone. Sean always wondered if the pair had been more than friends, but ancient history was better left in the past.

During mid-session training with swords, a page arrived with an urgent summons to Sean; council with the Queen on matters undisclosed in 30 minutes. Washing up at a barrel of water Sean did his best to clean up for the audience and rushed onward giving farewell to Cogarth. 'I wonder what is happening? We trained in using Earth yesterday, this must be important.'

Finding two guards outside the Queen's private study, Sean stopped, awaiting permission to enter. As the doors swung open, Sean saluted the guards who responded in kind and Sean strode inside the chamber. Taylor stood to the left of the Queen, her lips pursed; a strange man sat to the Queens right. Their positions flanking the Queen seemed natural, as if this was their rightful place and Sean had to focus elsewhere from Taylor. It being official business, gone were the usual trousers Taylor had adapted for training, and now a formal gown to match her mistress was donned. Beauty only outdone by the Queen, though Sean thought this on purpose. Staring only made Sean's face turn red and so instead he focused on the man standing effortlessly in full armor; face covered by a full masked helm. He wore chainmail that refracted the light around him, making it seem in an instant he could disappear solely by standing still. Bowing to the Queen, Sean stood upright waiting for introductions, and kicking himself for not changing out of the sweaty practice clothes. Sean wondered what the strange man's face looked like and as if on cue, the newcomer removed his helmet to reveal a withering face of leather. 'Price paid in the original Battle of Light and Dark? He looks old enough to have been there.' Sean thought, nearly speaking the question aloud. Sean studied the man more; his frame appeared willowy, as if he had not eaten in weeks but the toned muscle was intimidating and radiated strength. Sean believed this man could turn invisible in a moment's notice. all it took was the will to do so.

Bowing slightly, a raspy voice followed "Welcome to our ranks, Sean grandson of Orwick. May the light bless this meeting of fellow Ancients as Shadow nears our precious home. My name is Nesar, traveler of the world and Whisper of the Winds."

Returning the bow with a nod ,Sean spoke, "The light has blessed us, may our coming ride be to victory. It is an honor to make acquaintance with another Ancient, Nesar Whisper of Winds; please do comfort yourself around me."

"Many thanks young Ancient, my helmet protects what life is left in me. Your perception is astounding as always, no matter the life." said Nesar, returning helm to cover his face. "It also helps to keep the soldiers from thinking me a monster."

The last line nearly forced a chuckle from Sean who had not expected the dry humor, but Sean kept quiet and maintained his composure. The Queen sat with a smirk at Nesar's humor; it spoke of their long friendship; 'always those two together - plotting and scheming.' Sean shook away the thought, unsure where it came from.

"Nesar has journeyed long and far north to us with unpleasant news. Since your Proclamation, a rash of Wanderers have ventured further than ever before. Shadow responds to the Light that is beginning to shine bright and so with great haste your training must be completed, Sean. There are other elements to learn and master—something that is impossible to accomplish in our little paradise of stars," the Queen explained. "Our army is nearly ready for the march, but the need forces you to leave ahead and we shall meet on the road. Already our allies have begun to rebuild their long-disbanded armies to join; however, we may not be able to count on their aid for some time. It shall be the Land of Stars who strike at the Shadow first and lead the way."

"Who shall travel as part of the advance party with me, my Queen?" Asked Sean.

"Taylor of course, and Nesar for additional protection and guide. Do you require anyone else?"

"I ask for Captain Cogarth to join. He also will know specifics on the Army and its estimated strength to teach me battle tactics without need of time wasted."

"Agreed, Cogarth is a dedicated soldier and a benefit to the party. You shall leave at once, heed Nasar's words as mine and... do not forget our need for you; be careful." The last words of the Queen were softer than the rest.

With a bow accepting the terms, and a quick glance to Taylor in her gown, Sean left to pack for the journey. Servants ran around bringing a few changes of clothes for Sean—items that would survive the trip and allow Sean to blend in with the crowd. The last thing Sean needed was a gilded shirt saying "Lord" by the intricate scrollwork. Next, he put on leather bracers and light chainmail for armor, greaves were packed away with the cotton shirts. The gifted set from the twins would be taken along by the army so their trip load would be light for travel. In an hour, the group gathered the horses, all packed and ready to head out on the road. Sean raised an eyebrow seeing Nesar riding bareback with no bags at all, questioning the motive. Ignoring Sean, Nesar kicked the horse to a fast-paced trot which left Sean to scramble up or be left behind. Underway their party went out into the afternoon, heading south. Sean's nerves were harder on his stomach than the rough terrain.

During the ride, conversation was far more pleasant than trips past. Cogarth joined in more than Sean had expected, but Nesar remained stoic and only offered the occasional perfunctory nod. Keeping true to educating on the road, Taylor spoke of another Ancient named Tetral rallying an army to join them in the south. Other houses had been notified, but Gadriel was their closest ally; however, he had a great distance to cover from the West where his territory lay. Maddox and Gaddox who guarded the sea insured aid in any way possible, but they could not guarantee the Sea Terrans would join the fight. It made Sean's head spin hearing all the names with their current positions, but he absorbed it all, as this information was crucial. Cogarth listened intently as well. His training as an officer made him aware that knowing troop numbers and allies could turn a battle's tide. Oddly enough, Nesar seemed not to care as if it were old news, but did perk up at the mention of Sea Terrans. The Ancient offered no input on bringing forth any troops of his own, and Sean made sure to make a mental note, asking why this was at a later time. The politics on territory with Ancients still foreign and knowing who presided over which realm only placed a name, not their population or army size. As Taylor talked, Sean got the feeling that the Land of Stars had the most soldiers under its command at any given time. Gadriel was only second because of the peaceful nature found in the West.

The estimated combined army was 10,000 strong—a formidable enemy to fight alongside the Ancients against the Wanderers. Accurate numbers on the enemy troops was impossible to guess, as the unoccupied Southern Hemisphere was a breeding ground for the savage beasts. Light only knew what had taken place since the last war and they would need to be prepared for a horde; Sean feared this war could span decades. Entranced in the thought of fighting for years on end, Sean barely noticed the terrain, or the pace they were traveling. The landscape changed from mountains to desert as the sun began to dip below the horizon. Nesar pointed a willowy arm to a star in the sky as a guide to the fellowship's destination and Sean memorized its location in earnest. With a "whoosh," Nesar leapt into the cool evening air, leaving his horse behind and he naturally hovered above the ground with ease. Taylor, Sean and Cogarth gasped as the Ancient flew higher into the air till a slight glimmer could be seen like another star in the sky's tapestry. 'He can fly?!' Sean thought excitedly. 'Air will be amazing to learn!' The Ancient sped away like a shooting star faster than their horses could handle until it became clear to Sean that Nesar easily outdistanced them. Setting his mind to the task at hand of catching up to the Ancient, Sean led their group forward; following the star's direction, and each stayed alert for anything unusual. Using the power of Earth here to feel the ground movements would prove difficult as each trickle of sand seemed to make a large vibration that left Sean's blade half sheathed, ready for ambush. Night rode on for the three. The soft sound of hooves on sand began to wear away the tension of extreme vigilance and soon they fell into a rhythm, checking their surroundings of any sign that a Wanderer lay in wait.

    While riding, Taylor resumed her role of tutor and offered up what knowledge she had to Sean and Cogarth. That this desert realm was Nesar's home in which he had selected after the first war of Shadow on account that a wind always could be found blowing. Every inch was known to Nesar who dedicated years of exploration to build the Air Elemental's shrine. Upon mention of the Air shrine, Sean's ears perked up in hopes to get a little more detail to how it looked, or its location, but Taylor offered no more than the fact it existed. Further pestering about the shrine by Sean only made Taylor avoid the questions until rather bluntly she put the matter to bed. "That is yours alone to discover Sean, Cogarth and I may not enter except by invitation; which most Elementals are not forthcoming with."

    Silence filled quickly between the horses' hooves on sand as Sean got the hint from Taylor to let it be, the rambling questions awaiting hungrily for the next meeting with Nesar. Despite abandoning Sean, Taylor and Cogarth to their own trail, Nesar had taken to checking up on the trio on occasion by simply flying overhead or settling onto a dune far ahead. A quick watering of horses nearly turned ugly when large scorpions attacked in force; pincers clipping the air wildly and their tails ready to skewer anything unlucky enough to enter its range of attack. Sean, Taylor and Cogarth stood ready to defend their horses from becoming scorpion food, unsure how to kill the creatures. Luckily, Nesar stopped to check on the group at the right moment, letting loose a large fireball which zoomed past Sean and singeing the scorpions into an ashy crisp. Before Sean could hail the Ancient down to talk about the scorpions or even ask how far away the Air Shrine still was, Nesar soared into the air and out of sight. Once the horses had calmed down, Sean mounted along with Taylor and Cogarth to set out again on following the star and chasing Nesar. Dawn fast approached and the early morning light brought heat taking away the coolness offered by night.

By the next afternoon, Sean felt like those piles of scorpion ash; first experience in the desert heat and sweat poured out like a flooding creek while his lips remained dry and chapped. Topping a dune, Cogarth pointed off ahead in the distance to promises of lush greenery and cool water that lay only another mile off, lifting their spirits tremendously. Giving a spur to Star Shaker, Sean hurried to the oasis, hoping it was real. Taylor had spoken of the desert heat playing tricks on travelers' eyes, and this would be a cruel trick indeed. Sand turned to dirt, then came the green grass (a welcome relief from the baking heat) where Nesar sat gazing into the sky, checking out clouds. Horses and riders alike looked travel-worn to Nesar; they all needed to rest. Instead, however, Nesar protested the notion of relaxing to Sean with a single sentence: "To the top, climb for enlightenment." Sean's eyes followed the mountainside up to his intended destination which stood high above in the sky on a mountain peak. White marble could be seen glistening brightly in the sun, giving the shrine a look like a beacon of hope among the brown dirt and foliage. Taylor and Cogarth tied up the horses, taking Star Shaker from Sean, before they plopped down on the cool grass, taking a breath of relief and checking out the surrounding area. It was as Taylor had said—only by invitation would they be allowed up, and Nesar had no such invitation for the pair. Silently, Nesar lifted off the ground, soaring again in the clouds and leaving Sean to puzzle out how he might breach the Air Shrine.

Chapter 19 High Above the Clouds

    Groaning slightly, Sean took off what little armor he still had on, and left everything but his sword with Taylor and Cogarth. Sheer cliff stared back at Sean who decided it best to walk around this little oasis in search of a cliff that could support his climb. Heading toward the back of the mountain, Sean came upon steps set within stone and began to climb up, glad to avoid testing out how immortal he truly was. Wind gusted from every angle attempting to blow Sean off the side of the mountain. Like the cave of the Earth Shrine, Sean tried to find some pattern to the wind, a way to survive without exhausting what little energy he had. Tiled holes, bored into the cliff, gave the wind a path to pass through, howling as it forcefully pushed through. Sean marveled at how intricate these holes were spaced out and the difference in size making streams of wind blow with varying force and sound. As Sean continued to listen, he heard a pattern form as air currents moved around, almost like communicating his arrival to the shrine. The winding path leveled off, giving Sean a moment to see that he was sitting beneath a roaring waterfall that drowned out the pattern entirely. With his guard down, Sean was nearly blown off the mountain by another gust; with quick work channeling Earth Sean barely caught himself as a new rock ledge grew out of instinct. Wind subsided enough to let Sean get back on the path again, his ears straining to hear when another blast would be coming. Climbing for an hour, Sean took a break and looked down to see a world far below, causing him to cling more tightly to the wall; instinct might not save him this time. 'Such a distance down…maybe flying is not worth it,' he thought. Gathering his nerves, Sean looked up to the nearing peak and the white marble that lay only a bit further.

    Nesar sat perched on a wood platform held up by a long pole when Sean topped the last step. Air this high was thin and Sean gasped to catch his breath. Nesar chuckled softly, remembering how heights had unnerved the Ancient before he had learned to master the element. Not wishing to disturb Nesar, Sean searched for how he could sit on the other platform next to Nesar. The man was in such a trance, and meditation was exactly what Sean needed after the hike. No luck in puzzling a way up the pole to the other platform. Sean settled to the ground, listening as the air below created a soft chime noise. The howling from the holes below became soft notes which relaxed Sean. He tried to forget how high up he sat, and the near miss which would have caused his splattering on the ground below. Nesar remained still in his own meditation, platform swaying with each gust of wind but still the two held as one.

Softly, Sean heard Nesar whispering, "For this boy has come… Yes, Orwick … He knows not your presence, my friend … Remember patience…"

Confused, Sean strained to hear what mysterious voice was talking with Nesar. The only sounds Sean could make out were winds whipping past and the chime below, but nothing else; it began to frustrate Sean after some time. The wind seemed to mirror this frustration as the chime noise grew intensely, distracting Sean's calm meditation. Like a rising torrent, Sean's impatience flooded out and he opened his eyes to see Nesar staring back at him. Before Sean could utter a word, Nesar spoke in the same soft tone as before.

"Years of training to commune with wind is required, my friend; hence my title, for I have meditated in this place for centuries. Come, let us leave the doorstep, as there's someone who wishes to meet you," Nesar's voice was soothing and calmed Sean considerably.

With ease, Nesar floated over to Sean, landing gently on solid ground where he led Sean at a quick pace. From what Sean could see, most of the shrine lay open to the world with no roof other than a few marble buildings. Facing the west sat an arena fluted by marble columns, no seating on the sides for spectators or even a bridge to reach it. Sean wanted to stop and stare at its amazing design, but Nesar continued onward unaware of its existence. Sean followed reluctantly, fearing that the man would leave Sean to some sort of pitfall in his gawking. Reaching a lowered section of gleaming white marble, Sean could see a giant chasm set in the middle surrounded by more white marble structures several feet above the gleaming floor. Sean made out that they were buildings—some were clearly living quarters while a few others stood out oddly given the shape.

"Master Nesar, is all of this the shrine? I feel a presence. However so much of this seems grand compared to the Earth Shrine," Sean's question hung in the wind awaiting response from Nesar.

"The arena teaches fighting with Air but only those who can fly are accepted inside," Nesar offered softly. "The rest is sacred to the Air Elemental alone and any acolytes I feel are worthy to maintain it."

"I see Master Nesar," regarded Sean, confusion at the answer evident in his tone "But what of-"

Nesar cut off Sean by placing a finger to his lips as to quiet the boy for they stood in a sacred place deserving such revered respect and only when silence pervaded did Nesar continue onward toward the chasm edge. Sean, still confused by exactly where the Elemental was housed, looked over the marble edge to what was far beneath. Sean saw a small platform dangling above the ground from high above by a chain; exactly as he remembered from his dream. Here Sean could see that they sat perched upon not just a single peak but the tops of three; the marble Shrine spanning to connect each as one. Eyes back to the platform below, Sean strained to hear any sign that the Elemental was around. Slowly it swayed back and forth in the wind, leaving Sean hypnotized. Left, right, left, right, then a small bell adorning the top of the chain clanged along making magical music, the likes of which Sean had never heard in his life. The more Sean listened and watched the platform's gentle motion, the more he became lost in a trance. His body felt light as a feather. Strong winds caught Sean unawares and before he could struggle to hold tight to the marble beneath, he was picked up and he glided slowly to the swinging platform, making his stomach somersault end over end. Magic of the trance broken; Sean found himself alone trying to match the side-to-side movement in hopes of regaining his balance. The gusts subsided, letting Sean sit cross-legged. He was relieved to still be alive and far from a speck of dirt on the ground below. Wanting to find the peace of being weightless Sean started to meditate when a comforting breeze brushed his cheek and its gentle embrace alerted Sean to another presence. The warm sensation lingered a moment before leaving as quickly as it came to be replaced by a voice that whispered in Sean's head:

"Another Ancient to learn the power of wind, yet you do not listen... I expected more from the Proclaimer of Light..." came into Sean's head like a light breeze, an undertone of disappointment evident.

"My apologies, oh great Elemental; it seems my meditation needs further practice," Sean whispered in kind, adding as much admiration and respect he could muster. "I am a young Ancient seeking your guidance as Shadow grows in the South. My grandfather left many areas to be trained and knew those who possess greater talent would be needed."

Sean's request and compliment to the Elemental's prowess lingered unanswered for a time; even the wind seemed to calm down as if showing the Air Elemental contemplating its next action. Like the Earth Elemental before it was their decision alone to aid Sean, old ties to his grandfather no longer bound them to duty. Everything said about Orwick leaving Sean to be trained by those of greater power was truthful, even in the notebook left Sean found a scribbled note about this. No reason behind why Orwick planned it to be done this way; just that Sean needed to learn so as to not repeat past mistakes. What seemed an eternity passed before a breeze signaled Air's return to the platform and the voice came in stronger this time.

"Sadly, we have not the time for you to stay and begin mastery of listening to all and patience to attain this skill. Yet I stand strong on my training rules which shall be outlined by Nesar, my greatest pupil. Forewarning that a breeze must not be rushed else it turns to a gale with force enough to rip apart the lands and strip it bare; but alas, you are a Stormbringer…powerful storms remain part of your blood."

Sean remained silent for fear of offending the Elemental, trying to show patience and restraint despite question after question in his head. The bell rang on softly, adding to the sounds of wind below traversing through the open tunnels in the cliffs and Sean could feel the air currents all around. Their swirling motion gave Sean the idea that the Air Elemental existed in a form more advanced than a simple humanoid shape as other Elementals had taken prior. He knew not the limit to the Air Elementals unbound form, but it reminded Sean of a cloud floating free, high above the land.

"It appears you are a fast learner in puzzling out that my presence surrounds you, and your patience is deeper than I assumed… of the 6 Elementals I command the second largest domain, for all living things are in need of my domain. Only Death commands more power than I and is my sworn enemy…" hatred came with the mention of Death, giving Sean a picture of thunderclouds across the sky in his mind, sending shivers down his spine. The Air Elemental continued on, tone gaining force; "To fight my enemy I shall give my first instruction to sense what lies around you… The trait of Air lives strong in your line… Feel it touch your skin… Breathe in… Breathe out… Breathe in…"

Slowly Sean became aware of every bit of air; his senses searched, following the Elemental's guidance; only it seemed just out of reach. Frustrated, Sean tried to wrestle and capture the air like a calf on the farm. Without warning, a surge of energy flowed into his body and Sean gasped as if taking his first breath. Air currents began to swirl around him, changing that gentle song into a faster one; chaos on the edge of being released.

"Slow… your mind… quiet the storm…else you blow off this shrine…"

Reclaiming that slow breathing, Sean calmed down, energy stabilizing as the frustration subsided. The song returned to its gentle tune and the air was normal again. Still, it churned as if given the right push, it would erupt into a tornado of enormous power.

"Good… balance and control the power… maintain steady flows and feed a single current rather than all around you. Practice more in this and work with Nesar, then return here, Sean, so as to make beautiful tones with me… May the light guide you and listen for me always…" The Air Elemental's praise came from the winds this time and not from Sean's mind. "I also look forward to seeing how you handle the arena. Nesar needs a strong opponent."

Without warning, Sean felt light as a feather and was lifted in the air upward by the Air Elemental, settling on the main temple marble. Nesar had not shifted an inch since Sean had departed and watched Sean's landing intently, his awkward duck landing forced Nesar to chuckle. Sean let the power go and the presence he felt before dissipated making him feel like an empty husk. The solid floor beneath seemed to almost sway like the platform beneath, taking Sean a few extra minutes to let his body adjust.

"The Elemental chooses wisely in training one so young, we were much older so long ago that I was afraid it might reject you," Nesar's voice was gentle but strong, much like that of the Air Elemental, "let us hurry below to camp for the night and start fresh in the morning; it is a long way to the next temple, and you must regain your strength for the journey. What we seek next is the Water Elemental and for which I would be no help at all."

"I agree rest would be ideal; our prior ride has us weary and I feel I am about to collapse," Sean looked back down to the ground knowing the trip would take them till dusk Nesar, thanks for the advice on what we approach and for being the Air Elemental's selected teacher. I shall study what resources I have regarding the Water temple to prepare and look forward to our lessons on Air."

Nodding in acknowledgement, Nesar gathered air around both of them. Carefully he picked up Sean and they began their descent. Sean was nauseated from floating downward at such a fast pace. After his stomach began to settle, Sean felt pure exhilaration and started to enjoy floating through the air rather than walking. Sean had only known the ground beneath his feet and now he had the power to change all of that. 'More to learn but so rewarding' he thought excitedly 'plus training to fight with air; I can hardly wait!

Chapter 20 Ancient Ties and Friends of Light

    Taylor and Cogarth, uncertain of what to do when Sean left, decided it best to prepare a makeshift camp. Each could ride in a saddle for days, but the heat had drained their stamina and this oasis was pleasantly cool. Based on the miles of sand that stretched endlessly in all directions, this might be their one chance to relax before Nesar pushed them onward, and both were more than happy to take advantage of the situation. Heading deeper into the oasis, Taylor scouted a small clearing with enough trees for cover, the sound of a bell far away could be heard and she knew not where the tone came from. Looking into the sky above, Taylor's eyes squinted as she stared directly at the sun which seemed to block the source of the noise; leaving mystery behind, Taylor explored further. Beneath a waterfall at the base of the mountain they found a small lake to replenish waterskins and Cogarth contemplated a swim. Taylor looked after the horses, feeding them oats they'd brought, and making sure the horses drank their fill of water. Forgoing a swim, Cogarth looked up into the sky much the same as Taylor but could make out only a massive white shape that reflected sunlight. Refreshed, they returned to the clearing and each laid out a sleeping roll for a quick nap on the soft green grass. The sound of howling winds disturbed their sleep, and each awoke as if they could be ambushed at any moment. Then as Taylor and Cogarth began to ease back to sleep came another sound that started softly, gaining intensity with every passing second. Each sat stunned as Nesar and Sean dropped out of the sky directly above them, floating like birds. Scrambling to their feet, Taylor watched on as Sean plopped clumsily to the ground and Nesar with ease stepped down to the grass. Neither spoke of what transpired high above; however, to Taylor, Sean looked weary and on the verge of collapse. Taking up Sean's hand, Taylor led him to where she had set up his packed bed roll, and without hesitation, Sean dropped to the ground, immediately falling asleep. Nesar took to informing them of the intention to camp before flying off into the sky back to where they had descended.

    When Sean awoke sometime later he found wood stacked as a fire crackled. It was night and Taylor was cooking supper. Cogarth kept busy with sword practice. Nesar, it turns out, had come back to their camp at some point while Sean slept and left during the night to keep watch. Dinner smelled great to Sean who was hungry after all the mountain climbing, new power awakening, and he ate with ferocity.

Even if Taylor had prepared dinner; Sean thought it could be vegetable broth, but it was hard to tell because Sean inhaled it more than savor its taste.

Taylor waited for Sean to talk about what happened above, but he kept quiet, something Taylor was used to; how it was with Ancients and their mysteries that always seemed to follow suit. Sean's eyes seemed to be different somehow, almost like a storm brewed behind them and as the others ate, Taylor tended the fire—anything to keep from staring daggers at Sean to force out answers on what it was like to meet the Air Elemental. Nesar never disclosed information about the Elemental to the Queen of Stars so Taylor was woefully left in the dark and the library only had so much on the subject. To fly like a bird on the winds was one of Taylor's wishes but would never happen. After the pot had been scraped clean, Taylor took it to wash at the lake close by, moonlight reflecting on its surface making the oasis feel even more special. 'I should have brought Sean with me so we could enjoy this together' Taylor thought. 'Maybe I can get him to sneak away.'Returning to the camp, Taylor found Sean in a deep sleep again; to keep from waking Sean, Taylor took up Fate Avenger and started sharpening it, vigilant for an attack that would never come.

Eventually Sean fell asleep, belly full of food and the bell from the Air Shrine above clanging to create a peaceful melody. As he drifted off to sleep on the bedroll, a warm gentle breeze braced his cheek to remind him air was everywhere watching him... Sean woke up once to find Taylor intensely sharpening Fate Avenger's edge, each sweep casually stopping at the symbol before repeating the process. Sean rolled over to avoid a lecture on the necessity of blade maintenance and fell back into a dreamless sleep, the scrape of steel on rock replacing the soft bell and melody created by the winds. Tomorrow would be a hard ride in the desert, for Nesar made it quite clear they had to hurry on and there was no time to hold off for the cool of night. Sean hoped that Taylor could find time to rest; here they had no reason to fear an attack as the air lay heavy with protection from Wanderers.

Morning light broke into the clearing to wake their party who all had slept so soundly that the fire died, embers barely warm. Taylor still clutched the sharpening stone in one hand and Doomed Fate beside her within arms' reach. Cogarth looked rejuvenated, ready to begin the journey and Sean wished that a little more sleep was possible. After several prods by Taylor, Sean relented and sat upright, yawning wide to the world. They ate a light breakfast before clearing camp, dampening the leftover coals with dirt so as to not start a forest fire before mounting up to continue heading south. Nesar chose to stay far from their party and flew ahead, leading the way. Nesar had returned prior to sunrise not saying a word to anyone, grabbing only a quick piece of bread from the saddlebags for food. 'Do the Ancient sleep?' Wondered Sean, making a note to ask about sleep and the Ancients the next chance he got. While riding, Sean decided it best to train with Earth first, then Air and finally Life for a brief period. What surprised Sean was the amount of living creatures, small and large, that lived in this dry desert. Little evidence could be seen on the surface, but when Sean activated his Life eyes they popped up everywhere; buried in the sand even. Sean began to appreciate the delicate ecosystem through which they were traveling, and respected Nesar's decision to live in such a place. Taylor took time after training in the elements to educate Sean on combat techniques using two blades while demonstrating the slashes on Sean with sticks. By the end of their lesson, Sean's back and arms ached, Taylor left a few smart bruises to drive home the effectiveness of the combinations. Cogarth, whom Sean thought was a sympathetic friend, suppressed a smile when one strike made Sean howl in pain, for Taylor did not hold back.

Their trek across the desert sand lasted for two more days until grass plains sprawled in front of them as far as the eye could see. The heat was miserable but would have been unbearable during summer months according to Nesar. Traveling at night was the only option on particularly hot days during those months, which is why Nesar made sure to point out various star systems. The grass swayed in the wind as if welcoming the party to its home and they crossed southwards with only rolling hills to break up the terrain. Sean's training regimen continued in the elements and now Nesar came to give instruction on using Air while flying. Cogarth added a lesson on army tactics and formations which Sean found immensely interesting. All the books in the library at Sean's disposal and never had he thought to pick one up to study. When they concluded, Sean chided himself for ignoring such a crucial skill to lead an army; 'not every battle will end by my blade alone,' he thought deeply. Cogarth impressed on him the need for tactics, Taylor and Nesar nodded in agreement and just when Sean thought he had it, Cogarth came up with another surprise.

"There may come a time that you must lead, and I want you to be sure the simple maneuvers can be performed. Everyone overlooks the simplest movements," Cogarth offered kindly.

On the third day traveling in this sea of grass Sean begged to see a mountain or river for a change of scenery; anything to break up the monotonously waving tall grass. As if to answer Sean's desire for something new, a silhouette of a tower on the horizon came into view. Pulling up to a stop, Sean asked what the tower was and Nesar only confirmed it as their destination.

"There exist several outposts such as this in my realm, most abandoned to the wilds for I do not keep them staffed with soldiers like the Land of Stars does," Nesar spoke quietly. "I leave my people to govern themselves as much as they can; lacking even a proper army."

"What of any Wanderers that might attack?" Sean asked, shocked by the lackadaisical attitude of defending his territory.

"There are few villages, as the majority of this realm lies in the desert and is home to animals," Nesar responded. "Taylor, ready yourself, as I need you to be our envoy to some friends on behalf of your Mistress."

With that, Nesar floated higher up, leaving Sean with his mouth hanging open as to why no protection existed, even for the small population. 'This man is dangerous and careless,' drifted through Sean's mind as they continued. Looking to Taylor, Sean found her expression grim, a far cry from the usual cool demeanor Sean had grown to love. Clearly this did not sit well with Taylor either, and a quick glance to Cogarth read the same thought: 'This Ancient is careless about human life.'

In mid-afternoon, the tower was closer and Sean could see now what Nesar had meant by "abandoned to the wilds." Moss-covered gray stone on the tower standing nearly 150 ft high, parts of the walls were caved in and gave the structure a eerie feel. Animal trails in the grass could be seen going toward a number of the small cracks at its base and little traffic seen to the main door which hung half on its hinges. The other half looked to be broken apart by either age or weaponry; Sean could not tell. An algae-covered pond sat behind the tower with cattails overtaking the shore, and it left Sean with an uneasy feeling as to if the water was fit to drink.

"We are staying here?" Asked Sean.

"To rest briefly; the sea lies ahead yet it is where we must cross. The people in the next village are wary of weapons; do not draw your swords without reason," warned Nesar who looked at Taylor directly at this comment "it is time for you to depart and make our preparations known to the Captain awaiting us. Follow the Queen's command to the letter and no trouble should arise."

Stopping at the base of the tower, their party split ways; Sean begrudgingly let Taylor leave without his company and with a longing look of good luck, Taylor sped away toward the village. Nesar said the water was safe despite its sickly look, so Cogarth and Sean led the horses to get a drink. The tower looked even worse around back as a large section of it remained open to the elements, pitiful for any type of defense in Sean's opinion. Wasting no time, Sean took up sparring with Cogarth using one blade alone. Only a short bought for Nesar looked at them hauntingly as the sound of steel on steel clanged loudly in the wide-open plains. After their exercise, Cogarth took the opportunity to keep lecturing Sean on battle tactics and Nesar found it prudent to perch like a bird at the top of the tower, adding to the feeling of gloom this tower had for he looked like a terrifying gargoyle.

Taylor rode forward to the Village alone; her mission was securing a ship for passage across the sea. During the planning of this trip, it had fallen to Nesar but it seemed impossible to hold the man responsible for such a task so here Taylor was taking it on instead. All her Mistress had said for the Captain was that he could be quite mad.

"This whole world seems to be going mad." Taylor joked darkly to herself, habit begun after spending years searching for Sean.

Dismounting from Majesty, Taylor secured the lead on a sun-faded wooden post on the outskirts and ventured into the village on foot. A small village of roughly 40 buildings of varying size; each had the same raised foundation and what looked like irrigation pipes running off the roofs. The only building Taylor could see directly on the ground was a blacksmith shop, easily identified by the smoke billowing out the chimney and the clang of hammer on steel echoing through the village. The smell of fish permeated the air, only replaced by salt when wind stirred up to churn the stifled air. A number of Villagers would wave at Taylor until they noticed two blades on each hip and they would scurry into the nearest building. Mercenaries hired as guards kept a shrill eye on the newcomer to town, begging for Taylor to cause trouble so they could prove their worth. Before Taylor knew it, the sea spread far and wide in every direction, birds cawing, then scooping fish. Boats coming back filled with fish and sailors started unloading the cargo on docks that had seen better years. Quite the little village indeed, a far cry from those cities to the north and proof that Nesar truly let the people govern themselves. A little farther down the coast, Taylor wandered to a shack that had been built on solid ground overlooking the rocky water below. The boards holding up the structure almost reminded Taylor of driftwood, for none was the same material and all spoke to the years of being pummeled by storms. On the roof, Taylor could see a familiar fading mark, 'friend'; it meant to the Faithful 20, and the Ancient symbol beneath it only verified that this was her destination.

Knocking three times, followed by four more taps, Taylor stood on the strange stoop and wondered if anyone was home when no answer came. About to give up and leave, the door opened a crack, and a wrinkly faced man appeared. Taylor gave the secret sign of 'friend' and the door was thrown wide open to welcome her. Taking a gulp, Taylor stepped across the door threshold, hands to the sword hilts in preparation to fight for her life. Once clear of the door, it shut as quickly as it had opened to give Taylor's eyes only a moment to adjust to the dim, candle-lit room. Safe from danger, Taylor took a moment to further inspect the man's face: she saw years at sea mapped across it, tanned brown by the sun that must come with being on the water. The eyes seemed to be stark raving mad as if laughing at an unseen joke only known only to the man.

"Greetings, my name is Taylor, and the Queen of Stars has sent me as a friend," Taylor said, bowing to the man, she hoped was the Captain.

"May the 20 bless our meeting in the journey we both shall take. Preparations are made to take your party across the sea, surf be gentle and wind to match I may add," the man intoned with a laugh at the end.

"Many thanks, for the light shines on our good fortune," responded Taylor. "My Queen has thought of everything it seems. Food provisions for us and the horses?"

"Aye, ship stocked to take the journey in stride."

"Ships for the coming army as well?"

The Captain stood confused. Taylor was unsure what to do, as they were tasked with finding passage for themselves and to be sure, a number of ships were available to ferry the army. 'Damn you, Nesar!' Taylor thought in anger. 'If you were here then I would not be looking like a fool!'

"Afraid that order is too tall," the man said after a long pause "Many seasons have passed since war ships docked at this peaceful village. However, word was left to the Sea Terrains to strike a bargain for safe passage. My word carries weight to the tribes on fair bargains, never you fear, little lady."

Taylor responded with a deep curtsy this time, embarrassed at fumbling such a task threatening to turn her face red. "Much kindness indeed. My fellow travelers shall join us by nightfall, can we be underway then?"

"Aye! I shall start preparations now to be ready. Make yourself at home here or visit the town shops. By nightfall we set sail!"

"I am Taylor, servant of the Queen of Stars. May I ask your name?" Taylor asked, hoping to solve the mystery.

"I be Captain Maddox! Traveler of the sea far and near," Maddox shouted at Taylor.

With that, Captain Maddox left his shack, with mad, determined eyes. Taylor looked on in shock at being shouted at and then around at the contents in the shack. Deciding town or even the beach a better option than this drab, dreary place, Taylor followed behind to await Sean, Cogarth and Nesar. Something bothered Taylor about Maddox; his presence had a familiar feeling to it along with the face. Sitting in the sand by the docks, Taylor scoured her memories but could not shake this feeling of knowing Maddox. The breeze felt cool coming off the water and Taylor enjoyed the moment of peace that accompanied it; being alone for the first time in months to her thoughts was unnerving.

"Sean would really enjoy this view…" Taylor said to herself, checking behind as if waiting for Sean to pop up unexpectedly. Turning bright red in the face, 'Why do I keep thinking of him?' Shaking off the thought, Taylor decided to collect Majesty from her tether and be ready to depart as soon as the boys showed up.

The sun sat above the horizon when Nesar, Cogarth and Sean came into town from the direction of the tower. They had grown impatient waiting till dusk and Sean was ready to go full speed had Nesar let them. Reaching the village, it reminded Sean of another small village near the farm so far away. Minus the smell, that was definitely different for the fish and salt combined to be a pungent odor. Nesar led the way; people murmured as they passed by, heading to the docks. Walking their horses rather than riding in hopes of drawing less attention, Sean easily spotted Taylor eating an apple on an upturned barrel at the water's edge. Taylor waved them over and Sean eagerly returned the wave, freezing in mid motion at how silly he must look. Cogarth stared at Sean hiding a laugh, poorly, Nesar chuckled softly and Sean turned red as Taylor gave him an amused smile. 'How dumb could I be; smooth Sean,' he thought. Not a word had transpired of what happened at the shrine, nor anything further between the two. Their time was never spent alone to talk, and training had been the sole focus when they were one on one. Sean did once attempt to have dinner with Taylor who had brought Cogarth along, unbeknownst to Sean. 'I really know how to pick them,' Sean thought, face turning even redder. If anything, the more Sean tried to be with Taylor, the tougher Taylor would resist.

Reaching Taylor, she jumped off the barrel tossing Sean her apple core.

"Thanks for volunteering to dispose this," Taylor said with a wink. "Captain Maddox is ready to set sail before the tide turns. Majesty is on board already. Lead your mounts to the crewman."

Taylor pointed out a shirtless man in long shorts and no shoes walking down the dock. Cogarth and Sean dropped their horses following Taylor's direction, and Nesar met with Captain Maddox. Taylor kept a close eye on the greeting; she could not hear the conversation, but the salutations and introductions seemed short, especially for Captain Maddox meeting an Ancient. Nesar always remained a puzzle; any story of Nesar spoke of his power in Air and Fire only; never the mastery of using Life; so Taylor believed it because of the role Nesar played creating the Rebirth Chambers for Ancients. Those being a large well-kept secret discussed only in the presence of Ancients; Taylor had once tried to listen in on such a council, only to be ruthlessly punished when found out. Strolling casually, Taylor made it to the gangplank, prepared to board, Maddox and Nesar still in Taylor's peripheral all the while. Maddox was oddly familiar with Nesar but the same could not be said of Nesar; his body language well-guarded. Walking the wooden plank, Taylor climbed aboard the ship, stopping at its side where she began to drum fingers impatiently. Sean and Cogarth boarded after dropping off their mounts, Sean's gaze focused on Taylor but she kept eyes on the horizon, avoiding Sean's eyes. Both ended up standing next to Taylor. Cogarth chose to look upon the vessel while still Sean had eyes for only Taylor. As if reading Taylor's impatience, Nesar and Captain Maddox moved toward the ship, locked together by Maddox's hand on Nesar's back and their quiet conversation interrupted only by dock workers cutting in their path. 'I wonder how the two know each other,' thought Taylor who strained to hear anything as they came closer to the ship. 'Could they be old friends?' All Taylor could make out is the end of their conversation before Nesar shrugged free of Captain Maddox:

"… interesting party we travel with indeed. Our journey on the seas shall be adventurous!" Maddox laughed at this last comment, the joke still lost to all save him.

Taylor decided to finally check out the ship they were to sail on. 'Anything to keep from looking at that love-addled Farm Boy,' Taylor thought, 'and to keep me from acting a fool.' The ship was 100 feet in length and 40 feet starboard to port. Two large masts adorned the deck, each with sails furled, catching some light wind. At the stern, Taylor could see steps leading up to a top deck where a massive wheel was locked in place by a piece of rope. Here Captain Maddox stopped to check some strange instruments to the wheel's left side, muttering to himself all the while. The deck boards had been worn from years of sailors running up and down it while out on the open water, bolstering Taylor's confidence that Captain Maddox would be a seasoned charter to the Southern Hemisphere. A crewman scampered up to the top of the main mast via rope ladder and Taylor watched the swift, confident movements with wonder—even while moored, the ship rocked by waves of the tide would be sufficient to knock any green sailor from that height. An 'all clear' rang out, and the men began to cut their ties to the dock so as to give the ship freedom to roam as it was intended. Loaded for travel, the ship set sail across the Sea of Stars toward fate and all which awaited in the Southern Hemisphere.

Chapter 21: The Sea of Stars

Escaping from a hot sun in open water seemed impossible to Sean who had gone from excited to miserable. At night, Sean learned why it had been called the Sea of Stars: endless sky twinkled with starlight and a constellation of stars strung together was their guide south. Maddox took to explaining some of the intricate details involved with sailing a ship of this size, but a lot went over Sean's head, leaving him even more confused. Six days at sea had blistered Sean's skin raw. Six days of meditation, practicing with the powers and even gambling with the boat sailors, but now Sean was bored. Endless water stretched in all directions and made Sean long to see the grass plains they had left. In stories told of adventurers setting out into the great unknown there was action and not all this waiting around to be replaced by mere moments of adrenaline. On day three, a school of giant squid attacked the boat, but Nesar used fire to disperse the creatures. By the time Sean had shown up with sword drawn and shirt half on, the fighting had subsided; that brought quite some laughs among the crew and a few whistles as well. Cogarth had the same tension build-up as Sean, but neither could find a release and only so much sparring could happen in a day. So here Sean sat looking to the horizon, hoping that meditation might pass the time. Settling back to the railing on deck, Sean began to meditate, breathing deeply and feeling all around…

Commotion at the bow brought Sean back to reality. Sailors ran bow to stern, relaying messages from the front look-out and the navigator. Rising to check out what was the first distraction in days, Sean found only sea in front until a crewman pointed to an island a few miles out. White beach sparkling in the sun, broken by a small stone dock, not quite big enough for this ship shot into the water, waves breaking on it. Closer they moved to the island and Sean began to make out greenery past the beaches and a structure as well. The anchor was dropped, and two smaller boats were crowded with a landing party. Crewmen worked without a word to get the boats ready; to Sean it seemed this was a common stop, and he could not help but be amazed at their work. When the first boat was ready for departure, Nesar, Taylor, Cogarth and Captain Maddox joined Sean at the railing. The parties split into Maddox, Nesar, Taylor and a few other crew members in one boat, leaving Sean and Cogarth with the other crew members (some Sean had gambled with) to bring up the rear in the second boat. Ready to drop to the water below, the small craft were lowered by a pulley and rope on each end, which two crewmates handled while the rest waited to row. Waves rocked their boat, but the crew rowed on, unconcerned, the rhythm of oars on water soothing, and before Sean knew it, they were finally docked and tied off. Solid ground raised Sean's mood considerably; 'Hopefully time would allow for some of this pent-up energy to be used,' he thought with a smile. Catching up to the first group, Sean and Cogarth anxiously awaited word to explore this little paradise in the sea, the crew remained busy unloading supplies brought from the ship. With Sean and Cogarth now caught up, Maddox laughed and started inland on a dirt path that foliage had concealed until now.

  The party followed Maddox to a tower a short distance up the path, trees covering the tower made Sean wonder how many ships sailed past this island unawares. The square tower was built using smooth, tan sandstone; windows dotting the sides; attached to the back was a smaller structure of the same sandstone. Its layout made Sean feel that they were entering from the back rather than the front, and it seemed to be oddly placed. Nonchalantly, Maddox pulled open the door, disappearing inside, and the group followed behind. The room smelled of ocean air; light came in from those small windows coated by years of accumulated salt residue. Maddox had started lighting candles and Sean's jaw dropped. Fire flew effortlessly from Maddox's pinky finger as he pointed it across the room at every available candlestick. Looking at Taylor she seemed unsurprised, her face kept its same cool composure as wicks burned to life. Venturing further into the tower, Sean could see how truly mad its designer was: The entrance had a staircase winding up one side of the room, an odd assortment of chairs on the other side. Then came a door to the adjacent building which revealed a great hall built of glass. The ceiling was made entirely of glass, as was the floor which revealed the water below. The glass walls offered a nearly 360-degree view of the island. Sean, stepped carefully to avoid falling through the glass into the watery depths. A long table sat directly in the middle of this hall and even more chairs had been placed randomly at its edges. Nesar settled awkwardly into a stuffed chair on one end of the table and Sean followed his lead, sitting at the table, heart beating fast. This entire hall was one giant glass death trap, and it took Sean every ounce of courage to remain calmly seated. The crewmen ran around bringing in supplies from the ship and began preparing what Sean by now had surmised was Maddox's great hall. Taylor, Cogarth and Maddox sat down, filling the empty spaces; Sean grimaced at seeing Taylor sitting far away and leaving him to the company of Maddox. Pitchers of honey wine were placed on the dark wood table accompanied by goblets of various designs. Sean saw Nesar motion slightly with his right hand and a cold gust of wind blew across the table, chilling the contents of the goblets. Taylor let out a small squeal of surprise, at which Nesar chuckled softly. Embarrassed, Taylor shifted in her seat next to Nesar, and Maddox poured wine for each member before settling back into the chair. Sean could no longer hold back; he dared to speak aloud a question that was burning in his mind.

"Captain, you are an Ancient?" Sean blurted out.

The room fell deadly quiet, except Nesar, his body shaking with suppressed laughter; and Taylor, her eyes angry at Sean's idiocy. Swirling the wine before sipping, Maddox finally responded, tone muted compared to the usual boisterous sound Sean had grown accustomed to.

"It seems that you still are unable to sense Ancients ... Amusing," Maddox began. "Aye, my name be Rodrius Maddox of the family Maddoxis. May the Light bless our meeting and by the 20, your grandfather was an honorable friend. Welcome to my Island."

"May the Light bless our meeting, stranger, and future encounters as friends," responded Sean. "Many thanks to your hospitality."

"My Hall is always open and the hearth warm with fire. Now time be short, for your Queen arrives in days."

"What of negotiation to the Sea King for passage?" Sean asked, baffled at the speed of the army's arrival.

"A bargain has been struck! You are looking at such a Sea King, for the ships dispatched to make port long ago. I felt this place appropriate for introductions and to test your skill." Maddox's usual tone had returned but was still serious when speaking to Sean "Fewer prying eyes on this here island."

"Well, it's an honor to meet you, Maddox. Hopefully, I passed your test," joked Sean who received a laugh from the Ancient.

"Aye! Sense of humor like your grandfather to boot. We were young lads but a joke saved his life with me and started us as friends. Alas, there most likely are questions but leave them be for now, please, and until we head off again." Maddox drank a sip of wine to drive the point home. "We are here to rest our weary bones of the ship and sun; a greenhorn such as yourself could use the reprieve."

"As you wish, but I want to hear some stories of the old times with my grandfather." Sean had kept up the lighthearted demeanor on the surface, but a feeling of being overwhelmed built inside, the need for escape bubbling to the surface. "Then may we explore outside a bit, seeing as solid land is hard to come by?"

"By all means, have at it, Matey! Be warned of the crabs, for they bite!" Maddox let out a cackle before drinking more wine; the others joined in the laughter of the mad Ancient; except Sean.

Sliding his chair back, Sean stepped away, the joke having gone in one ear and out the other. A blank smile masked the building rage inside of Sean at being deceived again by Ancients and more so, by Taylor. Striding across the glass floor, Sean's quick exit left awkward silence between the others in the wake of his abrupt departure. Slowly, Taylor stood, excusing herself to follow Sean outside; a look of worry touching her face. Maddox decided to break the mood with some jokes, but the muffled words became inaudible to Taylor as she exited the tower.

Sean took a hard right upon exiting the tower door, direction unclear. All he knew was that heading away from the boat and dock a good start. Fists clenched tightly, he thought, 'How can I trust her? Even after promising to tell me everything she could on the Ancients.' Finding a log, Sean sat down, keeping his back to the tower, emotions surging through him. Sean wanted to shout. Instead, a single sentence escaped so softly that Sean thought only the Air Elemental would hear.

"Why, Taylor?"

"The truth?" Came Taylor's voice from behind. "All I had were suspicions about Maddox's identity. Rarely did he visit our realm and it never was stated openly. Being of legend has a cost, as you will find."

The answer—along with Taylor's sudden appearance—shocked Sean. Turning to face Taylor, they locked eyes and all the rage written clearly across his face would not be swayed by a mere admission.

"But even a hint! It could have saved me from looking like a fool!" Sean shouted back in protest.

"So your pride is injured and you use it to lash out at me?" Taylor asked angrily. "Information on Ancients is not found easily, and accusations of such association dangerous!"

Seeing the sun sinking closer to the horizon, Sean thought of what Taylor had to say, her words ringing true. "You are right, I am sorry for acting so childish."

"What is really on your mind, Sean?" Taylor's question was direct yet comforting; just the two of them alone, and she could feel the walls crumbling.

Shocked, Sean's expression softened, and he held onto Taylor eyes, finding those blue eyes that transfixed his heart. Sean's rage cooled, fists unclenching, letting blood flow back. Taking a deep breath, Sean tried to steady the fluttering in his stomach as a thought flashed across his mind: 'This is it, no turning back.'

"Since that night you have avoided me. Why? Am I to blame?" Sean asked.

His words struck at Taylor's core deeper than a knife and all strength left her. 'How could he break me so easily?' Tears streamed from the corners of Taylor's eyes. She began falling forward, when Sean caught her and they embraced, which only seemed to bring more tears. So many bottled emotions letting loose since that night, when Sean truly saw who Taylor was. Taylor began to compose herself as the tears ran dry, they ended their embrace and she saw Sean looking down at her.

"After that night, I could not face our future ahead the same as when we first met. Pretending nothing happened was the only way I thought that we both would move forward. To think of what lay ahead and what is... between us. In my heart, I know to protect this feeling. I would sacrifice everything in the world..." trailing off as a few last tears fell from Taylor's eyes.

Sean sat dumbstruck. It had never occurred to him that he was not the only one wrestling with the meaning of their relationship. A woman so complex after overcoming so much strife would naturally be conflicted, just as Sean was. Sean kissed her lips, hands locking tightly with hers, showing how he felt; words were not enough. Abandoning doubts of the future, Sean jumped into his feelings wholeheartedly and knew Taylor did the same. Breaking the sweet connection seemed impossible, but as quick as it began it ended."

"Taylor... for you, I would burn the world," Sean whispered in Taylor's ear.

Standing together as one, both Sean and Taylor looked at the setting sun, a scene of near perfection. At the back of Taylor's mind was a sole doubt as to what the future held, but it would not ruin this moment; Taylor would not allow it. Heading back to the sandstone tower with Sean, they came in to find dinner prepared. Taking their seats, neither spoke of what transpired for it was their business alone and only flitting looks passed between them. Sean looked much more relaxed to Taylor and the night proceeded without incident, filled with laughter from Maddox's stories.

"Fascinating fact on this yee Island—at high tide it disappears under water." Maddox began. "Enemies are unable to find us at night. Till this day I sleep like a babe during a calm storm. Full and swaddled!"

This brought a roar of laughter from the party around; even the crewmates of Maddox. Dinner concluded and the food cleared from the table, wine flowed in an endless fashion. A few crewmen brought out instruments that Sean had never seen before and they played music to add on to Maddox's tales, especially when he tried to tell serious ones. Sean could see that these men were loyal to Maddox and had spent years traveling together. They made Sean rethink his opinion of the Ancient and that maybe Maddox was the furthest thing from mad.

"Closest an enemy came to getting me at night on this island was Gadriel. I had pranked Gadriel by surrounding his castle with a 200-foot moat and no way to cross. I had help, of course; but he wanted to put a mountain over top me tower in retribution. Unable to find me exact location, he waited through the night until sunup. When I woke, his ship sat grounded by me doorstep and boy, Gadriel's face was redder than the sun! To this day I send a ship across land to him as a reminder," Maddox laughed louder than the rest, barely able to finish the punch line and Nesar chuckled along.

Maddox slammed down his goblet of wine and stood on shaky legs; the rest all chatted taking no mind to where their host was headed. Music played louder to fill the void of a loud tale and Maddox clapped along to the beat, making his way around the table stopping to tap Sean on the shoulder to talk. Maddox led Sean aside, facing the big window, away from prying ears, clapping all the while. Festivities like this warmed Maddox's heart and made him forget the seriously pressing matters at hand; but still things had to be said in private.

Taking advantage of their host's departure, Taylor grabbed Cogarth's hand, motioning him to follow. Secluded in a distant corner of the tower's first floor, Taylor released his hand, blushing slightly, as Cogarth looked on in pure confusion. To prevent Cogarth from asking any questions, Taylor jumped in, using a hushed whisper.

"Cogarth, this may be an odd request, but please hear me out and swear by the 20 it shall not be repeated unless…"

Maddox pointed Sean toward the window in the hall to show that they were underwater. Fish gently swam unconcerned by the two men staring at them through a pane of glass. Sean was dumbfounded; not that he thought Maddox was a liar, but at being submerged so far below the surface. Sean began to feel closed in. Out of the corner of

Sean's eye, he saw Taylor dragging Cogarth out of the hall. Before Sean could discern what they were up to, Maddox posed a question to Sean who heard not a word of it.

"My apologies; being below water seems to have rattled me slightly. What was the question, Maddox?" Asked Sean, somewhat embarrassed at having to ask.

"Aye, no worries, I only wonder how it felt being here as part of the fishes, but alas, that is my answer. Do not fear the water as Gadriel does; to you it is harmless. Blessings of the water element ensure drowning is nigh impossible," Maddox replied with a wink. "As to yee training on using water, the temple lies ahead, not far from here and our visit shall be brief. Like Nesar, I will teach you on our journey ahead to the southern continent, but only in water. 'Tis our bargain with Ancients—to rain you in months what took us years, nigh centuries to learn, for some folks."

"I appreciate any guidance you may offer. When I set out, I feared my path would be taken alone. I am confident that, with your help, I will be ready." Sean clasped Maddox's hand in a show of thanks and the man nodded.

"By the Light, you shall Sean, else the world is rotten."

"What of fire? Will that temple be on our way as well, Maddox? Can it be taught by you?" Sean asked, hoping to discover anything he could about it.

Darkness covered the man's face, pain creeping into Maddox's eye. Sean's hand hurt from Maddox's grip who squeezed hard as a vice at the mention of fire.

"No ... That be not my area to teach," tone dark as the look on Maddox's face "fire is not meant to be trifled with, for it only destroys."

"Then I will remember these words and never ask again. Now tell me more of the adventures long ago; you mentioned my grandfather?" Feeling guilt at bringing out this dark past in Maddox, Sean wanted to recapture the mood.

"Well, yee see, it all started on mine 20th year. Venturing to the great ocean I found a vessel trapped on a sandbar, 18 passengers total…"

"Remember, only if that happens to me are you meant to deliver this message. Agreed, Cogarth? Else I have no problem sending you home to wait our victory or our loss…" Taylor's threat hung in the air.

"I accept these terms on my own honor as a member of the Star Army and by the Light it will be done," Cogarth nodded and saluted Taylor.

Stifling a sigh of relief, Taylor returned the salute accepting Cogarth's oath sworn by the Light of the 20. Her mind at peace, Taylor joined in the festivities unfolding around them, humming along to the music and drinking some wine. Sean still stood secluded with Maddox and Taylor could see Sean intrigued by the Maddox's story. Eyes catching briefly, Taylor smiled at Sean who returned it with a wave making Taylor's heart skip a beat. 'I can face our future now, please understand,' Taylor thought, no longer feeling that prick of worry after speaking to Cogarth.

"You love Sean, do you not?" Cogarth asked.

Jumping at the remark, she replied "Is it that obvious, Cogarth? Guess I can't hide my feelings as well as I had thought…"

"Over these years I have laughed, talked and trained with you Taylor. Plus, your request speaks volumes…" Cogarth began.

Seeing the daggers from Taylor's eyes, Cogarth let his words hang in the air instead. After checking to be sure no ears were in range, Cogarth attempted to right the awkwardness in a much quieter tone.

"What I am getting at is that not a lot can be hidden from me, Taylor. For the record, Sean is lucky to have someone such as yourself. May the light protect you both." Cogarth left on the last word so as to not give Taylor the chance for one of her infamous retorts; much to Cogarth's glee at finally having the upper hand.

Taylor's mouth hung open in mid-insult as Cogarth left her there to join in the singing of an old Sea Folk shanty. Swallowing the leftover insult, Taylor decided it was high time to get some sleep and leave the party early. Exiting the hall filled with music, Taylor climbed the stairs and found an empty room to sleep in, a few levels up. Changing into a silk slip, Taylor wondered exactly what Sean discussed with Maddox in confidence. Before Taylor left, she saw Sean's eyes following her out of the room, so when the door creaked open, she did not turn around right away. Seconds ticked by and hearing no other sounds, Taylor turned around to see who had entered. Standing in the darkness was Nesar, helmet removed and eyes gleaming green revealing the use of his life power. Scrambling, Taylor covered up with a robe, ready to politely berate the depraved Ancient when Nesar spoke.

"Be wary young one, emotion is second to all but the Light. This young master your heart beats for can never know the deepest of truths, else the world falls…" Taylor understood Nesar's ominous words quite clearly.

In the blink of an eye, Nesar disappeared from sight and left Taylor unable to retort—the second time that night. The man's ability to make himself invisible worried Taylor, as she thoroughly checked every inch of the room. Relief flooded Taylor though, when Sean entered mere moments later. 'Surely Nesar would never spy on the Proclaimer of Light, or maybe he no longer has reason to.' The thought flickered away when Sean once more held Taylor close. She inhaled the smell of salt water, sun and pine needles, finding it oddly satisfying. Taylor kept Nesar's visit a secret from Sean—it would only lead to serious questions that were best left alone. Instead, Taylor hugged Sean tighter, as if to sear this moment forever in her memory. This time it was Taylor's turn to kiss Sean, feeling compelled to alleviate the aching in her chest. Taylor's heart beat so fast it hurt as Sean kissed back, into which he poured his soul. 'Getting the hang of it now, lover boy…' Taylor thought. Reaching out a hand, Taylor gently pushed Sean back, regretting having to do so.

"Not tonight…" she whispered.

"We can take it as slow as you want," Sean whispered back.

Sean took Taylor's hand and led her to the bed, and the crawled under the covers together. The warmth of Taylor's body comforting, as Sean wrapped his arms around her. Sleep came easily and dreamless slumber ensued until Sean's consciousness felt a strange sensation of light, which was, in fact, two lights; one rather large and one rather small. Focused on the second, smaller pool of light, Sean watched it pulsing, its origin a mystery, but it felt like an extension of Sean's own body, a familiar feeling. It faded away, leaving only the large pool of light to shine upon which Sean shifted focus, hoping to find some answers. One thing Sean knew was that the large pool felt like his own energy, the source of his Ancient power which he tapped into when using elements. Its pulsing light consumed Sean causing him to wake up in a gasp, sunlight streaming through the window, signaling the start of a new day. Taylor lay awake studying his face which horrified Sean. 'What if I have drool all over me!' Sean thought before casually wiping his face clean.

"Morning," Sean said through a yawn.

"Morning, farm boy," Taylor joked, mimicking Sean's movements.

Their laughter rang out through the early morning quiet, neither saying anything as each lay waiting until the sun finally rose. How beautiful Taylor looked in the morning light. Sean did not want to leave this place. Taylor made the first move (much to Sean's dislike) from the cozy bed, dressing to meet the day. Outside horns blared, signaling the arrival of Sea Terran ships transporting the army, and more importantly, the Queen. Sean groaned aloud, their presence meant heading back out to sea and away from solid ground. Duty bound, Sean rose from bed and dressed as Taylor had. She sat back on the edge of the bed, waiting for him to finish. Sean left first, with Taylor following a minute later; This was Taylor's request—not Sean's. Coming down the tower's staircase Sean headed toward the great hall to see who else had risen to the sound of the ship's horn. Seated in the dining hall was the Queen flanked by her generals who stood rather than occupying the empty chairs. Curt nods from Sean to the generals followed by a bow for the Queen; Sean then sat down in a chair opposite. Taylor entered the room shortly after, curtsying deeply to the Queen before taking up position to the Queen's right. An amused smile could be detected on the Queen's face, who saw right through the attempt at deception. 'Light Eyonka knows,' Sean thought, turning a shade of red.

    Food brought by other servants was placed on the table, followed by a strong smelling dark liquid Sean knew nothing of. Nesar popped in out of nowhere, sitting near the Queen, followed by Maddox who relayed the departure details. Sean agreed whenever asked and the Queen only interjected on supply transport issues as needed. With the final plan set, Maddox left to get orders delivered and fill in the captains on their routes. 30 ships sequestered to transport an army had been a tall order, but old alliances answered the call. Land promised North a main reason, for the Sea Terrans wanted the Dead Coast to set up trading posts with. A bargain to be paid after their victory in the South, Maddox sure had been sly on the deal.

    After a light breakfast, Sean ventured outside for one last look at the scenery before their voyage into endless water. At the tower's entrance, Sean found Cogarth and together they chatted while waiting to see if Taylor would join. Sure enough, Taylor met up with the two, face red from embarrassment it seemed, and Sean could only imagine what the Queen had said to Taylor. The three were in good spirits as they walked around the island, picking up shells and enjoying a rare, private moment.

    A 35-day journey on a ship awaited them, accommodations would be cramped, as their little ship was to remain behind. The Queen had planned for Nesar, Maddox, Sean, Taylor and Cogarth to be on the largest vessel with her in consideration of Sean's continued training regimen. Coming to the stone dock, Sean marveled as 30 larger-than-life ships sat anchored off the coast, orange wood brightly shining in the sun. They seemed ten times the size of the hundred-foot ship that had brought their party to this island. Each had four tall masts to propel the behemoths forward and half of them had small holes in the hull. Cogarth remarked that it was for rowing if they were ever stranded on open water with no wind. Time came to board small rowboats and leave Maddox's Island where it seemed the last semblance of peace existed. 'No, that is not entirely true; I have my peace with me always at my side,' Sean thought with a smile, as he and Taylor stood facing the next horizon together, regardless of what the future may bring.

Chapter 22: The Water Temple's Blessing

Ten days had passed, each morning, the same seascape. Sean had been thoroughly beaten in sword sparring, and was drained from using elements, as Nesar and the Queen trained Sean to the limit. Being a mountain dweller, Sean had minimal exposure to the hot sun that was always present on the Southern Sea of Stars leaving his skin nearly blistered. No time to waste meant endless training sessions and drills; not a moment with Taylor unless it was sparring against both swords reunited. Taylor had decided it best to use real swords going forward so that Sean could gain the experience with the combinations and the weight of the blades. Each made sure to only strike using the flat of the blade but a few cuts and scrapes resulted, nonetheless. Only news about landfall to the Water Temple brightened the ill feelings Sean had about this trip.

A horn blew, signaling the anchor drop of their ship alone, the others would continue South with a planned rendezvous. Maddox moved the rowboat into position over the side, motioning Sean to board. Running, Sean leapt in just as Maddox released the lock without lowering it using the pulleys, letting it freefall to the water below. Channeling Air by instinct, Sean applied air currents beneath them, slowing the descent, and the boat softly landed on the surface of the sea. 'Enough with the tests already,' Sean thought, stifling a groan. Maddox had surprised Sean in various ways to test how Sean reacted using elements to protect himself or solve a puzzle. Surprisingly, it helped more than Sean wanted to admit; but one night Maddox crossed the line in waking Sean up from a dead sleep with a punch. The shiner lasted a few days until Nesar showed Sean how to make the bruising disappear, healing it with a little Life energy.

"Ha! Luckily you saved us, big hero, else I might have drowned!" roared Maddox.

'He was mad!' Sean rolled his eyes relinquishing the power, a nearly natural sensation now like breathing. Sean scanned the water to find their destination but nothing close by spoke of land. Further inspection of the boat showed a lack of oars, and Sean wondered how they would approach an island so far off without guidance. In answer to this question, a wave pushed them free of the ship's side out onto the open sea.

Maddox took control by channeling water, eyes glowing blue, and the hairs on Sean's arm stood on end. Moving the boat at a fast clip, what appeared to be a small speck to the east began taking shape. Maddox slowed their speed when it sat a mile or so from the island, beaches reflecting the sun above like a beacon of light. A knot formed in Sean's gut, intuition as to what Maddox would do for his next test. Stripping off his gear, save the shorts, Sean waited for Maddox to make the next move.

"Now you swim the rest of the way, and find the Water Temple's entrance. I can't go any further as you must face it alone," Maddox said, confirming Sean's suspicions. "Oh, by the way, mind the current!"

With a heave, Maddox shoved Sean overboard into the frigid water, leaving no time to take a breath. Turning the rowboat around, Maddox took off just as fast back to the ship, apparently unconcerned about Sean's well-being. This truly was a trial at which Sean had to succeed, and Maddox knew the boy would survive.

"The blood of Orwick runs through his veins, time to sink or swim," Maddox joked darkly to himself.

Sean blinked twice, as a cold water surrounded him. He surfaced in a gasp, silently cursing Maddox. Sean could see the man off heading back to the ship. Shaking everything from his mind (except the thought of getting Maddox back), Sean started swimming toward the island. According to Maddox, Sean was incapable of drowning, but it was another ability Sean did not plan on putting to the test.

Hitting the shallows, Sean began wading in toward the sandy beach sprawled before him. Little greenery lived on this island—it was mostly small pools of water broken up by stretches of sand. Exploring the middle, Sean found what looked like remnants of a temple, fluted columns half destroyed, arranged in an odd pattern around a sandstone fountain, the water falling into a large pool below. Everything was exposed to the elements and it showed neglect; its condition was a far cry from all the other temples Sean had seen. Drinking from a handful of water, Sean found it refreshingly cool and salt free; he drank it greedily. White sand everywhere gave it all a bright look. Sunlight danced on the water. The sun rose higher as Sean searched for any sign of the Elemental. The water level in the pool seemed to be dropping, revealing only solid sand at the bottom. Meditating awhile, Sean felt no overwhelming presence or connection to the flow of water like elements past. 'Was it my imagination or did the surrounding water seem higher?' Sean thought, eyes now open to his surroundings. Channeling Earth, Sean felt for any clue to alter his decision that this in fact was the water temple, but the sand revealed nothing. Deciding to stretch the legs, Sean abandoned the pool's edge, pondering what Maddox said as to where the Water Elemental lay in wait.

Walking behind the fountain, Sean discovered a bridge of sand connecting a second smaller Island. No structures were to be seen or any sign a temple once existed on the plot of sand; however, Sean still moved toward it. Stopping in the middle of the sand bridge, Sean looked to his left and right; giant whirlpools formed on either side. Turning back to the fountain, Sean could see at this vantage point the temple as it truly was. Picturing how it would have looked years ago, an arrow pointed right to where Sean had stopped. Looking at the whirlpools forming to either side of the bridge, Sean could only figure the structures above ground had to be a decoy. That meant the answer to where the Water Temple's true location had to be….gulp. Taking a deep breath, Sean plunged into the nearest whirlpool, feeling himself being dragged below to its icy depths. Darkness blocked out all sunlight above and the strong currents pulled Sean deeper yet.

When the water relinquished its hold, Sean fell into a secret chamber of air directly beneath the sand bridge. Memory of the swim under the Tower of Resurrection and how Sean's lungs had ached came flooding back. Breathing in deep gasps, Sean moved toward the inner chambers, away from the whirlpool's wall and the roaring water. Dim light revealed a deep pool of water at the center, Sean searched the walls blindly for another clue. Hanging by one nail beneath an unlit torch was a wood sign warped from years of moisture. Covered in dust, Sean carefully cleaned it to read the text:

Struggle not,
The Pool Erases Sin,
Only the Worthy Survive.

A chilling warning to be sure, Sean wondered if it had once held more text, long ago. Piecing together the cryptic text's meaning, Maddox's words echoed: "good thing we can't drown!"

"That Madman fed me each clue," Sean said aloud, "and I had no idea; here is hoping it works!"

Diving headfirst into the pool, Sean braced to be "purified" yet there was no change or bright light as in the Resurrection Tower's pool. When the last vestige of air escaped Sean's lungs, they started to burn but it did not feel as if he were drowning. After several minutes, Sean could tell a change was happening as the burning sensation was replaced by that of normal breathing. Taken aback, Sean kept his eyes open in the water and saw a hole on the sandy floor near the wall, where water was moving freely. Getting closer, Sean felt compelled to continue, the symbol on his hand glowing brighter. Then a swoosh! Sean took off down a dark hallway filled with water, a current stronger than the whirlpools. It seemed as if a presence encompassed Sean, mentally and physically until… Sean floated outside a tunnel entrance deep under the sea. Before Sean sat an altar of stone, suspended from the seafloor by brightly colored rocks. To Sean, the rocks looked as if they grew from the sand and were almost alive. Beautiful shades of green, red, blue, pink and orange—the likes of which Sean had never seen. Movement commanded Sean's attention from the shrine itself—bright sea green eyes sitting above it then below and to each side they flowed around with ease. 'The Elemental…'

'Welcome, young Ancient, it is past time for our introduction.' echoed in Sean's head.

'An Honor to meet someone as wise as you, my Water Elemental. May the light bless our meeting.' Sean intoned while attempting a bow.

'Indeed. You have come to receive the power of water? The sea senses evil rising, and it appears that the 20 rides once more. Yes, yes power has been granted and your body washed clean of the vile curses left by use from Life power. Mind the use of such power in the coming days, young one, it may catch up to you in the future. Nesar is proof of that, although the man fears the depths of cleansing.' At this last line, the Elemental chuckled and churned in amusement.

'Many thanks, oh kind Elemental. Shall I return to complete my training as others have requested?'

'Hrmph. The Water Elemental has not the time to wait; nay, one must master the current alone with guidance of pupils that have come before you. Much strength lies within you, so the task is fitting and the products of water channeled to come from such work will be an even greater reward. Now be gone, feel the waves and will that water.'

All the while the Water Elemental spoke, those same eyes darted so fast in every direction that Sean got dizzy. When it finished speaking, they glowed brighter still and power filled Sean to the brim, his eyes able to make out an amorphous blob accompanying the sea green orbs. The way the shape of the Elemental shifted reminded Sean of a stream running over the ground to lower points, never standing still, and flowing as one.

Wasting no time, Sean did as he was told. The water's power surged through him, as bent the currents to his will. Rushing toward the surface out of the darkness, exhilaration filled Sean upon seeing how effortless it all was, bolstering his confidence. Breaching the surface, Sean blasted skyward 15 feet in the air before smacking back into the water. Groaning at the impact, Sean braced for the journey to the ship and lay on his back. Channeling, Sean pushed water toward the waiting ship some distance off.

Taylor stood vigilant, waiting for any sign that Sean was approaching; a few others did as well, but Taylor was certain it would be her who would first spot the Farm Boy. Maddox came back cackling madly retelling how Sean sunk like a stone when pushed out of the rowboat. Taylor held back punching the Ancient; barely. Channeling with air, Sean slowly began hoisting himself up the ship's side, staying clear of the onlookers who were anxiously awaiting his arrival. The trip up gave Sean time to drip-dry most of the water from his shorts. Clearing the railing Sean prepared to lower the air currents when a grinning Maddox ripped Sean from the air to a big bear hug, leaving Sean gasping for breath. Letting go of Sean after one last desperate pat on the back, Maddox laughed and went on his way. Sean, finally free to breathe, looked around to find Taylor standing guard next to Sean's gear by the opposite railing. Casually, Taylor tossed an apple to Sean. Channeling water energy, Sean lifted a single drop of moisture and flung it at Taylor jokingly. Laughing, Taylor strode over, then dumped a bucket on Sean in retribution which left him sputtering wet. A horn sounded signaling the ship to move forward, and crewmen
hauled in the anchor while letting loose the main sails. Exhausted, Sean went off to meditate and rest his energy; he channeled a lot of powers today. Their speed seemed faster given the wind, so Sean decided to investigate how it was possible. Focusing on the channeling performed by Maddox, it shocked Sean how much was being done. The currents churned around the ship and at its stern, a current pushed them ahead like a gentle hand. Before nightfall, they had caught up at the rendezvous point of other ships as if they never stopped in the first place. Then Sean got a true look at the power wielded by Maddox: the older ships in the fleet were being assisted by him channeling the water to maintain speed. Sean sat there amazed at keeping so many currents active at once; it only made him feel tired watching. 'Wait until I am that strong!' With

determination to match their prowess set, Sean doubled down on the training to push past his limits. What lay on the southern shores far across the blue sky and water days away was a mystery, and Sean wanted to be ready.

Chapter 23: The Southern Wasted Lands

A hint of a storm from the east could be seen from lofty banked clouds hovering in the distance. Warm wind were absent any strange scents as the Skulker checked the horizon for their intended target. Massive shoulders swayed as its head swept side to side, wondering if the landing point was wrong. A Clasher under the cover of night had flown out to sea discovering ships sailing south; the scout paid dearly for failing to discover the exact number, but still the dark wizard sent a welcoming party. Next to the 12-foot monster sat a shivering Grunt waiting for orders, nose sniffing salty air like the Skulker. Sunlight kept hitting the beast, causing it to let out small squeals of displeasure at the light. Only the fear of the Skulker's retribution did the creature remain; they preferred to scurry in the darkness of night. The Skulker growled as it retreated back into the forest which lay a hundred yards from the water, as Grunt scampered alongside, avoiding the behemoth's legs.

Rustling trees and a horrid stench revealed a horn of Wanderers in wait of fresh meat. Only a single Skulker amongst them stood in command at the tip, the rest a mixed bunch of Grunts, Hunters and Warrior Wanderers. Black eyes turned on their commander hungrily awaiting the signal for the ambush to commence, each opened mouth showing fangs, revealing their anticipation. In response, the Skulker beat his chest and roared angrily, picking up a leg. He brought it down on the nearest Grunt, leaving a mess of bones and flesh. The rest backed away in fear of falling to the same fate, a few Hunters, sniffing at the fresh meat for the taking, greedily licked their jowls. It would have to satisfy those strong enough to feast for the time being; the Skulker knew a Grunt could serve more than one purpose after all. Departing the horn, it walked a distance before the Skulker sat on the ground resting using a pine tree trunk to support its weight. From where that dead Grunt was, noise of eating could be heard, followed by small howls of the weaker Wanderers failing to grab a piece. One simple ambush to pull off and the glory was the Skulkers, a name written in legends. A rasping chuckle from the vile creature's jaw carried into the wind as thought to the upcoming feasts and bloodshed danced around its mind.

Sean sat on deck enjoying sun with Taylor, swords laying beside them and both were covered in a thick layer of sweat. This had become the routine for the last 10 days or so after word had gotten out about

Sean and Taylor's relationship; what else could be expected on a cramped ship? Taylor eventually eased up on the whole privacy thing, but it took a lot of convincing from Sean and passive aggressive jabs by the Queen. Staring at Sean's sweaty face, Taylor captured how it looked in the sunlight. With his eyes closed, Sean seemed relaxed and at peace, but closer inspection showed he was ready to spring into action at a moment's notice.

Since leaving the Water Temple, Sean spent hours training every chance he could, in channeling elements and sword skills alike. Proof of its success was evident as casting came casual now and Sean's sword skill vastly improved leaving Taylor sporting a bruise or two now. Smiling, Taylor took up Sean's left hand and she gazed South toward their destination about to appear. Maddox that morning said the continent would be vast and another day at sea should bring them to harbor. Storm clouds gathered west, moving in their direction which worried Maddox; he decided it best that Nesar be sent to investigate how far land truly was from the ships. Another measure taken, Maddox left the main ship in order to take half under concentrated channeling to establish a beachfront. They pulled ahead quite some distance to where a speck of sails could be seen from where Taylor sat at peace with Sean. Leaving Sean responsible to channel the other half forward, his body reverberated energy and it made Taylor's arm hair stand on end. 'You truly are impressive, Farm Boy,' Taylor thought, 'fighting me with swords while holding us on a steady course, it's like you were always a true Ancient.'

Sean sat with eyes closed and holding tightly to Taylor's hands. After a few days of practice with water he no longer needed to see what was channeled. Ships swaying from waves and the direction of the wind were all the telltale signs Sean needed to hold together the currents churning deep below. When spread this thin on 15 ships waters constantly misbehaved forcing Sean to use more power. Nesar did show Sean how to handle the air currents as well, but 15 sails blown at full mast was nearly as bad a drain on his power as when Maddox made Sean pull water against the ship's hull to slow its progress. 'That maniac throws a test every chance he can,' Sean thought bitterly. Yet his strength grew, and channeling did not drain energy as badly now. The exercise of pulling water back was why they were delayed a day and the Queen was livid. In penance, Sean was forced into more complicated studies with Nesar regarding the use of Air—something both were less than thrilled about.

Sean had not managed to float in the air since hoisting himself up to the boat after the Water Temple. Nesar had berated Sean for being reckless because a false step in the air current meant an unnecessary death. Air lessons consisted mostly of meditation and blowing little flags to annoyingly precise measurements. That led Sean into further study on arithmetic which hurt his brain; pressure, temperature, a value called volume. These factors changed how air itself behaved and left Sean to act by instinct. Now the Queen demanded it be done properly and Nesar followed her order. Nesar's tests were making Sean verbalize how and why he decided to use this much force or pressure and even the direction Sean pulled air from to perform the task. The time together did make Sean appreciate Nesar's quiet demeanor compared to Maddox's absurd laughter. Shrugging away the long hours of meditation, Sean returned his focus to the water channel as one ship started to break apart from the cluster.

With everything set to its correct proportions on the channel, Sean wrangled the lone ship to fall back into line before his thoughts drifted to their next step. Maddox would lead Group A to establish a perimeter, then a base of operations prior to the second group's arrival. Scouts led by Nesar dispatched in Group A should return by nightfall to report current threats; this worried Sean because rumors on what lay south were not good. The best armies can fail by not starting a proper march, or by being caught in battle early, or so Cogarth had told Sean. Three nights prior, the Queen gave a report on the South with what information existed, Maddox filling in what gaps he could. The Sea Terrans lived on the coast to the east, the exact location unknown and Maddox kept quiet if he knew. No other settlements other than a closed castle 30 miles inland could be found. Thick forests of pine, oak, maple, and a few other trees Sean knew the names of occupied much of the continent. More knowledge it seemed had been held back from the three elder Ancients which Sean would inquire about another time in private company. Sean had wanted to ask about where 'The Ancient 20' had fought in the last war, but he had a gut feeling they would never come across it. Centuries had passed for trees to grow tall, and untamed land to ensnare the bloody battlefield's grizzly contents of corpses. First came a march from the beach to that empty castle in order to establish a firm foothold in the campaign.

"LAAAAAAND HOOO!" shouted the lookout from his perch atop the mast.

Opening his eyes, Sean stood at the banister where he found the land growing more visible on the horizon. As they came closer, they viewed 15 ships at anchor. People awoke with new life and soon crewmen ran around readying the ship for landfall. The Queen joined Sean and Taylor, walking to the prow. All three remained silent as a white beach stretched far to the east and west. Even at this distance, the sizable forest beyond stood out to Sean; trees taller than he had ever seen swayed in the heavy wind. As Sean went to comment on their sheer size, a faint sound in the wind came to his ears—metal-on-metal, with shouts of men fighting. Blood drained from Sean's face and he gripped the railing firmly for support. Looking to Taylor and then the Queen, Sean could see from their expressions that they had heard the same.

"Wanderers are ambushing the first group," Sean whispered, to keep this news between them.

Nodding in silent agreement, the Queen stepped back, turning to face the crew and soldiers who gathered, the noise of the battle reaching them as well. Looks of panic spread across the less seasoned soldiers' faces while grim expressions on the veterans told of war. Taking a deep breath, the Queen steadied her beating heart as battle lay on the doorstep sooner than expected. Only when all eyes had locked on their fearless leader, did she speak, tone firm and full of encouragement.

"My warriors of the Stars and fellow Sea Terrans, it appears a 'welcoming party' awaits our arrival. Prepare for battle!"

Chapter 24: Crashing into Battle

A roar arose in unison from the gathered men as frenzied feet went about tasks with renewed purpose. Crewmates signaled the oncoming battle to the other vessels and along the line, a message of readiness flew. Soldiers donned armor before falling into formation, as each captain took account of his men. Sean hastened to strap on his light armor with Taylor's help. "How does she make this seem easy?" Sean thought, buckling on a greave. The full set of armor had been brought but it remained buried with the other cargo as Sean had seen it fitting to only wear what he left with. Regretting not having the pieces at the ready, Sean could only hope immortality and luck would suffice for this skirmish. Sean placed the helmet on his head and sat next to Taylor and Eyonka, sweat pouring out of his body as the sun beamed above. Those clouds to the west moved slowly to cover the sky as an omen to what lay on the beach.

"Sean, a favor if you can. Push this vessel faster than the rest; concentrate your power here and use Air as well," the Queen instructed.

"I agree on focusing all I have on one ship to aid as quick as possible, but two elements at once…" Sean trailed off at the monumental task of controlling them both.

"My queen, if I may, one is hard enough, but *two* …" Taylor protested.

"My young Taylor, please do not underestimate his abilities. Two is as easy as breathing while walking; one has to find balance," the Queen said. Then turning to Sean, she instructed him to "simply start one channel, then as it becomes self-sustaining, it can be left unattended for another to begin. I recommend Water first, as Air seems to take more control at your current level."

Adhering to his complex instructions, Sean closed his eyes concentrating on Water energy, using it to propel their ship forward, abandoning the rest. As it settled to a "balance" as the Queen had said it would, Sean found control could be dropped enough where only required energy was pulling and building of the water. Gathering Air energy, Sean feathered it until the sail almost burst. Using the wind from the west, Sean saw how easy it was to control both and the ship sped ahead with a lurch of momentum. Dialing air energy back, Sean monitored both channels, tweaking their flow only as necessary. The shore loomed closer with newly discovered speed and they all prepared to face what was to come. The Queen's eyes glowed brightly and the bloodlust in them scared Sean.

The beach erupted with noise of crashing wood, drowning out sounds of battle, and water rose to ankle depth, stopping every fight. A ship sat perched in sand, casting dark shadows over the men and Wanderers; after the initial shock wore off at its abrupt presence, fighting resumed. Next came a shudder in the ground itself as it split open at the Queen's command, trapping the chaos to the west of the ship. Channeling earth, a makeshift ramp formed to the bow and settled into place.

Seizing the opportunity, Maddox channeled the water to push back his Hunter opponent giving him time to kill the beast. Laughing wildly, Maddox moved on to the next Hunter, splashing in the water more than slashing down enemies, he took glee in finding combat. As another Hunter fell to Maddox's blade, a large, looming shadow caught his attention. Smiling wide, the man ran into danger leaving behind the smaller fish for others to fry.

Crashing the ship had not been Sean's intentions, but it was too late now. The Queen had taught how to double channel, but failed to mention how to end them both simultaneously. The army scrambled to disembark after toppling over at sand fall, but they recovered quickly and began forming ranks on the bow side. When every soldier sat in formation on the sand, their fearless Queen drew a sword and charged out to the fight, leading a thousand men. Shouting over the sound of battle, she began to turn the tide.

"To me! Rally to me!" The Queens voice soared above the metal on metal and noise of battle.

A roar of men responded to the rally call and Wanderers hesitated at the arrival of new foes. What was once a small band of men had grown to an army a thousand wide, each eager to prove his worth. More soldiers joined the procession heading west as enemies were dispatched in the commotion and others came from rowboats launched by the anchored ships which were now free to land. Like a storm front, the army pushed through blood and water, repelling the enemy backward to the trees.

In the chaos, Sean scanned for Maddox while cutting down vile creature after vile creature. No matter the class Sean took it down with practiced ease, blade humming in the air thirsting for blood. When a clearing opened Sean found his quarry gripped in the heat of battle far from the army's line. Maddox stood in a wide circle of Grunts facing a

Skulker: alone. Raising Ancient sword to the sky above a war cry escaped Sean's lips and soldiers on either side surged forward into the fray, hacking at the Grunts standing guard. Sean broke through, joining Maddox who was winded from deflecting blows; the opposing Skulker standing double his height made a formidable-looking enemy. It swung a thin, black sword, sharp on a single edge with an odd length hilt as if meant for two hands. Answering Sean's question as to why the blade was so peculiar, the Skulker lunged forward, holding the sword point first with both hands. A lethal move that caught Maddox and Sean unawares sped to pierce its target with deadly accuracy. The Skulker grinned sickly at catching the pair off guard. Using Air, Sean blew it off course, allowing both Ancients the necessary time to narrowly block this deadly strike. 'This Skulker is like none I have ever faced before,' Sean thought with a gulp.

Taylor attempted to follow Sean into the ring of Grunts; however, a group of Hunters trapped her alone on its edge. Four against one, Taylor was left with only one option—to use dual wielding. Taylor slowly drew the second blade from its sheath as one Hunter swung a black-bladed axe at her head. Taylor twirled the drawn blade across its midsection, slicing it open with ease. As it howled in pain, dropping to the ground, Taylor's second blade hit home as it sunk into the creature's spine.

"Three to go," Taylor said, laughing darkly at the thrill of killing the Hunter with ease. Her adrenaline was pumping to the extreme. "Such a disadvantage—for the Hunters, that is."

Teamwork between Maddox and Sean improved at each of their assaults against the Skulker. Blades combined with powers had the beast pushed up the beach to solid ground at the edge of the tree line; still it held ground and did not flee. It showed no sign of stopping or tiring, but Maddox did. Each step Maddox took was slower, his swings had less power, and each breath became heavy, displaying the Ancient's limitations. Though Maddox retained much power in elements, the physical restrictions from old age in his vessel and lack of combat training showed. The Skulker could see it as well, for each of its attacks focused on the elder Ancient rather than Sean whose sweat was only the result of standing in the hot sun.

So, the dance went on, a strike from Sean followed by a strike from Maddox and then came the beast's counter slash of its single-edged sword. Except this time, it swung the sword up diagonally rather than directly. Sean blocked it and was able to adjust in time but Maddox was not as lucky. Blood burst from the gash running up Maddox's right arm where the Skulker's blade made contact. It was the first wound on either side of the fight and Maddox dropped to one knee trying to stop the bleeding. 'Lucky to be alive,' Sean thought, his face wrought with worry. Seizing opportunity on seeing Sean's concern for the injured Maddox, the Skulker swung at Sean when an explosion of fire hit its right eye, causing the beast to howl in agony. Picking Maddox up, Sean carried him to a safe distance so the wound could be treated, and so that Sean would have no further distractions. His blood pulsing with rage, Sean relished in the Skulker's howls of pain at losing an eye. A single thought came to Sean's mind: 'You will harm no one else!' Returning to face the Skulker, Sean could see charred flesh from the burn and set in his heels for a long fight. Angrier than before, rage filled Skulker's remaining eye, and it attacked relentlessly, swinging the single-edged sword with all its force. However, Sean found helpful the blind-spot made by Maddox, for its attacks now landed wildly, spewing dirt rather than flesh. 'Now to hold until my opening,' Sean thought as he gritted his teeth.

The last Hunter fell to Taylor's feet as Doomed Fate finished its swinging attack, separating the head from his black, lifeless body. Taking a breath, Taylor watched as her Queen and line of renewed soldiers caught up to the pile of corpses. Wanderers scrambled to safety in the trees, forfeiting the battle to humans. More would surely die if an order to chase was given, but the Queen held the army at bay; enough blood had been shed on the beaches. Only the Skulker and Sean were left locked in combat with an army watching on in awe. Sean placed rocks at the creature's blind feet to trip it in hopes of creating an opening, slashing all the while, leaving small cuts across the Skulker's body. Taylor looked on impressed by Sean's skill at taking the beast solo and holding his own while forcing a kill move with the power. Impatient to join in the fight, Taylor stood at the ready. Upon further inspection of the crowd, Taylor found Maddox watching on with a look of amazement at the young Ancient's movements; fresh bandages started showing red with blood, but he was unconcerned.

The opening to join came in a flash; Sean stumbled on a risky foothold and the black blade bore down on him to chop off his head. Taylor jumped in without hesitation and parried the blow with a "cling" as her blades barely managed to stop the black sword. Looking back at Sean in triumph, Taylor saw the horror spreading across his face and turned to see why. The black blade swung around to strike again with no pause in between attacks, catching Taylor unawares as her face went white. Reacting out of instinct, Taylor raised Fate Avenger and Doomed Fate to defend the lethal blow. The blades were enough that it knocked the dark blade off its mark, but Taylor was not coming out of it unscathed. Warm blood poured out of Taylor's left arm and the pain soon followed. Her arm still intact, Taylor rolled just out of reach of the Skulker's perilous sword.

Seeing Taylor bleeding, Sean leapt up enraged, slamming the sword into the beast's side and turning the blade. Black blood oozed from the opening as Sean pulled the blade free. His face contorted in rage, he stood between Taylor and the Skulker. A howl of pain echoed across the beach as the Skulker staggered backward, dropping its sword. Sean made no move to approach, for the claws looked sharp as daggers and would rip flesh from bone easily. Instead, Sean remained where he was as a shield to Taylor who half held up Doomed Fate in a feigned attempt to show she could still fight. 'Your move, you bastard,' Sean thought, ready to unleash hellish fury.

An Army stretched in front of the Skulker and the old-young-one had a look of fiery murder in its eyes. Accepting death willingly, it bellowed a challenge once more to the old-young-one, ready to tear him apart with its claws. The injured woman uttered a cough before collapsing defeated. The Skulker smiled widely at killing another worthless human, the old-young-one dropped its guard for a second which is all the Skulker needed. At that moment, the Skulker welcomed the distraction, choosing to flee into the woods following the other Wanderers. News had to be reported of what transpired on the beach and another two horns to crush these humans would be needed.

Sean watched as the Skulker hobbled off into the woods right as Taylor collapsed to the ground bleeding. The beast was injured, so Sean did not fear another attack from the thicket and instead focused on Taylor's condition. The army moved forward to create a wall of protection from another wave of attackers while the Queen and Maddox conferred silently. Tapping into Life energy, Sean used his eyes to check on Taylor's wound and make sure her injuries were not critical. Finding only a cut of the skin and not the muscle beneath, Sean breathed a little easier. Gingerly, Sean channeled some of his own energy to stop the bleeding; he would have fully healed Taylor had Nesar not shown up to stop Sean. Calling it good enough, Sean leaned back to look over the beach where they landed to see piles of bodies strewn about, ready to be lit on fire. The first battle over and many yet to come, Sean prayed to the Light that they could triumph in such a deadly place.

"Welcome to the southern wastelands," Sean murmured, tired and weary from combat. "What a delightfully warm reception."

Chapter 25: Castle of Ancients Lost

The aftermath of the battle was positive in terms of casualties according to the Queen's generals; Sean, who never experienced more than a skirmish with Wanderers, felt even a single death was too great a cost. In total, 25 had died while another 40 had minor injuries that would heal by the time they reached the castle inland. During the fight with Sean and the one-eyed Skulker, more soldiers had landed. Now the full contingent of their army stood threatening any enemy foolish enough to attack. Immediately, picket sentries were set up near the forest giving those in combat a sense of security as they would not be caught unawares again. Further protection was provided by the Queen who channeled Earth by putting up a wall as extra security which let everyone breathe easier as tents for the wounded were set up.

Sean sat diligently by Taylor's cot, keeping a cold cloth on her head, waiting for her to wake. As the sun rose to signal a new day, Taylor stirred drinking water slowly before falling back asleep, Sean unable to follow suit. Two days passed, and the Queen ordered Sean to wash, eat a hot meal, and to get some rest. Sean reluctantly complied to the extent possible, but looking after Taylor was no small feat. It took a lot to stop the bleeding from her wound which ran 5 inches up the left arm and was slow to heal. Medics assured Sean that in time, things should return to normal but Taylor's fever remained, and it worried Sean. A similar cut proved fatal to Sean's brother Zach, who died of a fever so long ago; 'that was then; now I have the power to save her...' Sean shook the memory of his brother's death away. 'Curse or not I will use Life as I see fit.' Taking a small amount of Life energy, Sean channeled it into the wound, praying it would close up. Nothing changed on the cut that Sean could see, but Taylor murmured softly in response to the energy's flow, and he pulled back, afraid to disrupt her much needed sleep. Wringing the cloth, Sean dipped it back into the cool water by his side and returned it to Taylor's forehead.

"Fight it Taylor, I am here with you," Sean whispered softly, planting a kiss on her forehead, "Please do not leave me."

On the third day, Taylor awoke to see the canvas tent stretched above her. The sounds of seagulls and the smell of salty air told her they were camped near the sea. Taking it slowly, Taylor rolled over to see Sean on a stool fighting sleep just as he would on their first few watches together. Rather than speaking, Taylor squeezed Sean's hand and he jolted awake, ready for a fight. Taylor lay there sporting an amused look when Sean noticed it had been her hand and his face turned crimson. Sean explained softly that scouts reported no other signs of Wanderers and the castle appeared vacant. Their temporary camp had been transformed to a permanent wharf by the Queen and Maddox combined.

"Every ship docked directly; it was amazing to see the channeling performed. Wish you could have seen it with me, Sean said, brushing a strand of hair behind Taylor's ear. "I am glad you are safe."

"Ya See one Ancient trick, you've seen 'em all," Taylor jested, grabbing his other hand.

Taylor held on saying nothing else. She enjoyed just spending time with Sean who looked like he needed sleep desperately. How foolish Taylor had been thinking that she could fight a Skulker and now the greatest weapon of their army could become useless in a moment for lack of sleep. A shiver ran down Taylor's spine and not from the fever. Feeling this unease, Sean squeezed as if to dispel the growing doubt in Taylor's heart.

"I'm sorry I intervened," Taylor whispered. "I was so confident we could defeat that monster."

Sean heard what Taylor said but could hardly believe the words she uttered. Gripping firmer, Sean was at a loss how to respond other than holding on to his whole world. Throughout the journey, Sean had waited to hear praise from Taylor on his combat skills; each training session, sparring session or fight with other Wanderers. Hearing it now filled Sean with despair; 'this is not how I wanted it to happen,' he thought, holding back tears.

"The Queen says Gadriel is sailing now to join the march, but their crossing will take longer." Sean hesitated to add the next part. "I have been tasked to move on with an assault team to take up residence in the castle…"

"What of me? Am I to join?" Taylor shot up out of bed, heart racing wildly.

Sean gripped Taylor's hand tighter, eyes downcast avoiding those beautiful blue pools. It was an issue Sean had protested to no end until the final order was given firmly by the Queen who threatened to revoke her blessing of their relationship. The answer felt like poison on Sean's tongue, and he regretted every word as it came out.

"Until further notice, the Queen has requested your service at her side here." Sean could feel the heat of Taylor's eyes, as shock washed over Taylor and she pulled her hand free from Sean. Unable to believe that Sean, who spent days without sleep, would now just up and leave. It left Taylor feeling hollow.

"You, you are going without me?" The question posed by Taylor was heavy as a boulder, and tears welled up in her eyes.

"By her order." Sean replied.

Taylor turned away, facing the tent wall, and ignoring him entirely. Sean attempted to console Taylor but still she sat as if she were alone, a feeling of betrayal plagued her heart. One sole phrase caught Taylor's ears as Sean stood at the tent flap, sunlight streaming inside, cutting through the darkness.

"Thank you for saving my life," Sean said truthfully, letting the tent flap shut behind him.

"Just go already," Taylor whispered.

Taylor sobbed into the pillow at the kind words, how Sean could always cut right to the issue in her mind. Even after lashing out at Sean for leaving, Taylor wanted to fix her injured pride. 'If it is my mistress that caused our separation, then I will have to speak with her,' Taylor thought, tears beginning to subside. 'I must show the strength I have gained over the years out in the world!'

Sean left the darkness of the tent behind and set off to find his own quarters a few rows over. Taking direction from a page, Sean finally opened a tent that stood larger than the rest. 'Perks of being Ancient, I guess,' the sullen thought as empty as the void of leaving Taylor. Taking a look at the interior, Sean found the gilded armor set gifted to him by the twin guards first entering the Land of Stars, a larger cot than what Taylor had, his bags laid neatly on top. As Sean gathered the necessary supplies, his fingers briefly caught at a silk scrap taken from the dress Taylor wore that fateful, cold night when they met. Brushing it aside, Sean worked to contain the swelling emotion. 'It's safer this way.'

With his bag packed with a few extra undershirts, Sean dressed in full armor, for the Queen demanded vigilance on this mission. Finding Star Shaker, He fed it a carrot, gently rubbing the horse's nose while watching as the company gathered, placing finishing touches on their horses. Sean mounted and headed toward Cogarth who congregated with other officers. The gilded armor brought a raised eyebrow from Cogarth to which Sean nodded back. Conversation on the strategy seemed heated; especially from a few junior officers Sean noticed. Sean had been appointed second-in-command to Cogarth's squad, a position those junior officers had been hoping for. The opportunity lost with a snap of the Queen's fingers left bad blood between men who had never seen Sean fight and spent years working to hold the honor. Each had pledged loyalty to Sean, yet he could see the doubt behind the smiles, and the kind words regarding his skills in battle were all compliments passed on from stories they heard.

"What have you gotten yourself into, Farm Boy?" Sean said in his best Taylor impression.

The quip left Sean missing Taylor all the more; her pet name for Sean stung. Only Cogarth heard it fall from Sean's lips and he gave Sean a sympathetic pat on the back. Deciding it time to advance, Cogarth issued an order to march. Moving at an even clip, they advanced in columns of two with Sean and Cogarth in the lead. 100 men rode out toward the south. Banners flapped in the breeze and despite being up for three days straight, Sean felt wired, ready to ride until the morning next.

"I'm sorry…" Sean whispered and only Cogarth heard, pretending he had not.

His eye searing with pain, the Skulker tracked down each Wanderer who fled battle like pathetic grubs. Lunging his fist through a tree trunk he felt a spine crumbling as the Hunter hiding behind the tree wailed in terror. Thud. The Hunter's body fell to the ground in a heap; another dead and more yet to kill. A 10-day jot South West remained unless he reached a Clasher to carry his message of the battle outcome. Clenching his teeth, the Skulker surged onward into the woods, picking up a familiar scent which brought a wicked grin exposing its sharp teeth. Hunting deserters is the greatest honor for a Skulker, the brief pleasure at killing them breaking up the monotony of a long journey. Creeping forward, he kicked his found prey of one trembling Grunt covered by bushes. The Skulker pressed the Grunt into a tree and 'squishy' flesh dripped down the bark, coating it with blood. Wiping his foot on grass, the Skulker turned southwest. With the fun over, it lumbered on at a trot as the setting sun cast shadows and a cold wind ruffled the leaves, making them come alive.

Taylor flung back a tent flap, storming into the command pavilion without permission so that the guards standing on each side could not react. Looks of dumbfounded interest covered their faces, as they debated whether to intervene in the intrusion or not. The red pavilion walls matched the color of Taylor's face at being humiliated moments prior. 'In public, no less!' Taylor shouted in her head. A cool breeze wafted in from the open end facing the wharf and waves could be heard on the makeshift stone docks. Next, Taylor heard clinking metal outside, gradually growing louder. Scanning the tent, Taylor found four guards, half set in a protective stance, waiting for Taylor to make a move.

"At ease!" Taylor snapped.

None moved a muscle to relax; each held his hand over his hilt, ready to draw. They knew Taylor was the Queen's servant, but the abrupt entrance and heated expression gave them reason to be cautious. Rustling at the tent entrance caught their attention, flap gently opening and in walked four more soldiers standing to the other side of the tent. Regal as ever, the Queen entered, flanked by 12 additional guards. The Queen strode in, her face cool and composed. 'Sure takes her time! Sit already!' Taylor shouted in her mind, her rage boiling inside at the Queen. Taylor's face darkened as she watched the Queen sit down at her makeshift throne and as an afterthought looked at Taylor almost as if she had not been waiting inside. The Queen dismissed the guards with a wave, and Taylor turned to speak with her mistress.

"Enough, foolish girl. I have heard your piece, yet my position remains," the Queen began, her tone firm. "We shall join the rest of our encampment in due time, when our soldiers are ready to move and not a day sooner."

"Then let me scout ahead! Sitting here bored, acting as a doll, is driving me up a wall!" Taylor burst out, shaking with anger as she pressed on. "My tracking skills outclass any soldier here. Three-day cold trails speak to me. Please allow me to be of some use."

"Girl, you tire an old Queen and try her patience. Your skills are well known; however, your position in my army is Attendant to the Court. As Court shall be held here, at my pavilion, your place is here by my side. Gadriel plays tricks on us, for the ships at his command are faster than reported." Exasperated, the Queen poured a glass of wine. "Delayed messages, ships docked on the coast a day's ride from here. Caution is a necessity for Gadriel is known to hold a grudge against us; even years later …"

Now silence fell over them all, as the Queen was deep in thought. How Gadriel held a grudge. More so than any other Ancient, the man was vain. Brought back to the present from an intentional cough by Taylor, Eyonka weighed his plan. Gadriel was not above sacrificing an army for revenge, even if it cost the war. Sipping wine, the Queen continued on in a much softer tone.

"Nesar feels Gadriel plots against us. His intuition cannot be easily dismissed. The wind tells many secrets; more so in the old country where energy is wild," the Queen said, her cryptic message doing nothing to alleviate Taylor's anger.

"At least answer me why he had to continue?" Taylor whispered so softly that Eyonka spilled her wine as she strained to listen. Wiping away droplets of red wine from her dress, Eyonka wondered how she could reach the distraught girl.

"Must it be spelled out? Your romance on our voyage here was ignored only by my blind eye. Training that hard and fast meant high reward for all of our sakes." Drinking another sip of cool wine and fanning the air for relief from the heat, Eyonka continued, "that time has passed, war is upon the doorstep and it is the Army of Stars who knocks. Sean must be focused in the coming days without worrying about you, Taylor."

"We watch each other's ba--"

"Love will make a man do anything in order to save it," Eyonka said as she gripped Taylor's hand to drive the point home, thinking that the years had changed Taylor. "Worth mentioning the Fire Temple and element is our hardest path to follow as Ancients. Pure destruction, fire eats at a person's soul scorching it until a cinder burns and as the light fades a phoenix rises in place…"

'Two trail offs? Is she remembering Orwick?' Taylor wondered, emotions subsiding upon seeing the Queen's confidence in Ancient knowledge. Inside Taylor, rage still bubbled beneath the surface. One last chance to capitalize on the Queen's heart then. "Please…let me be by his side."

Releasing the girl's hand, Eyonka drank deeply, searching for a retort. How this girl tried to play such games with someone who had been formulating the rules for eons was baffling. It washed away all the compassion felt for the poor girl who nearly died trying to save the love Eyonka once held dear.

"Go rest, for your addled brain will bring only death," Eyonka said, her tone cold and distant.

Skulking out of the tent, Taylor headed towards a ship perched on land—the vessel Sean had not been able to stop in the rush to this beach. She smiled, letting out a small laugh which melted the rage, remembering how she berated him about it the previous day. Turning around, Taylor ventured into the camp and found the tent assigned for her use. Settling for another sleepless night, the battle played through Taylor's mind once more, Sean's look of worry frozen in time.

"Be safe," Taylor muttered to the wind.

A strong gust bustled into the Pavilion, shifting a few papers around, and without missing a beat, Eyonka spoke "how much did you hear, Nesar?"

Popping into the exact center of the large tent as if from nowhere stood Nesar, who cut the casting which rendered him nearly invisible. He was amused at being discovered so easily by Eyonka; sunset always posed problems in bending the light, but one had to know its telltale sign.

"I heard most of it, though Taylor rehearsed much more before approaching you outside. Poor girl never counted on your iron will, leaving a lot unspoken." Nesar shifted sideways, bowing, as he flourished a cloak in the Ancients' old-fashioned greeting lost long ago.

"Well, questioning my authority in public left little wiggle room to command," Eyonka said, rolling her eyes.

"There exist times that it sometimes appears that you two seem mother and daughter fighting," dry chuckling rose from Nesar at his jest.

"A thin line to draw conclusions with," hissed the Queen while shooting daggers with her eyes at the Whisperer of Winds.

"My deepest apologies for such a crass joke," Nesar spoke, bowing to add on to the apology.

Straightening, Nesar walked to the table where a pitcher of wine sat and poured a goblet. Removing his helmet, he began drinking slowly. Taylor and Eyonka truly held a relationship that transcended master and servant; Nesar enjoyed bringing light to it. Over the years, no other servant dared to speak to Eyonka in such a way except Taylor, and it brought back memories of days past before things were so serious. Eyonka now was the foreboding "Queen of Stars" who sat on the throne, commanding an army. Nesar never understood how one could sacrifice freedom of immortality for chains of ruling that bind one so heavily.

"Hmph. What news of Gadriel?" Eyonka asked.

"Troops converge in the southeast, but I estimate only half are here now with the rest to arrive within days. These forward troops had to have been sent prior to Gadriel's delayed message of departure. Possibly it was done deliberately for a sneak attack."

"I fear you are right, although in a darker way than outright combat here. Please continue observing their movements and tell Maddox we need one last favor."

Nesar listened, never interrupting to ask a question or offer advice to what Eyonka said. His skill set was gathering Intel and strategy better left to Eyonka—her specialty when dealing with Gadriel. Accepting the orders, Nesar drained the goblet before channeling Fire, Water and Air to shimmer from view, dropping the goblet with a clang.

Eyonka sat on the throne thinking long and hard, imagery of Nesar's rarely seen face sending shivers up her spine. How much that man sacrificed to the Light lay written across it, even taking a new host proved that using Life came at too great a cost. Years of training had given Nesar control over more elements than any other Ancient, save Orwick who picked up all six with ease. A talent lost on Eyonka who remained able to control only Earth no matter how much she trained. Life had given the reason that one's blood determined the capacity to handle greater power, something out of Eyonka's hands that could never be changed. Draining wine from the goblet, Eyonka set off to complete a long list of tasks requiring her attention for readying an army.

Further south, Sean and the soldiers worked toward the castle at a crawl, as they were forced to clear trees to make a path for the main army. Fifteen days chopping down trees, hauling stumps, and trampling underbrush to flatten it down was work Sean appreciated. This took him back to the days of clearing fields on the farm, the labor welcome to muscles accustomed to fighting. Whether Sean helped soldiers manually or by channeling elements, he began earning respect from those in the company. Each day it felt as if the heat had been cranked up a notch higher than the day before, the sun relentless as cool shade was cleared away. Sean got so sick of it one day he used Air to create a breeze which lifted everyone's spirit significantly.

Cogarth joined in the work as well, once orders to scouts were issued. He and Sean took turns swinging an axe to chop any tree in their path. Today, rooting out a large stump halted any progress. The tree had stood hundreds of feet high and the diameter across was twice Sean's height. Three attempts left the pair exhausted, and Sean searched to find a way to remove it using elements in hopes of conserving energy. The roots spread far beneath the ground, twisting to no end and Sean feared they would need to dig them up in order to cut it free.

"Cogarth, why does the Queen not clear our path? Her Earth power is incredible and she could create a road in no time," Sean mused while searching for the complex roots.

"Why depend on someone to do something we are capable of?" responded Cogarth with a laugh, as he jokingly punched Sean on his arm. "Us 'humans' rise to any challenge to prove we can stand on two feet without magic."

"That is why some men still stare at me when channeling…" Sean stopped his search using Earth and placed both hands on the stump, "well then, let's pull it up this time!"

Grabbing the chain wrapped around the stump opposite Sean, Cogarth gripped tightly and pulled, straining his arms till they seemed about to burst. As they found no give, and planned to release a failed 4th attempt, dirt cracked at the stump's base forcing them to push through with one last tug. The stump ripped free and Cogarth fell backward, landing in a 'thud', a dirt cloud forming around him. Grinning at their triumph, Sean extended a hand, picking Cogarth off the ground so as to marvel at their accomplishment. Hauling the stump to the side, Cogarth looked ahead to see all other trees removed, showing a path which ran to the castle perched next to a small lake. Turning to Sean, Cogarth watched as Sean's eyes glowed, and the earth filled the crater left by the stump so that a smooth, flat surface remained. All seemed calm; birds chirping, insects buzzing, and all other noises they had grown accustomed to in the trees fell away, leaving a void.

"Sean, ready for attack!" Cogarth yelled drawing a sword, "Men steel yourselves!"

Screeches rained from above, disorienting troops on the ground as they ran to pick up strewn bows and swords. Sean scanned where the noise came from high above to see giant-winged creatures carrying Hunters. Three beasts flew toward the men, each carrying two Hunters atop their backs. The lead descended to eat flesh and drink blood, its screeches louder now in anticipation.

Channeling Air, Sean lined up a concentration of wind, slicing the lead creature's wing like a knife and breaking it wide open. Tumbling faster now, the creature crashed hard into the dirt. Hunters wasted no time as they dismounted from the creature while attacking a cluster of soldiers, black half-moon axes finding flesh. The sight threw Sean into a rage and haphazardly by instinct he loosed another shot of Air to knock a Hunter down.

Soldiers loosed arrows at the other two flying beasts circling above, shots narrowly missing their targets. Running to the first downed beast, Sean received a better look at this wanderer class creature not yet familiar to him. Bat-like, the creature lay eight feet long, dark scales covered its body and large ears made Sean believe it could hear at least 100 meters away. As he drew closer to the beast, it shifted its red eyes on Sean, screeching louder still. Dodging the swing of a Hunter's axe, Sean countered with ease, using his blade. It hit flesh, and Sean ran the edge across its belly left to right and guts fell out before its body hit the ground. The second Hunter came next; roaring at Sean it charged swinging to cleave his head off, but it only whistled above, missing narrowly. Flourishing his blade, Sean sliced the beast's arm clean off and its head a moment later. The bat Wanderer backed off as much as it could, but Sean stabbed through its head and its body went limp.

"One down, two to go." Sean yelled and a cheer arose from the men.

The last Clasher (as Sean had been informed later) carried a message in its saddle. Up until the end it kept trying to fly on broken wings, forcing Sean to hold it down with Air as Cogarth finished it off. Three had died during the fight. A number had minor injuries, but none were life threatening. Still, it disturbed Sean that three good men had lost their lives. He didn't know their names; only their dedication to Cogarth. 'I have to be better; these men deserve better,' Sean thought grimly, wiping sweat from his brow.

Pocketing the message for the Queen to decode, Cogarth began setting their perimeter, ordering scouts who ventured off to track any other threats. Medics performed emergency treatment on injured soldiers while the rest carried carcasses to be torched per tradition among the Wanderers. When the wounded were tended and the fire died down, Cogarth arranged for new ranks to march forward to secure a permanent residence at this castle. They would not be camping in the forest if Cogarth could help it; the men needed rest, and so did Sean.

Sean looked upon the castle as if remembering an old dream; a feeling of nostalgia radiated through his body. The castle stood a hundred feet tall; three of the corners had towers while the fourth had an entrance connected by a bridge over a moat that emptied into the lake. A sole tower peaked above the castle walls, placed in what Sean guessed the middle; windows glittering in the sun offering a 360-degree view of the area. Near the east wall it appeared as if the tip of a tree could be seen sticking out, one nearly as big as the tree which left the troublesome stump. Small windows dotted the castle walls, breaking up the gray stone; from a distance the castle could have been mistaken for a giant, square boulder. The large, rusty gates on the bridge showed their age, but a color of what they once were came to Sean—gold. Origins of that image of golden gates were a mystery to Sean. Shaking it from his thoughts, he moved onward, excited to see the inside.

Reaching closed gates, it appeared not a soul had disturbed the castle for an eternity. Breaking locks with force, Sean pushed the gate open as hinges creaked eerily, and teams rushed ahead seeking enemy hideouts. Sean took a corner windowsill, closed his eyes, and channeled Life energy, feeling for any life forms. Thoroughly scrubbing each small life sign for malicious intent, Sean wanted to be sure no surprise new class of Wanderer lay waiting; exhausting work but after a few hours Sean was satisfied that the castle was safe. The teams reported much the same—that other than a few rats, the castle was empty, and everything appeared to be safe to occupy. Sean left the delegation of the soldiers to Cogarth and took up exploring the place for himself. Cleaning would happen after a night's rest, but barracks had to be set up along with a functioning kitchen in which to cook a hot meal.

Walking the dimly lit corridors, Sean found that same feeling of nostalgia, images of rich tapestries hung up and torches hanging in sconces. Sean found most of the rooms sparsely furnished with rickety chairs and tables. On a higher floor of the castle, Sean passed by large rooms, flanked on either side by two smaller rooms connected by wooden doors. Counting 20 large rooms in total, it hit Sean that these were once used by the Ancients, the smaller for any servants or private studies. Names had been etched in the wood which remained untouched by time. Blowing off the dust, he could make out odd letters. One such door caught Sean's eye more than the rest and the etched name read: Orwick Stormbringer.

Sean opened the door and ventured inside to find a collapsed bed, broken dresser, and a wooden chest. Bookshelves lined each wall and the tomes were crumbling to dust, Sean dared to not pick one up for fear it would be lost forever. Instead, Sean walked to the chest, his heart beating nervously as he contemplated opening it. Lifting the latch, Sean propped the lid open and inside was a journal carefully wrapped in cloth. Smaller contents littered the bottom, but most were in advanced stages of decay. Unfolding the cloth to reveal the book, Sean opened its cover and the familiar scrawl of Orwick's handwriting lay on the page. Closing the book just as carefully Sean hugged the book tightly; a treasure was found in the chest just like the stories he had been told as a child. Leaving the room, Sean decided it best to stay clear of the other rooms out of respect for the Ancients and he set off to find Cogarth. 'This floor belongs to the Ancients alone,' Sean thought with a smile.

By nightfall, temporary ownership of this castle was complete, bringing sighs of relief from the soldiers, who were afraid that they would have to spend another night outside. A hot meal and full bellies lifted everyone's spirit, and sleep came easy to those lucky enough to avoid the first watch while the rest took up posts with a torch. A storeroom had been discovered holding oil and all the makings needed to build torches. They might be far from staffing the fortress, but it provided enough security to last the night at least. Sean was lucky enough to miss the first watch as Cogarth took it upon himself to stay awake, planning to wake Sean only if a crisis arose. Rather than taking up Orwick's old room, Sean found a small room on the main floor and set down a bedroll on the cool stone floor. Sleep came, but Sean had a restless night where he dreamed of dying and he woke up in beads of cold sweat. Pinching himself to ensure he was awake and not dead, Sean relaxed again, choosing to stay awake a little longer. The night sky shone through the small window, casting light into the darkness 'what a day,' Sean thought, looking up at the night sky. 'I wonder if she is looking at the same moon.'

Chapter 26: Flames of the Undying

Taylor lay awake staring at the stars. The bright moon illuminated the camp. Taylor found the tent stifling, in all the travels she experienced sleeping in the open air always more enjoyable than any cot. Rolling over, Taylor's eyes fell on the grass, finding a new footprint of a familiar suspect. 'Nesar is back with news!' The thought exploded in Taylor's mind, all her senses hummed with anticipation. Jumping from the bedroll, Taylor dressed in a dark cloak for camouflage. Quickly Taylor tracked footsteps following the Ancient spy who had been gone some time gathering Intel. Cool night air brushed Taylor's cheek, freezing her in place between two tents; she checked both ways, then continued in a crouch before heading for the pavilion. 'No secret meeting this time; I want to hear the situation.' Taylor thought. Determined, Taylor moved like a cat in the night, avoiding sentries. Her eyes were fixed on Nesar's back. Taylor watched him entering the pavilion, light shot out momentarily as he drew back the flap. Sneaking toward the side of the pavilion, Taylor stuck an ear to the fabric, desperately trying to catch a word. Normally this would not be Taylor's style of receiving information, but two days ago a carrier rode in and not a word of his report reached Taylor's ears. It took a rather loose-lipped General seeking company in the Light-blasted Southern Lands to let slip three words: attack, Clashers and injured. Abruptly Taylor left the man with a look of confusion and anger at being played for Intel. Taylor ran from the tent, hiding her whitened face and with tears starting to form. Taylor used every chance to gather her own intelligence. With Nesar it had to be a treasure trove. Returning to focus on the pavilion, Taylor heard murmurs become clear as they moved closer to where she sat.

"...riders to aid must be sent at once. Gadriel plans to kill Sean outright so as to keep the Proclaimer of Light from becoming realized," Nesar urgently relayed.

"To think he held a grudge and uses it to justify killing Orwick's family." Eyonka placed her hands behind her back in worry, days of stress evident as she paced back and forth.

"Has Maddox responded to your request yet?" Nesar asked quickly.

"Nay, the man thinks this is an exercise to test Sean. What say you?" Eyonka paused her movements, waiting on pins and needles for Nesar to answer.

"The Fire Elemental forgives little and setting foot at the temple would find us crisped to the core," Nesar responded quietly, "though Maddox might get close enough without being burned alive…"

"I was afraid of that answer, and my power is of little to no help. Not since Orwick's death have I felt this useless." Sitting upright in the throne, Eyonka's eyes darted to one side of the tent. "May as well join us, Taylor."

Blood drained from Taylor's face; wondering at the penalty for eavesdropping. 'How could she possibly know I was there?' Lifting canvas slowly Taylor crawled into the light. As her eyes adjusted to the lamps inside, Taylor saw Nesar gripping a knife before casually hiding it in robes once more. Striding forward, Taylor disregarded the etiquette required with Ancients, forgoing a curtsy. Finding a small table containing honey-smelling wine, Taylor poured a glass and imbibed gratefully. Her nerves now settled, Taylor faced the Queen, eyes embroiled with rage.

"I agree, no sense in hiding behind formalities, for a crisis is imminent. Taylor, Gadriel has a plan to attack and kill --" Eyonka began.

"I heard it all. Gadriel's plan to kill Sean and stop the Proclaimer of Light. Our army sitting here for two weeks apart from each other has jeopardized the entire war it seems." These cold words left Taylor who spoke dark thoughts aloud but while the courage flowed, so did her words. "Permission or not, I leave tonight. Send any number of men that you wish."

"It is not that simple, his forces could turn their attention to us," Eyonka replied "Gadriel has had issues with me, Orwick and Nesar since the old days. Watching our armies die along with chances of our rebirth is a possible outcome and costly. Our only hope lies with the men under Cogarth's command holding on until Sean can complete the Trial of Fire."

"Ancient grudges be damned; it is Sean we are talking about here! Killing him could mean the world falling to shadow and we must rush to their aid in force," Taylor yelled, holding nothing back. "Let us not forget the 100 good men dedicated to the Army of Stars that we leave for dead."

"I have seen only a small force head toward the Fire Temple preparing an ambush. The rest poised for attack here. We've already killed five of their scouts," offered Nesar, interjecting before their fight could erupt to blows. "A small portion of troops sent could prove a difference in this fight."

"To prepare such a force at this hour would take too much time," Eyonka sat pondering what could be done, avoiding the eyes of both Taylor and Nesar.

"Then I go alone, by your leave," curtsying to mock the Queen. Taylor turned on her heels and made it two steps to the door before…

"Ride with the light, may the blessing of 20 guide you and save our world," these words came out as a whisper from the Queen.

Taylor smiled, well knowing that despite the disrespect shown, a newfound understanding between her and the Queen had formed. Outside, Taylor bolted to gather Majesty and her saddlebag which lay already packed; the thought of running was not new. With her armor bundle slung across her back, Taylor strapped on both swords and stepped out into the night air. Along the way, a large figure caught Taylor' s eye, silhouetted by the moonlight. A mad laugh only confirmed Taylor's suspicion to whom the shape belonged.

"Aye girly! We ride in five!" Maddox shouted.

"Maddox! Aye, aye!"

Beginning the journey to catch Sean seemed blurred in a blink of an eye and Taylor grinned wildly. Free to the open road, no more waiting and the excitement was exhilarating. If only it were under different circumstances. Maddox kept a hard pace, with horses lumbering along the recently built road, dark forest looming on either side. Twelve days hard riding with only moderate rest, and no real path existed to connect the Fire Temple. Traversing the wild forest at breakneck speed was a gamble, but they had no other choice, Maddox promised to make short work of any obstacles.

"Be safe, Farmboy," Taylor whispered as she kicked Majesty to a full gallop.

Sean stifled a yawn. Sleep had been difficult since they had taken up residence in the castle and after several days, he dreamt of the night sky paired with a fire. Orders came to send Sean out to the wild with a contingent of soldiers so as to visit the Fire Temple. Cogarth stayed back to hold down the fort and wait to be relieved from command as 5,000 reinforcements led by a General journeyed along the road. That left Sean in command of 75 soldiers heading southwest weaving through foliage following a narrow game trail. Seven days of riding toward the Fire Temple, and unless he soon emerged from the forest, it would likely be another five days at the same slow pace.

The sun sent down—mercifully, as the heat offered little respite but at night. Yet the closer to the Fire Temple they got, even night seemed as hot as the day before and the ground boiled with heat. Stopping at a stream to water horses for a brief reprieve, Sean looked around at the men. Each was, at one time, openly contemptuous of Sean. Now having proved himself in battle, they accepted him openly. 'This will make them worship me,' Sean thought with a laugh. Channeling Air, Sean sent cool wind around them breaking the relentless heat, even if only for a few moments. The men all smiled, a few laughing, expressing hope that Sean might keep it blowing the whole trip. Sean cracked a smile. Thus far, the trip was not as bad as Sean had feared. Signaling that the break was over, Sean mounted Star Shaker, brushing the horse's front gently and finishing with a pat. The company moved on in silence keeping a sharp lookout for any sign of ambush from Wanderers. Scouts reported small signs of activity but only tracks and corpses of other Wanderers. Despite their reports, Sean remained composed, though he knew the southwest lands held stories of danger. Occasionally Sean scanned his surroundings, using Life, but only small animals could be detected. A few had odd energy signatures causing Sean to inspect any game the soldiers had hunted before eating. Whenever they camped, it was quite the production, as a line formed so Sean could say whether or not a catch was healthy to eat.

  The tenth night at camp, Sean sat atop his bedroll, unable to sleep. The heat was intense, so most soldiers were also awake, mostly lying quietly, but a few told stories in hushed tones. One such story piqued Sean's interest and he strained to hear it without moving closer.

  "...they say our world was filled with the 'Folk. True as day is light and the 20 sealed dark."

  "Tall tales, Gray Folk are myths told to prop up blood line claims," this voice Sean recognized as a young lord officer.

  'Gray Folk?' It rang in Sean's ear, for though he knew not the specifics of the name, it struck true to his soul. All the hours studying in the library yielded next to nothing of Gray Folk other than that they lived in this land long before Ancients ruled—a civilization lost to the ravages of time.

  "Next you will say Giants still live in the Great North under their trees of stone," another soldier quipped, and the group laughed.

  With the story over, the group fell quiet, birds and insects filled the camp with noise. Now concentrating on the sky, Sean meditated, thinking of the next few days. Tomorrow they would reach the Fire

Temple, a mountain of fire if Sean remembered it correctly from the dream. Up until now, the dream had been only that—a dream. For some reason, though, Sean began to believe it was a premonition, and so far, had proven true. Maddox held tight on the temple and Nesar was even less helpful on what the Fire Elemental was like; both when asked had the same darkened look. In the journal one sentence was written, if you could call it that; "Run."

The sun sat high in the sky as men hunkered in the underbrush near the Fire Temple's sulfur field. It shook their nerves being so close to this mountain of fire and only for the King Gadriel would these men hold. A scout appeared in the clearing, donning armor of the stars, unaware of what lay in the shadows. 'Easy pickings,' thought Commander Braxter, smiling, no signs of ambush could be seen in this wasteland. Braxter's men were the best at stealth and used to assassinate many who rose against King Gadriel. Orders to be ready and to remain silent went through the ranks in hushed tones, 100 men waited anxiously for the command to strike.

The advance scout approached Sean who had stayed in the forest edge in case an enemy lay in wait. Reporting nothing but sulfur pools, Sean mulled over their next move. The temple lay 200 yards away. Every fiber in Sean's being screamed "ambush," and thanks to the sulfur, his visibility with Life provided little aid in proving it was a trap. Gripping the reins, Sean kicked Star Shaker to a trot, leaving the cool shade. Now, in the hot sun, beads of sweat rolled off his body. What lay in front made Sean stop dead, raising alarm among the waiting soldiers. A tall mountain topped by white smoke was oozing liquid fire which ran down to trenches below. Black stone shone bright as a star, sunlight bouncing off the surfaces giving the mountain a terrifying look; but something told Sean at night it would look even more gruesome. Continuing onward, Sean looked to find any entrance to the guts of the temple, spotting a square opening fluted by columns directly at the base. The men pressed on, staring at anything but the temple which lay ahead, for it was considered bad luck without blessing.

"Men, we ride to the Temple of Fire, look forward as is my blessing," Sean called out.

Relief spread among the men who were looking toward the fiery mountain in all its glory, each one resolved to die for Sean if asked. They rode farther into the clearing, avoiding the bubbling pools of sulfur. Smiling at giving the right command, Sean did not see the movement of foliage until it was too late. War cries echoed around them, followed by the sound of steel being drawn. Sean drew his sword and channeled Air to punish the foolish attackers. 100 men burst forth in a flanking pattern, the opening salvo in the unavoidable battle pushing Sean and his men backward to the Temple's steps. Only one maneuver came to Sean: they had to beat the flank or else all would be lost.

Sean charged in the direction he could—forward to the mountains. Reaching the rocky base, Sean turned his army to face the attackers still concealed by smoke. Using Air, Sean blew the smoke away to reveal their enemy. Years of training took over as his soldiers formed a barricade protecting Sean and the temple entrance. Neither side moved an inch to close the gap, they waited and the tension was palpable. Then one Terran surged forward, followed by another and another until lines clashed in full combat. The opponent's superior numbers surged ahead, but still they held formation and Sean joined the fray to turn the tide.

Sean cut down a man wielding a short pike and the next man who took his place. In terms of combat ability Sean gauged his men superior, but those lessons with Cogarth proved numbers could conquer even the best fighters. On top of that, time was running short for Sean who had to enter the Temple. Maddox gave only a single piece of advice: "Speak at noon or risk confrontation by the Fire Elemental." Moving to a junior officer, Sean tracked down his second in command, Drammal, who was locked in combat. Channeling Earth energy, Sean shot a rock at the enemy soldier, toppling him to the ground in a heap. Sean capitalized on the moment to issue an order to Drammal.

"Hold the line! I must complete this trial or we will all lose no matter what," Sean yelled over the roar of battle. "I trust in your leadership, Drammal."

Nodding, Drammal took up the charge and rallying of soldiers, their line shrinking with each clash of steel. They closed ranks and held tight to give Sean every second they could.

Orders confirmed, Sean raced up the slope to the Temple's opening. Sweat dripping from the heat and molten lava falling down all around the entrance, Sean pressed on into the depths with his sword in hand. The Ancient symbol glowed brighter than ever on Sean's blade along with the symbol etched on his hand. With each step, heat rolled out like a stove, light surging then falling as lava popped and boiled. Determined, Sean did not falter, for the world rested on his shoulders in this moment. Fighting sounds melted away in the black stone tunnel and a cavern opened revealing a pool of lava surrounding a patch of ground connected by a thin bridge. Walking out, Sean prepared to be spoken with or energy flowing as the other Elementals were approached. Silence was only broken by a "thump" of bowstring being released, followed by a wet feeling covering Sean's chest.

Taylor left Majesty with Maddox who stood in the trees outside of the toxic clearing surrounding the Fire Temple. Running forward fast as the wind, Taylor drew both blades, ready to cut down all who stood in her way. 'Please do not die,' Taylor thought as she ran exerting every muscle to the limit. What unfolded through the clouds of sulfur was Gadriel's 50 soldiers left fighting 40 or so Star soldiers. Advantage Gadriel as the Star soldiers held ground protecting the temple entrance for Sean. Minor relief came upon Taylor—there still was hope the day could be won and this helped unknot Taylor's stomach until one soldier wielding a bow broke through. Running right into the temple past the soldiers who could not give chase or the defense would collapse. Flying past both lines and killing two soldiers, Taylor raced to the Temple entrance doing all she could to catch him in time. She had a sick feeling in the pit of her stomach but pushed it away. Black stone engulfed Taylor and the noise of battle melted away except for one "thwap."

Braxter watched an arrow pierce the man in front of him—Sean, he believed, a shaft sticking out of the heart. Blood pooled on the man's shirt dripping onto stone and shock on the fellows face at being hit was priceless. Braxter took joy in seeing the pain and anger roll into one thought: I am dead. Of all the kills in Braxter's career this would be the most rewarding; King Gadriel promised an earldom to whoever could complete the task. Braxter would hold him to it. Before Braxter could take another step to claim his prize, a woman rushed toward his mark with swords drawn. 'The beautifully deadly Taylor?' Braxter mused, discarding his bow and drawing his own sword. 'Let us test how deadly you truly are."

Sean moved his hands to the arrow shaft protruding from his flesh, blood seeping out, the drops sizzling on the hot rocks below. Stepping backward, Sean stumbled and fell into lava just as he saw Taylor, her face streaked by tears, roar to a halt at the pit's edge. Smiling to show courage, Sean accepted his fate as he quickly sank into the molten depths, skin searing and insides boiling. Sean expected pain like when he burned hands on candles or adjusted logs in the fire but all he felt was a numbing in his body. Sensation of fire spread to Sean's soul, burning it to a crisp, leaving one sole cinder smoldering. As the cinder burned out, Sean felt something growing deep within, a change taking over in his body. Image of the scorpion's ash pile entered Sean's mind as he wondered if that would be all that was left of his legacy. Another image burst forth, emerging from the ashes of Sean was a flame phoenix radiating deadly force and renewed life. 'I…am…not…done!' raged in Sean's mind and the world turned black.

Taylor stood motionless as Sean sank below the lava surface, tears falling. 'No!' Turning around to face the murderer, Taylor raised Fate Avenger in time to block the oncoming sword.

"Bastard!!" Taylor howled and the cry echoed, forcing the man back a step.

Swinging Doomed Fate with all the hatred Taylor could muster, Braxter jumped, pushing Taylor back to avoid its strike. Taylor found her balance and hammered blows at the man, but he blocked easily, though Taylor's intensity caused Braxter to lose ground quickly.

Anticipating the combo of both swords, Braxter formulated how he could win the fight. The chamber wall behind was fast approaching and meant a dead end to his reward. The pool of lava seemed a fitting way to kill Taylor. It had, after all, worked on the so-called Proclaimer of Light. As Taylor began the second swing in her move, Braxter lunged right, feigning a counter before switching stances and striking left. Taylor behaved exactly how Braxter wanted; she blocked with both blades which he knocked from her hands, leaving her defenseless. No longer pressed by the wild animal of deadly grace, Braxter relaxed a little to let Taylor pray to the Light or the 20. It mattered not, for the victory lay at Braxter's feet; all he had to do was reach out and grab it.

Defenseless, Taylor played it cool, gathering every ounce of strength left, waiting for the opportune moment. Slowly Braxter closed the gap and Taylor punched him in the gut before he could finish her. Keeling back, Braxter struggled to find air while Taylor gathered swords once more. Fate Avenger raised Taylor pointed it at Braxter, tears evaporated, and with contempt she looked upon the face of the man who stole her whole world.

"For you, love," Taylor whispered.

Fire erupted around the pair, catching both by surprise as lava rained down from the sky. Standing atop the altar was Sean, the arrow shaft gone and he unharmed by the fire. A red aura pulsed from Sean and the heat in the cavern raised even higher as each second passed.

"Sean!" Taylor called, but there was no reaction.

Stepping down from the altar, Sean approached the pair who stood stunned watching the impossible, a man returning from the fiery depths of Hell. More lava fell as the pool bubbled faster, rising in temperature, it felt like the whole place would explode. Rocks above shook with anger and pieces broke off to fall into the sizzling magma.

Taylor noticed that Sean's eyes glowed red as lava to match his body aura. Laughter escaped Sean's lips, and his mad snarl cast wicked shadow across his face. This was not the man Taylor fell in love with; this shadow of madness itself seemed to be on the brink of eruption. Finding no words, Taylor could only stand there in awe, forgetting Braxter completely and the vow to kill him that had filled her being only moments before.

Raising his hand to the sky, Sean engulfed Braxter in flame, the man's screams echoing off the black rock. Braxter's flailing body dropped to the ground like charred tinder. The dark snarl grew wide on Sean's face as the sound of pain soothed his ears. Now it was his turn to take pleasure in hurting such a foolish mortal.

The stench of burnt flesh caused Taylor to nearly vomit, the horror at watching Braxter die in such a way made her cringe. The savagery and lack of compassion explained so much as to why the other Ancients feared this element; the pure destruction it contained unbearable.

"Sean..." she cried.

As if the world was set ablaze, Sean watched his attacker crumble to dust, vision red with rage. Laughter filled Sean's mind, 'could that be me?' Sean's thought echoed in his mind. Trying to move an arm, Sean now found that any movement was beyond his control.

"Do not struggle, Orwick. At last, you have returned to me, only spark to my favor. Watch as I burn your enemies and world as promised long ago..."

The voice filled was with rage and a torrent of power scorched Sean's mind. One single thought brought Sean to speak: "You think I am Orwick?"

"Have you forgotten me, dear friend?" Rage swelled and Sean's vision dipped darker. "Have thy wits burned away to see a lonely Fire Elemental?"

"An honor to meet you, oh Fire Elemental, but Orwick was my grandfather. My name is Sean, heir to his Ancient throne."

The words rang clear and true, but that rage only grew, vision blood red. Sean wanted to pass out being this close to such pain and madness in the intense heat of emotion as the Fire Elemental peered into Sean's mind, recounting his journey to the South. It took strength not to burn away as Sean sat as a helpless captive, body and mind trapped. Fire Elemental had true possession of his body.

"Sean you say. Whatever the name, your fire reeks of Orwick's scent. Welcome to the end, my old friend, take all my knowledge as requested."

Searing hot nails struck Sean's mind as he picked up every piece of information using Fire. It overwhelmed; sheer destruction incarnate that could rip apart the world. In the blink of an eye, the pain ended, leaving Sean straining to remain conscious, his body still a puppet.

"It appears strength has left you, my secrets nearly killing you. Rest now, friend. I shall handle burning the world. starting with a rat - who snuck into my home. Such vile filth; half-breeds roaming where they do not belong. That lot will burn first."

Panic gripped Sean as he was helpless to stop this creature from killing Taylor. 'Taylor...I would burn the world for you...' played in his head and Sean wept at such fated irony. No matter how hard Sean wrestled to gain control, the Fire Elemental was stronger, and the madness brought Sean to the brink.

Taylor watched in terror as Sean struggled, frozen in place, face holding that dark snarl. His eyes which were bright red, now turned a darker hue, flames popped up in random places, and a heat shockwave blasted Taylor. Struggling forward, Taylor focused on Sean's eyes as they went blood red. 'A little further...' When Taylor touched Sean, the skin burned her hand, his right arm grabbed her left shoulder .... Eyes locked, Taylor did the only thing she knew that might bring Sean back. Taylor kissed Sean. The struggle as he tried to break possession from the Elemental inside was evident on Sean's face. As it was on their first kiss, the connection between Taylor and Sean resonated deeply, Taylor feeding energy to Sean.

Sean's light grew stronger, and so did his strength to fight the Elemental. The color of the world started to shift back from red to its normal hues and Sean drank in all he could. Sean would not allow the Elemental to destroy the angel who sacrificed everything to save the world. The desire to save everyone deep within Sean was stirred by his newfound energy. He would start by saving the one person who meant more than the world itself.

Breaking contact, Taylor whispered, "Please, stop."

Infused by energy, Sean overpowered the Fire Elemental's control, banishing its spirit into the lava. With his mind now back in control of his body, Sean collapsed in Taylor's arms; tears falling and evaporating before touching her shoulder. Lava erupted around, threatening to consume them both. Sean reached out by instinct, channeling Fire. He countered the lava opposite and wrapped a tornado of Air around Taylor. Standing, they both sheathed their swords and leaned on each other they escaped the Chamber of Fire.

Wind touched their faces at the opening of the temple, both covered head to toe in soot and sweat. Taylor looked into Sean's blue eyes, 'my blue eyes,' the thought radiating happiness inside Taylor. Upon their exit, cheers rose from the remaining soldiers standing guard, awaiting their commander, Gadriel's army—either dead or escaped—no longer posed any threat. Raising his Ancient symbol in victory, Sean displayed the fully glowing symbol as a badge of pride.

"It is done! You are now the Proclaimer of Light," Taylor said, hugging Sean.

"I, Sean, first Ancient by my right and bloodline, am now claiming the title Proclaimer of Light!" Sean shouted which brought resounding cheers, especially from Maddox who sat there smiling wildly. "Now I know the cause of Maddox's insanity."

Taylor laughed at the joke, too exhausted to do anything but find humor after almost dying upwards of three times. Walking down the slope, Taylor was not sure who supported whom as both looked on the verge of passing out. The volcano rumbled behind but neither turned to look at it. With that part of the journey completed, they knew they'd never have to go back. Reaching the soldiers, an officer Taylor knew by the name of Drammal came up to Sean with a full report on casualties. How different it was not being in charge. Taylor liked it, nodding along as a list of names was recited. 35 men in total were unscathed, 10 had injuries but that left 30 dead, and Sean tensed up at the news. Taylor put a hand on Sean's back comforting him, and she could feel the tension ease.

Sean ordered Drammal in charge of burials, and soon the dead from both sides were stacked for a funeral pyre. Lighting the corpses, Sean said a quick prayer for their sacrifice to the Light and a vow it would not be in vain. While the fire burned, Sean took a moment to rest as Maddox took over the watch to be sure they would not be disturbed. The pain endured from the Fire Elemental having been seared into Sean and he wondered if ever it would dissipate, or if that was to be his fate—to be like Maddox?

Makeshift stretchers were crafted for the men too injured to ride and they were attached between horses. The rest took up positions to defend the caravan as they were still not out of the woods. Mounting their horses, the main contingent of both healthy and injured soldiers left to return home. On the trip back, Sean planned to cut it shorter as traversing through the dense forest growth meant trouble for the stretchers. Channeling Air energy, Sean held nothing back as currents began slicing trees down swifter than an axe clearing a path. This routine of trimming 50 meters at a time continued throughout the rest of the day while Maddox spent time burning the logs in their path. Working as a team made light work; Sean burning trees every so often as well to test out the fire power. Soldiers beamed with joy at avoiding the heavy work after a long battle and they kept an eye out for any intruder. Sean looked back at Taylor who, despite being travel-worn, seemed in good spirits; smiling, Sean thought 'Together, we return together.'

Chapter 27: Stirring Shadows

  Clasher wing beats lulled the Skulker to near sleep on a cloudless night. Report of the outcome already reached his Master; orders to return soon came by the beast carrying him to the castle of dark. Southeast lay vast forests spread and the Skulker ached for flesh to rip, knowing full well there were creatures to be found. Crossing the dark pits of birth where he himself crawled out of eons ago, a scent of death permeated the air, and he knew home was close. 'Soon I shall have revenge.'

  Standing in a dimly lit, circular room, the Skulker faced four others, each drastically different in appearance. On the left sat a Skulker with horns protruding from the crown of its head, narrow shouldered, it lazily leaned back in its chair. Next to the horned Skulker sat a larger beast whose belly jiggled with each breath taken. Then the oldest Skulker, with tusks rising from the jaw line and its face filled with wrinkles. The eyes, though, were as sharp as the tusks. Reaching the last Skulker in line who sat upright in the chair, left arm missing, it bolstered the one-eyed Skulker's confidence at the outcome for this tribunal. They winced as they saw the scab where an eye had once been. Whether he remained in command depended largely on his combat skills; ordering troops came second on the list of qualifications. One wrong vote would send him to fight for food against past Skulkers and challengers to power.

  The Master sat far behind the tribunal on a dais of bones, a dark cowl covered his face and at times it seemed the man would vanish from sight. Displeasure at the one-eyed Skulker's failure to kill his enemies and capture Sean radiated outward like heat from a fire. The Master would not interfere in these proceedings; however. he attended to ensure proper justice was done. The displeasure stung worse than the blade that had pierced the one-eyed Skulker's side. Since losing the war against the Light, the Wanderers had adapted ruling by their peers, unison among the Wanderer class needed to wipe humans from the planet. The Dark Wizard came years later and took command by killing the Wanderer King with a snap of his fingers. No Skulker dared to openly challenge the Wizard, their master, for fear of experiencing a similar fate.

  Hatred radiated outward as the Dark Wizard looked on at the pathetic creatures before him, their attempt to govern a far cry from a true society. Skulkers voted using hand signs, for the tongue was loud and the accused could not be given information on who voted against them else a blood feud started. Despite the feeling of contempt for such simple creatures, they were needed to fulfill the grand plan in his mind—death to the Ancients who ruled with even greater idiocy and shackled the world. The largest and oldest Skulker came forward after deliberation, and the Dark Wizard leaned forward in anticipation. It had been a short debate, for most of the council's judgments went on for days to reach unanimous conclusion.

Peering into its eyes, the charged Skulker searched for a clue while the elder read the verdict. Fists clenched at the ready to slay each Skulker if it was unfavorable, the one-eyed Skulker tried to keep its toothy smile.

"Found fit to command," came out groggily as words unfamiliar to this old one clumsily landed.

The Dark Wizard was shocked by the mercy shown from such filthy beasts. He held back a laugh; in days of old, this piece of meat would have been thrown to the pits for feeding the young Hunters. The tusked Skulker returned to his seat, a marvelous leader but old age seemed to soften its primal instincts. The tried Skulker's shoulders slumped in relief; the Dark Wizard knew this pawn would be successful for fear of failure, a powerful motivator. Leaving the chamber, the Dark Wizard took up humming an old dark tune used for singing criminals to death and the man took no notice as Wanderers knelt around his path. All the creatures existed to please him alone. If they did not, then the punishment of death always remained. Before entering the looming dark tower, the wizard looked back at the massive army gathered. 100,000 varying classes of Wanderers itched to go to battle against the Ancients, the sound of their cries a soothing lullaby. Humming once more, the Wizard retreated to find out how to capture Sean and stir up the Ancient hive. Only a few had come, but in time their blood would soak the earth and in doing so the rest would surely follow.

Chapter 28: Secrets and Ancient Alliances

Sounds of pitchers pouring wine bounced around the stone room, but not another noise could be heard. Servants ran around ensuring that each person in the room had something to drink and eat if they so desired before the council officially began. A breakthrough on the Wanderers' message came to the Queen while Sean visited the Fire Temple and summons to regroup had been sent out with haste. Sitting in the castle war chamber, Nesar, Taylor, Maddox, Sean and of course, the Queen, sat impatiently waiting to be alone. The last servant bowed, leaving more silence than before as no one wanted to be the first person to speak. So much had transpired since landing in the Southern continent and here they could openly decompress without fear of eavesdropping. Now if only Gadriel showed to complete the party, the Queen could begin. 'Where is that fool?' she thought, taking a sip of wine.

A knock at the door broke the spell of silence and in walked a page holding a scroll in hand. Taking it to the Queen directly, the page bowed deeply, then excused himself, shutting the door tightly behind. Rolling out the message, Eyonka read it silently before scoffing aloud and tossing it aside.

"Gadriel sends condolences and word that he is indisposed at the moment, unable to attend our summons." Then to emphasize the absurdity, Eyonka drank deeper of the goblet.

Gadriel's refusal of Eyonka's invitation to council was childish, especially since the message told them to keep communication open. 'Another blasted ploy to show his resounding independence from the 20,' The Queen thought darkly. 'How difficult it must be, always a need to be the center of attention.' Eyes slowly fell on those around the room, taking in each worn face with concern. Sean and Taylor both showed signs of recovering after the fight with Gadriel's men. Maddox and Nesar shared a similar sickly look after hearing Sean's recounted tale. 'An Elemental rooting for the dark...things must be worse off than imagined,' Eyonka shuddered at the thought. 'Best not dwell on missing company. Let us begin.'

"The message carried by that Clasher who attacked has been decrypted and Nesar has confirmed its contents. An army of Wanderers has been summoned to capture you, Sean, and kill the rest of us Ancients." Eyonka drank a sip, her throat dry like the desert, before continuing. "They seem more organized than originally thought and given our first skirmish, added to the recent news, we must strategize to win this next fight without losing our army. Nesar, if you would, please."

"Given a present troop count of nearly 10,000 Wanderers, our forces must join Gadriel, else we lose on both fronts," began Nesar, shaking free the ill will of the Fire Elemental. "They plan on attacking the Fire Temple ten days from now. I have scouted small groups running toward several rendezvous locations."

"We have no choice, but to offer a truce with Gadriel's camp and defend that Temple," the Queen responded with a sigh. Taking a sip of wine, she continued. "No matter the Fire Elemental's opinion we must honor the contract seal."

"Why not let the Wanderers come here?" Sean asked.

Three Ancients looked at one another, accepting that the truth would come eventually and better to face it now. None were happy to share the information, given their company included Taylor, but it was too late to exclude her. Long had this secret burdened the Ancients and it came second to the Blood Oath sworn, binding them to the Light.

"It seems pertinent to fill a few gaps on Ancient lore, Sean, given your recent status change," began Eyonka. "A contract was signed at the end of our war against the Dark, its purpose sealing Death itself. Binding to the Elementals who remained we placed a seal locking Death to his temple for what we thought was for eternity.

"Elementals supply the energy required to lock away a force such as Death and if one is destroyed that seal weakens greatly," she said, pausing to take a drink. "Therefore we are pinned, protecting the temple else our situation weakens. Already Elementals grow weaker each day, temples destroyed shall kill them entirely."

Silence as the words fell on Sean and Taylor who both looked shocked at this development. This secret held among the Ancients if discovered meant enemies would target other temples to crumble their power into dust. Sipping wine, Nesar and Maddox in unison looked down at the battle map avoiding divulging the details. 'Bunch of rotten help those two are; neither worth the information stored in between those ears if they keep quiet!' Eyonka continued on clearing her throat to grab their attention.

"Elementals are beings of environment. Compromises for the use of their power came only by us creating temples to honor them. Sean, the Fire Elemental temple constructed by your grandfather long ago is the first ever, and the only one in the Southern Hemisphere. As shadow grows dominant over Light in this wasteland, the Elemental changes with it."

"Then our path is set. No matter what, we must stand to protect the Temple," Sean answered.

"Indeed, any hope we hold to win the war lies in defending this temple to our last breath," Eyonka went on "All of our strategy must contain an aspect of defense which puts us at quite a disadvantage. Striking it down would signal other Ancients to rush to the call of battle. However, the cost is too great, for with Death released, the enemy will gain strength on a terrifying level from which we may never recover."

Sean sat taken aback at the information, how precarious it all seemed, and wondered why his grandfather chose to build the temple in such a dangerous place. Of all the other temples visited, the Fire Temple had a direct connection to where enemies roamed; it spoke of the arrogance held by Ancients' past. Shaking his head in shame, Sean thought of how to solve the problem rather than dwell upon the mistakes of his grandfather.

"I remember an open clearing further south; terrain fairly smooth and lacking the charm the sulfur pools," Sean offered aloud.

"Well observed, Maddox suggested much the same." Eyonka smiled appreciating Sean's wit and insight to the battle's stage. "As Nesar stated, estimates of 10,000 troops moving to positions at various rendezvous spots in semi-circles to the southeast presents a challenge. Attacking them in raid parties would be foolish, for the dense forest makes ambushes likely. Our only option is to use the spot south of the temple to draw in the enemy so as to strike them down with our force."

"It be wise to get trenches 500 yards off the temple for troops and one dug close by filled with lava," Maddox added.

Channeling Earth, the Queen changed the table surface slowly into their proposed battle strategy. Clay shifted, creating a mini–Fire Temple surrounded by one large trench at its base and at a distance, three more trenches formed. Looking up, Eyonka marveled at Sean and Taylor's faces; Nesar chuckled lightly. The table had been brought from storage in the castle at her request, age showing on the wood, but the clay still held like Eyonka remembered. Used during the first war to formulate battle plans, it brought back memories of the 20 sitting around it arguing whose strategy was best. Smiling at the memory, Eyonka finished channeling after adding a command tent for good measure with army figures showing troop placement.

Sean watched as the table's surface changed, bringing to life the plan as the rare clay held shape when molded by Eyonka's power. Tapping into Earth, Sean analyzed the clay, trying to ascertain what it was composed of and how to control it. A small bubble formed where Sean focused, a blemish on the perfect representation of the battlefield. Releasing the flow of energy, the shifting clay settled and Sean watched in admiration as the finishing touches held firm. 'Such finesse it takes to mold, but I think it can be done if I try this…' Sean thought.

"Another trench should be added behind the temple, where we can place troops to hide our total numbers and bolster the Wanderers' confidence," Sean offered.

Eyonka felt Sean move the clay, creating his offered addition as the table trembled, then the clay shifted, exposing a new trench with soldiers. It sat 50 yards in front of their command pavilion, deeper than the others to hide soldiers. 'A quick study, yet he lacks my finesse and details,' Eyonka mused. Looking at Taylor, Eyonka noticed a certain sparkle of jealousy in her servant's eyes, watching the clay intently. Shifting her gaze on Nesar, Eyonka saw his eyes hungrily focused, calculating every conceivable advantage and disadvantage.

"Yes, an addition to the plan Nesar?" Eyonka prompted.

"My Queen, if I may." Nesar stood and pointed to the pavilion. "As the battle commences, it may be best for you to hold back and let Sean take charge."

"May I ask why?" Eyonka asked coldly. 'He knows I wish glory at the front.'

"The sole reason being I feel a trap awaits us. A pre-emptive ambush signifies thought well beyond what we once fought; as we stated before." After taking a breath, Nesar continued. "Sean has earned your soldiers' respect. Let him lead off and fill their ranks with fear."

Eyonka hid a smile by taking another sip of wine, realizing the suggestion more than taking away glory at fighting on the front lines. 'You wish to use Sean as bait. Clever as always, Nesar.' Eyonka contemplated his proposed plan further. It was a good idea to use the Proclaimer of Light to divert the enemy's attention, but… conceding to the idea of holding back, Eyonka was slow in responding, an act to convince the others. 'Two can play at this, then, you old Whisperer.'

"Very well, but I require you to accompany Sean in order for this strategy to work. When they are unaware, I shall charge into the fray, dismantling their will for battle and splitting open the ground to swallow them whole." Eyonka looked to Nesar offering the challenge.

"Aye, but what now of Gadriel?" Maddox inquired, breaking the tension.

"Our hope is to have Gadriel push in as a sweeping boom into their ranks," responded Eyonka. "Our combined might on two fronts can tilt the battle to favor defeating the Wanderers with minimal casualties."

Adding troops representing Gadriel, Eyonka let the group soak in the inclusion and use of the absent Ancient. Hard pressed, their war council was for any other strategies; being forced to defend the Fire Temple left little room for creativity. Angle after angle analyzed, troop position set in various formations, equipment allocation came next as list after list was discussed until the sun dipped low on the horizon. In Eyonka's opinion, Sean may lack experience, but his assessments and insight remained deadly accurate. Breaking for dinner, Eyonka gently pulled Sean aside to speak, away from the others.

"My, my, quite a quick study in strategy," Eyonka teased.

"Well, it compares not to the wisdom you bring, nor the others, for that matter. Being awakened with each elemental power is nothing without guidance," Sean replied with a small bow.

"With a tongue of silver, now I see why Taylor fancies you," Eyonka laughed.

"Th-that … and other qualities," Sean blushed slightly while stuttering in embarrassment.

"Seems our invincible leader is still human, or is that you, Orwick?" Eyonka whispered.

Sean ignored the comment. Each time they had met it felt as if Eyonka was testing him to ferret out the truth of who Sean really was. Orwick had orchestrated a clever rebirth and played out a game with the other Ancients, something which Sean went along with. The real truth Sean knew was that his grandfather had died when he was a boy and yet it was never mentioned. Changing the subject, Sean chose not to dwell on the secret ploy.

"Tell me of the campaign last time. It must have been one not easy to forget. Are we using strategies strong against our old foe?" Sean asked casually.

Looking out a window away from Sean, Eyonka took to watching the sun set, deep in thought. So long ago they had fought and without the aid of armies or large-scale strategy. Other memories were obscured by time, but the carnage had scared every member of the 20 to remember it as if it took place yesterday; Eyonka was no different.

"Back in that first war there were three classes of Wanderer: Grunt, Warrior, and Hunter class being the leaders. Much later, Skulkers appeared, giant monsters who slaughtered everything in their path; by then it was too late, though. Fighting was simpler as our goal was to survive any means necessary and our power flowed freely. A small band of Terrans formed around us twenty, and the story spread of our triumph, light conquering darkness. In reality, what the stories fail to mention is we lost more than won, but it mattered not as we would pick ourselves up to fight again."

Eyonka breathed deeply before continuing. Sean could see the struggle of the fight and the memory resurfacing to her face brought a look of rage and regret. No book would give such a bleak detailing of the war. The truth of living through it must have weighed heavily on each Ancient.

"The creation of Rebirth Chambers, crafted by Light itself, changed the tide of our battle. None of us feared death, it allowed us to go all out fighting and reviving later if need be. Wanderer numbers dwindled every battle as the experience in fighting honed our skills with elements until we stood face to face with …"

"…Death." Nesar joined the story, adding, "true embodiment of Death rode to us, leaving a swath of decay in its wake."

"Gathering together, we battled, died, revived and repeated twenty days in total. Then on the twentieth day, the other Elementals joined us, offering strength; with their aid, Death was sealed far from our world..." Eyonka finished wiping a tear away.

Turning to face Sean, Eyonka saw a look of shock and ... 'recollection?'. she mused privately. Memory of the cloaked figure oozing blackness, dark enough to blot out the sun on a horse of pure white, began to make Eyonka's pulse quicken.

"Pact set with the Elementals in an oath binding us together, Death sealed out of thought, we ventured to explore a world unknown to us. Many years had passed since a fateful journey began of 18 noble ladies and lords to the South, setting off an adventure unimagined."

Staring at Sean's eyes, Eyonka saw hunger as he ate each word, blue reflecting pools of wisdom she could get lost in forever. 'Like Orwick…' the thought faded and Eyonka abruptly continued.

"Weary from the war, we disbanded to mentally recover. Dying a thousand times is no easy feat. Years flowed on as fewer contact came between the twenty, pacts of fealty offered by the humans awed by our presence established Kingdoms. Orwick was unseen for over 100 years, inhabiting mountains away from the world. At the 100-year mark we made true to honor our word and erected monuments to Elementals which turned to temples for their residence. Light ruled over all banishing Shadow. A beautiful time..." Eyonka's words trailed off as the sun dipped below the horizon out the window.

"What of the other twenty? Surely a call to arms has reached their ear by now, not much is told on their locations." Sean questioned them, hungry to learn more of their ancestry.

"After making the temples appease the Elementals, our twenty split once more; heading to what kingdoms they had established. Save one, Primordial, who remained south in hopes of conquering the wild lands as we called them. He was the first of our fellows to die of a mortal wound and proved how fragile we are apart from each other. The South became wastelands, filled by violent predators more so than the last vestiges of Wanderers who escaped our wrath. His kingdom was abandoned and in memory of Primordial, a new castle was built by a few of us who gathered to mourn." Eyonka watched the moon rising, lost in the memory, "although none planned to return, we did a few years later and found signs of increased Wanderer activity. In preparation of another war, the Castle of Light was reconstructed, housing a rebirth chamber to aid any Ancient in need. It shall be our next destination after the battle. To establish front lines against Shadow, we must travel farther southeast yet toward where Wanderers breed."

Eyonka turned and watched as pieces clicked into place in Sean's mind. History had not recorded mortality of Ancients for it meant utter destruction. Knowledge such as this could lead to subjects long under monarch rule rebelling to kill the Ancient King, leaving victory against Shadow slim. So much was riding on secrets layered within secrets, all to protect the world from falling into chaos. 'Heavy must be that burden to know so much and withhold it for the sake of the Light,' Sean thought, his mind spinning. A question came after digesting the story told, and before Sean could ask, Eyonka inquired.

"What plagues your mind, Sean?"

"Ancients can die outside natural choice?" Sean whispered. "How?"

"My young, young Ancient; being immortal costs dearly and does not exempt us from mortal injuries which destroy all life." Nesar chimed in matter-of-factly. "Only hope is a chamber to heal wounds or a vessel of transference. Every Ancient holds such assets dearly to survive. Vessels can only last so long given our power consumption."

"Have I vessels for replacements?" Sean asked, worry written on his face.

"At the moment, no. Creating vessels requires creating life, for it must be your blood alone," Eyonka stated, taking explanation over from Nesar. "So much to learn; Demi-Ancients born of our Ancient loins can sense and slightly use Elemental Powers. It is in them we are allowed to transfer our Ancient essence into a new body."

"Then…these vessels are living when taken over?" Sean's question hinting at dark intentions, a pit forming in his stomach.

"Not exactly; more steps are involved to perform a transference, but I feel more on this topic is unnecessary given the present company." With a nod, Eyonka motioned to Taylor. "Just know this: each Demi-Ancient birthed must be given away to another Ancient for training and servitude. Children soften us; were we to worry of their status during battle, one might find a sword blade and pay the final price. Old is this tradition agreed upon by the twenty, a grievance punishable by Death."

Words uttered from Eyonka's mouth were laced with doom and gloom. They reached Sean's core. "Death" lingered undisturbed around the three Ancients, sending shivers down each spine, for it carried ill will. Sean broke its bad omen, pondering a question aloud.

"Did this castle belong to Primordial?"

"Long ago, in fact, it did; however, never a favorite location of the peculiar Ancient as studies took him deep South."

"Was a body discovered?" Sean questioned, bad feeling growing larger.

"Nothing could be recovered," Nesar answered. "It was the Fire Elemental that related Primordial's death; warning us students… warning of our own death to come."

Silence fell between the three as each greedily drank wine, feigning thirst at mention of the Fire Elemental and the madness it created. As the conversation lulled, Eyonka checked for where Maddox had gone while such serious talks were taking place, she noticed him meditating quietly in a corner. 'That fool forgets protocol to the war council; seems he is too important to be disturbed by matters of Ancients.' Next, Eyonka found Taylor on the opposite side of the room, eyes hawking toward their meeting and ears straining for a word or two as to what was discussed. With a sharp look, Taylor turned away, her face turning red at being caught in such a way. 'That girl pushes every boundary…' Eyonka thought sullenly.

"Primordial, whom else can you tell me about?" Sean questioned intently breaking the reprieve.

"Well, Gaddox of course…" Eyonka began, eyes focused on Sean's and hoping that her heart would cease beating so rapidly.

Chapter 29: Taylor the Tactician

The sun was setting in the West as they broke for dinner, Taylor had remained quiet, letting the Ancients decide how best to fight at the Fire Temple. Years of experience had taught Taylor to listen and learn from those with decades of battle experience, though she could have offered to hide forces much sooner than Sean had. Looking over the battle plan, Taylor pretended to not see her mistress pull Sean aside and across the room, as the pair spoke in hushed tones. 'Like it will help - I will just make Sean tell me what was discussed later,' Taylor thought, ignoring that now even Nesar joined in the conversation. At least Maddox elected to steer clear of the Ancient pow wow, making Taylor feel a little better for not being included. So, Taylor found a chair on the other side of the room and pretended to look at the map, ears straining to catch bits of their conversation.

As the moon rose, Taylor caught her mistress' eye and Taylor turned away after the Queen shot her a look; blood rushing to brighten her face. Taylor knew the look all too well: 'Ancient talk only.' It had been used at court often, but Taylor always hid around corners to listen in as her duty was only to be at the Queen's call, or so Taylor argued whenever caught by other servants. Here at the war council, it proved a challenge as few presided to give ample cover for Taylor to eavesdrop. Not even generals attended tonight in case sensitive topics surfaced with Sean's new status.

"Proclaimer of Light..." Taylor whispered.

Heading to view the current plan that had just been hashed out, Taylor marveled at its simple genius. Attack waves would throw enemies off axis, hiding in and then rising from a covered trench to surprise them. This meant the Wanderers could be pushed back easily. 'That's when Gadriel strikes, taking them to a dark grave.' Taylor thought. Of course, Gadriel's role remained to be confirmed, but the messenger stood ready, anticipating plans at any moment. Gadriel always bugged Taylor; he was a man who changed vessels to keep looks young, which showed just how selfish he could be. But Gadriel's kingdom alone matched the Land of Stars and made one powerful ally - or enemy...

Moving her eyes to Sean's face, Taylor watched as his hands nervously brushed dust from his jacket. It seemed as if Sean wanted to be sick and Taylor could do nothing to help him without being punished for intruding. This killed Taylor inside, rage boiling until Sean's eyes caught hers and it all melted. In the torch light, Taylor noticed Sean's brown hair and a mix of blonde at its edge glowing like fire, as it had in the Fire Temple. Proclaimer of Light suited Sean well, and added to his growth in ways Taylor could not fathom. Strategy, leadership, fighting came to Sean like an old friend, and Taylor's admiration grew. His training was paying off in spades, as he prepared to fight Shadow, yet one piece felt forgotten. A nagging feeling like the simple perfect plan laid out tugged at Taylor.

"Clashers…" Taylor whispered aloud.

The barely audible whisper caught only one set of ears other than Taylor's; Maddox twitched uncomfortably and stared at Taylor. Her eyes looked into the Ancient seated on the floor away from the others. Maddox was sitting there so quietly that Taylor thought he was asleep. Getting up, Maddox moved to stand by Taylor over their current battle plan. It seemed Maddox had been contemplating this incredibly blatant hole since dinner as well.

"What of clashers?" Maddox asked louder to break up the Ancient conference.

"Signs of a large group remain to be seen; right now, investing valuable resources could be costly," Nesar responded coolly. "Better to let us Ancients handle Clashers along with a few archers equipped with long bows."

"I agree with we Ancients handling the Clashers, maybe a few catapults as well to be safe. Not enough to siege, but a rightly placed fire ball could save lives; soldiers' lives," The Queen added.

Each nodded in approval, Taylor sensed a tingle as clay morphed on the table until three catapults sat close to their pavilion. Taylor ached to wield power as her mistress did at times, shaping mountains to the users' will or flying, as Nesar did. Once the table quit moving, they all gathered around to check every angle, when finally a battle plan was laid out in full. Writing down details carefully and explicit instructions for Gadriel to approach, Taylor copied a rough sketch of the table. Gently putting documents in an envelope, Taylor handed it to her Queen, who sealed it shut, using wax and a sigil of stars. Tense faces relaxed as the envelope was passed to a messenger's hands and every member in that war chamber drank deeply, draining goblets.

Taylor thought of pouring another drink, her hand pausing near the pitcher hovering inches above Sean's hand. Letting her hand fall the remaining distance, Taylor held Sean's hand in hers, taking in how much bigger they were in comparison. Warm to the touch, Taylor intertwined her fingers with Sean and began to raise up Sean from his chair. Tugging at Sean, he slowly complied, setting the goblet down, and Taylor led them toward the door out of the room. None of the Ancients objected to their leaving, but as Taylor glanced at the Queen catching her mistress's eyes, Taylor saw a flicker of jealousy glaring back before they returned to Nesar and Maddox. 'Did I imagine that look just now?' Taylor thought as the door shut on the council room where battle plans lay behind them. In the torch-lit hallway, it was Sean and Taylor alone; save the shadows cast by dancing flames. Only here would Taylor let a small sigh of relief go; only when it was the two of them.

This time, Sean led the pair on to their prepared chambers, ready for a good night's sleep in a good bed because war loomed on the horizon and every moment together was a treasure. Squeezing Taylor's hand tight, Taylor followed in kind, letting Sean know they were in this together. Pushing tomorrow away from his thoughts, Sean walked forward, happy in the present, and humming softly.

Chapter 30: Ancient Wounds

Nesar, Maddox and Eyonka remained in their seats as the door shut with a clunk of wood in the frame. Having a drink, they absorbed the tranquility while it was available, a calm before the storm. Memories of their last battle disrupted their thoughts, bringing back forgotten emotions. Dying, reviving, dying, reviving, over and over endlessly to win a battle they never asked to fight. Since that battle, each Ancient had become formidable opponents, but now even fewer Ancients lived, and the foe was vastly different. This war had a much different tone; one for every race to survive and fought by all, meant that grievances must be put aside. No matter what each Ancient had done, Light had to win once more and combining forces was the only way. Long gone were their old vessels to take on the grueling rebirth process and only a limited number of replacements existed for each Ancient—a truth held back from Sean to save him from worry. Nesar left next. In a blink, he winked out of view and his position was indicated only by the door opening, then closing. Sound erased the last trace of his presence into the night air, off to scout and listen to the winds.

Fire crackled to fill the gap between Maddox and Eyonka who both feared breaking the quiet, though a question burned in Eyonka. Among all the Ancients lay a great feud long forgotten between Maddox and Orwick; one never mentioned openly but each knew it was lurking in the shadows. Eyonka suppressed a shudder at the thought, and offered up the question to probe the depths of Maddox's mind.

"Maddox, why were you so quiet with Sean?" Eyonka asked.

"Not much I can add to that lad's knowledge; if not for being Proclaimer would have given a wide berth truthfully," Maddox replied after drawing a slow breath.

"After all this time then?" Eyonka whispered.

Standing, Maddox emptied the contents of the goblet and set it back down on the table. In four strides, Maddox was at the door, his frozen hand turning the doorknob before he looked back at Eyonka. Locking eyes, Maddox studied fervently how the fire enhanced her beauty as shadows skated across her face like smoke in the sky. The eyes held the strength that had entrapped Maddox long ago; though Eyonka's face may have changed over the years, her eyes had not.

"If not for your request, we'd be out to sea yet," Maddox softly spoke. "Each day I relive losing the biggest catch of my life."

The words struck Eyonka, love lost in Maddox's eyes stinging her heart, the sound of a door closing came before she could answer, and a tear fell gently on Eyonka's cheek. 'What a sea-brained fool,' Eyonka thought, weeping on the inside. Years of living such a long life rushed forward, flooding Eyonka with every memory surfacing uninhibited and leaving ghosts of tears wept long past on her cheeks. Sitting alone in this empty war room, Eyonka let the emotion run rampant, holding it all internally, waiting for it to pass. 'How could I be expected to love anyone but Orwick?' Eyonka thought, wiping the tear from her cheek.

As quick as the emotion came, it left, the old wound on Eyonka's heart healing once again. Free of the pain, Eyonka focused on each second since the council convened, replaying events to ferret out any missed details. It had been Eyonka's decision to exclude her generals in the event of any sensitive topics; they normally were Eyonka's second eyes and ears—a trait ingrained in each man to aid in the heavy lifting of manipulating allies to do their bidding, an insurance policy, and how Eyonka had held such power for so long. This time it would be on Eyonka to find weaknesses to exploit, with little to no help from Taylor. The thought had crossed Eyonka's mind to use the lady of her court, but the allegiance to Sean was staggering. Taylor was an exception to the meeting only because Sean would tell her anyhow; deducting the Clashers was sheer brilliance speaking of Taylor's growth. Eyeing their battle plan across the way, Eyonka's mind drifted to Sean and their talks of Ancient secrets.

The boy surpassed expectations on strategy and absorbing knowledge of Ancients, understanding the need for secrecy being no small feat. To Eyonka, it seemed as though pieces fit together like a puzzle in the Proclaimer's mind, clicking in place to reveal one whole picture. 'I wonder if it is truly you, Orwick.' This thought had paraded through Eyonka's mind more than once. Ancient names lit up Sean's eyes, and rebirth by itself did not scare him away, back across the Sea of Stars. Even Eyonka knew not all that entailed chambers of rebirth; secrets for using Life foreign since coming to power and each bit learned a precious gem.

"At least Sean had not pressed further, else…" the thought trailed off as Eyonka breathed relief.

The birth of new Ancients had never been attempted, or even possible until Sean. Six lines once lost had given Eyonka hope they could be resurrected in their quest of Light versus Shadow; the outcome of their success still hung by a thread. With the full weight of 20 Ancients wielding power, that thread became a rope to save them from the edge of the cliff from which they'd been dangling.

"Pray to the Light they are on our side…" Eyonka whispered, and the flames crackled in response.

Thinking back to when Sean first came to stand in the Great Hall of Stars, Eyonka remembered the anxiety in waiting to see if the Ancient followed the Light or Shadow. Long ago, Orwick contemplated this choice, for Life itself drained much from the man as the years wore on. Happiness was replaced by grim anger, and disgust for the world. No other Ancients saw this side of Orwick—only Eyonka and Maddox, who had watched their idol fall to levels of darkness.

Days passed, turning to years, Orwick muttering curses to the Light and locked in a tower of his own accord, seeing none except Eyonka. So it went until at last, Orwick sauntered away forever; heading North East without equipment, save a sword and necklace. It broke Eyonka's heart in two, the sudden disappearance of the one she loved. Maddox, learning the news of Orwick's departure, loosed rage over the dissolution of a man he loved like a brother. Years went by with no word to Orwick's survival or mental status and image of the man before madness took control held firm in Eyonka's mind each day. Maddox journeyed away not long after, but his destination lay south to the Sea of Stars. Now here they sat in the Castle of Ancients where many laughs were shared; except nobody laughed these days…

Shaking off the memory, Eyonka stood up, toppling her goblet to the ground. It landed with a loud clang before rolling over to the wall's edge. Channeling earth, Eyonka gently moved it in front of her, then releasing more power, the goblet became a crushed pile of metal. Smiling, Eyonka shifted to the table and wiped it clean of the battle plan in a swift motion. It was replaced by an image of their world, a land mass to the north and south separated by the Sea of Stars. Ancient landmarks dotted the surface in great detail; the only known map of the world completed here for Eyonka alone to see. Six temples housing six Elementals, each crucial to survival, but the last most important of all. Out from the sea rose a temple, long hidden and sealed to keep Death from escaping.

Chapter 31: Restless Nights and Elemental Dreams

Sean lay awake next to Taylor, her soft breathing only interrupted by an occasional snore. Smiling, Sean brushed aside a strand of hair to expose a face like an angel who had come in what felt like a dream so long ago. Leaving Taylor to sleep, Sean began to meditate, dipping into each element, trying to hold onto as much as he was safely able to do. Channeling air to create some wind, Sean practiced moving air currents around the room in the moonlight. It was warm, just as every night had been, so this disturbance of air cooled Sean slightly, the breeze on his face offering comfort. Days had passed since the war council. After the commotion of traveling this far south sitting in wait for the signal had been great, but the nights offered little sleep.

After learning more about Ancients than books could tell, Sean had thought sleep would come easy. Instead, his mind flipped through each piece of information, searching to find any hidden meaning. Casually, Sean let wind die down and let go of the power, his senses readjusting to the darkness of the room. Without the power surging throughout, Sean's body felt empty as a dry keg—a feeling that he never grew accustomed to. Warnings from the other Ancients on dangers involved continuously holding power were deadly serious and Sean heeded their caution. Closing his eyes to absolute darkness, he hoped that meditating would subdue his restless mind before dawn. The rhythm of Taylor's breathing began to coincide with his own; in, out, in, out... No other noise pervaded Sean's mind and it echoed around him. Drifting in, out, in, out...

Breathing subsided and no noise remained; the corridors of his mind became a vast void. The world was silent as if no living being ever existed. Cautiously, Sean opened his right eye to be greeted by a bright white light. Shutting it tight, stars danced wildly in his vision in the dark space, flashing at him in odd patterns. This time, Sean narrowly opened both eyes at first, than wider as they adjusted to light. 'I have been here before...,' floated through Sean's head and he turned in a circle to find only an expanse of white light all around. Making the 360-degree scan once more, Sean shut his eyes angrily; 'angry at...what?' Sean thought, emotions swirling unchecked. Groping in front, arms outstretched, the feeling of bark touched Sean's skin. 'Bark?' Sean wondered, confused.

Opening his eyes a third time, ignoring the jabbing pain he felt from the light, Sean saw six figures standing in shadows. The images became clearer as light pulsed like a heartbeat until five Elementals stood, taking ethereal shape. The group's appearance shocked Sean, who was not convinced this was a dream brought on by Taylor's snoring. Sean looked on them with great interest, mesmerized by the forms chosen.

A familiar face of a living tree signified Life, its willowy branches for arms and trunk for legs just as Sean remembered. The flames spinning around a humanoid shape was Fire, glowing hot like embers in a forge, and Sean could feel the heat radiating outward. Tornados, contorted in a similar fashion, formed Air, which blew Sean's hair around as the wind whipped past. A gollum made of stone, showing glittering teeth of gold and sparkling gems had to be Earth. Next, Sean's eyes fell on a girl surrounded by swirling water; her legs switching between feet and fin. She had to be Water. Finally, Sean stopped breathing as his eyes focused upon a stone coffin concealed in shadow, evil pouring out. Shuddering, Sean hastily looked away to find Life again, absorbing the radiance of energy. Noticing that the bark Sean had felt was his hand perched upon an offered branch; the bark rough to touch spoke of how old the Elemental was. Pulling his hand back quickly, Sean's face reddened slightly at so brazenly laying a finger on the closest thing to a god. Taking a moment to compose his thoughts, Sean surveyed them all again in amazement. Bowing out of respect, Sean worked out what sat before him, his mind racing as fast as a horse at full gallop. Straightening up, Sean locked eyes with Life, opening his mouth to speak when the Fire Elemental burst in.

"Traitor! Foul liar, trickster to Elementals!" Fire Elemental roared, interrupting Sean and causing stir of unrest among the others.

"Quiet, fool!" responded a voice which sounded deep beneath water.

"If I may have the floor, brethren?" interceded Life.

All quieted at the request from Life, even the Fire Elemental. Like a silent tree, Life waited patiently to be acknowledged. An unnerving amount of time passed, and Sean held back, shuffling his feet in place as the light pulsed. Whispers barely audible came from each Elemental, not so many words, but a tongue unfamiliar to Sean.

"Sean, as I have requested, you have invoked Power of my brothers. Ancient name is your right, Proclaimer title earned and leader of Light's Army against Dark by our will," Life paused. "Trials ahead portend Evil; be warned as true enemies lurk in the Shadow."

"Search feelings, Orwick, know this enemy and understand their true destruction," stones crumbling like an avalanche; Sean recognized it as Earth.

"Wise advice, my masters, warning received. May I ask, who lies in the Shadow?" Sean asked, his mind absorbing every word and detail, only distracted by one thought: 'Orwick?'

"An answer better learned than told," a whisper of wind whistled past Sean's ear, "unless you inquire toward present company?"

On cue, the coffin shook violently, straining to break open and release its contents to the world of Light. The hidden meaning offered by the Elementals, Sean could not fathom. 'What enemy lay in the shadows?' Sean was puzzled. Attention focused on the locked coffin; the area seemed darker somehow, as if it had swallowed every beam of light. When Sean blinked, light returned, and that creeping dark edge disappeared entirely. Gulping loudly, Sean nodded in response, unable to speak freely.

"Death…"

That whispered word, barely audible, forced Sean to his knees, hands over his ears, as if attempting to block out the ill will. Sean felt sick, waves of rotting flesh invaded his nostrils at the thought of Death itself lying trapped, mere feet away. Sean would rather fight a thousand Skulkers than look upon the face of the Elemental who caused so much pain in the first war.

"You were not introduced, my apologies, Sean. Our brother, Death, lies trapped in a prison we created, something our students once informed you. As Shadow grows stronger, his essence follows, consciousness not far behind." Life took over to explain further.

"Death grew tainted in mad thoughts; before that, however, he remained in balance to me, Life, as is our cycle. Over time, Death grew distant from us, and this solitude caused his mind to break, fracture reality. Upon the blood pact of 20, a seed of hatred grew in Death, and in his fractured mental state, hatred proliferated, which brings us to our current position, Death's pain at being sealed is felt in all of us Elementals."

Sean looked dumbstruck as Life described imprisoning Death and their heavy burden at keeping brother alive, the sacrifice involved. How it must feel to be the warden of your brother's prison, the strain nearly incalculable. Sean would be hard pressed to do the same if any of his brothers were still alive. What terrible fate for any being, immortal or not, and Sean could feel a twinge of sympathy toward the Elemental.

The coffin shook harder in response as if feeling Sean's sympathy and Sean could almost make out a mad cackle of laughter deep inside. 'Someday I might just save you, Death; hold tight for that day,' Sean thought to himself.

"Come to us when ready; we can offer further training in aid of Light. Think of this story as well and puzzle out who the enemy is. Keep fighting bravely, Sean; our hope rides with you, Proclaimer of Light" Life intoned.

All five Elementals bowed to Sean this time—even the Fire Elemental. Before Sean could respond, light flashed around him and the room disappeared, leaving empty darkness. As if there was not enough on Sean's mind, the dream of Elementals sure added to the mountain of unknown. Image of the chained coffin rattling, and the laughter inside brought a chill to Sean; it was the stuff of nightmares. Cracking open an eye, Sean found the same stone ceiling of his and Taylor's room, morning light close at hand. 'As if my head did not hurt enough.' Sean complained internally, head pounding as if he had had too much wine.

"What am I?" Sean whispered, unable to fall back asleep.

Tossing aside his covers, Sean gingerly separated from Taylor's warmth, making no noise to avoid waking her. Once free, Sean began dressing for a walk around the castle in the early morning hours. Donning a light tunic, trousers, leather shoes and sword on his hip (out of instinct), Sean marveled at the Ancient symbol glowing faintly in pre-dawn light. Only one person could possibly give answers to what plagued Sean's mind and ensure that his identity was just that: his. As the last shoe hit the cool stone floor, Taylor rolled over, causing Sean to quickly glance over at her to see if she'd awoken. It took every ounce of strength to break eye contact from that perfect blonde hair, and Sean opened the door to leave, legs moving forward into an empty hallway, begrudgingly. 'The Queen has answers and owes me at least that much,' Sean thought, determined to start solving the mystery laid out by the Elementals.

Chapter 32: Stormbringer

Morning air flitted in through the hallway's open windows as the occasional servant passed by Sean who made slow progress to Eyonka's chambers. At each corner, Sean found himself pausing to question a thought or muse an idea over in an attempt to make sense of everything tossing around his aching mind. The servants bowed before scurrying on to complete tasks put off all night, each surprised by Sean's presence at such an early hour. Rounding a corner, deep in thought, Sean saw merely a glimpse of a raven-haired maiden headed into Eyonka's chamber.

Backtracking a few steps, Sean cautiously waited around the corner and channeled Life energy to view who all was in the room. Though brief, the maiden was not wearing attire fit for a servant, and Sean knew not any lady of the court with hair such as that. All the talk about Gadriel and plans to settle grudges quickened Sean's pulse.

"Oh, what games we Ancients play," Sean darkly joked to himself.

Three signatures of life blazed into Sean's eyes, one by the back wall and two toward where Eyonka favored sitting. The back wall life sign winked out of existence suddenly causing the hair on the back of Sean's neck to stand on end. Abandoning his place of concealment, Sean rushed the door, bursting in the chamber, sword half unsheathed to vanquish whatever enemy would be foolish enough to attack. Eyonka and the raven-haired maiden stood undisturbed by Sean's abrupt appearance, eyes barely noticing the blade half drawn; instead, they focused on his eyes which glowed with power.

Quickly sheathing the sword and power of Life, Sean bowed slightly waiting on permission to formally enter. What seemed an eternity passed before Eyonka beckoned Sean in by gesturing slightly with a wave. Closing the door, Sean approached the far side of the room, stopping next to Eyonka. As Sean settled in place, facing the unfamiliar guest, he began taking in the maiden fully for the first time.

Raven hair framed a face Sean could call noble, stoic features spoke of years lacking a smile and her eyes had a weighing judgment in their look. If Sean had to guess an age, she would be older than him by about 20 years. Sitting over her breast sat a broach that spoke of Ancient times long past, three prongs wrapped around the encompassing circle of metal keeping the travel cloak attached. Standing two inches taller than Sean, her face looked unconcerned at Sean's intrusion, yet the worn, leather, knife sheath she grasped told another story. Something told Sean to be wary of this stranger and not approach too closely else he would find how good with a knife she truly was. Metal clinked as the raven-haired maiden moved, revealing chainmail beneath the cloak, and Sean tensed up at being so ill prepared.

To Sean, Eyonka appeared cool and composed, seemingly unconcerned that the lady was fully prepared for war. In a dark blue dress that twinkled with gems to give the appearance of stars in the night sky, Sean wagered that more than one knife lay hidden in the folds. No other guests besides these two could be seen by Sean and he dared not invoke power to check again. A window opened wide enough for a person to fit through gave Sean an idea to who the third life sign belonged to.

"Good morning, my Queen, although early, it appears that the need for council is on several minds," Sean breathed out, containing his apprehension much like wrestling a bear. "May I ask to join or has business concluded?"

"May Light shine upon us this morning, for war always requires council, no matter the hour," Eyonka responded gently. "I must give introductions; Lady Sloane, may I present Sean, Proclaimer to Light and Ancient Ones."

Although the introduction was simply stated, power radiated from what Eyonka said. Shock was visible on Sloane's face; her eyes shot to Sean who was then appraised once more in careful detail. The weighing judgment of Sloane's stare made Sean want to run and hide far away in the castle depths. Knowledge such as this never brandished about casually meant Sloane was an ally, Sean mused, but for which Ancient he could not tell. Steeling his nerves, Sean made the necessary introductions, adding in a blessing to drive up the stock of his value.

"My Lady Sloane, may the twenty protect you and Light watch over you for eternity. I am Sean, Proclaimer of Light, Ancient heir to Orwick reborn against the Shadow."

This proclamation brought Sloane to kneel, tears rolling down from sow eyes at receiving such a blessing. Unashamed, Sloane stayed still, waiting for Sean's release.

"Please rise, the floor can be cold before early heat warms this castle," Sean said with a smile.

"My Lord, tales of your feats slaying Wanderers and being born again have spread far to our ears…yet…" Sloane responded while rising to stand. "May the Shadow curse my heart, for I feared they were nothing but false rumors to rally armies in this wasteland."

"The rumors you speak of, I myself heard some time ago, but my height was wrong. We welcome you daughter of Light; it is my hope that word of my existence spreads far, dispelling rumor…someday," Sean responded nodding toward her.

Catching Eyonka's eye, Sean could see it held a mischievous glint at forcing him to make such a formal greeting after her lackluster one. Ignoring Eyonka, Sean turned back to face Lady Sloane whose tears now had stopped. With a slight nod permitting him to speak, Sean settled in to hear the rest of what Lady Sloane had to say.

"Only the dawn knows for certain. I thank the twenty on this chance meeting, my Lord," Sloane said, bowing deeply, but returning upright, she rotated to face the Queen. "The answer shall be given post haste and my ride is long, but spurred on by hope."

"Implore my wishes to Gadriel and Light protect your journey. I await our next visit on pleasant tidings out from the shade of threat," Eyonka said.

After speaking, Eyonka raised her hand to grasp Sloane's slender fingers in an embrace. Realizing that Sean was watching her, Eyonka halted in midair, her cheeks becoming red. Sloane closed the gap to offer a tight squeeze of Eyonka's hand, the contact released quickly brought red to Sloane's cheeks as well. Neither enjoyed the idea that Sean sat intently watching the exchange, but time was running short and any longer would raise suspicions.

Sloane bowed again to Sean who returned it with a nod; no more words could be given as it was not his court to dismiss. Raven black hair swung across Sloane's shoulders, covering the back of her cloak as she turned away from the Ancients, her energy at the point of bursting with each step. Opening the door to the hallway, Sloane exited without turning around. Her mission to deliver an urgent message to her master took precedence. And if Sloane had to look into those dreamy blue eyes again, she might just swoon like all the other ladies in court would for a man so battle hardened.

The sound of a lock latching in place signaled Sloane leaving the two Ancients alone; no explanation came from Eyonka to Sean as to who Lady Sloane really was or what her purpose at this hour entailed. Silence enveloped as neither spoke, wills battling for dominance; but Sean could win, he knew it. Not seeking permission, Sean pulled a chair in front of Eyonka and sat, maintaining his composure despite the tempest of questions raging inside. Being face to face with Eyonka like this, some of those features on Sloane did share a little resemblance...mainly the eyes.

A sigh escaped Eyonka's lips as Sean sat; this boy turned warrior, turned Ancient now, challenging her as an equal. Taking a goblet of wine, Eyonka casually studied the face of a man she knew once long ago. Although a difference in the face could be seen, it was the eyes which unsettled Eyonka's stomach as they raged with intensity, just as she remembered. Control of every power came at heavy costs, the man's internal struggle worsening each day as elements would wage war to be Sean's primary strength. That is what made Stormbringer's honor their namesake—like a gale force hurricane, the power surged inside, and, in the middle, merely a man. Sipping wine, Eyonka drew strength to ask a question clawing to be released ever since meeting Sean.

"Is it you? Orwick?" Eyonka asked quietly.

Sean's brain exploded; the mere mention of his grandfather pushed all other questions away and he fought to hold a single one. The chamber spun as Sean struggled to form a response; Eyonka always seemed to thwart his plans. The idea that Sean, in fact, was not himself, but Orwick, and the reason for this meeting—it hurt his head thinking this hard, evaluating every action since birth to come to an answer. All the Elementals were convinced Sean was Orwick, but a deep feeling said that the confidence they offered in calling him Orwick was wrong.

"I...I..." Sean's voice trailed beyond the chamber walls, into thin air and in time itself.

"Hmm...then my suspicion will remain just that; the answer is one only you can give," Eyonka responded, a feeling of ages alive seeping deep in her bones. "Gadriel has countered our plan and wishes to join us but not as a pawn in battle."

"Then Gadriel shall not fight?" Sean let strategy instincts take over, brushing aside self-reflection...

"No, they will fight, especially after Sloane's stories spread of your stature, so I thank you for that." Pausing, Eyonka let the information sink in before continuing. "However, it shall be on his terms, not ours, as luck has it. Tomorrow, new plans will be drawn to depart sooner as I will ensure they have him in the perfect position for our plan."

"Then hope rides with us and our own luck is made..." Sean whispered, thinking deep about what preparations he needed done. "Lady Sloane is of Gadriel's charge, then?"

"Yes, unfortunately so," Eyonka said, her tone glum. "How my daughter ended up with such an arrogant Ancient to command her I will never know."

Sean nearly fell out of his chair. Sure, suspicions hung in the air, given their goodbye, but still. For a moment Sean forgot his own identity dilemma and his mind raced at the implications for having one's own blood under command of a man Eyonka loathed so much.

"I had my suspicions...but is that why you asked for Gadriel to make haste to join us?" Sean asked.

"Partly the reason; one I do not offer up to others with prying ears, though. Seeing the face of Lady Sloane always brings joy, but the goodbye is always a painful reminder that we may never enjoy a mother and daughter relationship..." Eyonka's voice trailed off, "but we need Gadriel's army and sheer force of numbers; that is why I hastened his addition to our ranks."

"My deepest condolences at the nature of this situation; someday, we will change the rules set so long ago," Sean replied.

Reaching out, Sean offered to embrace Eyonka who accepted in kind, both of their moods sullen and Sean feared it was his doing. Silence filled the distance between only broken by the crow of a rooster signaling morning light. A question formed in Sean's mind, and like reading a book, Eyonka pressed an inquiry.

"What else troubles you, Sean? A corpse contains more life than you this morning." Eyonka's piercing eyes looked into Sean's.

"I had a dream...a dream where all the Elemental's spoke to me while in a world of vast light. Even Death was there...but he said little." Sean spit out, afraid to continue on.

Cold crept in the room at mention of Death, fires darkened and both Ancients shivered in unison. The chill hung as an unwelcome guest despite the heat of the rising sun. Eyonka crossed her arm over heart in hopes of dispelling the mood.

"Then they chose to communicate with you outside our mortal realm, sensing the upcoming battle, I would guess." Eyonka proceeded cautiously. "Now you truly understand our next battle's importance, for without fire, Light is weak to Shadow."

"More importantly, what puzzles me is what they said about our enemy lurking in Shadow, Eyonka..." Sean told of the meeting, watching for any reaction.

Eyonka remained somber through Sean's telling of the Elemental's ethereal forms, soaking in details of Air, Fire and Water, as she had never laid eyes on them before. Upon reaching the part of the coffin cloaked in darkness, Eyonka made the same gesture of arm over her heart, an old custom of protection from her youth. It took strength maintaining a calm facade when Sean mentioned the blood pact of 20; 'Light, please say they avoided talking about how we came to power with that Dark Wizard in the tower….' Eyonka thought while praying to the Elementals. At the end of the story, Eyonka wished for another pitcher of wine and no responsibilities, allowing her to drink the day away. As always, Elementals spoke in riddles and their meaning with more truths than a Sea Folk silk trader. No wonder Sean had the look of a confused fish told to fly rather than swim—even Orwick would be at a loss.

"I will ponder this and seek Nesar's resources with information; one thing is clear at least," Eyonka finally spoke after the retelling.

"What might that be?" Sean asked.

"War rises as the sun does and it shall be harder than last time with us twenty." Eyonka slumped back in the chair.

Sean felt a little better after seeing the look on Eyonka's face from what was told by the Elementals. It seemed they confused Eyonka much the same as Sean and finally they both sat on equal footing. It could not be helped; Sean had to circle back to the question of his identity.

"Eyonka, you asked if I was Orwick. Elementals all ask this of me or think I am him reborn." Sean hesitated, "... Am I reborn?"

"Sean ... that remains for you alone to know. Furthermore, I venture to say, take the mantle of Orwick or Sean; actions and character will determine who you are." Eyonka paused, a good time to drink, his brow furrowed deeply, "another pressing question?"

"Regarding Ancient birth…if I am truly Sean and not Orwick then can we hope to rekindle our ranks?" Sean asked aloud, attempting to discover all he could of the dead house lines.

"Interesting…I have thought much the same question, let us order something to eat and discuss the theory of our Ancient blood."

Chapter 33: The Battle Looming Overhead

Sean sat in Star Shaker's saddle, next to Cogarth as they rode ahead of their men toward the Fire Temple. The plume of smoke coming from its peak was a sign that the Fire Elemental lay awake in the morning light and a shiver ran down Sean's spine. Cogarth looked on at the mountain, face painted with awe taking each detail in stride. Already a group of workers had been sent ahead of their procession in order to set up tents for the camp. Lying further to the south, rows of white linen and a signature red pavilion could be seen shining in the sun. Sean wrinkled his nose as they dodged past pools of bubbling sulfur, releasing a smell of rotten eggs and it took some effort not to cover up from the stench.

Preparations came faster than Sean expected, but their men rose to this challenge and knowing the moved up timetable for war required establishing guard on the upcoming battleground. Sean had been offered the option to take command of all troops until Eyonka arrived, but he politely turned it down, letting her generals retain that honor. Taylor remained back at the Castle of Ancients with Eyonka; Sean could not imagine their frustration at staying behind. The argument that ensued at this decision could be heard throughout the castle and guards had to separate each before they came to blows. The other Ancients would join as soon as possible, meaning Sean sat near the doomed temple by himself yet again.

Nessar worked with Maddox to bring the secret weapon forward, keeping it hidden in case enemy scouts lurked, requiring the cover of night. After the battle plans had been drawn to send on to Gadriel, no recent messengers came to change things; however, in a heated debate with the Star Army Generals, the Ancients chose to step up aerial defenses. Their combined opinion that three catapults and Ancient luck were lacking proper consideration of the threat that the Clashers posed. So, to offset the concern, a grand plan was devised; one that Sean still had a hard time believing. To keep all spies unaware, nothing had been written down officially and so the Ancients worked in the shadows.

"More secrets to keep," Sean grumbled.

Pulling up to the base of the mountain of fire, Sean nodded to Cogarth and took command over his half; Cogarth the other half. 'Time to start digging,' Sean thought wearily. The heat boiled around them, and for once Sean was glad not to be wearing full armor despite the last

215

encounter at the Temple. Dismounting Star Shaker, Sean took a spade from the horses saddle; soldiers followed suit making sure to hand reins off for a picket line being constructed. A page boy no taller than the horses midsection gladly accepted each rein leading horses away to wait until the small fence had been constructed. Scanning the faces of each man Sean took note of the looks; disdain, contempt and sweat covered a vast majority. Mainly the new recruits who had not spent weeks clearing trees and freshly assigned to Sean, another group to break in. 'Nothing like hard labor to pull men together.' Sean thought with a sigh.

 Directing men to locations of flat ground on the far side of the mountain, Sean started digging out a large trench just deep enough to hold 10-20 men. Strict instructions forbade using the power to dig, Sean would appear like an officer to avoid any assassination attempts. Sean did not complain, though; manual labor suited him fine and was a welcome relief from the pent up frustration. Two days had passed since speaking with Eyonka, yet Sean's mind raced faster than before; reviewing each moment in excruciating detail to solve the question of who Sean was. Taylor knew nothing, as Eyonka asked for their council to be held in confidence, but Sean knew his behavior had to be noticed by his love.

 Ancient knowledge was dangerous to those who had little value to its power or the meaning it held. Looking back on the past two days, everything rushed to ready the army to battle anyhow; no time was spared to get caught in a position where Sean would need to lie. 'Digging' this thought wiped away Sean's distraction and focus returned to the shovel scooping dirt. To build a better barricade, the loose sediment would be placed on the top of the trench, and any rocks dug free were placed to the side for the Ancients. Although dry, this dirt looked fertile as flecks fell off shovels and Sean wondered if a farm could be started here once the war was over. Despite the heat and current threat of dying at the hands of Wanderers, Sean thought building acreage to raise a family on would be enjoyable here. Wiping sweat from his brow, Sean listened as sounds of grunting men with scraping soil echoed around.

 "How I must sound like my grandfather," Sean joked to himself, letting out a small laugh.

 As the sun climbed overhead, more men joined in the digging as their other tasks had been completed. Each platoon stopped at Sean for orders of where to begin, which was welcome at first but by the hundredth interruption he ached to find his rhythm. Every break, however, did allow Sean to check on the progress of their semi-circle of trenches surrounding the Temple of Fire. They sat roughly five foot deep, running sixty feet in length and a space of twenty feet in between; their end goal was ten foot deep, so every added hand sped up the work. 'Another couple hours and it should be complete; if not sooner,' went through Sean's head while looking out across the field. Noticing several other soldiers doing a similar check, Sean smiled at how they all yearned to be free of the task at hand. Upon meeting eyes with Sean, they jumped back to work vigorously digging to catch up from their reprieve and Sean's smile grew wider. Casting a glimpse to the north, Sean saw their camp sprawling larger than when they first arrived. A sea of tents all centered around one large red pavilion structure. Cogarth had been assigned guard duty and Sean's mind drifted to how that must be, with only a sliver of envy at not being chosen for that responsibility.

Taylor huffed as she placed each item in a chest heading to her mistress's tent at camp. Every item packed away increased Taylor's huff, the intention clearly being to prove how pointless she felt to be used like a common servant. Days prior to being separated by guards, a decree went out that any verbal gripe or argument from Taylor at the task assigned meant a punishment of wrapping clean bandages for the medics. One chest full of them later drove the point home to Taylor, who decided she could toe a thin line by making as much noise as possible through exaggerated huffs.

The Queen, sitting at a map, either ignored Taylor or simply cared not what noise was made, as long as it was not spoken. Putting a chair down with a loud 'whoof' finally solicited a reaction from the Queen. No shouting or stern looks for Taylor, just more work and another chest of wrapped bandages. Tooth and nail Taylor nonverbally fought this role of personal Queen attendant until a threat by the Queen to make her battle naked came about. From that point on, all grumbling ceased until Taylor sat out of earshot from her mistress. This was Taylor's only means to rebel against the shackles binding her to the castle. The servants, guards and other ladies of court dared not cross paths by telling on Taylor. For fear of their lives, they would scoot past as Taylor sulked, carrying more linens and trinkets needed for the front lines.

"I hope Sean is at least enjoying being a soldier," Taylor grumbled, scaring off a serving girl.

Sean at that moment was not enjoying being a soldier, for the sun had set, but he stood helping to fix a partially collapsed trench wall. Other teams that had finished up their work and were not needed were granted permission to leave, yet they stayed to help wherever possible. Engaging in manual labor had brought together men under Sean in a way that he never thought possible. Prior looks of discontent now sported pride (and a little dirt) at accomplishing the fortifications. Sean was resolute about finishing this last task without aid of the power that hummed just out of reach, begging to be used. Cheers rose loud when the last scoop thudded outside the trench, finding home in the pile towering above. Climbing out of the trench, soldiers formed rank once more behind Sean who began heading to camp in the evening light. Smells of roasting meat wafted on the winds toward the group of soldiers, their onward march eager to eat a hot meal and drink water.

Sean found it funny at first that soldiers never drank anything but water; stories nearly glorified them as drunkards in the nights leading to battle. These men painted a new picture of honor to Sean, and he never broached its topic so as to not plant a seed of temptation. White tents soon engulfed their ranks, and as the last row entered the camp perimeter Sean dismissed them. Watching their departure, Sean briefly scanned each one; their physical condition as well as their attitude were taken into account while he formed opinions for each man. Sean knew not all their names at this moment, but it would be his personal mission to learn them; they pledged allegiance to die for the Light. It was the only honorable thing Sean could think to repay the debt owed.

"Men can be generals or soldiers; seldom both, else only commands would be issued, and nobody would follow," Sean muttered in barely a whisper.

Laughter erupted from behind Sean giving him a start; Cogarth came striding forward out from a row of tents into the torch light. Smiling wide, Sean crossed to meet up with Cogarth far from earshot of the other soldiers. Grasping forearms like old friends they carried off into the night relating their adventures of the day. Cogarth, it turns out, had to kill a few Grunts snooping around the encampment and Sean's jealousy grew at finding out about the conflict. Sean's only reports had been of the dirt caving in on a trench, which brought a slap on the back from Cogarth.

"If I remember right, you are better with a shovel than a sword," Cogarth jested.

"Well seems we might need to spar to settle this rumor," Sean joked back.

"Tomorrow then; tonight I head out on patrol again as they need the best Grunt killers we have," Cogarth laughed again, and Sean joined in.

Separating from each other they headed off into the camp in opposite directions, Cogarth to find his men and Sean to find a meal. The joking brought Sean back to when they went off to hunt and practice bow skills, no war looming overhead to kill the mood. So long ago those days felt and Sean hoped they'd survive to see them again.

Chapter 34: Little Moments

'Finding a tent should not be this hard,' Sean thought, trudging down row after row of identical canvas tents. The page had given directions, but three rows up and four over, Sean came across a tent occupied by a rather confused general. Leaving with a polite nod for apology, Sean recounted steps back to where he started off hoping to scare a little page when - CRASH. Linens fell to the ground everywhere in a pile. Sean lost his shovel in the accident and then tripped on a solid object buried deep. Mud covered more of Sean's body than before. He must have made quite a picture to the onlookers. Searching through linens, Sean pulled free a hand, hoisting it out gently came the one face he hoped not to see: Taylor's. Her blonde hair flickered in the firelight, framing a rather shocked face; half smiling it sat frozen in mid insult at the person foolish enough to bump into her. Seeing the culprit was Sean, the insult turned into a laugh and they both chuckled at the serendipitous encounter. Casually, Sean helped Taylor to stand, and using Earth, Sean removed the caked mud from her dress, stained much like Sean. Next came cleaning the linens as they were recovered and folded for Taylor to hold. Taking half of the load so Taylor could see properly, Sean took her hand again, this time out of affection.

Wordlessly, they both set off to drop Taylor's parcel at Eyonka's pavilion, Sean remained outside, wiping mud off his pants while taking in the scenery. Stone-faced guards sat unmoving near the tent flaps and Sean knew full well at a moment's notice they would kill any threat to Eyonka. Maybe not Sean, but any assassin who dared to approach definitely stood zero chance. Looking to the heavens above, Sean checked for any starlight, but only bleak darkness stared back at him. Shuffling of the tent flaps pulled Sean's eyes back to the pavilion as Taylor emerged; her face matching the color of the tent.

Her eyes meeting Sean, Taylor's rage dissipated, eliciting a smile instead, and they joined hands. The silence was broken by occasional voices, which suited them fine, making them feel closer than ever. Taylor stopped at an empty tent and beckoned Sean inside while he noted: 'row one, fifth tent from pavilion.' Striking flint and steel, Taylor lit a candle which illuminated their tent; two cots next to each other, a wash basin and a small table. Taylor set the candle on the table to pour water for Sean to wash up.

Stepping inside the tent, Sean began to peel off his dirty clothes. Before removing his trousers, Sean hesitated, unsure how much privacy they truly had here in camp. His actions brought a laugh from Taylor and embarrassed Sean as he hurried to be free of the dirty rags. Heat inside the tent was causing beads of sweat to emerge on Sean's brow. Taking leave so Sean could wash properly, Taylor scuttled outside, closing the tent flap.

Taylor took to starting a fire in front of their tent; a perk when lodging with a commander; after all, having room for a private fire is an obvious luxury. The rest of the men took to sharing fires and meals, but it would be ill advised for higher ups to join in with the troops. Taylor had not ever thought of this before as most fires in the wilds were private, save a few companions and her mistress who had not marched for a war in Taylor's lifetime. With the flames roaring nicely, Taylor thought about taking a peek inside the tent to spook Sean.

Sean stood in front of the water basin, naked head to toe, sword on the cot within reach in case of intruders. Up until this point, being dirty had never concerned Sean; a stream bath or swim in a lake always washed away most of the grime from the road. The water was cool, and Sean contemplated heating it with fire first, but thought of being this exposed overruled the option. While washing, Sean remembered the origin their journey, fleeing the farm and camping under stars while looking over their shoulders for Wanderers. Now it was different; a world's fate rested at what would come in two days time if they had luck. Washing the cool water over his face, Sean let it take away that large worry for a moment. 'Tomorrow's troubles are for then and not a moment sooner," Sean thought, happy to have Taylor watching his back.

Taylor sat by the fire, her back to the tent. She began humming gently, as the sound of water splashing signaled Sean bathing. Not an hour ago, Taylor was covered in mud, ready to tongue skewer whomever ran into her when her hand clutched another hand that she could know for eternity. Sean looked like the goofy farm boy Taylor loved, just as he did that fateful night. Taylor held what transpired in the pavilion from Sean, finishing her last chore. Of course, Sean using his power set some alarm triggers off to the Queen, and Taylor's answers only changed questions into a lecture, one that Taylor had no intention of relaying no matter how many bandages she'd be required to wrap. After a day like Taylor had in being ordered about as one does some new servant, she drank in their alone time, letting it soothe the edges of her bad attitude.

Deciding the fire and coals were ready to cook on, Taylor put one small pot in the hot embers while she dangled another over the fire. Meals had been prepared hours ago in anticipation of the soldiers' return so they could have a hot meal. Taylor had made sure to secure enough for them both and in doing so it led to their head-on collision.

"How Fate seems to find us," Taylor murmured to the coals.

Sean stood in the tent entrance, clean and wearing cotton clothes, disregarding the formal attire laid out for him. Exiting the tent, Sean walked over to stand by Taylor, as fire danced across both faces, creating odd shadows. Sitting together as their food warmed, they hummed in unison, a single star breaking into view in the dark night sky. Taylor leaned into Sean, his hand slowly stroking her middle back, which comforted her. No matter the number of tents that lay around them, Taylor only knew of herself and Sean.

"I love you…" Taylor whispered.

Sean responded with a squeeze and held on tighter, never to let go again, for this was peace. Images of a farm and children played in Sean's mind; picturing Taylor running after a little boy who held a wooden sword in each hand brought a grin to Sean's face. In the South, the cold winter would never come, and neither would the loneliness that crept in with it. 'This is why I would move to the South if given the chance when the war is over—to forever be ensconced in the warmth of those I love," Sean thought as a tear fell from his right eye.

Chapter 35: Swarm of Darkness

Wails rose up to the starless night sky as the Skulker passed through Wanderers, uttering a low growl. They opened up a path giving it a wide berth. Fatigued and angry, the Skulker had little time for their slow movement aside, an unlucky Grunt squashed beneath its feet sent a strong message to the others. The march north took longer than expected and only added to the rage felt by the Skulker. Finally, they would find blood and flesh to rip, it so badly wanted to shred apart flesh. The gunk of the dead Grunt between its toes brought a toothy grin to the one- eyed Skulker's face.

Hordes of every kind gathered in one giant swarm around a clearing where two other Skulkers sat atop a large boulder protruding from the ground. Approaching slowly, the one-eyed Skulker sized up the other two commanders sent along for the attack. On its left stood a fifteen-foot giant, a Skulker with claws reaching a foot in length and a battle ax strapped to its back. He was known to use claws first to rip flesh. On the right, thirteen feet in height with a three-foot horn protruding from its forehead and two small swords on the waist made it a fierce Skulker, crafty to fight. Its horn was enticing for opponents to rush in, but its drawn sword would finish them first. If not for these two to help command, their gathered force would kill itself by sheer madness and bloodlust. 'Though, that never would be admitted to another openly,' the one-eyed Skulker thought darkly.

Eight thousand creatures ready to devour flesh and prove their might vibrated expectantly as the one-eyed Skulker stepped upon the boulder. The other two Skulkers weighed the one-eyed Skulker's ability much the same, eyes coming to the single-edged sword attached to its back. On the one-eyed Skulker's hip sat another single-edged sword, on the other side were barbs of metal dotting its black steel. It was meant to pierce an opponent and rip any flesh upon withdrawal, gruesome to the fullest extent. Stopping once on top and next to the other commanders the one- eyed Skulker surveyed the clearing, having to turn in a circle for the full view.

A true swarm writhing in anticipation, waiting for the command to advance at any second. As the Skulker stare down ended, each raised a blood curdling roar signifying war and screeches rang from below in response. The One-Eyed Skulker let loose one last roar layered in bloodlust and beat its chest with a thick arm. Shooting in three different directions, the swarm broke apart as troops moved, followed behind by a Skulker each.

"War…" the one-eyed Skulker grumbled gleefully.

Thunder from above drowned out the noises made by the Wanderers marching to the North, giant Clashers descended out of the darkness scooping up Skulker's on their backs. The oldest and largest beasts had been given by the Dark Wizard to use however the Skulkers deemed fit. Resting its eye—the one-eyed Skulker let Clasher fly into the night far enough away to not be seen, the picture of Sean set firmly in its mind.

Chapter 36: Nightmares Before Battle

Taylor lay under the night sky, her head in Sean's lap, stomach full and embers from their fire glowing. Most went to bed already leaving quiet in the camp, voices less frequent except a sentry every fifteen minutes. Taylor held off going back into that hot tent which stood with the flaps wide open. The empty cots in the tent were its only occupants and neither made a move to change that. Besides, Taylor preferred the ground for some reason. Although here this far south it gave Taylor a bad vibe and made home seem so far away. Not only the ground gave off this feeling, but the heat and air as well in a way that seemed a chilling omen.

Sean's hands gently picked Taylor's head up. Catching the hint, she sat upright, at eye level with him. Smiling, Sean stood up, walked to his pack to retrieve … what? Taylor couldn't tell. Sean came back holding his arms behind him, and returning to the exact previous vacated spot, Sean revealed a wooden flute. Blowing air softly into the flute Sean started moving fingers along its holes to create music around them, sound coming slowly at first. To Taylor's amazement, the notes began to blend, picking up speed the song forging together until she recognized what Sean played.

"Winter's Melting Melody of Sorrow," Taylor whispered.

Picking the tune up, Taylor hummed along in harmony as each dark note carried onward a story of old. Taylor remembered reading it at a younger age from a book called "Tales of Old Wind" yet exact details of the tale eluded her. As they continued, their notes took on a new life like light shining through dark melodies morphed. Nearing the final act, Taylor began to hum the notes with heat, faster to evolve into … it was then she noticed that Sean had stopped playing.

"Well, Farm Boy...finish it already," Taylor teased.

"It seems odd to say...but you were coming in a little early…" Sean replied sheepishly.

Rolling her eyes at the comment, Taylor picked back up where they left off, followed by Sean, melodies joining together. All other sound died away except their tune which entrapped even sentries making the rounds. The last note faded into the night, heat radiating from Sean's face as he caught breath. It had been some time since he last played. Clinking mail signaled that their visitors were returning to duty in a hurry to get back to their watch. Satisfied at what they created together, exhaustion finally seeped into Sean's bones.

Sean stood and picked Taylor up, attempting to be romantic in going to bed. Closing the tent flap, the world fell away, leaving Taylor and Sean in peace. Worry pricked deep in Sean's mind as sleep fell. No matter how tightly he held Taylor, this worry smoldered like coals from their dying fire. The world of dreams banked this ember and Sean lay wrought with nightmares of places he knew not. They made Sean toss and turn, only from exhaustion did Sean stay asleep as night wore on.

Screams from a woman far in the distance raked Sean's consciousness and brought him awake, his sword in hand. Taylor met his gaze, alerted to other noises around them, and anticipating an attack; Sean shivered as cold sweat poured forth. That woman's scream fit his nightmare so well it made Sean's heart beat fast as if he had been running for days. In the dream, Sean had stood deep underground, rotten filth scattered about covering every surface and the smell made Sean queasy. Tortured screams of a woman echoed in what seemed a cavern beneath the ground and the woman relenting screams only to take breath. The screams were replaced by a soft whisper out of darkness, until more screeching drowned all other noise. Shadows loomed toward Sean eagerly…he gripped the sword even tighter.

Alarm horns sounded, bringing Sean back to reality of their tent, covered in cold sweat and feeling nauseated, Sean gasped, trying to calm down. In one swoop, Sean stood, donned mail and boots ready to battle whatever lay in the dark. Taylor was not far behind, strapped sword sheaths on her hip and back, a grim expression mixed with concern painted her angelic face into something darker. Shaking his head free of the dream, Sean opened the tent flap to find twenty soldiers running southwest. Sean checked to see that Taylor was right behind him, as both stepped out to discover what was going on.

Reaching a main road in the sea of tents they continued southwest as more soldiers fell in line. Some Sean recognized from his contingent or Cogarth's, but others seemed fresh to the camp. Among the throng, Sean spotted Cogarth ahead shouting orders standing by a bearded general who took reports of scouts before trotting toward the Red Pavilion. Seeing the man's calm demeanor, Sean did likewise; contorting features into a composed look, he reached Cogarth.

"Ho! What is going on?" Sean shouted over the roar of boots.

"Sean! Bless the Light!" Cogarth responded in kind.

Stepping closer, Cogarth lowered his voice to normal levels, keeping confidential information from prying ears.

"Sentries were found dead early this morning—killed by Wanderers."

Sean's blood ran cold with rage and anger. "Filthy beasts."

Nodding in agreement, Cogarth continued. "Alarm is raised, soldiers gather to patrol our picket lines to weed out any further intrusions. Sean, what was left…it's almost as if they had been tortured. A maiden found them just outside our camp perimeter near the woods."

"Where do you need us Cogarth? I can scour our perimeter using Life to find any vile beasts stalking the shadows."

"Nesar is already ahead doing so. The advance group has found tracks and a party will be sent out on top of our patrol scouts. Your presence is requested at the Queen's tent; both of you, that is," Cogarth added hastily noticing Taylor beginning to snarl.

"What of the Wanderers? My tracking skills and expertise could be needed?" Taylor asked, keeping her voice normal instead of yelling at her friend.

"Our Queen has demanded this most of all: for you and Sean to hold back in case things escalate."

"Humph! I grow tired of waiting on her to let us loose. What does she need, more linens?"

Cogarth's face darkened. "This is our Queen's direct order. Do not defy it, or else."

"Or else?"

"That's right—or else I have to escort you there by any means necessary."

Taylor's hand shot over Cogarth's mouth in a flash and words left hanging fell away. Taylor's face, full of murderous rage, brought only intrigue to Cogarth's eyes as he casually removed his muzzle. Sean watched the exchange in growing confusion, unsure how to separate the two from each other if they decided to fight. What Cogarth could be hinting at eluded Sean, but pressing matters took priority and Cogarth backed down.

"Hop to! I have other matters to tend and soldiers needing direction," Cogarth ordered, giving Sean a pleading look. "No detours, understood?"

Sean and Taylor nodded in unison, Cogarth, accepting their agreement, sauntered off to a group of soldiers donning armor and swords, awaiting orders. Turning back where they had come, Sean practically dragged Taylor toward the crimson pavilion. It looked blood red in the morning light, the sun peaking above the horizon. 'A bad omen,' Sean thought, mind whirling as if battle loomed sooner than expected. Triple guards on the pavilion clogged the road considerably as each one guarded its entrance, vigilance on high alert. Messengers filtered in and out, scrolls of new orders along with reports from scouting parties made Sean and Taylor's wait to enter unbearable.

Finally taking it no longer, Sean channeled air to create a path in; guards reacted immediately drawing swords as one messenger was knocked to the ground, hitting Sean's invisible barrier. Striding inside, Sean worried not that the guard's pride might be hurt for the intrusion, Wanderer sightings made it far more pressing to be in the know.

Helping the boy up, Taylor saw him scramble away perplexed at what happened and followed Sean inside. Gesturing to the guards as an apology, their swords returned in sheaths and commerce resumed as Sean released the air. Darkness closed, in causing Taylor to blink as her eyes adjusted to the tent light in time to see two corpses sprawled on a table, surrounded by several generals, the Queen, Sean, Maddox, and a raven-haired lady Taylor knew quite well. Reaching the table for a closer look revealed a disturbing site; corpse was an overstatement.

Sean clenched his jaw tightly, keeping down the bile, for what lay in front of him was gruesome. The two sentries' remains were riddled with maggots on flesh remnants, teeth marks on bone, but the eyes - gaping holes covered in black ooze stared back at Sean. Noticing Taylor opposite him, Sean backed away and moved to stand by her side. Reaching down his hand, Sean found Taylor's, and gripped it tightly. She reciprocated the motion, each taking comfort in the other's presence.

"Some may know the cost of losing those who do not take heed at this sight. Shadow consumes living, turns it rotten and creates more Wanderers here. These brave men paid a steep price for us never to forget." The Queen's words caused shudders around and reality at what lay ahead set ruin for those who thought Wanderers' danger had dissipated.

Summoning fire, Maddox burned the remains and Nesar used air to push smoke away, outside. Releasing fire, only ash sat on the table and Eyonka looked about at the faces gathered.

"Now then, to battle…" Eyonka spoke, issuing orders for war.

Chapter 37: Shadows Lurking Within

Cogarth pushed a branch away from his face, avoiding a spider web in the process. A hundred men marched through foliage heading southwest in pursuit of their enemy. Ten other groups advanced in similar fashion, spread apart by one hundred yards, checking for signs of Wanderers. Cogarth had been training for this nearly all his life, ever since a Wanderer slaughtered everyone he once loved. Small tracks and disturbed brush meant nothing, but big oozing blobs of filth told a different story. Mid-morning sun filtered through the treetops, adding more heat to the blasted southlands. Raising his hand, Cogarth signaled for the men to halt. He picked up a nearby stick, crouching. Gingerly, Cogarth prodded the black ooze to hear a hiss coming from bark, causing him to drop the twig immediately. An hour searching yielded this find and ahead another pool could be spotted. Rising, Cogarth drew a sword and patted his shirt pocket to ensure the letter had not fallen out. Taking another sweep at the surroundings, Cogarth signaled the men to move forward, for their trail was hot.... much like this weather.

Another half hour of searching yielded three more black ooze pools and now tracks much too large for any regular animal. Cogarth's pulse quickened, yet his face revealed nothing but courage; his men expected to die here, and if his bravery could change that then it was his sole duty. Selecting two soldiers out of the group, Cogarth ordered them to scout ahead twenty feet from the left and twenty-five feet from the right. Taking the middle, they advanced, preparing to kill any opponent foolish enough to cross their paths.

Brush began to fade away as trees opened into a clearing which made Cogarth gulp. In the middle of the treeless field sat a giant rock surrounded by grass, the rock surface broken up only by a hole here and there. What made Cogarth wary to approach the rock was how that grass sat lying down, blades bent showing signs of travel by lots of feet. Gazing across the clearing it appeared this was true of every blade, and as his eyes returned to the rock, Cogarth noticed the smell—rotting flesh wafted on the eastern breeze toward Cogarth, and he knew it too well. Turning left, Cogarth saw the soldier covering his nose, to the right much the same.

Taking a step back, Cogarth watched them follow, cautious not to make a noise on retreat. All was working until "Snap!" rang across the clearing which forced Cogarth to look right. The soldier sat pale faced and pointed toward the rock, his mouth frozen in a silent scream.

Cogarth turned to find a large Skulker standing on the rock, and from this distance it appeared to be smiling. With its presence discovered, all hopes of a quiet retreat was gone, and Cogarth could think of only one thing to do. A snarl grew inside to issue a challenge when the beast reared its head back and howled—a howl so fierce it could turn bone to jelly rang through the clearing and that was when the ground trembled.

Fifty Hunters surged forth into the grassy clearing from the rock holes Cogarth had seen, closing the gap at a frightening pace. Thousands of black scaly forms rushed in from the southeast to find blood and flesh in a frenzy. All Warrior or above at the front of the second wave leading the charge, black swords drawn, prepared to slay.

"Run!" Cogarth yelled, sword in hand.

The ambush of Wanderers was well set against the numbers in Cogarth's command. It meant instant death to any human and it was Cogarth's duty to report this. At the least, warn the Queen of where the enemy would attack from, for defying these odds seemed an impossible task. Soldiers picked through the terrain, retracing their steps till the brush again was thick; each man hacking and slashing to clear a path. Every swipe inched the human force backward, but still Wanderers closed the gap and yelps, growls and howls were heard as if right on their backs. Pulling aside one soldier, Cogarth handed him the emergency report and the letter.

"Be sure only Sean gets it. It's of the utmost importance you hold, soldier!" Cogarth ordered between breaths.

Saluting hand over fist, the soldier accepted his duty and began to run ahead when a set of claws ripped through his back, crushing the spine like a twig being snapped. Cogarth watched in horror, unable to stop the beast from killing his subordinate, the body crumpled to the ground. Cogarth snapped out of shock, and in a rage, slashed the Wanderer in half, as it spewed black blood everywhere. Shouting at the oncoming horde with fury, the Hunters paused, waiting to see Cogarth's next move. Stepping toward them, Cogarth took up a battle stance prepared to die for the information he had given up and avenge his soldier's death at least. One Hunter strode forward slowly, its companions bullied through brush all around, chasing men who ran in panic. Bellowing a roar, the Hunter then struck at Cogarth, sending the rest to follow suit, emitting roars of their own. Bracing for bloodshed, Cogarth swung at this first beast to find only ... air?

Cogarth's neck prickled sensing use of the power; it always happened whenever Nesar was around or Sean channeled wind. Looking to the sky, Cogarth found its source: a shimmer appeared out of thin air and Nesar sat floating high above. His blade still locked in place, Cogarth struggled to render it free; the baffled Hunter held back its attack, watching the sword hang motionless. Slowly Nesar removed his helmet to free a face of gnarled bark, his eyes alight with green madness, smile to match.

Nesar lowered himself to the ground. He had stopped the blade mid-strike without even raising a sword or hand—only by his Ancient power. The shock on Cogarth's face showed a fraction before the Hunter ripped him apart and Cogarth's corpse lay mutilated. Smiling, Nesar then honed his power to kill the approaching Wanderer horde; luckily, the group numbered a thousand, else Nesar would have been in trouble. Strong wind ripped through the trees toppling all toward the clearing where the ambush had struck. Bodies of Wanderer and man alike lay in the debris, none survived its strike save the Skulker standing atop the rock. The remaining men to the north scrambled to camp none the wiser at Nesar's intervention, only hearing the falling lumber coming from the south. The trees hid the dust cloud from sight and sounds of their labored breathing was all that could be heard. With the job complete and Wanderers' dead, Nesar placed his helmet back on to cover up his face before slipping back into the shadows.

"A fool's death to a fool who knew too much," Nesar whispered as tree shadows hid the Ancient once more.

Chapter 38: Fire Raining Above

Reports of the advancing Wanderers had reached camp before Cogarth's soldiers barreled into the perimeter, eyes mad and covered in scratches, they wept, screaming of ambush. Another group scouted around 7,000 Wanderers fast approaching and returned casualty free, but the latest group raised an alarm. Medics were set to treat any injuries of Cogarth's men and quiet their cries of terror. Nowhere could their captain be found and Eyonka feared Cogarth dead. Little time remained to search for the Demi-Ancient who remained. Issuing orders to the generals, troops took up position in the trenches, waiting for the sound of battle.

Sean sat in a trench hidden by the smallest layer of dirt held aloft using Earth. Darkness enveloped him and the men alike. His heart fluttering like mad, Sean tried to not think about his dream from the night before. Maddox squatted to Sean's right and a thousand men depended on the concentration he now used to channel this intricately woven deception. 'Light be with us now, the hour of battle is upon us,' Sean prayed inside.

Pieces set in place, Eyonka looked out upon the battlefield from the red pavilion surveying defenses and the traps set in place. To the south, 4,000 men in full armor lay in waiting to meet the Wanderer army, half in trenches and the other half lined up in neat rows to lure the enemy forward. To the north, another 4,000 men on horseback sat hidden by a tent waiting for the command to charge into the fray. Lady Sloane had been sent a message to warn Gadriel of the army and order his 10,000 men into battle. They would crash into the Wanderers from the east like a boom to end the battle. Eyonka hoped they had not camped far away from the temple and that news would reach them in time. Based on troop numbers alone, they held an advantage, but if the horde that approached consisted mainly of Hunters, it could prove a turning point for the enemy. Finally, Nessar, who reported the enemy advancement first, took up to his special post well beyond to the North of the encampment. At Nesar's command were several hundred Sea Folk who only joined by Maddox's request, the Sea King calling upon old fealties sworn.

"Is it enough, though?" Eyonka muttered aloud.

"Have faith, my Queen," Taylor replied, hands in knots of worry gripping her dress to keep them still.

Taylor's eyes focused on the far side of the mountain of fire where a wide expanse of dirt sat shifting, vibrating slightly. There Sean would be waiting on command to join in the fight and it was with him Taylor's heart lay. No more petty arguing over duties or position in the battle plan, Taylor knew they would find each other in the battle and now it was her responsibility to defend her Queen. Subconsciously, Taylor fingered the hilts of Doomed Fate and Fate Avenger at her hip. The Ancient blade hummed with life in expectation at the bloodshed to come.

Under the dirt covering, no other noise could be heard. The eerie quiet was discomforting to Sean. Channeling earth, Sean felt the shifting of the soldiers boots all around signaling that their position was set and the anxiety raging throughout the men amplified within him. Worry at Cogarth's disappearance seeped in, and he fought it away as if wrestling a bear. In the days prior, Taylor had insisted on joining Sean, but in the end, Eyonka ordered her as guard to the Queen. 'Safest place there is,' Sean thought tenderly. They said their brief goodbyes, vowing to meet on the battlefield when Eyonka's troops advanced, and with a kiss, Sean left to construct their trap.

Sean had been given strict instructions against using Life, for Wanderers could sense it a mile away like a moth senses a flame. Blind to what happened above in the bright sky, Sean waited for the signal to advance and join the fray. Slight trembles of earth signaled the horde's arrival—nearly 5,000 Wanderers, Sean guessed from the distant vibrations. They came from the southwest making a direct line to the Temple of Fire, aiming to fight the men waiting above the trenches. It wasn't until a second set of trembling from the southeast that Sean's stomach turned, threatening to empty what little contents it held.

"They are attacking from two directions…" Sean whispered to Maddox.

Chaos is what Taylor saw as a horde of over 5,000 Wanderers spilled from trees coming out of the southwest, making a line toward the Army of Stars. Her stomach was in knots at the sheer numbers, and the Wanderers made looking at that false patch of dirt hard to avoid. It was hard to gauge at such a distance, but their size indicated there were Hunters mixed with Warriors at the front lines, with the rear brought up by Grunts on all fours. As front lines clashed, Taylor saw soldiers hack and slash at the black mass, who in return used swords and claws. The Star Army's formation had been designed to propel men forward, a line at a time. Shield bearers yielded openings to swordsmen behind the attack, then covered them once more. This fluid motion laid waste to the first few lines of small-framed Warriors and Hunters until the larger, slower beasts caught up. Grunts leapt into the air, toppling shield bearers with their teeth gnashing, seeking flesh.

Eyonka's eyes began calculating their odds to win the moment lines met. The numbers were on their side, for only 5,000 came to fight. The army remained locked together as it took more effort to kill the larger Wanderers, but hope was not yet lost. Lines began to move forward, pushing hordes back, casualties looking light on their side. Men in the trenches had not joined in the main fighting—they slaughtered any who ventured to their depths over the mounds of dirt. Eyonka's heart sank as another horde emerged from the southeast to flank the main force of men, 3,000 strong spilled into the battle catching men held back in the trenches unawares. Distance closed in as both swarms of dark beasts pressed forward like a tidal wave. Apprehension hung thick in the air like smoke as the battle came to a climax, soldiers of the Star Army forced to abandon trenches were pressed back to the main force holding its ground.

Then everything broke as a Hunter emerged upright, swinging a dark hammer, smashing shields and bone, dismantling the front lines. Human soldiers bumped into human soldiers from the trenches as both forces collided, offering distraction enough for the Wanderers to strike amid the confusion. Taylor gasped as everything so meticulously planned out seemed to fall apart and she itched to join in the fight. Looking beyond the front line toward the tree line, her heart skipped a beat. Standing with no care in the world was ... impossible! A Skulker missing an eye, wielding a single-edged sword, surveyed the fight—an enemy who had nearly destroyed Sean and who Taylor foolishly thought she could match. The carefree attitude of the Skulker made Taylor shiver; they might defeat the horde to a point but a Skulker as skilled as this one was worth a thousand Hunters.

"My Queen, we must turn tides now, else the Shadow wins," Taylor said, her tone foreboding.

Beneath the ground, Sean thought he heard thunder. Concentrating, he felt hooves beating fast as the Queen surged to join the fighting. The lines had broken, and Sean knew the second wave of Wanderers had crushed the defenses set in the trenches, forcing men to retreat and regroup in the main force. Exactly how the main force fell remained unknown, though it would be disastrous if Eyonka chose to skip a few phases in the plan. Sean looked questioningly to Maddox who only shrugged, their signal to enter not yet given, and should have come before Eyonka's charge. Reflecting on the battle so far, it seemed to move in their direction, but it had slowed for a reason Sean could not understand. The next stage of their plan had been for Gadriel's forces to intercept the group of approaching Wanderers, but no sign of them arriving had been seen or felt. Even without their aid, it should be Sean rising up to spring the trap, not Eyonka riding out. Either way, Sean braced to react however this played out, hoping the signal to join would be raised.

"Please hold," Sean whispered, feeling helpless.

A thousand Hunters fought the front line, pressing the army back while spreading soldiers thin as more Grunts snuck past. Their bite was deadly, and Eyonka made sure to kill every Grunt she could by throwing stones large enough to crack skulls with her power. Letting guards fend off Warriors so Eyonka's concentration remained undivided, Taylor slew more than most. Blood thirst filled the girl's blue eyes and Taylor's sword singing through air gave an appearance of a devilish angel. The cavalry riding in to flank the Wanderers had bolstered defenses, but the battle sprawled outward into near chaos.

Inch by inch, the push back to the Fire Temple's base threatened Sean's hidden trench; it would be exposed any moment, revealing their trap prematurely. Eyonka could not let this happen or else the only play they'd have would be the secret weapon waiting in the wind. Searching the ground, Eyonka found a shallow magma vein, and using her power, created a moat of fiery magma, carefully carving the earth to control its flow. Like a snake of fire, the magma poured into a thin line sealing the Wanderers' fate in the depths of fire. Eyonka dared not make the trench larger, for it could swallow up her own soldiers as well. Satisfied that they pushed back enough to hold their position, Eyonka covered over the trench with solid ground. She then issued orders to the guardsmen to occupy the empty space with rows of shields held at the ready. Successfully shielding their trap, Eyonka focused again on killing Grunts, and now Warrior class Wanderers alike, with the stones all around. Like riding a horse, the motion flowed naturally to Eyonka, picking up a stone and loosing it with deadly force to meet its target; sometimes several at once.

"Almost time," Eyonka said, but nobody heard as battle raged.

The Skulker smiled at this wondrous feast spread out before him. Terran flesh tasted the best and he could eat for years on what lay on the ground. His single eye greedily scanned the dead bodies. Even the four-legged creatures would not be spared from death, for his Master demanded nothing less. Still, Sean had not shown up to the battle, and the Skulker grew impatient. The other two were working outward in the front lines but he had to sit back. They had not been given the mission to retrieve this Ancient for their Master. The one-eyed Skulker dare not tell them of it either for fear they would take credit from him.

"Arrugh!!" the one-eyed Skulker howled aloud.

"Maddox, Nessar should have arrived by now, but I do not sense him. What could be delaying the crafty Ancient?" Sean asked aloud.

"Patience Sean, he will come; hold a bit longer. We must have faith," Maddox replied.

Nodding in grim response, Sean held the worry at bay, amazed at Maddox disregarding his usual sea shanty speech. There was a lot to this Ancient comrade Sean still had to learn, it seemed … 'If we make it that long,' he thought darkly. Tremors in the ground had piqued Sean's curiosity and a feeling of heat came through the dirt. Moments later it dissipated, and he heard sounds of boots close to the trench opening. Vibrations told them of men in lines holding shields, defending their position; still no signal to join, which greatly irritated Sean.

Taylor breathed deeply after another Hunter lay dead at her feet, the procession of guards protecting the Queen all unharmed spoke of their skill in combat. Since joining this fight, Taylor had left a trail of corpses, felling Wanderers with both blades, no matter the size. Now three Hunters loomed ahead, gnashing black teeth as a threat to kill Taylor, but there was no fear of them inside her. Taylor drew breath and beckoned them forward, baiting a fight. The first howled while lunging directly at Taylor, claws extended to slice off her armor. Side stepping its attack, Taylor swung the right blade at its neck, making a clean cut. The next two attacked as one with blades drawn; retreating a step, Taylor blocked, then parried blows simultaneously. Going on the offensive, Taylor swung to the Hunter on her left, Doomed Fate slicing calf muscle open forcing it to the ground. The third struck with claws, sword abandoned. It connected with Taylor's armor, leaving a scratch in the metal. Its claw was not deep enough to pierce flesh on Taylor's shoulder, but the armor would be useless. Smiling, Taylor sliced off its forearm, then the head came next, black blood splattering everywhere. Coming back to the Hunter lying on the ground, calf muscle spilled out, Taylor stuck it through the chest and the beast died, bellowing a wail as air left its lungs.

"Now how about a challenge," Taylor joked darkly, looking for her next target.

More Hunters stepped forward to fill the void. They cared little that Taylor had just slayed three at once. The guards closed ranks with Taylor, forming a tight circle, allowing their Queen to rest a moment. As a unit they fought, and more bodies littered the ground. One Grunt attempted to jump above the defense, but its belly found cold steel, a warning to the others running around thinking the same thought.

Eyonka looked upon the battle, eyes calculating and searching for larger threats of Skulkers but only Hunters popped into view. Other groups of soldiers separated from the main unit took up similar formations to the guards surrounding Eyonka. Soon a rally cry would need to be issued to reform ranks. Eyonka's gut told her to hold off, as the time was not yet right. Rallying too soon could spell defeat. Taking up more stones, Eyonka channeled them to an approaching wall of Warriors and they crumpled to the ground. If defeat was a certainty, Eyonka knew opening the ground to swallow all would work; costly, but war meant sacrifice.

Finally, Sean could stand it no longer; Nessar was their signal to join, but he remained nowhere to be found. Opening to Life, Sean used its power invoking Life vision, and bright spots of life signs dotted the surface, showing the battle to him for the first time. Lines broke long ago as human soldiers and Wanderers fought mingled together in one single mass. Groups of soldiers sat linked up together in rings around the battlefield with dark masses of Hunters pressing forward. A quick count showed the numbers still favored the Army of Stars. A large force was held a hundred yards off but none of the smaller groups moved to join.

Then things shifted. Wanderers began to pull away, leaving fights unfinished heading toward a new direction. After watching them move, Sean realized they all congregated in a single place where a small number of men sat holding shields. Looking above, a large sign of Life signaled the presence of another Ancient, Eyonka, and her shape raised an arm high to the sky. Fearing that using Life was a mistake, Sean dropped its energy, letting lights blink out to leave them again in darkness.

"Maddox, ready for battle." Sean said, voice grim.

Eyonka watched in horror as the Wanderers' attention turned away from soldiers to one focal point: Sean's location. 'The idiot used his power of Life! He was supposed to wait!' Eyonka screamed in her head, anger threatening to burst outward. Channeling her rage, Eyonka summoned earth which exploded upwards. Giant rocks, guided by Eyonka, found targets, killing on impact, but still the Wanderers surged forward. 2,000 Hunters with blades drawn posed a challenge, but it offered an option Eyonka had held back.

"Rally! Rally to your Queen!" Eyonka boomed and banners raised to signal the main force.

Soldiers close by grouped in formation to their Queen and Eyonka channeled the ground, throwing up walls in the path of approaching Wanderers. There was a chance the main force, now free of combat, could pincer the enemy; it lay on generals to maneuver them so. Trusting them to read their Queen's intentions was the only hope; it had never come up during strategy sessions. Foregoing the planned signal, Eyonka removed the dirt that covered Sean and with her might she dumped it on the Wanderers, now twenty feet away.

"March in the Light and vanquish the Shadow!" Eyonka roared, setting off a fury of battle cries down the line from officers in her wake.

Taylor yelled loudest of them all. Watching those Wanderers turn in their direction brought butterflies to her chest. Though a layer of men separated Taylor from the Hunters at the front lines, she knew their concentrated force would drive in like a nail. This might be the final fight of the battle and Taylor's adrenaline pumped wildly, ready to dismember any who tried to reach her love.

Fresh air filled Sean's lungs as the dirt flew up out of his control, the bright sunlight above a welcome relief. Words lost, Sean took his sword up to lead men out of the trench into the fight and he set upon the task before him: killing Wanderers. Topping the dirt, Sean saw a sea of dark, writhing figures coming at every angle, threatening to close the gap of dirt between his force and Eyonka's. Years of fear, regret and hate filled each swing of the sword as Sean hacked each Wanderer that crossed his path. One goal was on Sean's mind: to back up the men who had defended their position for so long.

The blade hummed to life at the first contact of blood. A Grunt that Sean sliced in half rolled down the trench, spilling black blood in the dirt. Soldiers followed his charge into battle, tearing into the beasts as if they were made of paper. Sean sensed he needed to channel Air around their swords and his group became Wanderer slayers. Hunters stopped to challenge Sean, but he felled them easily like swatting an annoying bug. The disarray of Wanderers from every side forced his thousand men into a tight line defending the Temple, and like a single organism, they pressed forward, hoping to meet up with Eyonka before they were cut off from each other. Using trenches to gain a foothold, the progress was slow; up one, then back down to regroup on the other side.

Maddox chose to fight with the power rather than a sword. Fire leapt from his fingers, burning Wanderers to death. Atop a dirt rise, Maddox closed his eyes, gathering power to a focal point above his head till it wanted to burst. Opening his eyes, Maddox let free a fireball, spanning 10 feet in diameter to the left horde of Wanderers and an explosion followed as flames scorched the ground. Warmed up, Maddox began firing smaller balls of fire in a similar fashion, taking care to not hit the soldiers close by. A Hunter who had come too close forced Maddox to draw a blade, and using Fire he lit the sword to a blaze, slicing through easily. Sean seemed to use a similar trick with Air on the soldiers' blades and it worked for Maddox, too; grinning wildly, the mad man joined in the bloodshed.

Boots marching caught Sean's attention and he spared a moment to look at what was happening. Eyonka rode headfirst to the Wanderers toward Sean. At Eyonka's right stood Taylor, grinning, both swords out and armor slightly dented. The afternoon sun gave Taylor's blonde hair a look of fire which added to her haunting beauty, but Sean's seed of worry grew. Rallying to Sean's line, they joined together, leaving the slightest of gaps to allow Wanderers who dared to die through the space. Their focus was on Sean alone and they no longer paid attention to the Fire Temple. In the distance, Sean could make out the remaining main force marching to pincer the Wanderers whose numbers were dwindling quickly.

Releasing the channel of Air around soldiers, blades Sean counted on their skill to be enough to finish off the remaining Wanderers. 1,200 Hunters swarmed the groups led by Sean and Eyonka, the toughest left of 7,000 who charged into battle. Taking a breather, Sean scoped out the biggest target to take down. Energy was best invested on focusing on them first. Among the swarm, several stuck out above the rest, but two caught Sean's eye: a fifteen-foot-tall Skulker with claws a foot long, a giant black axe strapped to its back and a thirteen-foot Skulker with a three-foot horn lumbered in the mass of Hunters. One to the left and one to the right, they meant to split apart the Star Army's rally. The clawed Skulker swung at soldiers, knocking them aside with ease while the horned Skulker ran through soldiers, blood glinting off the tip in the sunlight.

Maddox took to fighting the horned Skulker, sending more fireballs at it and ordering men to retreat. There could be no repeat of the last fight with a Skulker, concern for troops would only get in Maddox's mind. Fire engulfed the Skulker who screeched in pain but still it moved onward, not totally fazed by the burns. Channeling full power, Maddox began a deadly dance with his sword in hand, staying out of reach from the horn's sharp point. Frustrated, the Skulker drew two black swords and fervently struck at Maddox with every blade at its disposal. Such an attack left it poorly guarded, and Maddox released a pillar of fire on the beast, so hot its scales melted to the ground. A charred husk sizzled at Maddox's feet, the horn resembling a half-burned candle, and cheers rose from the men around. Filled with renewed energy, they set out to finish off the remaining Hunters.

The clawed Skulker moved in on Eyonka's position, each lumbering step tore the ground up, leaving large footprints. After joining up with Sean, Eyonka had positioned herself to protect the temple so as to leave Sean free to move about. The group held strong as a Skulker stopped fifty feet away and Sean saw the Skulker settle on his next target: Eyonka. Just as Sean was about to order a full retreat, a shadow covered up the sun.

Dropping from the sky came a massive Sea Terran ship and at its helm sat Nesar. The Ancient had to properly hold wooden beams with Air to move it so the ship would not break in half. Maddox's men jumped into action, firing cannons at the horde surrounding the clawed Skulker, breaking their lines with ease. The Star Army watched as iron fell to the ground, killing Hunters, decimating numbers and leaving corpses strewn about. Maddox jumped up from the trench after resting and began slicing Wanderers as well. The battle had broken into full swing and over 6,000 Wanderers were dead, but Sean knew it was far from finished.

A cannon fired at the clawed Skulker and it knocked aside the projectile with ease, releasing a bellow to rally its troops. Cries rose to answer the call and they pushed on, discarding the thought of fleeing. From deep behind the enemy lines another roar erupted; the one-eyed Skulker had joined the fight at long last. The clawed Skulker grinned, knowing reinforcements were on the way. How wise it had been to leave a thousand good swords behind at the meeting place. The vile human trash would fall this day yet; then the conquerors would revel in a feast the likes of which no one had never seen.

Eyonka looked at the massive vessel now sailing above and marveled at its cannon fire taking out Wanderers. Their last trump card played, it would be on soldiers' will and strength to determine the outcome of battle. Gadriel failed to show and would pay dearly for the cowardice; on Eyonka's honor he would. Eyonka had lost track of Taylor during the commotion, but she knew the girl would be at Sean's side fighting. Enough men sat around to protect Eyonka in case anything dared approach; the jury was still out on whether there would be any punishment for abandoning post, but Eyonka would handle it after the battle.

Smoke filled the air and Wanderer stench everywhere made focusing difficult. The clawed Skulker was clearing a path with ease to where Eyonka stood. 'How did we do this in the old days?' Eyonka thought. Smiling, she summoned her full power of earth and the world began to quake. Directing the quake to where the clawed Skulker headed, Eyonka shifted the channel and the ground shivered like a wave in water. Wanderers lost footing, scrambling to keep their balance and as the wave subsided, a large rock wall appeared, cutting off all access to the temple. Focusing on the fight in front of her once more, Eyonka chuckled as the clawed Skulker howled in frustration at being thwarted.

"Well my friend, I am your opponent and don't you forget it," Eyonka said with a laugh.

Amid the fighting and converging of armies on both sides, Taylor found Sean and formed ranks hacking at any Wanderers who came close to him. Both swords glistened with black blood and each swing flung specks in the enemies' eyes. Soon they developed a rhythm taking Hunters and Warriors down with practiced ease. It was in such harmony that corpses piled around them. As the last close Hunter fell,

Taylor breathed deeply, taking brief reprieve at their work and Sean followed suit. Catching his eye, Taylor nodded toward the next group and grinned as he took off to lead the way. It was here that the ground shook and Taylor's skin prickled, sensing something happening. Glancing at the Queen, she knew the source and quickly clung to Sean as the ground shook in a violent wave. Worry spread through Taylor. She had left the Queen's side and now a steep price might be paid. Dust settled to the ground, the world no longer shook and a vicious howl went up 200 yards ahead. Disengaging from Sean, Taylor turned to face what she knew would come next.

  The clawed Skulker turned back on the armies and it ran forward, raking all in its paths with razor sharp claws. Bodies of humans and Wanderers alike dropped to the ground in heaps before it stopped running, anger in its eyes. Warriors popped in front of Taylor and again their rhythm of block, slash, hack resumed, creating a deadly melody. Taylor checked on the clawed Skulker out of the corner of her eye; it had to be dealt with. Her muscles ached from killing so many in this meticulous dance, powered on by adrenaline and sheer will. She nudged Sean to communicate their next target. Then a sword broke through as Taylor tripped on the corpse of a dead Grunt and she raced to block with her other Fate Avenger. "Clung," Sean's blade came into focus, deflecting dark steel. Gathering herself, Taylor killed the foe that almost ended it all. 'Farm boy will never let me live this one down,' Taylor thought jokingly. Together they headed off toward the clawed Skulker who sat in a circle of dead bodies, eyes filled with rage.

  Sean had saved Taylor's life by mere fractions of a second, and luck had everything to do with it. Sean had no clue how many died by his hand, but it was refreshing to use a sword for life rather than death. The onslaught of Wanderers never ceased, but he knew the battle's outcome fast approached. From what he could see, their soldiers now had to deal with the best of the Hunters, numbers were to the advantage of the Army of Stars, but the beasts left could kill 3 to every 1. The ship had ceased firing some time ago and looked to be landing on the ground, fear of friendly fire evidently the reason for its cessation. Taylor and Sean both tried to level out the playing field while walking to the clawed Skulker. Sean's blade greedily devoured each Wanderer it came across, slicing flesh with ease and Taylor's deathly grace split them in two.

Sean was glad he had released Air from blades long before this point as the strain was great and his energy was needed for this final push. As another pair of Hunters fell to Taylor's swords, Sean could finally see the enemies left to defeat. The clawed Skulker sat alone, waiting on a challenger, debating to attack Eyonka who channeled ground to intimidate the beast. Around 400 Hunters loomed behind them, held at bay by the Star Army who had joined to become one force as more enemies perished. The pincer move had done its job. Eyonka's small force would soon meet up and push to finish them off. Sean could no longer deliberate on where to attack; each moment was costing lives. Sean stepped forward with Taylor right behind; the clawed Skulker had to die.

Hastily Sean released Life as the Skulker drew a pitch-black great sword. The blade had one side of sharp teeth like a saw and the other side sharp-edged; deadly looking on its own, but in a Skulker's hand…Taylor led off the fight, both swords deflecting its sweeping blows, but no opening presented to counter. Wanderers and soldiers alike watched the exchange as steel clanged. The saw edge grazed Taylor's damaged shoulder, scraping through to meet flesh. She let out a great wail and Sean rushed to take over. Air surrounding blade, he sent Skulker backward. An angry snarl graced the grotesque beast's face at being deprived of his kill, but Sean struck faster, rage boiling for Taylor's injury. The snarl fell away to be replaced by 'worry?' Sean thought.

Slowly approaching the clawed Skulker, it fell back a few steps and crouched, ready to run at them. Sean circled left while Taylor circled right, keeping distance so as to not be taken out in one swoop. They hoped it would give the other an opportunity, whomever the clawed Skulker chose to attack. Charging forward, it went after Taylor. Channeling Earth, Sean placed a rock in its path and the clawed Skulker lost footing, presenting Sean a long-awaited opening to kill. Its right claw still carried on, grazing Taylor's left shoulder. The damaged armor broke free and blood dripped from the claws tip. Taylor never cried out in pain; Fate Avenger fell out of her hand in reaction to being hit. Thrusting forward, Sean's sword pierced the armored hide and the clawed Skulker roared loudly in pain. Sean had missed the beast's kill shot by an inch and as the blade pulled free, a new blade protruded inches from Sean's face. Much like how they first met, Taylor's sword hit the Skulker's kill point and its black eyes rolled back. The "thud" could be heard as it fell to the ground dead, and no Wanderer rushed forward in revenge; rather they seemed confused.

"Always the hero making a grand entrance," Sean joked between deep breaths. "Don't collapse on me now."

Taylor gave a smile, kneeling out of exhaustion, red blood trickling from the wound on her arm. With no medics in sight, Sean tore off a piece of fabric from his shirt to bandage the wound. He did the best he could with first aid, all the while fearing using Life in such an exposed position to check Taylor's damaged arm. Patched up, they retrieved Taylor's blade Fate Avenger when thunder crackled from overhead, louder than their cannon fire and Sean looked quickly for its source. Descending above was the largest black bat Sean had ever seen, and on top sat…a Skulker?

"Clasher!" Taylor yelled over the noise.

Sean's stomach leapt into his throat at the sight of the giant Clasher. The beast crashed headfirst into the floating ship, as splintering timber echoed across the plain. Then came creaks and groans as the ship plummeted to earth. Fires raked the vessel and Nesar struggled to hold on. It landed 100 feet from their position, causing Wanderer and soldiers alike to pause fighting. Without thinking, Sean sprinted toward the vessel and Taylor followed, killing Wanderers he left alone. Foregoing the fear of using Life, Sean found survivors and began to pull boards to save the wounded, searching for Nesar. As the last living soldier was pulled free, Sean frantically searched the sky to find his ally.

Locked in mid-air combat was Near fighting Clasher and Skulker, blood dripping to earth below. Sean noticed Nesar healing his wounds with Life, while simultaneously dodging a fatal blow. Then with a twist of his hand, Nesar sliced the Clashers wing using Air. Black blood poured out, and the beast tumbled downward as its one good wing flapped furiously to remain afloat. Fifty feet above the ground, Sean watched in horror as Skulker jumped free to land ahead of Taylor unscathed. It looked on at the army of humans, ignoring Sean and Taylor as if searching the bodies for someone. The Skulker was smaller than the last, but its presence gave an eerie vibe.

Hastily, Sean released Life as the Skulker drew a pitch black single-edged great sword. The shape of the blade had a familiar look to it. Deadly looking on its own, but when in a Skulker's hand… Sean shivered. As the Skulker turned to face Taylor, Sean got a look at the beast and his blood ran cold. It had one eye; a scar ran up its side from a sword stab that Sean knew all too well.

"It can't be…" Sean's voice trailed off.

The crashed ship had brought a party of Hunters to investigate, Sea Folk able to walk picked up swords in an attempt to fend them off. Sean could not leave them alone to take on these beasts and Taylor agreed. The one-eyed Skulker would have to wait. Hopefully allies could come to their aid in time. Sean led the fight, sword swinging to take out Wanderer flesh, with Taylor covering his back. The Sea Folk soldiers watched the exchange as steel clanged. They gathered up the wounded and took up defensive stances.

Eyonka took in the battle, suppressing a smile as the Skulker fell. 'We might just pull this off,' she thought hopefully. Number of casualties Eyonka knew not, but this afternoon had been long and the enemy wavered on the brink of collapse. The falling ship and screech of a Clasher had pulled them back to reality, reminding them that the battle still raged. At first glance, Eyonka saw Sean and Taylor pulling free Sea Folk from the wreckage, a group of Wanderers broke free to kill the easy prey.

Another screech brought Eyonka to look above as Nesar fought the Clasher; it suffered a fatal wound and fell fast. From its back dropped a Skulker and her heart sank as it stood pulling free a sword. Signaling a rally once more, her troops marched forward to execute those Hunters that remained. They could tackle the Skulker next; victory over the horde lay so close at hand. A scout report told of Gadriel's approach and that reinforcements were imminent, but Eyonka feared they were too late. Over the years in battle, experience told Eyonka not to count chickens before they hatch, but a spark of hope ignited her to push further.

Glancing back at Sean, Eyonka saw battle ensued with the group of Hunters that had broken free. Taylor stood out of combat; a bandage wrapped thickly around her arm gave Eyonka pause that they might be in trouble. Without speaking a word to the guards, Eyonka ran to meet up with Sean and Taylor, her heart beating as if it were about to leap out of her chest. The guards followed, leaving other soldiers behind to do what they did best. Time slowed for Eyonka; the distance away was seemingly endless as she watched the fight unfold like a nightmare.

Sean slayed the largest Hunter, air swirling all around him and eyes glowed thick with power. The other Hunters hung back as the Skulker pushed its way into the circle challenging Sean, dark blade casually slung across its shoulders. Turning back to see all who had followed, Eyonka prayed their numbers would be enough to push ahead into the ring of Hunters. Issuing an order to the captain of the guard, Eyonka waited to ensure he had heard and watched a soldier drop back to the main force to carry it out. Knowing help would soon come, Eyonka looked back to the ship wreckage to find an image of Orwick standing over the corpse of…

"No!" Eyonka screamed.

Their victory over the large Hunter was short lived. Sean panted wildly, fending off Hunters who were trying to kill him and Taylor. Fifteen surrounded them on all sides. Using numbers to keep Taylor and Sean at bay, they formed a ring of steel and gnashing teeth. With her arm hurt, Taylor was back to using her right sword only, and things looked bleak. The Hunters kept aid from reaching Sean and no other Ancients were in sight. Wounded Sea Folk had retreated a safe distance away. Gulping, Sean summoned a power he was not fond of—fire. His sword blazed as an inferno engulfed it and rage fed the flame. Slicing through a Hunter's hammer, Sean kept momentum going to cut the beast in half. Turning to his next target, Sean ran a sword through its body and flames leapt to burn the Hunter. The rest looked on in worry as the creature withered in pain until only ash could be seen. Another fell and Sean could breathe once more. With fire sapping his energy fast, he relinquished the power and cut through the Hunter in front of him. Eleven more to go and they would be safe, able to take on the Skulker who lurked just beyond the ring. As Sean moved to his next target, a great black body cleared through the horde. Standing in front of Sean, the one-eyed Skulker held a single-edged great sword comfortably on his shoulder.

Sean's blood drained from his face. Locking eyes with Taylor, and nodding in encouragement, both attacked as one force. Hefting its sword, the one-eyed Skulker easily deflected their combined blow to counter in a wide-arched swing. This forced Sean and Taylor to take steps back, dodging its deadly sharp point. Another swing pushed them further back and on the third, Taylor ducked to counter a strike in the Skulker's blind spot. Her sword sliced the Skulker's left side and black blood gushed outward in force. Sean then struck, taking the Skulker's arm off, cleanly forcing its sword to the ground, all the while Skulker sat growling in pain. Using its right arm, the Skulker pushed Taylor aside like a rag doll and drew a second single-edged sword, black as night. This one had black barbed metal on the other side. Sean was sure it meant to rip flesh more so than cut it.

Sean deflected mighty blows, yet the Skulker relentlessly hammered at Sean, like the first fight on the beach. Each blow pushed Sean a step back, another step, then another, the Skulker advancing with every blow. On the last step, Sean's heel caught on a corpse. Losing his footing and finding ground beneath his knees, Sean knew this was the end. Taylor had not joined back in the fight and her injured arm meant a saving double sword move was completely out of the question. Sean's arm burned from blocking; a mighty blow knocked his sword and it fell away, clanging loudly on stone. The blade seemed darker to Sean somehow, like what radiated from Death's coffin, as it closed in to strike his head.

A smirk graced the Skulker's face, for victory was going to be his at long last. It cared not for the punishment the Dark Wizard would impose; this kill was his. Thousands had been sacrificed for this moment and the terror in Sean's eyes made the Skulker giddy.

Closing his eyes, Sean waited to feel flesh being torn by the Skulker's blade. As air rushed toward Sean from the swing, he heard it make contact with flesh, but nothing hurt.... from all he could tell, his head remained intact. The sound of battle and smell of fresh blood invaded Sean's senses; listening closer, Sean could hear light grunts of strangled breathing.

Sean opened his eyes to horror; standing between the Skulker blade and his head was Taylor. Her face frozen in smile, Taylor's hands held the blade's edge protruding through her front. Blood dripped to the ground in red drops, a crimson spot formed on Taylor's chest spreading slowly by the second as the blade vacated her body.

"Always...saving..." Taylor mumbled, before she fell to the ground.

Sean's eyes were locked with Taylor's, gasps escaped her lips and Sean could see the life fading without the aid of his power. Unable to muster the words, Sean lost himself in the sky-blue pools of her eyes, memorizing every inch of them.

"I ... love ..." Taylor gasped.

The light faded from Taylor's eyes and her body became limp, her chest no longer struggling to draw in air. Sean trembled from emotion; hate, rage, sorrow, love all flowed through Sean.

"Taylor..." Sean whispered.

Skulker looked on in triumph, licking the blade clean of Taylor's blood and Sean stood upright. A maelstrom of emotions swirled inside, forming a snarl in the back of Sean's throat. Starting low, it grew into a feral roar. Then a thought from long ago echoed throughout Sean's being; "I will burn the world."

The Skulker prodded Taylor's corpse with its blade, a mad smile showing yellow teeth to further taunt Sean over killing Taylor. Like a twig snapping, Sean immersed himself in the pool of element energy that flowed within. As if retrieving an old memory, Sean started channeling a combination of fire, air, and a little earth for good measure; all fueled by emotion. The ground began to tremble, thunder crackled overhead once more and this time the Skulker looked to find its source as no Clasher or cloud was in sight. Sean cared not what this foul beast did, for he only knew one thing—it would die in agony. Cold rage fueled every action, and power filled Sean till he felt it would burst out. Rumbling thunder grew deafening until it finally stopped; electricity could be felt in the air.

"Burn" Sean's cold voice distant from the world or any thought was not his own.

Lightning rained down from a clear sky and struck the Skulker, exploding it into a million pieces, leaving nothing but a strong smell of copper. More bolts came down on the battlefield striking every Wanderer still standing. The world turned black as Sean passed out. Devoid of any will to live and accepting death, a welcome outcome to the fight. Taylor's frozen angelic face covered in blood, dirt and battle grime was the last thing Sean saw as darkness settled.

"You were my world…" Sean whispered to the darkness; the tone used was his once more.

Lightning fell from a cloudless sky, killing every last Wanderer on the battlefield as Gadriel's troops came into sight. Leading the men, Sloane pulled their procession to a halt, looking on in awe at the sight of exploding flesh. Electricity crackled through the air. The battlefield was a grizzly sight. When the last bolt fell, a roar rose from the Army of Stars soldiers signaling their victory. Sloane, concerned about the events that transpired, spurred on ahead to find out what happened. Reaching the Queen, she forewent the usual formalities in greeting the Ancient ruler as it seemed no one else of importance in the army could say what happened.

"We have won the day," Eyonka said before Sloane could speak, "but at a great cost."

Looking upon the wreckage of the ship, Sloane could see a pile of corpses, Wanderer and human alike intertwined. Soldiers moved to separate out the bodies with the help of Sea Folk who all looked on the verge of tears. A sole body was lifted from the top; at this distance, Sloane could make out Sean's hair, and her heart sank like a stone. Beneath it, blonde hair glowed like fire in the late afternoon sun, and Sloane felt the Queen's hand grip hers tightly. 'Such a great cost.' Sloane dared not say this aloud, the pain felt by the Queen was all too evident. Slowly, both bodies were carried to the main force standing in silence, barely breathing for fear of disturbing the solemn scene.

Depositing Sean and Taylor on the ground carefully, the men knelt out of honor for the sacrifice of these two brave souls. Like a wave, the rest of the soldiers followed suit, taking a knee, some openly crying at the sight. Many had died this day, but these two saved so many more and even the three Ancients gathered, their heads bowed in respect.

In the silent weeping, Sean's eyes opened as if being struck by lightning, and a deep gasp bellowed forth. Eyonka fainted at the sight of Sean's eyes; electric blue, they surged with power and life. A moment later they closed, his chest slowly rising and falling signaled life was still with the Proclaimer of Light.

Chapter 39: Aftermath In the Darkness

Night was best; shadows could move freely at night without worry. The Skulker hissed impatiently as Grunts scoured foliage to find their quarry. On a hunch, the Dark Wizard had released another horde of Wanderers to investigate the meeting place. Strong winds that had reached the castle of darkness reeked of Ancient power. Looking over the large clearing, it could see felled trees surrounding them due to the wind. The Skulker remembered the weak horde it held not long ago, now defeated. Yelps caught the Skulkers' attention and he charged through fallen trees to its source; a necklace of skulls jiggling with the motion. A Grunt stood over one soldier's body, sniffing eagerly to be rewarded. Swatting the Grunt aside, it pulled the body up by its neck, using massive paws to search its contents. Chuckling, it pulled free two scrolls and after pocketing them it threw the body away to feed the deserving Grunt. Scampering to its perch on the boulder, the Skulker waited for a sound of wings as Clasher approached in the moonlight. Battle may have been lost, but the war far from over and the Skulker's reward would be great for finding such treasures.

Made in the USA
Monee, IL
04 August 2021